Mildred the Crazy Cat Lady

K.S. Horak

First published in the United Kingdom in 2022 by Wolf House Publishing Ltd.

Copyright © K S Horak 2022
SECOND EDITION
The moral right of K S Horak to be identified as the author of
this work has been asserted in accordance with the
Copyright, Designs and Patents Act 1988.

A catalogue record for this book is available from the British Library.

ISBN: 978-0-9557769-7-7

Wolf House Publishing Ltd
8 Shoplatch Shrewsbury Shropshire
SY1 1HF
United Kingdom
kshorak.com wolfhousepublishing.com
katchamber.com

Cover Art by Lyndon White (front) and Dan Butcher (back)
who has granted exclusive license for perpetuity to K S Horak.
This is a work of fiction, any references to historical events, places and incidents are used
fictitiously, any resemblance to actual persons living or dead is entirely coincidental.

Printed and bound in Great Britain by Bell and Bain Ltd, Glasgow.

Contents

For Lauren

K.S. Horak

Chapter One:

EVERY CAT HAS A NAME

He stared down the dark and eerie road that ended abruptly in a semicircle of trees. The summer moon dimly lit the well-maintained tarmac as the tops of the trees over 30 feet high on either side of him swayed gently in the early morning breeze.

A white cat in the tree's roots stirred, seeing the cloaked figure that had suddenly appeared moving closer in the dark. She knew what he was, having seen his kind before. The heckles on her back stood up. She hissed aggressively and, unseen, quickly moved away, disappearing into the undergrowth.

The barefooted figure stepped onto the grass verge at the end of the empty road and waited. He had heard the cat and knew he was exactly where he was supposed to be.

The sound of the treetops gently brushing against each other was suddenly disrupted by a buzzing from above.

Four red dots grouped closely together started to descend towards him. His breathing became more audible as the red lights of the drone, now only 15 feet or so above him, stopped.

He looked directly at it as he wiped saliva away from his chin on to the floor.

A sudden blinding white light came from the drone, making him flinch as he pulled at his cloak to cover his skull. He peered through a gap in his cloak just as a pulsing fire of white light struck him. He instantly fell to the floor.

In pain and unable to move, his fingernails scratched at the tarmac as the trees in front of him started to shake. With foliage falling to the ground around him, he could hear the sound of heavy gates opening. The cluster of red lights rose and disappeared back over the trees.

As he drew breath, the sound of footsteps quickly surrounded him. His vision started to fade, but he recognised the uniforms that stood on either side of him. He caught a glimpse of a large figure moving towards him, weapon drawn as he lost consciousness.

NEARLY 3 YEARS EARLIER...

The display on the navigator told Nubia that she has arrived at Rocke Road. The car parked itself at the bottom of the cul-de-sac on the opposite side to number one. She sat nervously in thought, still unsure of what she was doing here.

It was rare that Nubia left the safety of Loxley Manor and she felt anxious exiting the car in this foreign environment. As she took a couple of steps forward, the car door closed by itself, auto-locking immediately.

She looked at the immaculately presented house at number one and glanced around to make sure she wasn't the focus of anyone's attention. Undoing her waistcoat, she reached in and took a phone from her inside pocket.

Chewing at her lip, she surveyed the well maintained front garden with a recently cut lawn. The small gate at the front of the path was closed and the pathway leading to the blue front door didn't have a weed in sight.

She glanced down at her phone and inputted her security code. Distracted by a wood pigeon in morning song, she glanced over at the neighbouring garden and the rose bushes in full bloom. Many of the houses on the street clearly took pride in their gardens. It was quaint and peaceful at this time of the morning.

She redialled the number for Lady Ebonee, who answered immediately after one ring. Lady Ebonee sounded very pensive.

"Are you there?"

"Yes, my Lady, the car brought me to the house and I was able to leave the Manor undetected." She paused briefly for thought, looking around again. "I know you are concerned, but maybe you çan now tell me what I'm doing here. I don't feel comfortable on the outside."

"You are there, Nubia, because it's happening again. I know the Grand Council does not share my views, but I have insights and connections away from them and their bureaucracy. I fear great change is about to happen and it's long overdue."

The secrecy of the call prompted Nubia to look over her shoulder to confirm that she wasn't being watched. "A great change of what Lady Ebonee? You are worrying me, let alone not knowing what I'm doing here."

"The prophecy of old; events that happened a long time ago are going to resurface, terrible things."

"Things? The last time there was even an inkling of the prophecy was over 350 years ago and even then there were a great many losses. Are you sure of this?"

"Yes and that house right in front of you will play its part. To what extent I am not yet sure."

"The house?"

"Yes, well, rather she who lives there."

Nubia chewed at her lips again whilst looking at the two-storey house that was fairly unremarkable compared to the others. "Who is she and is now the right time for her?"

"Apparently so and this is a factor that concerns me. Plans for her initiation are already underway and would you believe she has a job?"

"A job?"

"Yes, a job. I'm not happy about it and it's a risky strategy that the Grand Council are taking! However, wheels are already in motion and we have seen to that. Today will be the last day of her work; soon, she will have all of the time that she needs. This is why you are there. I want you to keep an eye on her and report back, what she is doing, where she is going and…."

"Wait, Lady Ebonee, there is movement next door." Nubia moved to the other side of the car as a man appeared in the front garden next door to number one.

"Well, who is it? Is it the neighbour?" her words were spoken anxiously.

"How should I know." She started to whisper, ducking down out of view.

11

"He's looking at his rose bushes and picking up some litter, cursing for some reason."

"Nubia, the word curse we could do without, as you well know!"

Nubia flushed a little with worry. "I know. Sorry, I'm not comfortable being out here!" She watched him turn around to smile as the woman from number one appeared.

"Lady Ebonee, a lady has just appeared outside number one."

"Get out of sight, don't let her see you. Quickly!"

Nubia depressed the symbol on the lapel-badge on her waistcoat as the car door unlocked and opened automatically. She quickly walked back to the front of the car, got in and pressed her lapel again. "Come on, come on." Her encouragement did not increase the speed of the closing door. She waited for it to close and lock before continuing. "I'm back in the car."

She watched the two people conversing; it was clear from the body language that they spoke regularly. He looked to be talking about the rubbish in his garden and she was full of sympathy and smiles. "Are you sure this is our girl, my Lady?"

"I'm reliably informed so. Why do you ask, what does she look like?"

Nubia scanned the very well dressed lady up and down. Her auburn shoulder-length hair was cut in a perfect line.

She wore makeup and was probably the early side of middle age. Nubia frowned at her clean presentation. "She doesn't look like most of the new ladies, more like a banker than anything else."

"Mmm, some of them start off like that, but it never lasts."

"So, what happens now, my Lady? This is against regular protocol and I still don't know exactly why I'm here?" There was silence at the other end of the phone, "my Lady?"

"You are there because I have my suspicions. She is being fast-tracked and for some reason, things are being kept from me."

"Suspicions of what?"

"There is something about her from an earlier timeline that makes me uncomfortable."

"So why are you uncomfortable about her?"

"I cannot say how I get my information, but something has been flagged in the archives. I've privately assigned Lady Tempest to investigate it; I sense menace at work. In any event, change is inevitable and I sense the Watchers you have secured at Loxley will soon sense it. If they become self-aware, I fear we will not have a hold over them anymore."

"You think they are trying to unite?"

"I think it's a possibility. All I know is that the woman you are looking at right now will play a part and possibly not for good!"

Nubia looked on at what appeared to be a pleasant, smiling lady from the relative safety of the car. "She's still catless, presumably?"

"Her cat is with her Elder; it will be delivered to her soon. You need to check on those arrangements beforehand, Nubia."

"I will." She quickly bobbed her head down to the steering wheel. "Hang on, she's moving!"

She watched the lady walk to the end of her path, closing the gate behind her as she waved at the man next door. She started walking down the road in the opposite direction. "She's moving off, going to work, I guess."

"Probably and for her last time. Look, follow her, will you?"

"What? What for?" She could hear anxious breathing from down the other end of the phone.

"Nubia, please. I need to be sure of something."

"I don't mean to speak out of turn, my Lady, but if you wanted someone followed, you should have spoken with Raysmau!"

"I'm sure she is very busy already with the gathering approaching."

"And I'm not?" Her question fell flat without response.

Where are we at, Nubia? What's happening?"

"I'm watching her in the rearview mirror. She is heading towards a bus stop. I'll try and get you on the camera so you can see for yourself."

"Good, well, follow her then while you do that!"

"Ebonee, I'm really not very good at these things!" She pressed the button on the navigator as the car started and inputted directions for it to turn around. The car did a 180-degree turn to the other side of the road. "She's stopped at the bus stop. Some male youths in school uniform are talking to her. I'll move the car a little closer." She pressed the forward button on the control panel as the car edged slowly forward. "They are offering her a seat. If I didn't know better, it looks like they are trying to impress her. Right, what do you want me to do?"

"She's obviously waiting for a bus. Follow it when it arrives. Try and get me on the camera as we need to observe her and what she does."

Nubia, who was not one for technology, pressed impatiently at the phone buttons, noticing a red bus turning into the road ahead.

"There is a bus on the way!" she spoke with panic in her voice as the phone screen lit up and the very worn face of Lady Ebonee appeared.

The bus passed her, then turned back on itself in the cul-de-sac, making its way back towards her. She watched it pass by and pull into the bus stop. Nubia watched the young boys step to the side to let the well-groomed lady get on the bus. "Well, I never. They are letting her get on the bus first."

"Why are they doing that? Are they scared of her or something? Hold the phone up, will you? I can't see properly. Does she have some sort of power over them?"

"Of sorts, I think my Lady, I wouldn't know the first thing about teenage boys, but watching them blush, I think they are intimidated by her."

"Intimidated?"

"Yes. Like they like her."

"What on earth do you mean?"

"Well, you know..."

There was a brief silence. "Oh my word, perish the thought."

"I know; it makes me shudder." Nubia watched the lady get onto the bus and walk to the back seat next to the rear window. The boys, giggling with their lack of bravery, sat some seats in front. The bus started to move away. "The bus is moving."

"Follow her. Quickly!"

"Alright, alright. Remember, I can't drive." Nubia frantically pushed at the buttons on the navigator as the car started to creep forward, quickly gaining speed.

"Are you close to the bus?"

"I'm working on it, Ebonee."

"Well, work harder and don't forget who you are addressing!"

"Sorry, my Lady, but I've got to my old age without the need for driving a car and I'm not going to try and learn now. Besides, my feet get nowhere near the peddles."

The car followed up behind the bus and Nubia leant forward to see what was going on. A frown appeared across her face. "She's got one of those portable make-up things. She's looking at herself in a mirror."

The bus turned the corner and headed along Benbow Street.

"What's she doing now? Can you zoom the camera in a bit?"

She watched the lady on the bus pull lipstick from her bag as she resumed looking at herself in the portable mirror.

"Yep, she's still applying make-up!" Nubia let out a big puff of disapproving air as she spoke.

The bus and car drew to a halt at traffic lights. Still craning forward over the steering wheel, Nubia quickly dived for cover dropping the phone as she went as the lady turned around to look out of the back window.

"Nubia… Nubia! Why has everything gone dark?"

Nubia struggled to reach the phone in the footwell and could hear the bus moving away in front of her. "Hang on, I've dropped the phone!"

"NUBIA!!"

Clambering to the floor, she snatched at the phone. "Got it, my…" she quickly sat up and froze, focused on the police officer staring at her. "Er, I may have a problem here, my Lady. A policeman is knocking on the window."

"What does he want? We need to stick to the task in hand, Nubia!"

Nubia tried to lower the phone out of sight, "that's not going to be possible. He doesn't look very happy."

"What? What did you say, Nubia? I can't hear or see you."

Nubia glanced across to the other side of the road and could see a parked police vehicle. He knocked on the glass again as Nubia watched the bus turn the corner and drive out of sight.

A car chase would bring unnecessary attention and she would be at the wrath of the Order; there would be many consequences; it was not a risk worth taking.

"Nubia, what's happening?"

"My Lady, I can't talk. Hold on."

The policeman knocked on the glass again, looking at the small lady's guilt-ridden face driving the large unusual car. Nubia pressed the button for the window to come down on the passenger side.

"Driving while on the phone and no seatbelt. I'll need to see your driver's licence!"

"Erm..." Nubia looked in front and behind. Cars were now passing her at the lights, but there were no pedestrians to be seen.

"In fact, what type of car is this. I don't recognise it at all?"

Nubia dropped the phone on the passenger seat and fiddled with her handbag. "Erm, it's an import."

"An import? Say, I don't mean to be rude, but can you even reach those peddles?"

Hands shaking, Nubia pulled an old looking camera from her bag and looked away as a bright flash lit up the car.

Dropping the camera onto the passenger seat, she quickly turned around to see if anyone was watching. Swallowing hard, she reached for the phone again and could see a look of panic on Lady Ebonee's face.

"That's taken care of him. I had a camera with me, my Lady. I think I should leave here very quickly. I won't have long."

"Definitely. We'll be in all sorts of bother if this gets out. Move away Nubia, there's nothing more that can be done for today. However, listen to me very carefully; that lady you have just seen is of utmost concern. I am told she may be bearing the mark and if she isn't someone close to her is. This could be for good or for evil and maybe our undoing. Remember her face and remember this place. I suspect you will be meeting her in the future. Others will help you when the time is right."

Nubia inputted the address for Loxley Manor into the navigator as the car pulled away. She glanced in the rearview mirror; the non-moving policeman was not attracting any attention for the moment. "I sense your concerns, my Lady. I will see that the area and this lady are monitored. Tell me, do you know her name?"

A few seconds of silence passed before she heard the Scottish accent on the phone again. "Her name is temporary, of course, but for now, she is known as Mildred."

PRESENT DAY

"MISSY!! MISSSSYYYYY!!!" the screech of Mildred's voice travelled the length of Rocke Road, Shrewsbury, in the middle part of England.

Over the last three years, the residents of the usually quiet road had become accustomed to this daily early morning wake-up call. The sound of a spoon clattering against an empty cat food tin added to their suffering.

"MISSYYYYYYYYY!!!"

At 7am and 7pm, this daily racket, caused by the solitary and unusual lady, could last anything from 2 – 15 minutes.

"MISSSSSSSYYYYYYYYYYYY!!!!"

Although hearing the call from Mildred, Missy chose to ignore the dinner bell ringing. She did not care for being called 'Missy' and generally would not react to it; she would prefer to be called by her real name of Nahla. She knew that Mildred did not know her real name; maybe she would be told in time.

Except for Mildred's intervention into the daily peace, Rocke Road was a closely-knit community where many of the neighbours mingled with one another. They practically ignored the cat lady who lived on the corner at number one, although she was often the subject of conversation and gossip.

In a strange quirk of timing, nearly three years ago, she abruptly lost her job and within a matter of days, a complete stranger arrived at her door and gave Missy to her, on the condition she joined the local cat club. Ever since that time, it was a very rare occasion for anyone to visit the house and for the most part, Mildred kept herself to herself.

In the apparent loneliness of her life with her cat, Mildred kept a daily routine, ensuring some structure in her life. After Missy finally returned home for feeding in the morning, she would read magazines and talk to her cat until lunchtime. After lunch would be the daily visit to see Mr Franks, who owned the local convenience store. The highlight of her day was her television game shows, especially 'Bang Goes Your Money.' It was usually on after tea, followed by her bedtime somewhere around 9pm.

Any modern-day technology had been substituted over the last three years. Inside her home was sparse of any material objects and more of a shrine to cats' lives, from books that she bought from charity shops to cat-themed window stickers. Her duvet has multiple pictures of random cats and she has a cat-shaped hot water bottle that she liked to hug in winter. Her mug for drinking tea has a smiling face of a cat that would appear when warm water was poured inside.

The mat outside the front door said 'Beware of The Cat' although there was nothing to be 'beware of' in Mildred's house.

In the dimly lit, musty, unkempt home, there was only one object that took Mildred's attention daily; her framed certificate that she polished each day. She would often smile to herself when she polished it. Her being awarded the certificate and the events surrounding it still begged her curiosity. Her membership to the United Kingdom Kat Chamber had not happened by chance; she was certain of that. After all, Missy would not have come into her life had she not joined or rather been told to do so.

The only exception to the daily routine was an outing once a month. She would leave for the day, taking the bus or train to meet colleagues from the Chamber. These monthly meets were informal catch-ups with other members from the 'local' area that spanned over 100 miles. There would usually be 6-8 of them at each meeting.

There are many other members of the Chamber within the United Kingdom and the rest of the world. Her own district (or chapter) covered Central England and Wales; the larger gathering of everyone from the district would happen once a year. The next was this coming Friday.

Approaching her 3rd anniversary of membership of the Chamber, she found how they conducted the running of the club to be highly strange. For reasons unknown to her, their monthly meetings and yearly gatherings were always arranged at the last moment and held in private. They may use hotels but would never meet publically in a bar or restaurant. It would always be within a hotel conference room, away from the prying eyes of the uninvited.

In consideration, lack of cat-related conversation among the elder members made little sense and Mildred questioned why they were there or even members in the first place.

Nearly every day, in conversation with Missy, Mildred would mention the Chamber. On many occasions, she would freeze and stop talking, shaking her head saying, "I'm not supposed to talk about that."

Much surrounding the Chamber and their apparent rules didn't make sense, including being told she was not allowed another cat. For Mildred, a mild-mannered lady, this upset her and as time progressed, started to anger her. Rules apparently cannot be broken, although she had no idea what would happen if they were.

Nahla, when she had peace in the evenings, away from Mildred's prattling, would question herself about many aspects of her own life whilst patrolling the surrounding streets. Her early memories were extremely vague. She remembered being held by another before being passed to Mildred. Anything before this was absent from her mind and details could not be recalled no matter how hard she tried. She had no idea who the lady was who passed her to Mildred or how she ended up in her hands. She could not remember her mother at all and it was a constant irritation that her memories failed her. Her dreams, on the other hand, were very vivid; recollecting them made her shudder. These unnerving dreams, especially of late, were of dark places and tunnels below ground with no idea why or what they meant.

For both of them, the time was coming when they wanted answers. Hopefully, the strange characters involved in the Chamber would have them very soon.

Chapter Two:

SLIPPERY AT THE SWAY

MONDAY

It had just gone 11am when Mildred's phone rang. Unlike usual phones, her cat-shaped phone meowed when it needed to be answered.

"Hello Daphne," Mildred said excitedly, "how are things?"

"Well, I'm looking forward to the forthcoming gathering on Friday; it will be lovely for us to get together again. I can't believe it was almost a year ago since we all met. Time passes by so quickly."

"It certainly does, Daphne. I can't wait; I'm so excited. I've knitted a lovely new cardigan just for this special occasion."

Mildred always looked forward to the gatherings, although she felt she had been largely ignored by everyone at the last two that she had been to. It played on her mind constantly and her formal invitation had not arrived as yet.

"I've been told nearly all from our region are attending, most have confirmed so far."

"Well, that's a lot of sandwiches and cakes!" Mildred's tone was etched with concern knowing that someone would have to make them. Being relatively new to the club, chores were undertaken by new members. Daphne had been a member for seven years and she had two cats called Aziza and Binky.

"I will call you back with the exact numbers once I'm told. Mildred from Merewood Close in Coningsby, Lincolnshire, will also be helping and we have a new Mildred that you've not met as yet. She's from Alpine Grove in Stratford-Upon-Avon. They will both help you with providing supper."

"That's good to know. I appreciate the help. May I ask, what is the new Mildred like?"

"I don't know, Mildred; it's not my place to speak with her. She has her own Elder. I'm sure she'll find her way on the right path very soon. Everyone does with time."

For some reason, newish members of the Kat Chamber were all called Mildred, Daphne or Jessica. Mildred had overheard it said at a previous gathering that you will find a Mildred, Daphne or Jessica in every major town or city.

"Daphne, I must ask, do you happen to know if there will be an awards ceremony?" Mildred spoke with anxiousness in her tone. She had been told that receiving awards led to more cats.

"I'm not sure as yet. I haven't been told; these things are always last minute arrangements. I understand there has been some disturbing news that is delaying things."

"I understand," Mildred responded politely. Still, she didn't really understand why these things were so disorganised and what could be disturbing about being a cat club member.

"I must go, Mildred. I have others to speak to and much to do!"

"That's okay Daphne, thank you for taking the time to call me."

"You are most welcome. Goodbye for now, Mildred and may peace be with you and Nahla."

"Thank you, Daphne."

Mildred The Crazy Cat Lady

Mildred put the cat phone down on the side. Her mind was racing with so much to do and less than a week to prepare. She put her thoughts about sandwich making temporarily on hold as a frown appeared across her face; who exactly was Nahla?

The letterbox at the front door chattered into life. Mildred leapt to her feet from the comfy old sofa and immediately let out sounds of glee upon seeing what had arrived in the post.

"Oh Missy, it's here!" She held Cats Quarterly Magazine aloft, beaming with excitement.

Nahla was not impressed with this revelation, having been awoken with this most uninteresting news.

"Missy, oh look, there are pictures of Savannah cats, Minx cats and Birman cats," she announced with glee clutching at the magazine as though it was a priceless artwork. "What a beautiful Siamese, Missy. One day I would love to own another cat. I'm sure you wouldn't mind, would you?"

Nahla's ears twitched. She knew full well that the atmosphere in the house was about to descend into a rapid downward spiral, namely why Mildred was not allowed to bring another cat into the house.

"It's just not fair, Missy; why am I not allowed?"

Nahla's eyes were half-open, watching Mildred flicking through the magazine, shaking her head as she went.

"It's just not on. What could..." Her words stopped abruptly as a leaflet fell to the floor from the magazine.

"Hello, what's this?" She picked the flyer up from the floor. The photographs on both sides gripped her instantly as she slumped into the old sofa, sending dust into the air.

Mildred's eyes widened with shock; it was unusual for Nahla to see her react like this.

"20,000 cats are abandoned each year. Even more have to be taken into shelters!"

Her tone and body language became agitated with frustration. "How can this happen, Missy?" she waved the flyer in the direction of her cat. "I appreciate some can't cope and let's face it, I know how difficult you can be, Missy. Look how long it takes you to come in for feeding and I know you slip out more at night now. Don't think I don't notice!"

She brought her knees in together and let the flyer fall into her lap. For ten seconds or so, there was no sound to be heard.

She drew in a large breath and sighed. "It's not right, not right at all. We have a nice home here and I tell you, Missy, I will be speaking to the Chamber about this at the gathering on Friday. There's plenty more room for paws here."

It was rare that Mildred's words drew Nahla's interest. It hadn't escaped her attention that Mildred had become more agitated about the most mundane of things over the last few weeks. But this was clearly not a mundane matter and Nahla could see that she was deeply upset. She pulled herself into a ball on the single-seater chair and watched Mildred rise to her feet.

"I've not used it in years, but I've got a cheque book around here somewhere." She watched Mildred turn in circles a couple of times, eyeing up all of the piles of paper in the very disorganised mess.

"Let's send that charity some money," was the last thing Nahla heard as she drifted off to sleep again.

Mildred had retired for the evening; she always did around 9pm.

Downstairs Nahla sat in anticipation, waiting for the sound of the upstairs light to be switched off. Regular as clockwork, off it went and she headed for the cat flap. Mildred was wise to her antics and she knew she worried about her. Truth be told, she was pampered way too much for her liking and of late the evening escape from the house gave her time to think.

Exiting the house, she hopped up onto the wall at the front of number one. Approaching the overgrown bush, she inhaled deeply and took in the last warmth that the August evening had to offer. Natural light was fading and a few bedroom lights were already on. There were dark clouds in the distance and with the humidity of the last few days, a storm was probable sooner rather than later.

As she looked down from the troubling skyline, she noticed a lady moving quickly away from her.

She had seen her loitering a couple of times before. Her dress sense was distinctive, neither smart nor casual. Rather, it was strangely awkward and out of place.

She leapt down from the wall, positive that she had not been seen and headed towards her. She paused as the lady stopped moving and took something out of her pocket. Nahla tucked herself in behind a wall a few doors down. Once out of sight, she peered her head around the wall to see what the lady was doing. She shrunk back behind the wall as the lady looked over her shoulder suspiciously. Peering back into the road, she watched the stranger look up and down the road a couple of times. Nahla's eyes narrowed in concentration; this lady clearly did not want to be seen. The stranger was now holding a black box-like shape in her hands and looked to be pressing buttons on it as a car engine started on the other side of the road and started to move forward.

The car turned around, stopping next to the stranger. Nahla blinked a couple of times as the lady started to move towards the driverless car. She moved from the cover of the wall and crept towards her. The driver's side door opened by itself as the lady walked around the rear of the car. As she went to get in, she froze immediately, seeing Nahla. Nahla's tail twitched as they both stared at each other. The lady smiled at her and nodded, paused for a few seconds and stepped into the car. Nahla moved quickly towards the car as the driver's door automatically closed. Hopping up onto the wall opposite the car moved away, the stranger never took her eyes off her.

She perched on the wall in contemplation, watching the car disappear into the distance, perturbed that the stranger seemed to know who she was; it didn't bode well with her. Her dreams over the last couple of weeks had become more disturbing and she sensed change with the usually calm Mildred. Something was troubling her as well.

Hearing a rumbling of thunder in the distance, she looked up and down the road. A dog barked from one of the gardens in response to the thunder, but none of the other cats that lived within the two surrounding streets could be seen.

The breeze was picking up as the dark clouds moved closer. She watched a flash in the distance and counted down, reaching eight before she heard the dog bark again as the sky rumbled.

Hopping down from the wall, she walked to the corner of Rocke Road. There were 54 houses in the street, which was an average amount for the area. From here, she could survey the length of Benbow Street. The stagnant life of Rocke Road became a distant memory when passing through Benbow Street. Here you could find Mr Franks' shop, The Tudor House Café and the Futility Public House. The shop and café would be closed at this hour, but there was always something happening at the Futility.

She had wanted answers for a long time. Not knowing how she ended up on Mildred's doorstep or who the stranger was that delivered her was a quest for understanding every night. Other cats from the local streets all remembered their mothers. Some recalled their stories with affection, even though the chances of them seeing their mothers again were slim. But it didn't worry them and they sought no reason to raise questions about it. The only thing she had in common with them was that they all used their real names. She knew she had a strong connection with cats, just not the ones that lived locally.

As she started to walk along Benbow Street, a few people scattered on both sides of the road walking quickly, anticipating that rain was imminent. As she passed the Franks' shop, the road lit up in the evaporating light quickly followed by a crash of thunder; she only counted to four this time.

As light raindrops started to descend, she hopped up onto one of the tables outside the Futility. She often sat there looking inside the busy, very noisy place. She could remember the face of the lady who delivered her to Mildred and pondered whether she would see her again.

There was a flash directly overhead with an instantaneous bang as cheers erupted from inside the pub. A few came to the windows to look overhead as the sky lit up again. She had seen many of the faces before, they were regulars. But the lady who she wanted to see, the lady who delivered her to Mildred was, as usual, nowhere to be seen.

The sky lit up overhead, drenching her coat in an instant. The regulars were becoming noisier as the music started playing from inside to which they all sang along.

Glancing upwards at the dark clouds, this was not going to be a short shower. Nahla shook her soaked coat and glanced over to the archway that led to the car park to the right-hand side of the pub. She needed cover quickly and would wait there for the rain to pass.

She moved through the old archway and peered her head around the corner of the wall. Two men were smoking and looking at the sky as they talked about fishing. She ran as fast as she could across the cobbled stones towards the car park, ignoring the "Hey kitty" from one of the men as she passed.

She hopped onto the bonnet and roof of a parked green van before leaping on the wall that surrounded the rear of the Futility.

Known locally as 'The Sway,' she surveyed the outside of the rear of the pub, watching one of the men slip on the wet cobbles as he crashed to the floor. Both men were in fits of laughter, allowing her a welcome diversion to run the whole length of the wall towards the outbuildings. She froze momentarily as the man helped his friend back to his feet and opened the rear door to the pub. The music blasted out across the car park; she'd heard this before. Everyone inside the pub was chanting about a 'Sweet Caroline,' whoever that was.

From the end of the wall, she hopped onto the roof of the pub kitchen. With the rain pouring down even harder, she would need to tread carefully to get to her hiding place.

Looking down from the roof, the mossy concrete below was littered with broken glasses, rotten beer towels and discarded beer kegs. The light from the kitchen windows helped light this dull and neglected place as she gingerly leapt to the floor and weaved her way around the obstacles. Shaking her coat and clearing her eyes, the wall in front of her was covered in thick ivy. She crept underneath an old shopping trolley, stepped over a rusty fire extinguisher and started moving the long lines of ivy to one side.

With a final shake of her coat, she entered the damp, musty room that had not been lived in by anyone in a very long time.

As the rain dripped from her coat to the filthy floor, lightning passed overhead, lighting up her new hideaway. It was no accident that she had found this place a few weeks ago. She walked towards the far wall, fascinated by what was inscribed into it.

She stared at the wall, totally absorbed in thought. The only distraction being the sound of the rain falling against the broken glass outside.

As the room lit up again, the inscribed symbol was as clear as day. She didn't know what it meant or whether it was a warning, but she was drawn to it nevertheless. The noise of the thunder reverberated against the walls. She would wait there until the rain passed.

The symbol on the wall gave her the shivers. She had seen it many times before.

It was the same symbol printed onto the certificate that hung on Mildred's wall.

The lake's surface was on fire. The surrounding trees of turquoise were ablaze as the flames from the boathouse roared into the sky. The heat was so intense that she could feel herself moving backwards to escape from it. On the right, an old mansion house burst into flames.

The sound of glass shattering forced her to cover her ears. White pulses of light shot across the lake of fire directly at the shape moving across the surface.

She pulled her robe over her hair as a dark cloaked figure appeared in front of her with an outstretched hand. Something moved inside his palm as a painful wave of heat passed through her......

Mildred immediately threw herself upright on her bed, putting a hand to her chest with worry. "What on earth?" She coughed a couple of times and lifted a shaky hand to her brow, wiping away beads of sweat. Reaching out to her bedside table, she fumbled around in the darkness for a hair tie. She could feel her thick, knotted auburn hair was damp at the roots as she tied it up. Pausing for a few seconds in the silence, she had no idea what time it was.

"Missy!" She coughed a couple more times as she got to her feet and walked over to her ancient windup alarm clock and held it towards the moonlight, rubbing her eyes. 03.09; she couldn't recall the last time she had been up in the middle of the night.

"Missy, are you home?" Her voice echoed in the silence.

She put the clock back down and walked out to the landing, flicking the light switch and instantly shielding her eyes from the bright light. "Missy?" The only sound she could hear was the clock ticking from downstairs. "Are you out again?"

The lack of response suggested this was the case.

Mildred headed back into her room and looked out of the window, her overgrown garden glistened in the moonlight; there had clearly been rain as she slept. But the sky was clear now. She stared at the moon and took a deep breath, closing her eyes, but opened them instantly on hearing the hissing of a cat outside.

She looked out of the window to see a dark hooded figure staring up at her. Her heart skipped a few beats in fear as she wiped the sleep away from her eyes and blinked a few times. It was gone. She must have imagined it. She drew a few deep breaths and sat on the end of her bed.

Her dream was starting to fade as she rubbed at her eyes again and looked up towards the moon; there was no sound to be heard.

Lying down on her bed, she turned her thoughts to Missy. The fading dream was unnerving.

She could use a hug with her cat right now.

Chapter Three:

FISH PASTE SANDWICHES

TUESDAY

"MISSSSYYYYYY." The daily alarm sounded out across Rocke Road at exactly 7am. "MISSSSYYYYYY." The clattering of a spoon on an empty cat tin was added to the wake-up call.

"MISSSYYYYYYYYYYYY!!!!!"

Mildred looked up and down the road waiting impatiently. She saw the neighbour opposite at his bedroom window. He didn't look very happy.

She opened the front gate, stepped into the road in her fluffy slippers and crouched down to look under the parked cars. Hearing her left knee crack as she got close to the ground, she immediately stood back up, pulling upwards at the clicking knee. "Oww, I'm getting old!" she said, wiggling her leg to encourage circulation. The tin was hit a few more times, but there was no sign of her absent cat.

Glancing up to her right, she could see the man opposite, shaking his head at the window.

"Don't know what he's staring at. Isn't everyone up at this hour?" She shrugged, but it did occur to her that yelling for Missy balanced on one leg may look a little unusual. The banging of the tin stopped and she lowered her leg. She stood in silence, looking down the road.

"Where on earth could you be?"

Closing the gate behind her, she headed back to the house, muttering as she went. The tin was tossed into the recycling bin. It was time for an anxious cup of tea while she waited for Missy to return.

Startled, Nahla jumped quickly to her feet, her heart beating at speed. There was a crash of what sounded like metal on porcelain. She could hear running water from inside the kitchen of the Futility. Her pulse started to slow as she gathered her thoughts. The occasional shard of light had made its way through the thick ivy; the sun must have risen some hours ago. Hearing a glass breaking, she peered her head gingerly through the ivy, the bright sunlight shocking her eyes as she lifted a paw up to them for cover. As she adjusted to the brightness of the morning, she could see a lady cleaning inside the kitchen.

She knew she was late and that Mildred would be worrying. It was the first night she had slept soundly in some time. She pulled her head back inside to look at the scratching on the wall. It was the symbol of the head of a cat, as seen on Mildred's wall. However she did not recognise what it wore around its neck. Another cat had used this den before. Nahla was certain the clawed symbol on the wall must have meant something to the previous resident. She knew she had to go but would return again very soon.

Making her way through the ivy, she crept past the fire extinguisher and made her way under the trolley. She would have to jump on top of the empty beer kegs and climb a short section of the wall to make her way back to the car park. The sound of traffic on Benbow Street confirmed that she was much later than usual. Mildred fussed around her far too much for her liking, but she knew that she was harmless.

Having made her way to the top of the wall, she inhaled and stretched in the summer sun. It was sure to be a beautiful day.

Mildred poured the hot water from the kettle as a smiling face of a cat instantly appeared on her mug. Dropping a tea bag and spoon into the water, she didn't have a lot to smile about, unlike the happy cat.

Full of worry, she stirred at the teabag briskly. Missy not returning on time was commonplace, but now she was over an hour late, which was troubling.

She pulled the filthy net curtains to the side for about the tenth time, looking out across her overgrown front garden; there was no sign of Missy. This was all she needed, that and her bad dream last night. She felt very uncomfortable and nervous.

It was at worrying times like this that she missed her old friends and her work colleagues. They had steadily vanished from her life over the last few years; she was surplus to requirements, it would appear. The only time the phone meowed was something Chamber related. If it did, it was always Daphne or Mildred from Merewood Close. None of the other members had ever called or even tried to get to know her.

She had stirred the tea bag for far too long; the stewed brown liquid in her mug was not going to soothe her concerns. Worryingly, the clock had just gone 8am. This was now becoming a crisis and positive action needed to be taken.

Hearing a door slam next door, she rushed outside.

"Mr Jenkins!"

The startled man whom she had not spoken to in ages turned to her.

"Yes, Mildred, whatever is the matter?"

"Have you got an air horn or a loudspeaker?" It was the best she could think of off the top of her head.

He blinked a few times, "I'm sorry, have I got a what?"

"An air horn?"

"I'm an accountant Mildred, why on earth would I have an air horn?" He shook his head, wondering what was going on in the mind of his peculiar neighbour.

"It's just I've lost my Missy and she's never home this late."

Mr Jenkins, somewhat aghast with the mental picture of Mildred sounding an air horn to look for her cat, couldn't help but notice how upset she was.

"Mildred, look; she always comes home, you know that." His words were softly spoken in an effort to reassure her. "I must get to work now, Mildred. I do hope she shows up soon."

He opened the gate at the end of his path and turned back to Mildred.

"It's just a thought, but old Ron further down the street remembers the nightly bombing in the war. I don't think a repetitive air horn will do much for his heart condition."

"Oh, I hadn't considered that."

"Well, good luck Mildred."

She watched him close the gate and walk off down Rocke Road.

Hands on hips and minus an air horn, she was at a loss with what to do next.

✛✛✛✛

At speed, it didn't take long for Nahla to get back to Rocke Road. She slowed her pace and looked down to the far end of the road towards number one. There was no sound of a food tin being banged or any sign of Mildred.

Distracted by bushes twitching erratically behind the wall at number nineteen, intrigued and on impulse, she darted across the road to investigate. Suddenly, the loud noise of car brakes made her jump, followed by tires skidding to a halt. Freezing in the middle of the road, she stared at the driver of the car. He did not appear to be in shock and stepped calmly out of the car.

Nahla looked up at the dark-suited figure as he moved towards her. She tilted her head to the side with her eyes firmly fixed on him as her tail began to twitch. The driver looked down at her, "You should not be in the road. This is a dangerous place for you." His statement was spoken quite firmly and she noticed saliva running down his chin from bad dental work. Nahla took a step forward as he bent down towards her and took off one of his gloves. "I mean it. This is no place for you." The driver's voice was calm as he extended his hand towards Nahla's head.

She felt drawn to him and moved closer, his hand now just above her head. They were both suddenly distracted by a car horn coming from behind the driver's car as he quickly drew his hand back. Nahla stepped backwards a couple of paces. The driver still crouched down, turned around and hissed in displeasure, looking at the driver of the car whose horn had suddenly rung out.

"Get out of the road!" The driver yelled, shaking his head, hitting the horn again, "I'm late for work! Honestly, some people," he grumbled under his breath. "The road is not a place to play!" he said whilst looking at the figure and the strange glasses he was wearing.

Nahla moved to the kerb, her gaze never leaving the stranger who wiped saliva from his chin as he slowly got back into his car.

As the car moved away, the driver turned to look at her and continued staring until he moved out of sight.

She hopped up on the wall where the bushes had been twitching as the other car sped by. Just as she was about to peer over the wall, she froze, gathering her thoughts about the stranger in the glasses; something seemed oddly familiar about him.

✛✛✛✛

The cat flap sprung into life. The sudden burst of noise made Mildred jump, spilling a freshly made cup of tea down her blouse.

"MISSY!!!" She put the mug down abruptly onto the kitchen table and ran towards her cat.

"Heavens above, I've been so worried." She bent down and gathered Nahla into her chest. "Where on ever have you been?"

Clutching her tightly, she brushed a tear from her eye. "Please don't ever do that again. You have no idea how much I worry about you. I'm meant to be your protector after all!" She pushed her hand across Nahla's head and stroked her repetitively.

Mildred's nose twitched as she brought her head down to her chest, sniffing in the air. "What on earth have you been rolling in?" She moved her head away and lifted Nahla up to her face to smell her again. "You smell like stale beer and look at the state of your coat. Someone needs a bath. I'd love to know what you get up to sometimes; I really would."

Despite the stale smell of her fur, Mildred was delighted. Missy was home and that was all that mattered as she blew out a huge sigh of relief.

"You must be hungry?" She stared at her cat with an inquisitive smile. "I've got you herring in cod roe today; I know how much you love it!"

Mildred blinked twice, having thought she had seen Missy's eyes roll, but she was quick to discount it as a lack of sleep.

She placed Missy on the floor and ushered her towards her food bowl as she reached into the overhead cupboard for a food tin.

"I have a busy day of sandwich making today, Missy. It's only three days before I meet with everyone." She spoke with excitement, knowing that she would push for some answers from the Chamber this time. "Maybe having another cat will stop you from running off all of the time?"

Nahla looked on as Mildred absorbed herself in prepping her food bowl.

"I also need to speak with two of the other Mildreds today; Mildred from Merewood Close and there's a new Mildred from Stratford-Upon-Avon." Mildred shook her head. "Mildred from Merewood Close only has one cat as well for some reason." She looked towards the ceiling, daydreaming. Shaking her head to quickly snap out of her broody cat daze, there was much to do as everything had to be perfect for Friday. She faffed with her hands in excitement, but it was short-lived as a strained look appeared across her face, her hands falling to her sides.

"They never really talk to me, Missy," she spoke with sadness, "and some ignore me. I've never spoken to them at all!" She bit at her lower lip in concentration. "A renewed effort is needed. I need to make a good impression!" Although she was at a loss, why she may not have done so before. "Good impressions are the most important impressions, Missy." She bent down towards her cat with an index finger raised as if she were a politician making a very important point.

Reaching in the drawer for the tin opener, she glanced out into the street through the kitchen window. Ever since Daphne came into Mildred's life, things had changed for the better, very much for the better. "Missy, the day Daphne brought you to me, was my happiest and…" she spun around instantly, noticing that she wasn't being heard.

"Missy… Missy?" Mildred left the kitchen and walked into the living room. As predictable as ever, Missy was curled up in a ball on the sofa. "Well, how about that. Missy, I was talking to you!" she spoke with sadness after her last couple of hours of worry. "I'm sure you don't care for me sometimes. I really do."

Mildred about-turned back to the kitchen with much to consider regarding her sandwiches.

"Fish paste. Everyone loves fish paste." Mildred said to Mr Franks.

"We don't sell as much of it as we used to, Mildred. Not by a long margin. Fish paste is a dying food. Not all developments are progress. It's all microwave meals and the like these days." Mr Franks, the owner of Franks Convenience Store, asserted.

Not owning a microwave, Mildred chose to ignore his comment. Ladies love fish paste, she thought to herself.

"How much do you need then?" Mr Franks enquired, rasping his breath at the end of the sentence. He was not a figure of fitness.

"I think about 10 pots of the Salmon and 10 pots of the Sardine and Tomato please."

"20 pots, Mildred? That's a big spend; I'll have none left." He put his hands on his hips in amazement at the scale of the fish paste order.

"Well, if it's not selling, then it shouldn't worry you too much," Mildred quickly asserted.

Mr Franks gave a little smile. "I'll just check the sell by dates, Mildred." Something he clearly didn't do very often.

She waited deep in thought, thinking about Mildred from Merewood Close providing cakes again and the new Mildred providing sandwiches.

"I'll need around 20 loaves of bread as well, please."

"Right you are." Mr Franks' hands were back on his hips as he surveyed the bread shelf, hoping he had enough. "White or brown?" The frown across his forehead indicated that he may be a little short of completing the order.

"A mixture will be fine, thank you."

As Merewood Mildred was very nifty in the kitchen, it would be difficult to compete against her amazing cakes. She may need something else to accompany the sandwiches, perhaps a few...

"Mildred? Hello... Mildred?" Mr Franks coughed out loud to get her attention. She looked to be lost in thought.

"Oh, I'm sorry. My mind drifted somewhere else." She turned and smiled at Mr Franks, fluttering her eyes.

"Do you need anything else?"

"A couple of pots of butter, please."

"So what's going on, Mildred? Why do you need so much fish paste?" he asked with his gruff voice.

Caught off-guard with the question, Mildred's eyes widened. Think, think, think; she wrestled with her thoughts. "Oh, I'm donating sandwiches to the Church for the fete."

"I didn't know you went to Church, Mildred" he responded politely, putting his hands back on his hips.

"Well, you don't really know me, Mr Franks!" Mildred retorted with a snap. So much so that Mr Franks was unsure where to look.

"I meant no offence, Mildred."

"None taken, Mr Franks." She smiled politely, but her tone was clear enough; there were no more questions for today. "I'll probably be back tomorrow for some more supplies."

"No worries at all. I'm open most hours and your TV magazine will be here tomorrow as usual."

If it's usual, I'm not sure why he's telling me. Mildred considered with some paranoia, let alone this 'open all hours' type of talk.

She counted her money as Mr Franks bagged up the bread, butter and pots of fish paste.

"I'll have to charge you for the bags again, I'm afraid. As I say, not everything in life is progress."

It certainly wasn't. Mildred remembered that she had over 50 empty carrier bags at home gathering dust, all bearing the 'Franks' logo.

Laden with her newly purchased carrier bags and placing her purse back into her pocket, she turned to leave.

"Goodbye, for now, Mr Franks."

"Goodbye, Mildred," he responded as she left the shop.

Mr Franks watched as Mildred passed by the window as a puzzled expression appeared across his face. "I'm sure the church fete isn't until next month."

Without giving it a second thought, he shook his head and returned to reading his newspaper.

Bags in hand, Mildred started the walk back home, mentally berating herself as she went. You need to be much more prepared for questions; she was annoyed at herself following the brief exchange with Mr Franks. Why does he want to know what I'm doing anyway? For reasons that had not been made clear, the Kat Chamber was private, very private and outsiders were not welcome. Daphne had made this explicitly clear to her nearly three years ago. The first and only occasion that she had visited Mildred's home.

'You were chosen, Mildred.' Daphne said, looking her straight in the eye; her well-kept hair could not shield the ageing lines across her face.

'You've always known you were different from others. You must have felt it.'

'I'm not sure what you mean?' Mildred had responded as she reflected on their initial conversation.

'As a youngster, you didn't have pets did you?' Daphne spoke very softly and clearly.

'No, I didn't, my parents would not allow it and my father had an allergy to animals and a temperament that would not suit.'

'It concerned your mother, didn't it?' Daphne said with a smile, nodding her head as though she already knew the answer.

'She always thought it would be good for my development, for my path for the future. How could you possibly know that?' Mildred responded, her voice breaking a little with emotion; the question had clearly upset her.

'All will be revealed in time. We are not so dissimilar,' she smiled and stepped forward to Mildred, lowering her chin to make direct eye contact, 'but you are special, Mildred. More than you know. You have an affinity with animals.'

Mildred's eyes widened in utter disbelief at what she was hearing. 'All animals?' she enquired.

'No, just cats,' was the quick and matter of fact response. 'But it's only cats that matter to us, Mildred.' Daphne spoke with confidence and touched Mildred on the hand, offering reassurance that what she had said was a fact.

'There are many others like us, Mildred. Yes, people keep cats. You'll find one or two in every street, in every town the breadth of the land over. Some guardians are more enlightened than others and you are enlightened, Mildred.'

Mildred took a step back, shocked with what she was hearing and not understanding a word of it. 'Guardians?'

'I know this is a lot to take in. It was the same for me when I was visited by my Elder.' Daphne smiled, offering reassurance that she was not a complete crackpot, although she was failing miserably.

'And I have something for you, Mildred, something very precious. Please do look after her at all times.'

Mildred stood in silence, stunned as Daphne left her in her kitchen. The cogs of her brain whirring with so many questions for which she had no answers. Irrespective of the beautiful new kitten she was now holding, she did know one thing for certain and she was very sure of it.

She would never let complete strangers into her home again.

Mildred's home had changed somewhat following that meeting nearly three years ago. Her front and rear gardens were unloved and overgrown. The paintwork around the windows was flaking and the glass in the window frames had taken on a misty and dusty sheen. The house had generally fallen into a state of disrepair and its unkempt appearance was noted and regularly discussed amongst the locals.

The hedge at the front of her garden would grow out of control and hang over onto the pathway. Mr Jenkins took it upon himself to tend to it. Tutting under his breath and shaking his head, seeing the ever-decreasing state of Mildred's house and gardens. He often wondered what had happened to her. She used to be so house proud and presentable, but now she always wore the same clothes. Something had changed with Mildred over the last few years noticeably after she got her cat. She never had visitors any more and her appearance had changed dramatically from the lady he used to know. Something was amiss and the formerly sociable lady now kept herself to herself.

In all honesty, Mildred couldn't bear the sight or smell of fish paste any more.

Knowing that Missy loved them so much, her nose had become accustomed to the smell of luxury fish related cat food. Well, as luxurious as Mr Franks' shop had to offer.

But sometimes in life, a line may be drawn and Mildred's line had run right out today as far as the fish paste was concerned.

She sat down wearily on the stool next to the kitchen table, surveying what can only be described as the Mount Everest of fish paste sandwiches.

She was confident that she had made enough but wasn't sure if she should have added something to them. Fish and cucumber go well together, don't they? The very thought of going to see Mr Franks to buy a dozen cucumbers, with the risk of him asking more questions, was something she really wanted to avoid.

So, plain fish paste sandwiches it was, with no fancy trimmings. With Merewood Mildred focusing on cakes, it also fell on Mildred from Alpine Grove to provide sandwiches. Suddenly, nerves jangling, Mildred paused, her body becoming rigid. What if she has made fish paste as well? On no, I never thought to ask, she thought.

Whilst it was not a competition, the Chamber wanted to see new members taking their roles seriously, ensuring they would be positive role models for the future. This made no sense at all. Yes, she was asked to join, but her interest was in cats. A positive role model; a positive role model for what?

Oh, this is no good. Mildred's mind chattered away. I'd better call the other Mildreds and see what's going on. With no time to waste, the cat's bottom was pressed firmly towards her mouth.

"Hello, Mildred? It's Mildred from Rocke Road in Shrewsbury!"

"Hello, Mildred," said Mildred from Alpine Grove, followed by a brief pause. "I'm sorry, from where?"

"It's Mildred from Rocke Road."

There was a brief pause. "Oh, good afternoon Mildred, my Elder said someone may be in touch. There are so many Mildreds you can never be too sure," she asserted with a chuckle.

Mildred joined her in laughter. "Well, the only Mildreds I know are you and Mildred from Merewood Close."

"Mmm," was the short response.

Mildred pulled the phone away from her face in shock, staring incredulously at the cat's bottom at what she had just heard. 'Mmm' she thought, 'mmm,' what could that possibly mean? This would suggest that Mildred from Alpine Grove may already know other Mildreds. That would be somewhat disconcerting when the others never spoke to her. "Err... um, well..." she stumbled with her words.

"Whatever is the matter, Mildred?"

"Well... I was just thinking about the meeting on Friday."

"The gathering, you mean?" Mildred interrupted.

"Yes. That's right, the gathering. I'm not fully aware of how many will be attending. Can I ask how many sandwiches have you made?"

"Well, I think everyone is coming from across the region, so that will be 45 in total."

How could she possibly know that. Mildred thought to herself as a scowl flashed across her face. A couple of comments in their conversation were starting to concern her. "I see and how many sandwiches have you made?" she asked.

"Three plates," was the instant response. Mildred breathed a sigh of relief. I've probably done more, she thought.

"Yes. Three plates of cheese, three plates of ham and three plates of cheese and ham."

Damn it! Mildred waved a frustrated fist in the air. Her victory was short-lived as worry started to set in.

"I see," said Mildred as she bowed her head towards the floor and composed herself, "that's good," she mumbled, trying to think what to say next.

"And what have you made, Mildred?"

"I've done three plates of fish paste sandwiches," she responded proudly, holding her chin aloft.

"Fish paste Mildred? Fish paste, you say?" She scoffed with a little shrill of laughter, "I didn't know anyone ate that any more, let alone that you could buy it, ha-ha. You could have at least added cucumber."

Mildred's scowl deepened with teeth clenched. She could visualise this new Mildred on the other end of the phone, shaking her head in royal disapproval, laughing at her expense.

"It's very much the thought that counts, Mildred!"

There was silence at the other end of the phone.

"Yes, of course. You're completely right, Mildred. Besides, you can feed any leftovers to your cat."

She scowled once again and it was at that very moment that Mildred realised that she really didn't like the new Mildred very much.

Sitting in the kitchen in silence, Mildred decided not to call Merewood Mildred after all. She was staring at the floor and had been doing so for some time. Other Mildreds? She knew the exact number going to the gathering. She knew that fish paste was not very popular anymore, confirming what Mr Franks had said.

How does she know all of these things when she's only just joined? Mildred bit at her nails in a state of worry.

The sound of ticking fluttered into her ears, breaking the silence. She looked up at the old clock on her kitchen wall; it was approaching 7pm. She stretched her arms above her head, time to go and call Missy. I hope she comes in quickly this time, she thought, knowing her favourite programme would soon be starting on the television.

Pushing her toes into her scuffed brown shoes, she straightened the wrinkles on her stockings, got up, walked through to the front room, switched on the television and turned the sound up. She returned to the kitchen and reached into the overhead cupboard, taking out a tin of cat food and grabbing a spoon. It was now time to call Missy.

In the background, she could hear the music to her favourite game show starting. She dropped the spoon on the counter in shock. She glanced up in a panic, looked at the clock and saw that the second's hand was moving too slowly. "Oh no, the clock must be slow!" Now in a quandary, flapping her arms like an insane penguin, she was torn between watching the show and finding Missy.

"MISSY!" She snatched the spoon and started banging the tin as hard as she could. "MISSSSYYYY!" She was practically screaming. The full tin didn't provide enough volume, so she hit the kitchen counter with the spoon instead. Her eyes were still firmly fixed on the television.

"MISSSSSSSSSSSSSSSYYYYYYYYYY!" she hollered.

"MISS..." She was immediately drawn to the presenter as he came forward on the screen. With his usual beaming, cheesy smile and outstretched hands, he proclaimed;

"Welcome to Bang Goes Your Money!" The studio audience roared with approval.

Mildred was smiling; she had stopped yelling and banging the counter. Transfixed, she listened to the presenter and focused on the words coming out of his mouth, the very same words he says every time he is on television.

She liked him. He was okay. Well, for a man anyway.

Chapter Four:

Mr. FRANKS TARDIS EMPORIUM

WEDNESDAY

Mildred's behaviour had become rapidly more excitable over the last hour. Opening the fridge, she looked at her plates of sandwiches and tugged at the cling film from one of them.

Prodding the sandwiches with her finger, she smiled, satisfied with her work from the previous evening. "Pretty good, pretty good." She placed her hands on her hips and kicked the fridge door closed.

Glancing at the clock, she quickly clapped her hands together with glee; it was 8am.

"Well, Wednesday is upon us Missy, I'll need to collect my TV magazine this morning and probably some more supplies." She turned to look at her black cat, curled up in a ball on the couch, a commonplace sight with her white-tipped tail resting across her body.

However, this was not a regular Wednesday. The gathering was in two days and Mildred would be celebrating three years of membership. The longer she was a member of the club, the more 'benefits' came with it, or so she had been led to believe.

47

She stepped into the living room to look at the certificate on her wall that stated her membership in the Kat Chamber. Focusing on the logo of the Egyptian looking cat she started to chew at her lower lip.

"What to wear, Missy, what to wear?" she said in a concerned tone as she glanced down at her cat. Nahla, who had been happily asleep on the couch, opened one eye.

"I need to be sure that everything is in order." She raised both hands to her head, fully outstretching her fingers and ran them as best as she could through her knotted hair. "Wait a second…" she said, waving a finger at Missy. A big grin spread across her face as she left the room abruptly.

Yawning and getting to her feet, Nahla stretched her legs forwards and backwards, hearing the floorboards creak as Mildred ran up the stairs. Mildred was undoubtedly going to her wardrobe again; for about the tenth time this week.

Yawning again and extending her tail, she leapt down from the couch. The crashing of coat hangers from the wardrobe upstairs meant it was definitely time for fresh air. She headed towards the cat flap, catching a casual glance at her food bowl full of the usual inedible offerings.

She headed out of the Mildred house.

✜✜✜✜

Nahla pulled the ivy back and peered through into the dark. She felt the temperature change as soon as she stepped inside; it was cold. As the ivy fell back into place behind her, the temporary light she had created was instantly withdrawn. With such a hyperactive mind and disturbing dreams of late, Nahla had no idea why she was at peace in this damp and unused place. Although this was now her private place, noise from the kitchen of the Futility reminded her that humans were never far away.

She stepped towards the logo on the far wall; her thoughts and concentration fixed on the faded scratching. She knew from the certificate at home that Mildred was part of this, but Mildred hadn't carved this symbol into the wall; someone or something else had.

Lifting her left paw, she gently scratched at the neckline of the Egyptian looking cat and gazed into its eyes. She recoiled feeling a burning sensation inside her, as her heart skipped a beat, something didn't feel right.

++++

"Good morning," Mildred said, striding through the doorway of Franks Convenience Store.

She was mentally prepared for any questions that Mr Franks would throw her way today. She had rehearsed them in her mind beforehand whilst trying on different clothing combinations at home.

There was no response. Mr Franks was engrossed in his newspaper.

She coughed under her breath and caught his attention.

"Well, good morning, Mildred," he responded, looking up from his paper, "sorry about that, something strange is going on."

"Such as what?"

"There was an accident outside here recently. According to the paper, the Police have no leads and all the CCTV footage has gone missing."

"That's odd." Mildred responded, but she was not as enthused by the story as he was.

"Anyway, what can I do you for today?"

"My TV magazine, please and I need a few more supplies."

"Supplies? Supplies for what then Mildred?" he politely inquired, "ha, ha, you creating an army?" he chuckled away to himself, shaking his head.

Oh, I wasn't prepared for a simple question like that, Mildred thought to herself.

"Err, just for home, that's all," she nodded her head, smiling politely.

"Well, okie-dokey. I'm guessing you will not be needing any more fish paste now will you?" He smiled and continued to giggle to himself. Placing his hands on his hips, he looked up in thought.

"Have you considered adding cucumber to your fish paste sandwiches, Mildred?"

His question was met by a long and vacant expression. "No, I hadn't," she said, gently clenching her teeth. His thoughts on all things sandwiches were not appreciated.

"Oh, right you are then." He had stopped giggling and had the slightest of well-meant smiles on his face. With a little fake cough, he returned to reading his newspaper.

Mildred turned her gaze away from him and returned to her thoughts. Mildred from Merewood Close will be cake ready, the new Mildred from Alpine Grove is ham and cheese ready, what can she possibly add to fish paste ready without the cucumber?

Looking through Mr Franks' convenience store was like stepping back in time. The shop that time forgot. Mildred amused herself with this thought. There was a musty smell in the air and faded postcards of old Shropshire littered the walls. There were remnants of Christmas decorations from celebrations of years gone by and creaky floorboards with sticky lino on the floor; it was not a plush shopping experience. However, it was comfortable and safe with no unexpected surprises. Mildred was happy in knowing that she had a routine and, like many, was a creature of habit.

She walked down the toy aisle, which hosted old children's trikes, bright orange snowboards, even though it was summer, and build your own tree house sets complete with hammer and nails; no doubt a health hazard and probably circa 1980s.

Approaching the back of the store, where some of the cleaning products had no doubt passed their use by date, she moved on quickly to jams, marmalades and peanut butter. The very thought of spending the rest of the day making sandwiches filled her with dread. She wanted to excel and impress, but there is a limit to Mildred's usually very calm demeanour.

"Do you have little sausages on sticks, Mr Franks?" she shouted across the shop.

He looked up from his newspaper, "I have some sausages, yes, but not on sticks." He paused briefly in thought before resuming. "I've got a woodcutter out the back and some wooden tent pegs I can cut up for you if you like?" he shouted.

She stared at him, realising that he was quite serious with this clearly absurd suggestion. "No, I think I may pass on that, thank you," Mildred responded with a frown across her face. She shuddered at the very thought of spending the afternoon putting shards of wood into little sausages. Mr Franks was a breed apart.

"I'm glad to hear you are not prescribing to this modern-day living Mildred," he added.

"Whatever do you mean, Mr Franks?"

"Well, this 'veganarisum' or whatever this newfangled thing is called. I just don't understand youngsters anymore. As I say, not everything in life is progress." With that, he returned to his newspaper.

Mildred was starting to get a little frustrated as she continued to work her way through the tardis of Franks Convenience Store. There were many nooks and crannies you could rummage your way through. She let out a large puff of air; nothing was jumping out at her to make a clear and memorable statement for everyone at the gathering. That was until she saw a rack of very old cards. Birthday cards, anniversary cards, congratulations on your newborn type of cards; there seemed to be a card for everything these days. Some of the cards had been on display for some time; the plastic wallets meant to protect them were looking somewhat old and discoloured. But poking out from behind a 'sorry you've lost your job' card was what looked to be a pair of black ears that stood out proudly behind the old cellophane. She quickly pulled it out from the rack with excitement.

They were indeed what she hoped they were; cat's ears.

"Mr Franks, do you have any more of these, please?" She waved the card with the little black cat on the front in the air.

He lifted his head from his newspaper. "No, Mildred, some of those cards are quite old, if I'm honest, but you are welcome to buy it all the same."

"Would you be able to get any more... by tomorrow?" She gave him a pleading look.

"Well, I would need to speak to my supplier if they are still in business, that is. It's been a while since I called them." He pulled up his trousers, his belly hanging over the sides of his belt. "Don't sell many cards you see; it may be a tall order in this time frame, Mildred," he shook his head in unison with his regular rasping voice.

"I just need a card with a beautiful black cat on it, just like this." She walked over to Mr Franks, thrusting the card in his face.

"Well, why don't I make a phone call. You go for a nice cup of tea in the café next door and come back in 10 minutes or so" he smiled. "I'll see what I can do for my best customer."

"Thank you. Oh, I need some more batteries; my clock is slow again."

"Really? You only bought some last week, Mildred."

"Yes, quite."

"When you come back, I'll have those ready for you."

"Can I take my TV magazine with me?" she asked.

"Yes, of course. Pay me when you come back. If I can't trust someone like you, Mildred, who can I trust?"

He smiled as he passed her the magazine, which she put into her bag.

"Well, thank you, Mr Franks." Mildred's smile of glee was much like the young girl who had just found chocolate in her pocket. The shop bell tinkled as she opened the door.

"Oh, Mildred, exactly how many cards do you want?"

"Forty-four," she responded.

Mr Franks' mouth fell open; "How many?" his voice quivered.

"I like cats, you see."

With that, the cat lady was gone.

There were around twelve people in The Tudor House Café as she entered the quaint tea shop.

Holding her usual oversized bag, she took a seat next to the front window. Waiting to be served, she enjoyed watching the world go by. It was a welcomed break and took her mind off the forthcoming gathering.

A young girl approached Mildred's table wearing a badge which said, 'here to help you' and her name, Chloe.

"Hello and welcome to The Tudor House. How may I help you today?" Chloe asked whilst looking curiously up and down at what Mildred was wearing.

"I would like a cup of Earl Grey, please."

Chloe scribbled on her note pad. "Would you like cream with that?"

Mildred recoiled in horror, "Heavens above no."

Chloe almost took a step back in shock at the outburst.

Mildred coughed slightly under her breath and offered Chloe a smile, "some lemon if you have it would be fine, please."

"That's no problem at all. I'll just be a jiffy." She headed off behind the serving counter.

Earl Grey with cream, what on earth is happening to modern society? Not everything in life is progress, Mildred said to herself. She snapped the saying out of her mind, realising she sounded like Mr Franks.

She dived into her TV magazine, quickly skipping the features at the start and heading straight to the programme listings. She wanted to be sure that 'Bang Goes Your Money' would be on again in the forthcoming week. Relieved to find that it was, she lowered the magazine and looked around at the other people in the café.

A couple of people were sitting by themselves. There was one group of four and three couples. Almost all of them were tapping away on phones. Laughter would occasionally erupt, inevitably followed by someone reading a quote aloud for the others to hear, or they would show a picture of something they had seen that seemed to be absurdly funny.

There was plenty of noise but sadly hardly any conversation about natural things. Mildred shook her head, thinking about the art of conversation, which seemed to be lost in modern society.

A sign on the wall read, 'Our WiFi code is Fri13n2dys;' she had no idea what that could mean and equally had no use for anything WiFi related. As she had gotten older, many things in life just didn't seem to add up. To the right of the code, there was a white poster with a red border advertising the forthcoming church fete, the very same fete she had claimed she was making sandwiches for. She gulped, noticing it wasn't until next month. She shook her head in annoyance; she really must get her stories straight and be more prepared for questions. She really didn't understand the need for all of the secrecy about the Kat Chamber, but Daphne had explained this not long after their first meeting.

'One simply doesn't join this organisation, Mildred; it is not for everyone. You need to be invited. It's a calling, really.'

She recalled that Daphne had put a reassuring hand on hers when she made this point.

'We are proud to be invited. That pride extends to our commitment and above all our complete discretion.'

At the time, and still to this day, she found all of this behaviour a little odd. But she didn't ask questions, didn't make waves and guessed that this was just the way it had to be, as strange as it all sounded.

A very traditional white china cup of Earl Grey was placed in front of her with a thin slice of lemon. Chloe had listened and thankfully it was without cream.

"Here you go," said Chloe, "can I get you anything else?"

"No, thank you, that will be fine for now."

Chloe headed to another table.

Bowing her head to take a sip of tea, Mildred enjoyed the warm and smooth taste of the tea leaves. Letting out a sigh, she straightened her head and smiled.

She found herself drawn towards an advert on the wall that had a photograph of a dog on it.

She read the lines printed across the top. 'Do you understand your pets? Do you know what they are thinking? No? Well, you should because they understand you!'

What a bizarre statement, Mildred considered with a smile as she stood up and walked over to the wall to read the small print.

'I'm Doctor Bethany Birks, the animal psychologist. I would like to introduce you to my human training programmes where I teach you to understand your pets and communicate with them.' There was a small picture of a woman smiling with a stethoscope wrapped around her neck, presumably the doctor in question.

'My 1-2-1 programmes will enable you to understand your pets and in so doing, they will understand you more.'

She was quite fascinated by the advert as it occurred to her that Missy ignored her on occasions. She mentally wrestled with the thought for a moment. Well, I'm sure Missy doesn't ignore me. She just has a funny way of showing it; that's part of her character. She mentally reassured herself there were no flaws in the way she tended to her cat.

She carried on reading with interest. 'Whether you own a dog, a budgie, a hamster, or a cat, call me today. I will change your life forever or your money back!' ★

She looked around the café. Still engrossed in their phones, no one was watching or paying her the slightest bit of attention. She quickly pulled the advert off the wall and placed it into her jacket pocket before sitting back down.

She stared out of the window, having a momentary wobble of guilt that she may have just stolen something.

Missy was perched on top of the wall opposite. Mildred leaned her head towards the window with a perfect smile on her face looking at her beloved cat.

Missy's attention seemed to be focused elsewhere. Mildred brought her teacup to her lips. Her hand started to shake. "Missy, whatever is the matter?" She watched from the window as Missy crouched down, her tail extended. She started to scratch at the wall. Mildred put down her cup, spilling tea over the sides as she watched on. Missy was hissing at something. She looked scared. In a panic, Mildred leaned against the glass and looked in the direction of whatever Missy was looking at. There was a lone figure on her side of the road. She strained her face against the glass to get a better look. He was tall, dressed in a black suit and was wearing the strangest sunglasses. For a moment, she felt like the figure looked at her and she felt instantly cold. Worried for Missy, she got to her feet and quickly snatched at the door, stepping out onto Benbow Street. The figure turned to her and wiped what looked like saliva away from his mouth. He lifted his hand to his glasses as Missy hissed from the other side of the road.

Mildred had never heard her hiss before. Seeing her cat in distress was unnerving. Without thinking, Mildred ran straight across the road as a car skidded to a halt. The noise of the car horn drowned out Missy's hissing as Mildred grabbed hold of her from the wall and brought her to her chest.

"Whatever is the matter, Missy?"

She ignored the angry voice coming from the car and looked over to the figure. It felt cold outside for the time of year.

She watched him look around at the people staring at her and the angry man in the car. She blinked, having thought she saw a flash of colour from his right palm as he turned to walk away.

"I could have killed you, you crazy woman!"

Others were watching the event as Mr Franks came out of his shop. "Are you okay, Mildred?"

Clutching Missy as tightly as she could, she nodded at Mr Franks and watched the car drive away. "You must be careful Mildred, I just told you there was a nasty accident outside here recently."

She nodded again at Mr Franks.

Looking down, she could see that Missy was distressed. Her heartbeat was pumping so fast it almost felt like two beats.

The dark-suited figure had disappeared. She needed to get Missy home.

*subject to status and mental health assessment.

Chapter Five:

THE NOOK AT THE COACH AND HORSES

WEDNESDAY

It was a rare occasion for Daphne to meet with her Elder away from the monthly meetings or yearly regional gathering. As such, she was looking forward to seeing her again in person. In fact, she was surprised when she called asking for her time. It must be important.

There were no hard and fast rules to extraordinary meetings. Gathering business took place at gatherings and more generalised topics occurred at the monthly meet-ups. There was always the phone if necessary.

The monthly meet-ups were informal and members within the local district would attend. For Daphne, it was the Shropshire region where Jessica, her Elder, also lived.

The Shropshire meetings are reasonably popular as it is a large county in England. Landlocked and sitting next to the Welsh border, there could be a crossover of accents and the occasional musings of the Welsh language.

Within the Shropshire local area, some had been members of the Chamber for much longer than Daphne. For that reason, the monthly meetings were usually well attended.

The Shropshire group members also included Mildred from Rocke Road and one other Jessica, from the new intake. New members were considered as such if they had been a member for anything up to three years. The yearly gathering always had an air of formality about it and all members across the region were invited. Unless due to ill health, every member is expected to attend. In total, within the region of the middle sector of England and Wales (including the new intake), there were 8 Mildreds, 5 Daphnes, 11 Jessicas and 21 other Elders, all of whom went by different names.

Daphne was preparing herself in anticipation of this unscheduled meeting. She was due to meet with Jessica at 3pm at the Coach and Horses on Swan Hill in Shrewsbury. It was also unusual to meet in a public house. Still, Jessica had advised her of a quiet area towards the back of the pub, where they would be able to drink tea and talk privately. Looking at the pendulum swinging back and forth on her grandmother clock, she re-read the familiar words engraved upon it; 'Tempus Fugit.' That was as much of the Latin language that she knew. Indeed time does fly; much too quickly, she considered. Some of the other Elders, who were much more senior to her, spoke many of the old languages and followed many traditions passed down through generations of enlightenment.

As an 8th degree Elder, Daphne had responsibilities and she took them very seriously. This included assisting other Elders, usually of the same level, with whatever their needs may be. She also had to liaise with the new intakes, especially Mildred, who was her direct responsibility. But there were also responsibilities to the Chamber that Elders often referred to as the 'Order.' Those responsibilities were to ensure that rules were followed; after all, anarchy would prevail. The system would fall apart without discipline within the membership. Jessica had informed her of this some years ago.

She buttoned up her jacket and checked the food bowls for her cats before she left; Aziza and Binky were nowhere to be seen. Not uncommon for this time of the day as she glanced at the two certificates hung up on the wall. As she reached for her door keys, she still pondered what this meeting could possibly be about, as well as the sense of urgency.

Built on a narrow road surrounded by Georgian and Victorian manor houses, the Coach and Horses consisted of two bars. The main bar could be accessed from the main road and was for recreation with a dart-board and sports on the television. The other bar was the restaurant area, accessed via the side street. Tucked away in the restaurant was a little nook. Hidden from prying eyes within this narrow cut out in the brickwork, Daphne was sitting at an old oak table waiting for her Elder to arrive. Old posters hung on the walls from a bygone era. The posters proudly promoted the health benefits of drinking beer. The design and colour indicated they were probably printed just after the second world war.

Within the nook were framed paintings on the wall of old lawyers with references to old acts of law. There was a huge, green plaque inscribed with names of lawyers, going back as far as 1760. Deciding to read a few lines of the old English language from one of the acts of law, she became goggle-eyed very quickly, blinking a few times.

A couple of minutes of her life had just passed by that she would never be able to reclaim.

"Tempus fugit indeed," she muttered to herself.

7th Degree Elders had certain privileges and lifestyle changes were encouraged by higher members of the Order. The higher the status, the more privileges were offered with higher security clearance to access information.

One of the notable benefits was the use of a motor car. New members and 8th Degree Elders rarely had motor vehicles and were usually solitary people.

Televisions were commonplace, but computers, mobile telephones and the use of the internet were not encouraged. New members led a simplistic life and did not require the complications of modern-day living.

A car became necessary once progression had been offered. There would be a larger area to cover and people of influence within the Kat Chamber have to be seen. Sitting on buses and other forms of public transport could, at times, encourage complete strangers to start speaking with you. Let's face it, no one wants to be bothered with any of that. Members of the Order led private and quiet lives and kept themselves to themselves.

Jessica, currently a 7th Degree Elder, got out of her little black car outside the Coach And Horses. She composed herself, straightening the tartan design on the long skirt she was wearing as she stared at the front door. Lifting up her right leg, she removed a piece of dirt that had attached itself to the front of her new high-heeled shoes. She brushed herself down, leaving bread crumbs and the remnants of her lunch on the pavement below. Locking her car, she dropped the keys into her expensive clutch bag and made a point of checking her navigator was inside. She noticed two security cameras above the front door and could see another one down the side road. Ignoring them but noting their presence, she wobbled on the uneven cobbles as she crossed the road and went inside.

Daphne was overjoyed to see her Elder walk in. With a huge smile, she stood up to greet her friend and Elder. "Good afternoon, Lady Jessica."

"Good afternoon, my friend."

Both had checked that no one was listening before they addressed each other and then hugged like old friends.

"Can I get you anything?" Daphne enquired.

"Mint tea, please, if they have it."

"Of course. Please take a seat." Daphne politely requested. "Would you like something to eat? I noticed they have fish paste sandwiches on the menu."

"Oh, no, thank you, I've already eaten," although she did momentarily consider it.

Daphne nodded and headed towards the bar area to place the order. Looking back, she could see Jessica surveying the pictures of lawyers and reading the same legal jargon that stole her attention only moments ago.

It had been some years since Jessica came into her life; Daphne smiled to herself at the thought of it and turned to place the order at the bar.

Bored of reading, Jessica turned her attention to the interior of the pub. There were a few small security cameras in domes fixed around the ceiling and above the bar area.

They were discreetly nestled between the painted black beams that wove their way around the ceilings.

A couple was sitting at a table just out of ear's reach.

Pleased to see Daphne returning with a cup of tea, she quickly gathered her thoughts.

"It's very quiet in here," Daphne said, placing the cup down on the table in front of Jessica.

"I thought this would be a good place to meet at this hour of the day," she smiled. Jessica was itching to talk.

"I have news," she proclaimed, "and it's exciting, Daphne, very exciting," she grinned, "although somewhat sad at the same time." She softened her voice and shook her head a little with sadness. She bowed her head slightly to make sure the couple on the other table could not hear. "You wouldn't have known her, but Lady Tempest a 6th Degree Elder from Cheshire, has passed over."

"Gosh, I'm sorry to hear that, Jessica," Daphne said, hearing this sad and uncomfortable news.

"I know; I only met her once. It has come as such a shock to everyone, the Elders especially. She was a perfect role model and most respected."

"Oh, this is very sad news; I'm shocked. Was it ill health? Could she not have been healed?"

"No, I'm afraid not; her health was quite perfect. Unfortunately, the world of men did for her."

"Oh, that sounds most terrible," exclaimed Daphne.

"Yes, she was hit by a bus."

They both fell silent for a few moments.

"This is terrible. What became of her cats, Lady Jessica?"

"Of course, at her Degree Level she had four cats. I'm guessing they have been returned to the Keeper; I'm not knowledgeable on these things, I'm afraid. This is why I wanted to meet with you," she said quietly. "I have been selected and I will be presented with my real name at the forthcoming gathering."

"Oh, Jessica, this is amazing news!" Daphne grinned and put her hands together, clapping gently with excitement. The clapping was short-lived as she realised she had caught the attention of the couple sitting having their dinner.

Jessica lowered her voice to a whisper. "It's more responsibility, of course and there are many perks and benefits, most of which have not been explained to me as yet." Jessica shook her head as she spoke with speed and excitement as she reflected on becoming a 6th Degree Elder.

Moving up a Degree Level only occurred when another Elder passed over, so this was by no means commonplace. The forthcoming gathering was annual, but on occasion, it could be as long as 13-14 months before the collective regions would meet.

"I long for my real name," Daphne mused.

"It will come in time, my friend, when you become a Level 6 Elder." Jessica added, placing a supporting hand on Daphne's arm, although never looking her in the eyes.

She was deep in thought when she gave out a little nervous cough for attention. "Tell me, how is Mildred progressing?" Jessica asked.

Daphne, who had lifted her cup to her mouth, paused. "Fine," she said, sipping her tea before stopping at such a random question. "Wait, which Mildred?"

"Mildred from Rocke Road." Jessica gave a nervous smile, took a sip of her tea and quickly returned her gaze to her cup.

"All the Mildreds are fine across the region; well, to the best of my knowledge." She looked at Jessica with some curiosity. "You've never asked after the Mildreds before, or the Jessicas and Daphnes for that matter; is everything okay?"

"Yes! Just doing my 'Elderly' bit." She offered a broad unconvincing smile. "I just thought with this new level of responsibility, I should get to know that particular Mildred a little more, as I do you. She's right on my doorstep."

"I see. That's very nice of you," she said with suspicion. Surely, it was her role to look after the local Mildred. After all, she was Mildred's direct Elder.

Jessica stirred at her tea. "Nothing strange going on? You don't need to confide in me about anything... at all?" she muttered quietly.

Daphne's eyebrows lifted. She had a confused expression on her face at hearing these strange questions.

"No, Lady Jessica. Everything is well." She offered a gentle nod and an awkward smile.

"Oh, that's good then." Jessica took a sip of tea. "You will tell me if something is not right or if you need to share any concerns with me?"

Daphne leaned forward. "Of course. Are you quite sure that everything is okay?"

"Yes. I'm just tired, please ignore me; much to do and not enough time." She looked at Daphne with a tired smile. "There never is."

"There is never enough of what Lady Jessica?" Daphne looked at her with further curiosity.

"Time, my friend." Jessica looked ponderously into her cup. "I may offer Mildred a lift to the gathering," she said, looking up from her tea. "Just part of the getting to know everyone type of thing."

Daphne's eyes were fixed on Jessica. In all of the time she had known her, she had never once offered her a lift anywhere.

Daphne cleared her throat to break the long silence. "It really is amazing news for you, Lady Jessica and it's always wonderful to see you, of course. May I ask why you decided not to tell me these things on the phone?"

"The Watchers, Daphne. The Watchers."

"But the Watchers see Lady Jessica?"

Jessica turned her head towards Daphne. "No, my friend, they are moving and they also hear."

Daphne knew that something was seriously wrong.

Mildred carried Missy all the way home. She sat on her sofa, stroking her up and down, stopping around her heart to check the heartbeat had returned to its normal pace, which it had.

The earlier event was perplexing. She had never seen Missy hiss before; it was clear that something had unnerved her.

She leaned back into her sofa; the coldness she had felt previously had passed quickly. She thought about the man on the other side of the street. She could have sworn that Missy was hissing at him, but that would make little sense.

After returning to pay for her cup of tea and a brief conversation with Mr Franks, who confirmed her cards would be ready for collection the following day, she talked to Missy all the way home. Forty-four cards with the lovely black cat on the front would certainly make an impression. The cat on the front looked just like Missy and would be a talking point for sure. She intended to give a card to every member. She would have to write 'with best wishes' inside as she didn't know the names of most of them, even after all this time. As the monthly meetings were far more intimate, everyone had got to know each other, but it was different at the gatherings. Those who had been members of the Chamber for longer would usually sit in their own groups. Even the local members from Shropshire, most of whom were older than her, would peel away to sit with others of their own rank.

She had noticed a certain level of mutual respect between the members who had been involved for longer. Pleasantries were exchanged, of course, but newer members knew their place; quite odd for a cat club. She had considered this in the past but had not dwelled upon it. But this coming Friday, she would make an effort and do something that at least all of them would remember her by.

Missy was sound asleep as she got to her feet to go upstairs. Sitting on the end of her bed and facing her wardrobe, she was reasonably sure of what she was going to wear on Friday. She kicked off her shoes and pushed them to one side with her feet. They looked somewhat tired, but so did the other three pairs of the exact same colour and design.

Standing up and stretching, she turned around and flattened out the creases on the bed, making sure the cats printed on her bedspread were all perfectly in line.

The old wardrobe doors made their usual moaning sound as she pulled them open to survey the minimal amount of clothing inside.

Seeing her outfit brought a smile to her face.

She looked forward to an evening of all things cat related.

Chapter Six:

DRIVE OF THE NAVIGATOR

TUESDAY – APPROACHING MIDDAY

Jessica felt quite lost as her car stopped beside a grass verge. Concerned, she looked at her watch, which confirmed what she already suspected, she was behind schedule.

Only two days had passed since the knock at her front door, which took her by surprise as it was rare for anyone to knock on her door, more so on a Sunday. A notice hung in her front porch clearly stating 'No salespeople, no leaflets and no politicians,' which typically guaranteed she would be left in peace for the best part of the day.

Scrambling with her dressing gown and bright red, fluffy slippers, she tripped over one of her three cat bowls and scowled, hoping she hadn't chipped her nail polish. She opened the front door to discover that no-one was there. Stepping out of her porch on Porthill Crescent, she looked left and right, but there was not a soul in sight.

Frowning and reasonably positive that she hadn't imagined it, she turned to go back inside and noticed a small package on the doorstep.

It was not distinctive in any way, bore no postmarks and was hand-wrapped in brown paper fastened with string. She picked up the square package and took it inside, placed it on the kitchen table and stared at it, wondering what it could be.

'Jessica, Number 13 Porthill Crescent'

The package was definitely for her and it was clear that whoever had dropped it off didn't want to wait around; that alone intrigued her.

Jessica jumped, startled by her eldest cat Khepri's tail brushing past her ankle. Their eyes met momentarily; "shall I open it?" Jessica whispered. Khepri stared at her and without breaking eye contact Jessica nodded her head. "Okay."

She pulled at the string and the package began to unfold. She removed a hand-written note, a shiny metal badge and a smaller black box that equally bore no markings of any distinction.

The badge had a symbol on it that she did not fully recognise, though there was something familiar about it. At previous gatherings, she observed that some of the other Elders, who were of a higher degree than she was, wore badges, but she did not wish to appear to be rude by staring at them. It occurred to her that this may be one of them.

'Staring is very rude!' her mother regularly used to remind her, (her adopted mother that is) and to this day, she was very self-conscious about looking at people directly.

She unfolded the handwritten note. The handwriting was immaculate and pleasing to the eye. Every single word was equally spaced and every line a perfect millimetre apart; quite a feat on unlined paper.

'Dear Jessica

Following your selection and forthcoming appointment to degree level 6, you are required to attend an informal meeting this coming Tuesday at 14.00 hours. The contents of the box enclosed will help you to find our national headquarters. It is paramount that you do not discuss your appointment with anyone else and the contents of the box are to remain on your person at all times day and night hereafter.

In order not to be late you should leave Porthill Crescent at midday using your motor vehicle. It is advised that you have an appropriate amount of fuel for the journey. Do not switch on the navigator until this time. Thank you for your cooperation.'

Her Elder had only very recently given her the amazing news that she was to become a Degree Level 6, but this was the first 'official' communication she had received to confirm this. The note was to the point and she was being told what to do, with no idea where she would be heading, but she smiled upon receipt of the clarification of her new position.

She took the small black box into her hands, lifted it and lowered her head to look underneath. All she could see was a tiny gold dot, which presumably was an indicator to where it should be opened.

She lifted the flap just enough to see a well-padded compartment inside. In the centre of the padding was a silver-coloured object, not much bigger than the size of her palm. Taking it out and studying it carefully, she could see a push-button on the side, she picked up the note again.

'Do not switch on the navigator until this time.'

With the navigator in her left hand and the note in her right, she stood frozen in a perplexed state. She considered what would happen if she were to push the button.

That was something she would have to contemplate for the next two days.

Kherpri stared at her constantly during the ten-minute box opening ceremony, she remained unmoved throughout.

Present Day

Jessica stepped out from her car and wobbled slightly on the uneven road resting both of her arms on top of the open car door to regain her balance.

All she could see were masses of huge cedar trees as she looked up and down the road; the gentle summer breeze passing over her. She moved away from the car and stood in the middle of the road completely confused by the dead-end road she had just driven down, or rather that her car had chauffeured her to.

Putting one hand on her hip and the other to her head and pushing it through her long hair as if for some sort of inspiration, she felt that she was forced to consider what sort of clueless place she had been brought to. She knew that she had passed over the Welsh border some 30-40 minutes ago in what initially seemed like a great motoring adventure as it was rare that she travelled very far. She had driven past wonderful landscapes and mountains to get to this, not so much lifeless, but very quiet place in the middle of nowhere. She pushed her hand through her long hair and placed her hands on her hips. What sort of clueless place had she been brought to?

She looked up and noticed no birds singing from the very well maintained trees that stretched in a perfect line on both sides of the road, possibly for at least half a mile. Were it not for the noise of the gentle breeze that blew through them, she could have heard a pin drop. A rabbit stared at her from the edge of the road that ended in a perfect 180-degree curve of trees. Nose twitching with some greenery in its mouth, it was unmoved and curious that its day had been disturbed by the presence of another. Markings on the tarmac at the end of the road directly in front of the rabbit suggested that others had driven down this road in the past and had abruptly turned around.

The rabbit disappeared. The only disturbance she could now hear was the bleeping noise coming from the inside of her car. It was then that she realised that she had left the door open and the engine running.

She returned to the car, switched off the engine and closed the door to silence the beeping noise. She then walked the short distance to where she had seen the rabbit. The greenery below the trees was well-kept. Someone had gone to a lot of trouble to maintain this dead-end road. She stepped onto the grass verge towards the trees on the right-hand side of the semicircle and attempted to peer through them in a fruitless attempt to see if anything lay beyond. Seeing anything further than a few feet in front of her was impossible due to the immense depth of the trees. She glanced at her watch and felt a wave of anxiety come up through her tummy. Five minutes to two. She was definitely going to be late.

Earlier In The Day

Jessica had stared at the box referred to as the 'navigator,' for two days. To say she was excited to switch it on was an understatement. She knew, as all higher degree level members did, that rules had to be followed, as rules ensure balance and stability. It would not be the last time that day that she would feel waves of anxiety, but the time to switch on the device was finally upon her.

Nervous at first, she picked it up and stared at it for a little while. Taking a deep breath, she pressed the single button. The silver 'navigator' immediately lit up and a clear white screen appeared, which said one word at the top left-hand side 'Videmus.'

What could that possibly mean she thought to herself. She touched the screen but nothing happened and switching it off and on again three times yielded no further clues either.

Khepri was back at her feet looking up at her as she did a couple of days beforehand.

"What is it Khepri?" she asked. Unsurprisingly, no response was forthcoming and Khepri just continued to stare back at her. Frustrated, she continued to press at the mysterious device.

Khepri broke their stare upon realising that she had been joined by Neith and Tabby.

Jessica looked down at her cats, surprised to see three pairs of eyes were now firmly fixed on her.

"What do you all want?" she questioned in a rare display of ill-patience.

Firmly clutching the navigator, she looked directly into the cats' eyes, something she found much easier than looking directly at humans.

"Why are you all staring at me?" Her voice had now softened but her frown remained as she etched a hint of a smile from the left corner of her mouth.

Jessica had a great connection with her cats, but she had never witnessed all three of them staring at her in unison before. "Are you all trying to tell me something?"

She blinked and returned her gaze to the navigator. Looking at the white screen and re-reading the word, she shook her head in frustration.

She recalled a recent conversation with her Elder after she had been informed of her progression up the Order. "When the time is right, you will have the ability to see." At the time, she thought the comment was a little odd.

Jessica snapped back to the machine; 'enlightened,' 'to see,' 'illumination,' were some of the words bouncing in her head. 'To see...,' 'To see...,' "TO SEE!" she said out loud and lifted the navigator to her face. She brought it close to her eyes and speaking loudly and firmly; "I have the ability to see!" she said with confidence. Instantly, the white screen disappeared and was replaced by the same symbol that appeared on the badge. She snatched the badge off the table and affixed it to her jacket. A message appeared on the screen;

Time for you to leave, make haste Jessica.

A huge beaming smile stretched across her face; "Ha–ha" she exclaimed out loud, stamping her feet up and down. Excitedly, she peered over the kitchen table to speak to the cats, but all three of them had disappeared.

"That's odd!" Without hesitation, she reached out for her car keys. It was time to depart, to where she had no idea.

She was certain she had followed all instructions. Having cracked the entry code to activate the navigator, she went directly to her car without any hesitation and climbed inside. She placed the key into the ignition, whilst mentally preparing herself for what may well be a long drive. She turned the key clockwise and the engine fired into life. At that very moment the air vents sprang forward, flipped around and snapped back into the dashboard revealing a new hidden panel. Jessica was startled; this had never happened before. The new panel had a cradle in it as well as a small screen to the right.

Securing the handbrake, she picked up the navigator noticing that a small entry port had appeared directly below the screen. She assessed the panel and its cradle to see if it would be a perfect fit. It was!

The accelerator pedal immediately fell from beneath her right foot as the car started to jump uncontrollably. Nervously, she released the handbrake. The words 'auto–drive' appeared on the screen next to the navigator and the car hurtled towards the end of the drive.

Slamming her foot on the brake, she grabbed the steering wheel, but the car continued to gain speed.

She shielded her eyes with her hands and squealed as the car turned right onto the main road. Puffing and panting she pressed one hand on the window next to her and the other over her heart in a complete panic; she had no control of the car.

She recognised the elderly gentleman waiting at the pedestrian crossing with his walking stick preparing to cross. The car was not slowing down as the lights changed from green to amber, to red.

"GET OUT THE WAY!!!" she screamed at the top of her voice in a panic, pressing the button to wind down the window. She cocked her head out of the window, her hair flailing behind her; "GET OUT OF THE ROAD!" she screamed waving her arm and sounding and looking like a crazy person, but it was all too late as the man had already started walking slowly across the road.

"AHHHHHH!" she yelled, slamming on the break and covering her eyes. The car came to an abrupt stop. Heart racing at 150 miles per hour, she gasped for breath as she slowly removed her hands from her eyes. The car had stopped dead at the stop sign.

The man stopped in the middle of the crossing looking directly at her in a state of shock; "What's the matter with you crazy woman?" he gesticulated with his stick.

"Sorry, sorry!" she repeated with much sincerity and embarrassment whilst flapping her hands in the air, eyes partially weeping with tears of shock.

He finished crossing, the lights changed back to green and the car lunged forward again. Without holding the steering wheel, Jessica turned around and could see through the rear windscreen that the man was still waving his stick at her.

Oh heavens, what on earth is happening she thought to herself and with that, the car made its way in the direction of the Welsh border.

Present Time

Perplexed, she took another glance at her designer watch and walked back to the car and opened the door. The navigator was still in place and the display that once said auto-drive had now disappeared. She got in and sat in the front seat to consider her options. She had no number to call and no-one she could speak to as the instructions were quite clear;

> **'...do not discuss your appointment...**
> **box to remain on your person at all times...'**

'At all times...' She considered. Pulling the navigator from the cradle the panel immediately turned back around revealing the air vents.

The navigator was still lit but offered nothing else, so she placed it towards her mouth.

"Navigator help," she spoke into it and then pulled it away from her mouth looking longingly at it for guidance.

"Navigator... err... navigate?" Nothing. All that could be heard was the breeze outside and the cursor light still flashed on the screen.

Scratching her head, she stepped outside, away from the car and noticed that the rabbit had reappeared, munching something in its mouth. She started at a pace and walked right up to the rabbit. It swallowed whatever it had been eating before disappearing into the undergrowth.

As she drew close to the trees, she saw something that she hadn't noticed before. The tarmac ended at the semicircle, but there was a dip in the grassed area to the right, exactly where the rabbit had disappeared, almost as if it were an entry point to somewhere. To the right of her, she could see a camouflaged green post with a tiny symbol on it. Crouching down, she recognised it instantly.

She held the navigator next to the post and leaned down so that her pin badge was level with it. Immediately, she heard a loud clicking noise followed by the sound of grinding metal coming from the ground below. She was unsure if the ground beneath her feet was moving as the trees shook in front of her. She took a couple of steps backwards in panic. The trees directly in front of her started to part and move backwards, she could see twigs and foliage falling into the gap that had now appeared as the trees gave way either side of her. The mechanical rumblings from below became louder as the gap that had appeared was now being refilled by a huge slab of tarmac that was being pushed upright from below. The twigs and dirt that had fallen into the gap only moments before were now resting directly on top of what was an unblemished tarmac driveway.

There was a loud crunching noise and everything came to a standstill.

Jessica looked around to see if anybody else had seen this unbelievable event that had just happened right in front of her.

The trees had given way to reveal what Jessica had been summoned to see. Adrenaline raced through her veins.

"Oh my!" were the only words that could be heard drifting down the eerie road.

Chapter Seven:

WORD OF THE ORDER

WEDNESDAY AFTERNOON

Mildred tilted her head towards the stairs. She had only just finished putting her clothes away in the wardrobe when she heard the not too familiar noise of her phone meowing.

It was reasonable to assume that it was probably someone trying to sell something as she was not due a call from Daphne or the other Mildreds.

All the same, she shuffled down the stairs to answer it just in case.

Mildred had been a reasonably sociable person in her former life, before becoming a member of the cat club, which has slowly led to her happy but virtually solitary life with her cat.

"Hello, number one Rocke Road" she answered.

"Oh, hello Mildred, it's Jessica."

"Hello, Jessica," the cogs of her brain turned over, "I'm sorry, which Jessica is this?"

"Oh, yes, sorry Mildred, its Jessica, you met me at the gathering last year. I was speaking with Daphne, do you remember?"

Mildred pulled the cat's bottom away from her mouth, staring at the phone in confusion, yes of course I remember, but what would Daphne's 'Elder' be doing ringing me, she thought?

Composing herself, with a little cough to clear her throat, she answered "Yes, of course, Lady Jessica, I remember you very well. How are you? How are your cats? I'm very sorry, I do not recall their names?"

"That's okay Mildred, my cats are fine, thank you for asking. I wanted..."

"How many do you have, I can't remember?" interrupted an over-excited Mildred.

Jessica had to remind herself that Mildred was still new to the Order and there were a great many things that she was yet to understand.

"Well I have three Mildred; a person of my degree level always has three."

"Oh, how wonderful, I just have Missy, she's my company. Daphne has two cats you know? Binky and Aziza."

Jessica smiled to herself hearing Mildred speaking at motormouth speed, knowing all too well that Daphne has two cats and that Binky was not her real name.

"Yes, I am aware of this Mildred."

"Although bit of a shock yesterday; Missy had a bit of a funny turn, started hissing at a complete stranger. Never heard her do anything like that before; most odd."

"Oh, I'm sure it's nothing, Mildred. Cats are very independent and occasionally like to make their presence felt."

"Mmm, maybe. Some strange chap wearing weird glasses."

Jessica's eyes widened immediately with concern. "Strange glasses you say, Mildred, such as?"

"Oh, how would I know, I'm not a fashion person. Anyway, I've been thinking about getting another cat; company for Missy as well as for myself. I can afford to keep another one. I've seen some beautiful cats in Cats Monthly, they're..."

Jessica's eyes widened further; "No, Mildred, you do not need another cat at this time!"

Realising that she had snapped her answer and interrupted Mildred she composed herself. "I'm quite sure in the future this will not be a problem."

Mildred's upbeat mood was instantly withdrawn. She had heard it mentioned before that she should only own one cat; why it was such a problem in this club that celebrated cats she did not know. Surely the more cats the better?

Jessica remembered that it was only five years ago that she had been at the same point of membership within the Order as Mildred. She knew that she would need patience for the remainder of this phone call.

"I wanted to call you to see if you are keeping well Mildred?"

"I'm fine, thank you," Mildred said softly, still somewhat curious as to why Lady Jessica had called her in the first place. So far, all she had gleaned from this call was that she was being told she couldn't have another cat.

She removed that from her mind and picked up the tone of her voice "I'm better now that I've finally settled on what to wear on Friday."

"Oh good, so you are looking forward to Friday, are you? It should be a very good night and well attended." Jessica smiled to herself pleased to have got the conversation back on track and with the added knowledge that Friday would be her naming ceremony.

"Oh yes, I have my new handmade cardigan and my hat. It's always exciting to meet other members in the region; I've not had a chance to speak to many of the older members as yet."

Jessica sensed Mildred's curiosity, "That may well be the case right now, but that will most certainly change. The longer you are a member of the Order, the more valued you become." Jessica was nodding at the same time with a smile of contentment across her face.

"I'm sorry, the Order?"

Jessica froze, the smile disappearing from her face as quickly as it had arrived. Putting one hand to her face, she reminded herself, yet again, that Mildred did not know these things yet. "Er, yes, the order... I'm so sorry, I am reading a takeaway menu at the same time as talking to you, I was thinking of ordering something to eat. How very rude of me. I do apologise, I meant to say the club."

"Oh, that's okay Lady Jessica, I've done it before when speaking to the other Mildreds. Mildred from Merewood Close likes to talk about her cakes. Now I'm not much of a cake person, but she is and she does make a wonderful jam sponge…"

Jessica was pleased that she had gotten out of that one, but had to pinch herself as a reminder that she needed to be patient. She mentally tried to rejoin the conversation whilst Mildred was still talking away at 100 miles per hour.

"...She is quite remarkable with her baking skills. Anyway, I did the same thing to her recently. I was flicking through Cats Quarterly as she was talking away, she asked me a question and I didn't even hear what she said, ha-ha, can you believe it? I felt so silly." Mildred was still laughing but seemed to be the only one doing so. "Jessica? Lady Jessica?"

"Yes, Mildred I am here." She responded, realising that she had drifted off for the second time during the phone call. The thought of the stranger with the glasses concerned her. "That is a very amusing story."

"Isn't it?" Mildred said with a frowned expression as she was rapidly coming to the conclusion that Jessica didn't appear to be paying much attention.

"Well, I guess I had better get to the reason why I called. As part of my new and expanding role within the club, I want to spend more time with our members and get to know them more on a personal level. This includes you, Mildred. So, I wondered if you would like a lift to the gathering on Friday?"

"Oh, do you have a new role Lady Jessica?"

She raised her hand to her head again, realising for the second time, she had spoken out of turn. Her promotion was supposed to be kept quiet for now. She had informed Daphne of her move up the ranks earlier in the day at the Coach and Horses, but she had used that as an excuse to meet with her to find out how Mildred was doing. She contemplated that she was not particularly good at this sneaky kind of behaviour, but she had been asked to do it, and it was for the benefit of the Order after all.

"Yes. I'll find out more on Friday, it's still a little vague, to be honest."

"Well, I'd be delighted to accept a lift from you. I would also like us to spend more time together, you must know a great deal about cats."

"Yes, I guess I do."

But Jessica knew a great deal more about other things as well as cats.

"I'd better get going. So, I'll see you on Friday."

"I understand Lady Jessica. Do you know where I live so you can collect me?"

"Oh yes, we know where you live."

Mildred was staring at her phone again.

Chapter Eight:

THE CURATOR AND THE WATCHED GARDEN

TUESDAY

Standing at the front of a very imposing driveway, Jessica could see that it was a short distance to walk to a very elaborately decorated archway with huge gates. Stepping forward beyond the tree line, the walls that ran from either side of the archway stretched for as far as she could see. They had to be at least ten feet tall, keeping uninvited and prying eyes at bay. Looking back, the tree lines to her left and right looked like an immense never-ending forest, secluded and peaceful. She could see the archway was made of huge pieces of weather-worn sandstone. Triangular like turrets pointed towards the sky from the very top of the arch and in the centre lay a huge crest and a small decorative shape below it. She was unable to work out what it was; an old family crest presumably.

The trees sat motionless behind her save the breeze that passed over them. She guessed they would resume their position as soon as she had entered. Set beneath her feet were metal tracks that guided the trees back and forth.

The tranquillity of the surroundings was interrupted as the gates underneath the archway started to open inwards, the sound of moving metal forcing her to take a few steps back. There was a loud crash of metal hitting metal as the gates drew to a halt. It was reasonable to presume that this was her invitation to enter the gardens that came into view beyond the gates.

The mansion house in the distance looked to have a grand entrance with too many windows to count and huge chimneys breaking up the skyline. The detail of the gardens in front of her and how well they were maintained either side of the main driveway, was equally impressive.

Jessica was amazed at the stunning beauty of the old mansion house that lay peacefully hidden away from the eyes of others. She strained her eyes to see the finer details of the enormous building that stood probably half a mile away. It was intimidating but just as impressive as the well-maintained gardens.

She looked down at her clean, expensive heels, which were not especially practical for walking such distances and considered her options. The trees behind her had not closed back on themselves, as she looked at her little black car sat alone on the road with no name. Jessica scratched her chin, looked at her car, then back at the house and made the decision that the car would take her the length of the driveway. This would preserve her heels, not to mention she was already late for her meeting. She turned her back on the house moving quickly towards her car. She got in, turned the keys and waited for the hidden panel behind her vents to reappear and the engine to start. She placed the navigator in the cradle and felt the car move forward. I'm getting good at this she thought, although nerves were starting to get the better of her.

Her car drove straight through the main gates. Jessica looked out of the rear windscreen to see the trees shaking as they moved back into place. They had to be at least ten trees deep, how on earth could that be possible? She was now being auto driven towards a place she did not know, with no idea as to whom she would be meeting.

The gardens on both sides of the driveway were stunningly impressive; she had never seen grass so green and cared for. The bushes had been carved into shapes, or possibly symbols that meant something to someone. Between some of the carved topiaries were occasional statues that sat almost within their own gardens.

She spotted a huge statue in the distance holding one arm aloft with what appeared to be a cat in the other, but at that distance, she couldn't be sure. The car must have been moving at 30 miles per hour down the driveway as the imposing size of the grand mansion house came more into view. She giggled to herself at the thought of receiving a personal invitation to this most grand place.

Jessica was admiring the perfectly trimmed, pyramid-shaped bushes when something caught her eye moving towards the large statue. She pressed her face closer to the glass, positive that she had seen a cloaked figure.

"Car stop, stop!" she yelled. "Navigator, stop the car!" She said with authority though it was duly ignored.

Without thinking, she hit the car horn and the black-cloaked figure spun around and stared directly at her. She froze to her seat. The car kept moving until the cloaked figure disappeared from view.

Jessica gathered her thoughts as the car approached the grand main entrance doors. She was very nervous and could feel her heart beating in her chest. Preparing herself, she ran her hand through her hair and down the length of her jacket. She was practising her smile when the car veered to the left away from the main entrance.

"Wait, where are we going?" she exclaimed with some panic, watching the main entrance disappear over her right shoulder. The car moved at speed down the driveway along the side of the house. Her hands started to shake as her adrenaline spiralled out of control.

There was a lake on the left with a boathouse and more stunning gardens, but there are only so many gardens you can admire in a state of panic. The car made another abrupt turn and stopped dead, lunging Jessica forward as the engine cut off. Small plumes of dust settled to reveal a series of doors. Her knuckles had turned white from gripping the steering wheel, though it served little purpose.

"Is this it, do I get out now?" she said to the car not expecting a response.

She took a deep breath and opened the car door and looked up at the grand old house and its stone construction, cornices and huge windows, some probably 12 feet high. The building must be at least 4 or 5 storeys high. There were many busts on plinths, carvings with shields and gargoyles on every tier of the house. She grabbed her bag off the passenger seat and closed the car door.

She was drawn to an arched doorway inset to the rear of the building. No-one had appeared to greet her, so she went to investigate for herself.

She walked towards the abandoned looking building, there were no other vehicles, which was quite odd for such a huge place. Someone must have controlled the gates as well as looking after these immaculate gardens. Suddenly, she remembered 'the navigator must remain on your person at all times.'

She returned to the car and snatched the navigator out of the cradle, dropping it into her bag. As she walked back towards the house, the car engine started and the car drove off by itself, passing her before it dipped out of view. Jessica shook her head, not giving it another thought. She was adapting to all things new on this very strange day.

She walked up to the archway and looked at the incredibly strong oak doors that lay before her. On the wall, she noticed the familiar symbol that had been opening doors for her all day.

She leaned towards the symbol with her badge and waited. A loud click was heard, followed by the sound of huge wooden doors moaning as if being disturbed from their resting place of some hundreds of years. As the doors moved inwards, her eyes opened wide as she surveyed whatever she could see inside; not surprisingly it appeared to be a very old room and it was empty.

Taking the initiative with this newfound courage, Jessica stepped through onto the wooden flooring that creaked under her weight. Dozens of mahogany coloured wooden panels covered the walls. There were flickering candles supported on wall-mounted, silver holders offering enough light to brighten the room. Multiple black wooden beams ran the length of the ceiling and it was cool for this time of year. The reflections and shadows on the mahogany panelled walls made the room feel eerie.

Jessica turned abruptly to the sound of the groaning wooden doors banging closed, causing an echo to reverberate around the room. Her pulse increased and she swallowed to wet her dry throat. She was startled by a figure looking back at her. The figure, partially silhouetted by the candlelight, was short in stature with its hands behind its back.

"Don't worry about the car. It has a beacon when on the grounds of the Order," the figure said looking directly at Jessica, who was frozen in fear.

The figure took a step forward, it was a woman.

"It's good to see you again Jessica, it's been quite some time. I'm Nubia, the Curator. Welcome to the Great Manor Of Loxley and thank you enormously for bringing it to our attention that you had arrived by banging your car horn; quite the entrance!"

She beamed an enormous smile that bordered on terrifying.

The smile slowly disappeared from Nubia's face as they stood in silence.

Still, with her hands behind her back, Nubia spoke quietly, "Look at me, Jessica."

Jessica shifted her body weight and stuttered a little cough, reluctantly turning her eyes towards Nubia. Their eyes met.

"That wasn't so bad was it now? There's much to discuss. Follow me." With that, she smiled and turned on her heels.

"I am taking you to the long walk, which is the main corridor and the heart of the house. You have access to everywhere from there," she stopped abruptly and turned her head, "well, permitted areas of course." No eye contact was made, but Nubia flashed a smile before she started walking again.

The next room comprised of very old furniture with an unlit fireplace, which took centre place in the room. There was a viewing balcony above with an immaculately carved balustrade. Old artworks hung on the wall depicting scenes and events from days past. The ever-quickening pace of her house guide did not allow time for her to see much more.

Jessica left the door open behind her as she entered a carpeted corridor with wall to wall portraits of older distinguished ladies. Many of them wore decorative chains around their necks or emblems and badges displaying some form of common order. The corridor smelt old and musty. Whether this was caused by damp or just a lack of use over many years, she could not possibly know. She could only imagine the generations that had passed through these corridors over the course of time.

The surroundings were incredibly quiet with the only exception being the sound of ticking coming from multiple clocks placed throughout the long corridor. She paused to look at an extremely old looking clock, watching the pendulum sway back and forth steadily. Suddenly, the clock came alive, chiming into action. Within a fraction of a second, the other clocks chimed, ringing throughout the corridor, bringing this silent corridor to life.

Beside the clock was a portrait of, what she guessed to be, an Elder. She stared at the old eyes.

It reminded her of someone from her past. The sound of the clocks became more unnerving than reassuring; she did glance at one informing her that it was now quarter past two. The clocks fell silent in unison.

"Keep up!" Nubia asserted. Her pace was considerable for someone of such small stature.

They passed a study, a library and what looked like some form of weapons room, which Jessica stopped to inspect with curiosity. Peering through the slightly open door she could see swords, shields and a few other antique battle items. A shield displaying a damaged crest caught her eye. She leaned her head closer to the door to read the inscribed plaque directly beneath it; 'The Gate Of Souls...'

The door slammed shut before she could finish reading it. Startled, Jessica jumped back. Nubia had stopped and was staring at her once again, bolt upright, chin aloft, hands behind her back. "You'll find nothing of use to you in there." As she said this immediately all of the other open doors within the corridor slammed shut with a loud thud; there was no smile on her face this time. "Come, we are nearly at the long walk."

Jessica made a mental note to keep looking forwards from now on.

Approaching the end of the corridor, Jessica noticed a huge tapestry on the wall that depicted a mountain scene with a grey-haired lady holding her arms in the air with a spear in one hand and something that was not very clear in the other. She had a cat at her feet and dark cloaked shapes were coming up the mountain towards her.

No time to assess it further. Nubia had turned the corner to the left and stopped. She turned around, looked at Jessica and proudly proclaimed;

"Welcome to the long walk of Loxley."

Jessica's mouth fell open letting out a small gasp. It was the most elaborate corridor she had ever seen.

Nubia stood back, allowing time for Jessica to absorb this rich paradise of decadent splendour. She smiled as she watched Jessica take in the architectural spectacle for the very first time.

Jessica took a few paces forward, her initial shocked expression quickly changed to a beaming smile.

The corridor that Nubia had called the 'long walk' ran the whole length of the house. Stunned at the enormity of the place there were equally spaced multiple grand arches that lay ahead and further corridors peeled away to the left between each arch. But one grand archway stood out above the others. Approximately half way down the length of the corridor there was a large opening that looked to be the central point of the house; it was the only place where the movement of others could be seen.

There were doorways directly to her left and right and there were two staircases directly in front of her; she suspected that many more lay beyond. The staircases had the most incredible amount of opulent detail.

Gold carpet runners with millimetre precision secured a patterned, thick carpet that weaved its way up the stairs and around corners out of sight. The wooden panelling above heavy oak handrails had elaborate carvings of shields and words that were in an unreadable language to her.

Nubia watched Jessica lift her head to look at the ceiling; those that had the rare chance to see Loxley always reacted in the same way. The smile across Jessica's face was all telling as she surveyed the ceiling that featured the same mahogany panelling she had seen on the walls in the other rooms, chandeliers hung down from multiple panels on long black chains. Jessica noticed the candles on these chandeliers did not flicker in the same way as those in the first room she visited, these chandeliers were powered. She could not help but notice how clean everywhere appeared; upon first inspection there didn't appear to be a speck of dust anywhere, an incredible feat for a place clearly so grand in scale and age.

The musty smell of the corridor of clocks had long since disappeared. The long walk corridor was clearly more lived in and had purpose.

She took a couple of further steps forward on the deep red carpet that ran the length of floor up to the main grand archway. Beyond there the flooring was tiled and it looked like the area between the grand arches served as the central lobby of the house, she presumed the main entrance doors could be found there. Jessica shook her head in disbelief. It must cost a fortune to maintain this place, an observation that she thought it wise to keep to herself.

"Come, let me show you to my chambers," said Nubia resuming the lead.

There was too much for Jessica to take in. The further they travelled the more fascinated she became with the enormity of the grand house and the elaborate display of wealth. She marvelled at the opulence of it all. This was not a manor house, it was a palace.

All of the doors ahead were closed. She could see the familiar symbol of the Order on the right-hand side of every single door. These were not your average 'turn handle to enter' doors, a passcode or similar was needed to enter. She was curious to find out whether her pin badge would open any of the doors, but with Nubia watching her every move, it was unlikely that she would find out.

The domed skylight high above the large lobby area, brought a smile to her face as she admired the balconies that lay below it. Everything was so grand in scale it was almost unprecedented; the wood carvings, the opulence of the archways and the four hooded people sitting at a huge, old oak desk. She paused and looked at the white cloaks they wore, noticing the symbol etched in black on the top of their hoods. She could not see their faces as all four heads were bowed down busy working. Jessica swallowed not knowing what to say. She turned to Nubia, who was standing by a flight of stairs with her hands behind her back. To the left of the stairway, Jessica noticed a metal sliding gate with a lit compartment right behind it and push buttons inside.

"Follow me." Nubia started up the stairs.

"Do we have far to go?" questioned Jessica.

Nubia stopped climbing up the stairs and turned around looking quite perplexed.

"Why ever would you ask?"

"Oh it's just; it looks like there is a lift here." Jessica shrugged her shoulders and half-heartedly pointed towards the lift. "I was just curious." She offered a smile.

Nubia descended a couple of steps. "The lifts only go down." She gave another fake smile.

"Oh, that's unusual for such a large building." Jessica attempted a smile, exposing more teeth than she meant to. Nubia was unmoved, once again, looking Jessica in the eyes with one eyebrow slightly raised. Jessica averted her gaze.

Nubia's response was very firm and composed. "We only go down when we choose to go down and if we choose to go down we are carried. We are always supported when entering the lower places and that is the way it has been for a very long time. When we ascend we do it on our own terms. We are ascending, so we walk." Another fake smile appeared across her face as she turned around and proceeded up the stairs.

Chapter Nine:

THE LONG HAIRED MAN

WEDNESDAY EVENING

Roy Jenkins was tapping his watch, staring at it quizzically; he took it off his wrist and held it to his ear. It was 6.45 pm. He walked into his kitchen to check the clock, which read 6.46. Lifting an eyebrow, he returned to the front room and pulled back his net curtain to take a look next door.

He could see Mildred in her front garden holding a tin can, standing on her tiptoes, craning her neck to look up and down the street. As standard, she had on a pair of brown shoes, crumpled stockings, a plain skirt, a blouse, a baggy cardigan and a knitted woollen hat with a flower pattern on it. What was not standard was the time. It was not yet 7 o'clock and she was already banging the cat food tin. He checked his watch again to make sure.

"What on earth is that woman up to now?" he said out loud knowing this was the first time he could ever recall her being out looking for the cat ahead of schedule.

He sat back down and mentally prepared himself for anything up to ten minutes of noise.

"MISSYYYYYY" could be heard up and down the length of Rocke Road followed by a combination of banging and clattering noises.

"MISSSYYYYYYYYY."

Mildred walked to the end of her path and poked her head over her gate looking up and down the road. Missy was nowhere to be seen. She stepped onto the pavement still surveying left and right, noticing for the first time that her hedge had been cut back. She knew it was rare that Missy would show up straight away, but just in case, Mildred always made a point of looking up at people's garage roofs and in trees, or bending down to see if she was sitting under a parked car. She wished Missy wouldn't do that.

She looked down the road towards the bus stop and could see youths playing around; they usually were around the bus stop these days. One had a skateboard, a couple had bikes and the other three were sitting down. She was fairly sure they were not waiting for a bus.

She continued to bang the tin with her spoon. "MISSY!" She looked over to see the youths laughing and making fun of her. She did not like it, she did not like it at all.

"Mildreddddd!" One of them yelled in her direction.

As usual, she chose to ignore it.

"Oh Mildreddddddd, are you the crazy cat lady?"

"Crazy cat, crazy cat..." A couple of them jeered in unison.

It was most unpleasant. Quite what she had done to receive this regular abuse she did not know. She had no idea who they were or how they knew her name. She went to bang the tin again but they were all still laughing.

"That's enough!" Someone shouted from behind the boys. "Leave her alone, she's done nothing to you."

The boys shouted back but soon moved off in the direction of Benbow Street. As Mildred watched them head off down the road, she saw a figure appear on the path from where the noise had come from. She recognised him by his long curly hair and leather jacket. He looked towards her. Embarrassed, Mildred looked to the floor, but looked up again and caught his eye. He took one hand out of his pocket and waved. She looked at the floor again and took a couple of steps back towards the gate. She was a little flustered.

Mildred lifted the spoon ready to beat the tin can when she looked down to find Missy staring up at her.

"Oh good Missy, let's go inside. It's time for dinner. I don't want to miss Bang Goes Your Money." She looked back towards the man just in time to catch a smile before he disappeared down his driveway. She didn't know his name but had walked passed his house many times. All she knew was that she was very grateful for his help.

Chapter Ten:

THE PASSING OF LADY TEMPEST

TUESDAY

Jessica considered that she was not making the best impressions and that she should probably keep her mouth shut. Before following Nubia up the stairs, she glanced across at the buttons on the lift panel. Strange that in such a grand house, the lift only went down.

"There are five main floors in the house, hundreds of rooms and two attic areas. My office and my workers can be found further down here on the second floor." Nubia said, reaching the top of the staircase.

There is clearly an area below as well Jessica considered, but thought it wise not to mention it. She had a feeling that the area would be off-limits.

They proceeded into yet another red-carpeted corridor, with more wooden panelling, which led to a large diamond-shaped opening with corridors at every point.

Like the floor below, four figures sat at an enormous oak desk working in unison, keeping themselves busy. Again, they wore white cloaks, and their faces were not visible. They did not look up.

Jessica could not help herself; "Madam Nubia, I must ask, who are they?" she whispered.

"Oh, you don't need to whisper Jessica, you cannot offend them. You won't have seen them in recent times, but these are some of my Clerics." Nubia stopped and turned to face Jessica, "I have many."

The closer they got, the more there seemed to be an icy and unnerving presence around them.

Jessica turned her attention to the ceilings and artwork as they resumed their pace down the left fork of the diamond-shaped lobby. Jessica looked back to see the Cleric furthest away from her had lifted its cloaked head and was staring straight at her. She instantly felt a chill and the hairs on the back of her neck stood up as she looked at the deathly pale face.

They approached a large doorway set into the wall on the left. Pillars ran up the sides of the walls leading to a highly elaborate five-feet deep archway with a lit symbol on the right. It was different from the other symbols she had seen so far.

The solid oak door bore heavy scars with ancient fortifications that must have served a purpose in the past. There was a huge crest in the centre of the door chipped in places. A large crack ran throughout it. The doorway was cold, vacant and unclean, unlike everywhere else she had seen on this floor.

"May I ask what this door is for?" Jessica asked.

"Why, that is the office of the Reeve, my dear." She smiled and tilted her head slightly to the right, almost as if Jessica had asked an obvious question.

"The Reeve?" Jessica repeated as frown lines appeared across her forehead.

"Yes, the Reeve. Come, this way, we are nearly there."

They moved to the final door at the end of the corridor. Nubia pushed it open with ease and although Jessica could see the symbol lit up on the right-hand side, Nubia did not need to use it.

"Please take a seat." Nubia ushered Jessica towards a very old high-backed chair that stood about 6 feet in height.

"Thank you." Jessica gave a little smile as she took a quick look around the room. There was a couch under the main gothic-looking window that she suspected Nubia may stand on to look outside. The shelving was quite low down, presumably so that she could reach her curious-looking ornaments.

The old, heavy curtains were tied back and there were various portraitures of very imposing looking women hung on the walls.

The hard seat was uncomfortable. Jessica crossed one leg over the other, wriggling in the seat, but she knew this was probably a formal meeting, so she uncrossed her legs and resumed the former position, looking like someone of importance who was sitting on a throne.

She could hear the ticking of an old clock behind her and quickly glanced over at it. Clocks seemed to be a prominent feature in this mansion house, but she didn't dwell on it and considered it best to keep her focus on the lady in front of her.

Nubia glanced at notes on her desk before sitting back in her seat. She placed one leg over the other and pulled her hands together into a ball, resting them on her knee. A curt smile appeared on her face.

"Your naming ceremony and appointment to Degree Level 6 is imminent following the very sad passing of Lady Tempest. An appointment, which was not mine to make. Council presides over such matters."

Her words lingered in the air. "Your being here today is due to that very sad occasion." She paused briefly. "I understand you met Lady Tempest once. An intellectual who undoubtedly would have proceeded to higher Degree Levels. Most unusually, she was very popular with the Grand Council for someone of such a lesser degree." Nubia spoke with clarity and conviction. "She most certainly shined. It's immensely sad that she has passed, even more so in the manner of how it happened." Nubia looked down to the floor and took a deep breath. The passing of Lady Tempest clearly upset her.

Jessica noticed Nubia's knuckles became white as she gripped tighter with the ball of her hands.

"What happened?" Jessica asked.

With a sorrowful face, she looked back up at Jessica. "She was the victim of a most tragic road accident."

"That is terrible." Jessica was quite upset on hearing this. Abrielle, her Elder, had informed her that Lady Tempest had passed over but not explained how it happened.

"Was she in a self-drive car at the time?" Jessica questioned without thinking, remembering her own experiences just an hour or two before.

A frown crossed Nubia's face and her eyes widened. She resumed her composure. "No, she was hit by a bus."

They both sat in momentary silence.

"We are most disturbed by this," Nubia mumbled deep in thought. "She was in a place where she was not supposed to be. In fact, she was far from where she was supposed to be. The very thought that such an intellect would walk out onto a road so carelessly. We all had high hopes for her. We are still looking into this." Nubia shook her head in disbelief but spoke with some certainty.

Nubia broke from her thoughts. "Tea?"

Jessica looked back up.

"Would you like a cup of tea Jessica?" Nubia enquired.

"Oh, yes, that would be wonderful, thank you."

Nubia stood to her feet, walked the short distance towards a table on Jessica's right, picked up a tea-pot and poured black tea into small china cups.

"And here we are, Jessica, only nine years since you received your first visit from your Elder Abrielle. I'm informed she supports your appointment."

"And you do not?" shot straight out of Jessica's mouth before she realised what she had said. Nubia lowered the tea-pot and stopped pouring upon hearing this spontaneous remark.

"There are others more qualified than you, but my opinions are not taken into account. That is not the role of the Curator. My role within the Order is clearly defined as are those of Clerics, the Keeper and others."

She resumed pouring. "Order and process have not changed for a very long time and we ensure balance and prosperity. Recent events of this nature are most troubling indeed," she said, shaking her head. She reached for the silver tongs and dropped a slice of lemon into Jessica's tea.

She walked to the main desk, placed a cup of tea in front of Jessica, laid one on the table for herself and took her seat.

"Presumably, this is why I was brought here, to discuss my appointment? I have never seen this place before, but things seem familiar for some reason."

"Really?" She looked directly at Jessica with a concerned frown and did her best to keep eye contact. "You have been here before, Jessica, but it was a very long time ago. It would be most peculiar if your memory served you after such a long time has passed."

She paused as she tried to assess Jessica's face.

"Memories fade, but history will always remain!" Nubia said with surety as she took a sip of tea. "More trust will be placed with you and upon you, more responsibilities and more knowledge. That is why you are here today, for preparation for what is to come in the future."

Nubia placed her cup on the saucer, crossed her legs and rested her hands in the ball position.

"You will have your own office here. Your navigator will bring you whenever you wish. How to use it properly will be explained to you in due course and you will be informed as to when you do need to be here; most come when a time of reflection is needed."

Jessica nodded and tried to hide a smile that was itching to get out on hearing that she will have her own office in the grand house.

"Is that why it is so quiet here?" she asked.

"There are many in the Order, as you know, but this special place is our quiet home and has been for a long time. It is a very rare occurrence that the house is full. I do not like the noise if truth be told," she lifted an eyebrow at the very thought of the calm tranquillity of this place being disturbed.

"I remain here with the Lady of the House, other essential members of the household and of course the Clerics. They never leave the grounds."

They both sat in silence, drinking their tea.

"I must ask Madam Curator," Jessica shuffled in her seat with curiosity. "My car, how on earth did it do that? It was almost by magic."

The Curator slammed her cup down on the saucer with such an abrupt noise that Jessica jumped in her seat, spilling tea down her top.

"We do not speak of those things here!" Nubia said, enraged, her face red with anger. Jessica sat aghast from this outburst.

"I'm sorry, I meant no...."

"Your car and its devices are nothing but technology from the world outside of here, produced by our specialist teams and their experts, nothing more. Whilst I do not embrace technology, we have no choice but to accept it and utilise it. The world outside craves new developments and technologies; they have a thirst for it." Nubia scowled. "Our principles and our goals are unchanged, but regrettably, we have had to evolve, if we do not, others that seek to disrupt our way of life may do so." The noise of china hitting china filled the room as Jessica struggled to compose herself, her cup and the saucer shaking uncontrollably in her hands following Nubia's outburst. Jessica made an attempt to break the silent deadlock.

"I'm sorry about banging the car horn; I thought I saw something in the garden."

Nubia looked up to hear more.

"Someone wearing a black cloak moving towards a large statue."

Nubia shook her head with a dismissive smile. "You tried to get the attention of a Watcher by banging a car horn? Most peculiar, I've never heard anything of the sort; it is those actions that concern me about your appointment," she scowled.

Jessica could not bear the sound of china on china any further and placed the cup and saucer on the desk.

"What you saw was a Watcher performing daily chores, although strange that it was alone close to the great statue of Salma."

Nubia's body language had an air of concern about it as she looked at the floor in consideration.

Jessica coughed slightly and shifted uncomfortably in her seat. "May I ask Lady Nubia, why are they here; Watchers, I've heard of them, but I don't fully understand?" She was confident that she had asked a sensible question this time.

"It's time you were informed of some things, Jessica, so I will say this on the matter."

Jessica looked on with interest watching Nubia's fingers tighten in their little ball. "The Watchers are the last remnants of an old poisonous bloodline that sought to damage the Order a long time ago. They do not like us; they do not like our ways or what we stand for. If they had their way, we would all live in darkness."

She paused, staring at Jessica; "They are evil."

Jessica swallowed, listening intently.

"There are more of them and they all have their appointed duties. Some maintain the house, some the gardens and farming area and others have chores that we assign to them. They are outcasts, so they wear black robes as a reminder of days of old. Our Clerics wear white as they represent purity and passiveness. Underneath their dark robes, the Watchers are quite unpleasant to look at up close, I'm afraid." Nubia paused.

"We try not to talk about them. Their bloodline was corrupted a long time ago. In time, you will have access to information that will explain more. Still, for now, all you need to know is that they serve their place, and on occasions, need to be reminded of their place, but they are servants nevertheless. Watchers try to resist harmony and balance, which is why they are here to remind them of such. Their place here in the lower parts of Loxley goes deep underground and that is where they belong, in the dark places."

She looked at Jessica with concern, "They always become more active close to a gathering as they can sense when we all meet. Many roam freely on the outside of here, but we detain them when we can. A poisonous cast from a long time ago, they endure and that is why the Order is necessary to ensure they do not succeed in their overall goal."

"And what is that?" Jessica asked with some concern and curiosity.

Nubia looked to the floor, "I cannot say."

With that, the room fell silent.

Nubia stretched her fingers and curled her hands into a ball, placing them on her knees. "There is one more thing before you leave. This is vitally important and requires your most utmost care and attention."

Jessica nodded her head with interest, "I understand, Madam Nubia. What is it?"

"Although you are here today as a matter of degree process, something has arisen that is most unusual. I've been here a very long time and I've not seen the like throughout my time as Curator." Her head shook a couple of times before she looked up. "What I'm about to tell you is secret. It must remain between us; do you understand?"

Jessica tried to conceal her surprise, but she was excited nevertheless being entrusted with private information. "Yes, Madam Nubia, of course."

"I spoke with a member of The Grand Council a few days ago. I do not want to go into the full details about it right now, but she was very specific with what she told me."

Nubia placed both hands on the desk and looked directly at Jessica.

"You know the Lady of whom I am about to speak of as you are her Elder."

Jessica recoiled in shock, "Daphne?"

"Yes, Daphne; you are to keep a personal watch over her, but we are more interested in the one who calls herself Mildred. Daphne is Mildred's Elder. We want you to make contact with Mildred and to watch her. Do I make myself clear?"

Jessica swallowed with worry, "Erm, yes, Madam Nubia, are they in trouble or have they done something wrong?"

"It is too early to tell and the reasons why you are being entrusted with this will tell us more about your suitability in deserving this new Level 6 appointment. Your progress to higher degree status in the future will depend on your personal diligence in this matter. This is your duty, Jessica; this is what you need to do for the good of the Order. Watch both of them, especially Mildred."

Jessica swallowed the saliva in her mouth. "It would be my honour Lady Nubia" she offered humbly.

Nubia nodded, "Despite my misgivings about your early appointment to this level, I'm assigning you to this task and I need you to observe her. See that it is done."

The look on Nubia's face suggested the meeting was over.

Jessica stood up to leave, straightening her skirt with both hands before grabbing her bag. Inside the bag, she noticed the navigator cursor flashing as if awaiting instruction.

"I will escort you out. Your car waits for you outside." Nubia stood to her feet.

On their way out, Jessica noticed that the Reeve's door was open very slightly and the Clerics were nowhere to be seen. Jessica could feel Nubia's eyes bearing down on her back, watching her every move as she walked behind her.

As they descended the last step, Jessica looked across the grand lobby and the main entrance at the front of the house and took a couple of steps towards them.

"Where are you going?"

Jessica immediately stopped, hearing Nubia's voice and turned around.

"You arrived through the back door and you leave in the very same manner."

Jessica gave an awkward smile and a nod of embarrassment. She headed down the long walk in the direction of the tapestry. When she reached it, she turned right into the corridor of clocks, noticing all of the doors were still closed. She could hear Nubia's footsteps a couple of paces behind hers as she headed towards the exit rooms.

She felt somewhat relieved to be leaving as she reached the final door. She turned to Nubia.

"Thank you for your invitation and your time Lady Nubia."

"The invitation was necessary Jessica," she smiled. "But the time was mine and you are welcome to that," she said, nodding her head a few times, almost approving of her own excellence.

Nubia stepped forward and the heavy doors moaned once more as they opened. Jessica could see her car was already waiting for her outside.

Nubia looked up at her. "Good luck with your endeavours Jessica and please keep watch over Mildred."

Jessica was considering a handshake but thought better of it as Nubia's hands were behind her back once again.

"Thank you." She said, walking out of the doors towards her car.

"Oh Jessica, one more thing."

Jessica turned around, noticing Lady Nubia's short stature in the archway towering above her.

"Do inform us if you ever see a figure wearing peculiar glasses." The familiar tight-lipped, horizontal smile appeared across Nubia's face. She stepped back a few paces as the doors came to a close with a loud thud.

Jessica sat in her car, started the engine and took the navigator out of her bag placing it inside the cradle. The pedals moved from under her feet and the car took her away from the most amazing grounds. At the forefront of her mind, all she could think about was two key things, how incredibly rude Nubia was and the fact that there was not a cat in sight.

Chapter Eleven:

THE PALM OF DUAT

Mildred looked over at Missy with some concern, her bowl was full of cat food, yet she seemed mostly disinterested in it. "What's the matter, Missy?" Nahla looked at her, but was unmoved.

Mildred banged the empty tin of cat food down on the side and grabbed her teacup and saucer; "We'll resume this conversation later." On hearing the starting music for Bang Goes Your Money, she rushed towards the front room and there he was. What a nice man Mildred thought, looking at De'Hoof Monterrey, the presenter of the show.

He ran down the stairs, showing off his sparkling gleaming teeth, jumped in the air clicking his heels to one side, then threw his cane off-screen for someone to catch. 'The Hoof,' as he liked to be known, opened up both arms.

"And let's meet today's contestants." With that, the cheesy smile appeared as he turned around, lifting his arms in the air as the contestants peeled in waving excitedly at the camera.

Mildred, so engrossed with the programme, had now taken a seat looking at these lucky people on the show; she was tempted to wave back at them were it not for the cup of tea in her hand.

"So tell us all, what's your name and where do you come from?" De'Hoof's smile was beaming even more than usual.

"Hello, I'm Julie, and I'm from Wiltshire." Julie flashed an enormous smile upon hearing the rapturous applause coming from the audience. She began clapping for herself with excitement, overwhelmed by the occasion.

"And you can call me Hoof." De'Hoof spun around, pointing at her. Julie was absolutely blown away at this personal invitation.

"Thank you, Hoof!"

"No, thank you, Julie." He kissed her hand and flashed his cheesy smile.

"Good luck, Julie!" Mildred shouted, clapping and spilling tea down her floral-coloured skirt.

Suddenly, three loud bangs came from her front door. Mildred jumped up spilling even more tea down her top. She froze and looked over towards Missy, who was sound asleep. She turned the volume down on the television and walked briskly towards the front door, frustrated that her programme had been interrupted.

"I really hope it's not those boys again, Missy," her skin was flushed with anxiety, "quite what I've done to them, I just don't know."

She snapped open the door, but no-one was there. A wave of anger came over her. She went to slam the door shut when she saw an envelope on the floor written in the neatest of handwriting.

'Mildred
Number 1 Rocke Road
Shrewsbury
Shropshire
United Kingdom'

She took a step forward and leaned her head outside of her doorway, looking left and right. She couldn't see anyone and could only hear the light noise of the road starting to wind down for the evening. She bent down, picked up the envelope and closed the door.

She walked into her kitchen, reading her address over and over again. Frown lines formed over her forehead and she looked up at her clock, it was 19.09.

In a very soft voice, she muttered to herself, "Strange time of the evening for the post." The white envelope was sealed with wax, with a crest stamped into it. She recognised it instantly and with excitement, sat down at the kitchen table. She broke open the seal to reveal a solitary piece of heavy card. The card had a gold seal going around it with the familiar crest of her club in the centre.

By permission of the Grand Council of The United Kingdom Kat Chamber, it is with great honour that we invite you to our yearly gathering.

To be held within the Dogpole Suite at Dovercote Mansion, Wroxeter, Shropshire.

Time 19.00.

Date 13th August.

You must present your invitation upon arrival.

Failure to do so will not permit entry.

Dress code optional.

Please do not bring cameras.

She had received two invitations like this before and never understood why they left it so late to send them out. Quite why they never used the postal service was a mystery.

She had never been to Dovercote Mansion before; it sounds very grand she thought to herself with a smile. She looked at the invitation again; 'The Grand Council,' still smiling, she shook her head. She had never met any form of Council from the club, let alone a 'Grand Council.' They were certainly very strange, she thought as she giggled to herself.

Unfortunately, she could not keep her two former invitations as they were always taken from her on arrival. Shame really, as they would be very lovely mementos to keep on her wall next to her certificate. She stared at the card almost brooding, biting her lip deep in thought. She never asked to join this club, it was practically put upon her as though she didn't have a choice, not that she minded of course.

'You were chosen, Mildred.'

She recalled the very first time she met Daphne. Shaking her head slightly, she realised that she had never really questioned anything. They definitely had some strange ways about them in how they ran their cat club.

'You've always known you were different from others.'

Mildred reflected on the meeting nearly three years ago. How could Daphne have known that she was not allowed to keep pets as a child? There were quite a few things that just did not add up and more questions were developing the further she considered it. Why was there so much secrecy and why do they meet in quiet places out of others' view?

'All will be revealed in time.'

She looked up at her clock oblivious to the time then looked over at Missy, who was curled up in a ball. She looked to be dreaming heavily judging by her stomach moving up and down.

"Why were you brought to me, Missy?" She continued to labour the point in her mind. It was clear that Daphne had not come from the local cat shelter and there was a presumption on her part that Mildred would take Missy from her in the first place.

When presenting Missy, Daphne informed her that she had an affinity with animals; that came of some surprise as she would have liked to have had pets as a child and had considered getting one to keep her company as she got older. Mildred was surprised when Daphne informed her that the club would pay her a monthly bursary to cover her living expenses. The roof over her head needed to be paid for and her daily living, so it was perfect. Apparently, she was the guardian of Missy and therefore would be rewarded as such; it was a strange scenario but, to date, she had never really questioned it.

Daphne informed her at that first meeting that there 'were many others.'

However, Mildred's certificate did not display a membership number and her phone was quiet for the most part. The other members didn't call her, save Daphne and Mildred of Merewood Close.

She stood up and went to the wall in her front room where the certificate hung; it was in pristine condition as she cleaned it more than anything else. Very gently, she took it off the wall and stared at it. She could see her curious reflection in the glass and her cloche hat with woven flowers embroidered into it. She never used to dress like this, she thought thinking back to her former life.

The crest of the club took pride of place on the certificate. Mildred's name wasn't on it and neither was Missy's. Printed in simple, clean text, it said:

MEMBER OF THE UNITED KINGDOM KAT CHAMBER

So much didn't add up. Mildred had a good relationship with Daphne, but Jessica seemed to be a little odd. Most members attending the monthly meetings all seemed different in their own way and didn't speak with her regularly.

Placing the certificate back on the wall, she resumed her seat in the kitchen, looking down at the invitation. She turned the card over to find a handwritten note:

'Don't forget sandwiches'

Sandwiches, sandwiches, sandwiches! The words kept turning in her mind, so much so that she was completely oblivious to the closing credits to Bang Goes Your Money on her television.

Julie had lost.

Duat was undisturbed, sitting in his chamber deep below the ground. He had been brought below as all the Watchers were before the fall of darkness.

Since his incarceration and when he was not being forced to carry out mundane tasks for the Order, he would spend most of his time thinking of events past and the days to come.

Vapour emanated from the exposed holes in his skull that vaguely represented his nose. He lifted his head and turned it to the side, left first and then to the right, stretching his neck muscles until there was a large cracking sound. He pulled down the hood of his robe and let out a huge but almost silent sigh, shifting his focus to the old walls of the room he was sitting in.

His security restraint measures had been removed for the day. He could now take off the gloves he was forced to wear for many hours whilst performing tedious chores for those above. He flexed his fingers inside the gloves.

He, like other Watchers, took great care in protecting his hands, especially his right hand. Through the sense of touch, some had abilities that could allow them to read, feel, and control others to some degree. All Watchers had different abilities but never had there been one blessed with them all. For this reason, those who imprisoned them from above made them cover their hands as they feared what they did not know.

Those who resided in the grand hallways, directly above where Duat was sitting, were incredibly nervous of these gifts, abilities and powers; all art forms within their own right. Duat knew they feared Watchers and their fears were real. "As they should be," he muttered, watching the warm vapour appear in front of him again.

Every day without fail, the Escarrabin would take him and other incarcerated Watchers up to the above. The Reeve's security officers would ensure his hands and thin skin were not exposed to the light of the sun or to other Escarrabin.

He took off his gloves and placed them neatly by his side. Stretching his right arm out in front of him, he thrust his fingers forward as far as they could go.

He stretched them to the point where his finger-tips were now veering upwards and curved against their natural movement. He looked at his nails, they were very long, sharp, and filthy; they disgusted him.

Turning his hand, he looked at the turquoise colouring of his palm and the life that moved throughout it. It was this colouration, this gift that made him unique. No Watcher possessed the high level of abilities that he did, in fact, he knew none ever had.

Bringing his right hand towards his face the dark green and blue blood vessels that moved throughout his palm fascinated him. The gift he bore never stopped his curiosity and he spent many hours watching the life move around inside his palm, while imprisoned.

He was reasonably sure that the Reeve and others were not aware of his chamber. The lift from the above only goes to the first floor where the Watchers assemble every day to be collected by the Escarrabin and taken above. The Escarrabin never ventured deeper and he knew they feared the darkness. They dressed as soldiers but had the hearts of cowards. Over hundreds of years, the Watchers had created tunnels and chambers that stretched as far wide as they did deep; they were quite ingenious. He smiled at the thought as saliva ran from his mouth.

The original rock and iron walls were created by others from another era when times were not so dark, not so suspicious, not so threatening. They were laid in times of relative peace. The manor house detained Watchers for a long time.

All they had left were the old tools that had been left behind from the past. Progress had been made with a new tunnel system that would lead to the surface beyond the house's walls above, but there was further to go and not enough time. Having close proximity to the Order and observing its inner workings had been useful; watching them, studying them and despising those who call themselves the enlightened.

He stood up and walked over to the solitary wine glass on his table, it had been empty for only a few hours. He breathed in deeply as he picked it up, gripping it tightly with his right hand. He could feel the deep colours moving throughout his palm as he concentrated hearing the faint sounds of clocks chiming from above. He put down the glass and lifted his right palm to his eye. He flexed his fingers and watched turquoise patterns move to the end of his fingers.

"Time," he muttered, staring at the objects on an old shelf cut into one of the walls in front of him.

The clocks above in the manor house were a constant reminder to the Order that time is precious, time is short and time will always bring change. It was a leveller of balance and it had been foretold. He was well aware of the prophecy; it had been explained along with their fears of it. The chimes strike to remind them of their inadequacies. "We do not need such devices," he spoke, whilst looking at a very old pair of weighing scales and an ancient unturned hourglass.

Chapter Twelve:

PALE HANDS OF CLERICS

THURSDAY MORNING (EARLY)

Nubia was keeping a watchful eye upon her clock; it was almost time.

Placing her teacup down, she stood up and walked from her study to the desk in her office.

She pressed one of the many buttons on the old phone. Her finger remained on the button for 15 seconds.

"Yes, Madam Curator?" A voice sounded from a speaker next to her phone.

"Well, you took your time!"

"Sorry Madam Curator. We have been very busy."

"My office please. Thank you." She released the button, instantly terminating the conversation.

She walked over to her hat and coat stand, removed her jacket and gracefully put it on. Even though it was always clean and shiny, she took a handkerchief and polished the badge on her lapel.

She knew that it would be a long day; it always was the day before a gathering. She would be thankful once it had passed and peace and quiet returned to Loxley.

Her role as Curator was to ensure procedures were followed. Her direct responsibility covered the whole six regional areas of the United Kingdom and Ireland, which included assisting all the Senior Elders when called upon.

She stood in front of the only mirror in her chambers. I look old, she thought to herself. She ensured her outfit was precise as was expected of a Curator of the Order.

A knock at the door distracted her from assessing her 'laughter lines.'

"Come." She said, returning to her desk and taking a seat.

"You called Madam Curator." The Cleric's head was bowed towards the floor, her face unseen underneath the hood.

"I did. Have you seen any movement from the Reeve this morning?"

"No Ma'am. Not a sound."

"Well go and give her a knock. I will be along shortly."

"Yes, Ma'am." The Cleric left the office, closing the door behind her.

She crossed her legs, placing both hands into a ball on her knee and looked blankly at the door. She disapproved of this new Reeve, but her considerations in these matters were not taken into account.

She sat waiting patiently in contemplation.

Mildred clicked her teeth together with some concern and placed her hands on her hips. Missy appeared to be sleeping but looked to be in some sort of discomfort. Her paws were constantly twitching and on occasion, she would snarl from the side of her mouth. Whether it was bad dreams or she was in pain, Mildred could not be sure.

Her concerns had started earlier that morning when she didn't have to call Missy in to be fed. She was already asleep downstairs and hadn't moved since. Mildred wondered if gently banging a tin would help. She pulled a tin of cockle and tomato flavoured cat food out of the larder and gently hit it with a spoon. There was no response from Missy, even after she tried it for a second time. She became more concerned by the minute.

She reached out and stroked Missy. She was warm and her pulse was too fast, almost as though she had a double heartbeat.

"Whatever is the matter, Missy? How can I help you?" her voice was hopeless and flat. She knew from past experience that Missy did not like the vet; just its mention would often stir up a reaction.

She stood up, deciding that a purposeful and assertive voice would be the best course of action.

"Missy I am going to wait for one more hour and if you do not get up or start to feel better, I am calling the vet." She waited for a response, but none was forthcoming.

"Oh my, this really is not good." Concern etched across her face.

"Come!" the Curator glanced over her shoulder as a white-hooded figure stepped into her office.

"Ma'am, the Reeve is aware that you require her presence."

Nubia frowned as she turned to face the Cleric. "Aware that I require her presence?" Impatience lingered in her tone.

"Yes, Ma'am." The Cleric bowed her head further.

"Well of course she's aware if she understands protocol. The Curator always meets the Reeve the day before a gathering." Nubia's feelings about the newly appointed Reeve was well known throughout Loxley. "Did she say anything else?"

"No Ma'am."

"Very well, off you go."

The Cleric moved to the door.

"Damn useless creatures," she said under her breath as the door closed. She checked her clothes in the mirror a final time, doing up her white shirt's top button. Her frown lines became her primary focus again; they have multiplied of late, she thought to herself.

She closed the door behind her fixing the badge on her lapel one last time. Hands clasped behind her back, she strode down the corridor. She always walked with purpose and dignity. She would often inform lesser degree Elders and Clerics that standards must be kept and respect shown at all times. In her opinion, they needed a constant reminder of their place.

She approached the diamond-shaped lobby area. The archway for the Reeve's offices came into view on the right. She scowled at the state of the decay on the doorway not always approving of the Reeve's traditions, noticing with some frustration that the door was also slightly open.

She shook her head in disapproval and glanced behind her, three Clerics were working at a desk, but one was missing. She walked towards them.

"Where is the other one?" she said, nodding in the direction of the empty seat, "and why is the Reeve's door open?"

There was no response from the Clerics who continued to work, heads down.

"Excuse me!" she shouted impatiently. "Am I talking to the wall?"

Their heads remained bowed.

"You there on the left, look at me!"

The Cleric lifted her head.

"Where is she?"

"I'm sorry, I do not know Ma'am."

"There should always be four! No excuses, no exceptions."

"Yes, Ma'am."

"Why is the Reeve's door open?"

The echo of the question bounced off the walls throughout the diamond-shaped lobby with no answer forthcoming.

"Hood down so I can see you."

The Cleric looked up to meet her gaze.

"Pull your hood from your face."

The Cleric lifted her pale hands and pulled her hood back to reveal her deathly white face and the whites of her eyes.

"I'll ask you one last time. Where is the fourth Cleric and why is the Reeve's door open?"

"Probably because I left it open, Nubia."

She spun around to see the Reeve leaning against her doorway with her legs crossed.

"And your missing Cleric has been doing some cleaning for me."

The Reeve spoke very calmly looking in the Cleric's direction; "pull up your hood."

The pale hands pulled the hood back over her face and the Cleric returned to work.

Nubia scowled and headed towards the Reeve's doorway.

"I really wish you would address me by my proper title in front of others."

"I'm very sorry, Curator. You know, you can be quite rude to the Clerics at times. You'll never get their trust or respect like that." The Curator maintained eye contact with the Reeve. "One day, you may really upset them and we don't want a break from harmony now do we?"

"I know what I'm doing Reeve; order and process."

"Yes, yes, I know all of that. However, stress is not good and has no place here." She paused momentarily, "I do wonder if you could ever handle the responsibilities that I have."

Nubia, completely un-amused retorted, "Well, I'd make sure the security doors were closed for a start." She pushed the Reeve's door open and walked through.

I really miss the old Reeve, she thought to herself.

✝✝✝✝

Mildred could not take her eyes off the cat phone as she considered what to do next.

She knew that Missy did not like seeing the vet, in fact, Mildred found the vet to be quite a strange individual. Both of them were happier away from her.

Mildred didn't own a car so she would have to take Missy on the bus in the carrier, or ask the vet to make a house call. Missy was clearly in distress. Mildred brought the phone back into the kitchen, its long wire trailing behind. "Right Missy, do you see this?"

Nahla's eyes remained closed.

"If you do not open your eyes right now, I'm calling Miss Fennaway." She waved the phone around at Missy with her idle threat. There was still no response.

"Oh come on Missy, do something please, you are worrying me." Her voice was wavering as she crouched down to stroke her gently. Missy's tummy was moving up and down and her pulse felt very unnatural.

She walked over to the sideboard and started searching through the piles of receipts and bits of paper that she has hoarded over the last few years. She was pleased to find the handwritten number for the vet.

"Last chance Missy." With a futile gesture, she shook the phone one last time before dialling.

She didn't relish the thought of the odd lady she was about to invite into her house for the first time.

'Fennaway Veterinary Practise, how may we direct your call?'

"Oh, good morning, it's my Missy, I would like to..."

'Please press 1 for appointments.'

"What?" Mildred was staring incredulously at the cat's bottom.

Returning the phone to her ear quickly...

'Press 2 to speak to Miss Fennaway.'

'Press 3 to have your pet put down.'

'Press 4 for anything else.'

She turned to see Missy's leg twitch and accidentally hit a random button on the phone.

"Missy...Missy, are you okay?"

'You have selected option 3; you wish to have your pet put down.'

"What? No, wait. Stupid phone!"

'Please tell us the name of your pet.'

"Miss Fennaway, I want to speak to Miss Fennaway." She yelled down the phone.

'Thank you. We understand you would like Miss Fennaway to be put down.'

"What? No, customer service, customer service!!" she yelled, stomping her feet in frustration.

'Please tell us what type of animal you would like to have put down.'

"It's a cat and I don't want her to be put down!!"

'You wish to have your cat put down. Thank you, directing your call.'

The last thing I want is for my cat to be out down, she thought, looking down at Missy on the sofa.

She looked at the phone, willing for a human to answer.

Nubia took a seat in the Reeve's main office.

"Please, do take a seat." The Reeve said, smiling.

Nubia looked forward very unimpressed at the chair behind the Reeve's desk, "I see you have a new chair."

"Yes, the old one was uncomfortable to sit on."

She shook her head disapproving of the Reeve's decision to not follow custom. Nubia was impatient and wanted to proceed with matters quickly.

"As you are aware, a new Elder must be appointed to maintain balance, following the sad loss of Lady Tempest."

"If I am already aware of these things Nubia, why are you reminding me of them?"

"I like to ensure that processes are followed as they always have been. It's important and I need to be sure that you have made the appropriate security related arrangements."

"I may be new to my post and I am aware you did not support my role, but what makes you think that I wouldn't have, Nubia?" The Curator looked towards the floor with a slight admission of guilt and the Reeve leaned forward to regain her attention. "Let me assure you so this is not mentioned again. My Order has full belief in me and what I do, which is why I was appointed." She settled back in her seat.

"The fact remains that you are of a new breed," Nubia said bluntly.

"New?" The Reeve interjected. "New, you say?" The Reeve smiled, "I am hardly new and neither are you for that matter. Let's not lose sight of that." The smile left her face and the room fell silent as the Curator stared at the floor.

"Would you care for a cup of tea Nubia?" asked the Reeve, breaking the deadlock.

"No, thank you, Reeve. I've just had one." Was the succinct response.

"I see," she smiled, "let me stop you worrying Nubia. My Escarrabin have their orders regarding their duties for all of the gatherings. I will also inform you that the Keeper is on her way, she carries word and will be here very soon."

The Curator looked up; "The Keeper is coming here, already?"

"Yes, she is. You should have more faith. Everything is in order." She said confidently.

"Faith is for dreamers and for the weak, a word misused by them outside. A Reeve should not use such words. It has been foretold that the time may come where we will all be tésted and therefore we must be ready!" Nubia smirked.

"I think you mean the time will come, Nubia!"

The Curator swallowed hard, her body language remained resolute even though she knew that the Reeve was right, if the old prophecy was to be believed.

The only sound that could be heard in the office was the ticking of a clock. She took a moment to think. "Do you have any idea who they may be?" Nubia mumbled.

"Who are you referring to?" The Reeve asked curiously.

"The ones who will ascend up the order?" The Curator looked at the Reeve inquisitively.

"No, no, I don't. I have no feelings on the matter. Elder ascension is not the business of the Order Of The Reeves," she replied in a calm and controlled manner.

They were interrupted by a knock at the door.

"Come in." The Reeve watched as the door opened.

"Ma'am, the vehicle of the Keeper is at the main gate."

"Good, thank you."

"She's here already! Well, don't hang around, go and let her in." Nubia snapped at the Cleric.

"Nubia, I assert instructions in my office, not you!" The Reeve was not impressed.

"Please go down and assist Raysmau in opening the front doors. We will be there to meet her shortly." The Reeve offered a gentle smile, an apology for her guest's behaviour.

"Yes, Ma'am." The Cleric bowed her head and left the room, shutting the door behind her.

"There. That's how easy it is. Speak nicely and you will be treated the same way."

"They need to be reminded of their place," Nubia growled under her breath.

"And it seems you need to be reminded of yours, Curator."

Chapter Thirteen:

THE ARRIVAL OF MISS FENNAWAY

THURSDAY APPROACHING 11AM

Having been infuriated earlier by 'phone technology,' Mildred was now sitting with a cup of tea in hand having regained her usual calm demeanour. She looked down at Missy, biting her lip. She had no idea what was wrong with her. She had fed her the same food as the previous night and she seemed fine when she went to bed. What could it possibly be?

She sat in silence waiting for Miss Fennaway, listening to the clock ticking in her kitchen with its newly replaced batteries. She surveyed the kitchen, anxious to be having a visitor to the house. The thought of Miss Fennaway in her home frustrated her.

She had met her twice before when Missy was having her health injections.

Mildred phoned Daphne for advice not long after she had delivered Missy and was told that protecting a cat would come naturally to her, that it was in her blood.

She insisted that if there were any problems, she should call Miss Fennaway. She read the number for her to write down.

'Without exception Mildred, always call Miss Fennaway if there are any problems. Don't ever call anyone else.'

119

After finally being able to speak with her, she was surprised that Miss Fennaway was available straight away. She was not sure why Daphne was insistent on her using the Fennaway practice, it was at least an hour's ride away on the bus. There were closer practices that she had read about. However, she was sure the other vets charge for their services. Miss Fennaway never took a penny. Mildred pondered whether she'd prefer another vet all the same, considering Miss Fennaway always leaves the room with Missy to carry out treatments, which made Mildred very uncomfortable.

She moved quickly to the kitchen window on hearing the click of the front gate. Miss Fennaway was coming up the pathway.

She rushed to open the front door happy to see Miss Fennaway's beaming face looking straight at her.

"Hello Miss Fennaway, thank you for coming at such short notice."

"It's Dr Fennaway, Mildred, but you can call me, Kamilah."

"Please do come in, I'm sorry about the mess," said Mildred, apologising for any shortcomings.

"Don't worry, I'm used to it," she replied.

"Oh, I see, well hopefully it's not too bad for you." Mildred said worriedly.

"Mmm!" Miss Fennaway gave a gentle shrug.

Mildred was not enthralled by this response as she watched the stranger walk through her kitchen surveying her home, almost in a judgemental way.

"I will take you to Missy."

"Please do. Cats usually hide like Ninjas when I show up," she laughed.

Mildred didn't join her in laughter as she had heard the 'joke' last time she went to see her.

Mildred showed Miss Fennaway into the front room and pointed to the couch where Missy lay. "Nice cushion." Kamilah beamed her almost black teeth on seeing the homemade cushion with the white cat on it.

"Thank you," Mildred paused momentarily, "what about Missy?"

"Of course; I'm quite sure it's nothing, people who look after cats can worry somewhat."

"You mean people who own cats presumably?"

"What now dear?"

"People who own cats Dr Fennaway?" Mildred decided not to address her by her first name as informality didn't really seem to be getting her anywhere fast.

"Yes, of course, you are right," Kamilah swallowed and returned her gaze to Missy knowing that Mildred was new to the Order and as yet, knew little of these things. "People who own cats."

Kamilah placed her workbag on the couch and sat down beside Missy. "Right Missy, what is all this fuss about?" She took a stethoscope from her bag and placed it on Missy's chest moving it around. She didn't keep it in one place for very long. She glanced at her watch then turned to Mildred and smiled.

"Well, everything appears to be in order here!"

"Do you not have to put the other end of the stethoscope into your ears?" Mildred asked, puzzled.

"What now, dear?"

"The other end with the ear things, do you not need to listen through those?"

Kamilah's eyes widened slightly upon hearing this, "well, yes you can, er, of course... some do; but then I have done this job a long time. I work a lot on instinct and feelings, all good vet's do Mildred" she was nodding as she spoke. Mildred stood over Kamilah with her hands on hips following the vet's bizarre comment; she would keep a close eye from now on.

"But seeing as you have asked, I will."

Mildred nodded. "Seen as I'm not a complete fool that would be appreciated."

Kamilah averted Mildred's gaze. "Yes my dear, I meant no offence it's just many of my clients trust my judgement."

She placed the ear tips into her ears and started dabbing the chest piece over the cat again.

"As I say, everything seems in order."

Kamilah rummaged in her bag. "Would it be too much to trouble you for a cup of tea, Mildred?" Mildred smiled politely. "Yes, that would be fine," she paused briefly reluctant to leave Miss Fennaway alone with Missy. She noticed Miss Fennaway hadn't looked up from the bag.

Once Mildred was out of sight, Kamilah took a Signapher out of her bag, an oval shaped, electronic device that had been made especially for her. The screen lit up immediately. She checked the sensors on the bottom, then looked behind her to check that Mildred was still in the kitchen.

"Would you like a fish paste sandwich?" yelled Mildred, knowing she had a couple to spare.

"Oh yes please, that would be lovely Mildred, you are very kind. I love fish paste" she said, deep in concentration with the fakest of smiles across her face, knowing full well that she couldn't stand fish paste.

Kamilah ran the sensors over Missy and watched the different colours move up and down as a graph appeared on the screen. She froze and swallowed heavily when a red warning light appeared on the screen. She switched it back off.

Mildred came back into the room to see Miss Fennaway quickly scrambling to put the device back in her bag.

"What's that?" She enquired.

"Oh, it's nothing. I took a blood test, just to be sure." It's all she could think of, off the top of her head.

"I don't think Missy likes needles."

"Come now, Mildred, it's not like the old days, blood tests are painless now, new technology and all that, completely pain free these days." Kamilah was talking with her hands doing her best to reassure Mildred.

"I see!" Mildred responded suspiciously, handing her a cup of tea and four, curly fish paste sandwiches.

"Thank you very much Mildred." Kamilah said taking the cup and saucer. Mildred noticed her hands were shaking a little.

"Would you mind terribly if I made a quick phone call?"

Mildred paused to look at her with concern.

"I have another client afterwards you see."

"No, not at all, you can use mine if you like," and she pointed at the cat phone.

"That's a phone?" Kamilah smiled.

"Yes and it meows as well if someone calls!"

"I see; how extraordinary." She was shaking her head slightly as the certificate on the wall caught her attention.

Kamilah attempted to place the cup and saucer on the table without bringing attention to her shaky hands. She stood up and pulled out a phone. "I won't be long." She made her way to the front door.

"You can call from here if you wish, there's no need to go outside." Mildred shouted after her.

Kamilah stepped back towards her, "client confidentiality, Mildred; you wouldn't want me to be talking about your Missy in front of others would you?"

"I guess not." Mildred sat down looking worried.

"By the way; your cat is perfectly well, it's just a passing bug and I'm quite positive she will be fine in a few hours." Her smile was somewhat reassuring as she turned her back on Mildred and carried on towards the door.

With the exception of the ticking clock in the kitchen, Mildred sat in silence looking down into her tea. "You see Missy, Miss Fennaway said that you are going to be okay." She looked up and smiled at her cat but she was troubled by the quick diagnosis; something did not feel right about all of this.

Curiosity brought her to her feet. She looked out of the front room window to see Miss Fennaway further down the path on the phone.

She had a very concerned look on her face.

Mildred shook her head in worry.

As they left the Reeve's offices, Nubia was very quick to notice that all four Clerics were now sitting back at their desk, not that it changed her mood in any way. Slowing down her pace, she could see that the former missing Cleric on the right hand side was not busy with her work unlike the others, instead her head was raised up and she was looking back at her.

"Nubia...Curator," the Reeve elevated her voice on the second occasion to make sure she was heard.

"Yes, coming" she responded and quickened her pace still looking over her left shoulder at the Cleric. "Something not right with that one," she muttered under her breath.

At the top of the stairs the Reeve looked at the Curator. "I thought it was you that was always in a rush," she smiled, "is something bothering you?"

She shook her head. "No, I'm sure it's nothing."

"Very well." The Reeve offered a brief smile as they descended the stairs and headed towards the main entrance.

As they reached the bottom of the stairs Nubia lifted her head to look at this new Reeve. Despite all of the grandeur on display, the Reeve never once looked impressed or daunted by Loxley Manor. She hadn't been long in post and many aspects of this new and non-traditional Reeve still puzzled her.

All the Clerics were in place. Six always sat at the main desk when a special guest was due to arrive. There would be three either side of the entrance doors and a further three would wait in the centre as aides, should their assistance be needed. A handful of Elders loitered on the balconies having heard that the Keeper was due to arrive; her visits were rare.

The Reeve visually assessed the lobby area ensuring that the security positions were covered. Nubia was glad to finally see some form of reaction from her for the importance of the occasion.

Whilst the Reeve was one of a new breed that embraced technology, no cameras were ever allowed inside the grand mansion as headquarters was the most private place of all. That was not true of the road outside of the grounds where security measures were in place to help protect and conceal the hidden entrance to the mansion house.

The Reeve glanced to the upper tiers of the house and surveyed the ground level to ensure her security officers were in place. The security officers were known as the Escarrabin, elite soldiers that protected the Order and the grounds of Loxley. In full ceremonial wear they blended in where possible.

The Curator glanced at the three Clerics standing in line behind them and then looked up at the Reeve.

"Shouldn't your head of the Escarrabin be..."

She was interrupted by the sound of a gate moving, unseen to both of them from behind a heavy security door. They looked directly across the lobby as the huge oak door started to open.

Behind this fortified door was the office of Raysmau, Chief Security Officer of the Escarrabin and the protector of Loxley.

The Reeve turned her head to the left and looked down. "As I told you Curator, everything is quite in order."

The sound of heavy footsteps came from the doorway and a loud crash echoed through the lobby as the security door was re-closed remotely by the Escarrabin.

In full ceremonial clothing, Raysmau, only answerable to The Reeve stepped forward wearing the colours of the Keeper. With the lower half of her face and neck shielded in a black mask, she walked towards the main entrance doors of the grand lobby with her cloak trailing behind her.

She turned and nodded at the Clerics on the front desk. The very old and heavy oak doors slowly parted opening inwards. The sound of creaking wood and moving metal could be heard as the sheer weight of the doors moved across the tiled floor, creating a harrowing sound all around the lobby.

The mechanical parts that drove the heavy wooden doors were silenced as the doors found their resting place. Everyone on the ground level of the lobby could now see the Keeper's immaculate car directly in front of them.

Her driver remained in place as the huge frame of Raysmau approached the car and opened the door. She took a couple of steps backwards before offering her hand to the Keeper.

"Thank you Raysmau that will not be necessary." The Keeper stepped out of the car and composed herself, looking at the frontage of this grand old home. "I know that I'm getting on a bit but I can still get out of a car by myself, even if I do have to use this cane on occasions."

She tapped the wooden cane, that bore a cat's head at its tip on the gravel a couple of times.

"Yes Madam Keeper." Raysmau said with her head bowed.

"You are well, I trust?"

"Yes Ma'am well and here to serve."

"That's good to know." The Keeper smiled looking up at the enormous size of the Head of Security. "I do not have any bags, flying visit today."

"So I am led to believe, Ma'am."

She walked forward before turning to face Raysmau with a big smile across her face. "And how is our Curator?"

"The Curator is very efficient at her job" she said with polite tact.

"Mmm" she smiled, "no change there then." She took a step closer. "At least you answer to the Reeve and not to the Curator."

"Yes Ma'am," Raysmau offered the hint of a smile.

"I trust that she is settling in well?"

"Yes Ma'am." We have bonded and I have a good understanding with the new Reeve."

"That's good to know."

The Keeper walked towards the grand doors of the headquarters, the sound of Raysmau's heavy boots crunching behind her at a slow pace. As she got closer to the doors, she could see the Reeve's security team watching her every move from the lower balcony. The Clerics to her left and right had their heads bowed. Ahead, she could see the smiling face of the Reeve and the usual serious stare of Nubia.

"Madam Keeper, how lovely to see you." The Reeve nodded her head slightly in reverence.

"I would say it was lovely to be here Reeve, but given the circumstances..."

"I know, we are all quite troubled by recent events."

"Hello Nubia, I trust you are keeping well?"

"I am also as concerned as the Reeve," Nubia responded.

"I'm quite sure that you are." The Keeper was unmoved by this response.

"Please come this way Ma'am." The Reeve extended her arm towards the stairs.

"Thank you, Raysmau." She nodded towards her Head of Security, who took three steps backwards before returning to her doorway.

"I'm very sorry that Lady Safiya was not here to greet you today," the Reeve offered her apology to the Keeper. "The Lady of the House is away on business at the moment and not due here until tomorrow morning."

"Yes, I am aware she is very busy, but thank you all the same, Reeve. It's not her that I've come to see."

The loud thud from the heavy doors re-closing behind them made Nubia turn around. She raised her arm to dismiss the Clerics. She briefly looked up and noticed out of the corner of her eye, that one Cleric was stood back watching them from the first floor balcony.

A frown appeared across her face, she was sure it was the Cleric that had been staring at her earlier. She made a mental note to investigate it later.

Chapter Fourteen:

THE REEVE'S FIRST SCROLL

THURSDAY: LATE MORNING

The Keeper studied the Reeve's main door with a wry smile across her face, she leaned forward on her cane to run her right hand over it.

"This old door tells many stories." She spoke very quietly and calmly studying the worn markings and battle scars. She rested her hand on the cracked seal of the Reeve's. The Reeve directly to the right of her offered a smile. "Shall we?"

The Curator stepped in front of them and pushed her weight against the door. The door groaned upon opening as most did within this old house.

"Please, Madam Keeper," the Curator extended her arm, ushering her to come inside.

The Reeve was silent as the Curator invited the Keeper into her private part of the house.

The three of them moved forward as the door behind them started to close. They continued passed other rooms that held historical records of the Reeves' and their Order.

The Keeper could see other Clerics were sitting working in a room on their left-hand side before they passed the grand security briefing room of the Escarrabin.

In ceremonial dress with her helmet under her arm, one of the Reeve's personal bodyguards stood with her head bowed as the Keeper passed by.

The Reeve's main office door was already open (much to the Curator's displeasure) as they walked in and took their seats.

"Would you care for a cup of tea Madam Keeper?" The Reeve asked as she watched the Keeper steady herself with her cane and sit, letting out a little sigh.

"Yes, thank you very much, Reeve." She wrestled with her long gown before she was comfortable.

"I'll summon a Cleric to see to that," the Curator said as she went to get back up.

"That really won't be necessary Nubia, I'm quite capable of making us some tea." The Reeve spoke with a smile and the Curator sat back down directly to the right-hand side of the Keeper.

"You are both probably aware that I met with members of the Grand Council this week, as terribly saddening as it is at this time."

The Reeve listened with interest as she poured the tea.

"We are most concerned about events regarding Lady Tempest. Reeve, I trust that you are still investigating this?"

"I am, but factual matters are still a little vague at this time. I have assigned Kalara, one of our most skilled and loyal security team, to devote her time to this one matter."

She brought a cup of tea over to the Keeper and passed it directly to her.

"I'm sure that in time more facts will present themselves, but for now, it is classified in public records as an accident."

"What about outside involvement? Are questions being asked?"

"There has been some curiosity, but my team entered Lady Tempest's home and removed her certificates and work files. We replaced her main computer with one of our sterile models, so there are no records or association."

There was an audible tut from the Curator.

Both the Reeve and the Keeper looked at her with some displeasure.

"Nubia, you have made your feelings very clear about the use of computing and the changes to our processes. This is the way it is and will continue to be," said the Keeper.

The Reeve frowned as she passed Nubia a cup of tea. She poured one for herself and sat at her desk.

"I have accessed the civilian policing records and there is no inference of foul play at this time. However, we are monitoring this and I've recovered all available CCTV footage of the incident."

"I see. I do not need to tell you that we do not need outside Police looking around into our affairs, so I guess that is something to be thankful for."

The Reeve nodded. "It is currently listed as an accident on the public record. We, however, will keep an open mind until I am fully satisfied."

"Good. Thank you, Reeve."

"And what of her cats?"

The Keeper looked directly at Nubia in some astonishment. The Reeve shook her head and looked at the floor.

"The cats were presented back to me Nubia as is common practice. Why do you ask of such matters that do not concern you?"

Nubia met her eyes briefly before looking downwards at the cup of tea balanced on her knee.

The role of the Keeper was very important and like the Reeve, she conducted her affairs in secrecy. Secrecy was paramount, as long as Nubia knew about it.

The room fell silent as they all sipped their tea.

"Most troubling," the Keeper muttered, staring into her tea.

The Reeve, anxious to ask, looked up towards the Keeper. "Have the Council given their advice? Do you bring word?"

The Keeper looked directly at the Reeve; "Yes, I bring word."

She reached into the left inside pocket of her ceremonial robe and pulled out a very small gold-leaf scroll that was secured with a wax seal.

"You can open it now, Reeve," she said and passed it to her.

It was her first time being entrusted with the opening and security of one of the scrolls. Before her appointment at Loxley, her Elder had prepared her for such delicate and important matters.

She pulled at the seal that cracked and opened quite easily. A few fragments of wax fell onto her desk as she brushed them aside.

There was a singular name and an address inside.

The Reeve looked up at the Keeper and met her gaze.

"She's reasonably local to here."

"Yes, she is. Not at the other end of the district."

Nubia was attempting to read what was printed on the scroll when there was a loud knock at the door.

"Come," said the Reeve, averting her gaze from the scroll to the doorway.

A Cleric appeared at the door as all three turned to look with interest at the interruption.

"I'm sorry to disturb Ma'am, but there is a phone call for Lady Curator."

"What, right now? Can it not wait? Can you not see we are having an important meeting?" the Curator blasted at the Cleric.

"I'm sorry, Madam Curator, I'm told that it is most urgent."

"Well, it had better be!" she said, spilling some of her tea on the Reeve's desk as she put the cup and saucer down in anger.

"Please excuse me, ladies," she offered by way of apology as she turned around towards the door. "Well, show me the way then!" she fluttered an arm at the Cleric, berating her for interrupting their meeting. The Reeve and the Keeper watched as the Curator slammed the door closed.

The Keeper turned back to the Reeve. "This is why she was never placed into the Order of the Reeves!"

The Reeve offered a faint smile and resumed reading the few words perfectly written on the scroll.

Mildred was talking into the cat's bottom for the second time that day.

"I've made an amazing luxury chocolate truffle cake. Honestly, it's to die for!"

"Well, let's not go crazy!" Mildred said to Mildred of Merewood Close as they burst into fits of laughter.

"And I've made some lovely cupcakes and some cat treats that all of the members can take away with them."

Suddenly Mildred's laughter stopped. Oh, that's much better than giving everyone a card, she thought to herself and she started biting her nails again.

"You okay, Mildred?" she asked, noticing the sudden silence.

"Yes, I'm fine. Well, not really, my Missy is unwell."

"Oh really, what on earth is the matter with her? Did you call Fennaway's?"

"Oh, you know Miss Fennaway as well then?" Mildred asked with some curiosity as Merewood Close was in Coningsby in Lincolnshire, quite some miles away from Shrewsbury in Shropshire.

"Oh yes, my Elder recommended her."

Very odd, Mildred thought to herself.

"Well, she came over and prodded her with a stethoscope and assured me that she would be fine and that it was just a passing bug. She then made a call and had to leave abruptly."

"Well, I'm sure she is right. I trust my Elder's recommendation on these things."

"Yes, me too, I suppose. I hope she is right. Miss Fennaway can be a little peculiar, can't she?" Mildred said, laughing to herself, albeit fake laughter.

"I wouldn't know. I've never met her; she was just recommended. My Misty has never needed to see a vet."

"You didn't take Misty for injections?"

"You had your Missy injected, heavens on earth whatever with?"

"Well, I don't know. I read it in a magazine and overheard a couple of ladies talking about it in The Tudor House Café. Apparently, you are supposed to." She was waving her arms in the air, clearly clueless about these things. "Stops them getting bugs or something..."

There was silence before Mildred, queen of cakes, decided to speak up.

"My Elder said that my cat was mine to keep and protect and to only call the vet if I need to. Apparently, Miss Fennaway understands these things. She also told me that our cats don't like injections, so I never did."

"Oh!" Mildred sat in silence, looking worriedly over at Missy. "Well, I had better go and see to Missy."

"Okay, Mildred, I do hope that Missy feels better again soon."

"Thank you, Mildred, that's very kind of you."

"I'll tell you what, I'll make extra special cat treats for you. That will perk Missy right up." She could almost sense Mildred down the phone, happy with her marvellous creations.

"Thank you, Mildred. I'll see you tomorrow evening."

"Looking forward to it Mildred. Goodbye for now."

Mildred put the cat's bottom down and stared helplessly at Missy. An eyebrow rose as she reflected on the call, what exactly was meant by 'our cats'? She was now lost in her thoughts.

What was I thinking by getting everyone a card? Her homemade cardigan and cards will be outshone by cupcakes and cat treats; she was sure of that.

"Daphne
Number 27
Crosshouses Road,
Much Wenlock,
Shropshire"

The Reeve read out aloud.

She looked back at the Keeper as she gently put the scroll down on her desk.

"She will fall into the Shropshire and North Wales local region and of course, the middle section of England and Wales for larger events and gatherings." The Keeper spoke in her usual calming voice.

The Reeve nodded in agreement.

"She will be in good hands. The local region is well supported and of course, has Jessica, who is about to be elevated to Degree Level 6."

"Indeed," said the Reeve, still nodding in agreement with everything she was hearing.

"The Grand Council have sanctioned this new member. Daphne apparently came of age within the last couple of months, so her time is now."

The Keeper looked assertively at the Reeve. She leant forward on her cane and took a more serious stance. "Reeve, always around the time of the gatherings, the Watchers are more active, always trying to find out if there are new lines of ascension. You know of quite a few occurrences recently where reports have been made of them being seen on the outside. To our knowledge, they are not aware of the new Daphne, but it's safe to presume they may know of Lady Tempest's passing and the suspicious manner in how she passed. If that is the case, we need to be extra vigilant. They will roam more than usual, especially in the hours of darkness."

"I understand, Madam Keeper."

"Her new Elder will be disclosed tomorrow night and until such time that she is presented with her cat, we need to keep this close to our chests; it mustn't leave this room."

"Of course Madam Keeper. I will see that it is done."

"Well, thank you for the tea. I need to depart as I have others to see and I have to travel down to the lower section now. Much to do with so little time."

The Reeve smiled. "There never is."

"Time?" The Keeper smiled back and steadied herself to her feet. "I know."

The Reeve stood up at the same time. "Do you need a hand, Ma'am?"

"No, no, thank you. My envoy will be here to see you on Saturday morning with four new cats, one for Jessica along with Daphne's first cat. She will, of course, have two other cats for the other two Elders that will be promoted."

"Do you know who is being elevated from Degree Level 8 to 7 and from 9 to 8?"

"No, I'm not aware as yet. With the course of events, the Grand Council are leaving their decisions until very late. All will be announced tomorrow evening at the local gathering, I am assured."

"I see," the Reeve nodded.

The door bursting open startled them. They turned around to see the Curator red in the face and panting.

"What on earth is it, Nubia?" The Reeve said, startled.

"I have just been informed of something most troubling."

"Well, what is it?" said the Keeper.

She took a brief moment in the knowledge that she knew something that both of them did not.

"I have just had a phone call from Fennaway. A cat in this district is showing the signs."

The Keeper fell back into her seat and they all fell silent with worry.

Chapter Fifteen:

LADY EBONEE

THURSDAY AFTERNOON

Having gone through her wardrobe yet again and still arriving at the same conclusion, Mildred made her way downstairs to her front room.

Looking across to her couch, she could see that Missy was still unmoved. It upset her looking in the kitchen at the untouched food and the full water bowl. Glancing up at her clock, she could see that it was approaching 2pm. The cards should have arrived at Mr Franks' shop some hours ago, but with Missy being unwell and Miss Fennaway's visit, it had slipped her mind.

She sat down next to her cat, placing a hand on her tummy and could still feel that her heart was beating too fast. Mildred felt helpless and alone and distrusting of the vet's opinion.

She had been staring at the wall for far too long. She blinked and shook her head to snap out of it. "I do hope you are better soon. I can't go to the gathering with you like this." She stroked Missy gently. "I have to go and see Mr Franks now, but I won't be long." She bent over and gave Missy a gentle kiss on the head. "See you in a bit."

She walked into the kitchen, grabbed her oversized purse bulging with receipts and dropped it into her equally oversized bag. Straining to get her shoes on as the buckle was too tight, she fidgeted with her feet and ankles until they were forced on. She felt guilty about leaving Missy while she was unwell but had promised Mr Franks she would pick up her large card order. She had no choice but to leave.

She set off down her pathway completely oblivious to everything and slowly walked down Rocke Road towards the shop. She didn't notice a couple of the youths from the day before as she approached the bus stop.

"Here she comes!" one said, laughing.

"Helloooo Mildred," the other one cackled as they both laughed away at her expense.

"Leave me alone, please," Mildred said very quietly, looking at the ground as she continued to shuffle forwards.

"Oh, Mildred, you not banging your cat tin this afternoon?"

"Nah, it's not feeding time yet," said the other, "feeding time is always at 7pm; you can set your watch by her!"

Mildred looked around. The man with the long hair was not there to save her this time.

"Say, where is that stupid cat of yours anyway?" one of them said.

Mildred stopped. "It's my Missy and she's not stupid."

The boys fell about laughing. "Oh my days," one of them said, playfully punching the other.

Mildred looked on at them as a couple of tears rolled from her eyes down past her cheeks.

The one who had said about her 'stupid cat' suddenly stopped laughing and nudged his mate. Both of the boys were looking at her as the laughter and their smiles faded away.

Mildred continued towards the shop and brushed a couple of tears away hoping that her cat would be okay, she also wondered why people could be so mean.

"Are you alright, Mildred?" Mr Franks enquired, noticing that Mildred did not seem her usual self; something did not seem right.

"Yes, I'm fine, thank you," she said, putting on a brave face.

Mr Franks could see that she looked upset.

"What on earth is it, Mildred?" he asked, putting down his newspaper.

She shrugged, looking towards the floor. "It's just the boys at the bus stop. They make fun of me."

"Well, boys will be boys, Mildred," he rasped.

"That doesn't make it right, Mr Franks!" His response caused even more upset.

"Indeed, it does not, Mildred and one day they will learn to better themselves."

Mildred wondered if the boys would ever better themselves.

"Is that everything Mildred, unlike you to get so upset about stupid boys?"

"My Missy is very unwell. I had to have the vet round earlier."

"Oh, I'm sorry to hear this Mildred, did you call vets at Castle Hollow?"

"No, Fennaway's Veterinary."

"Mmm, not heard of that one." He shuffled with his newspaper, suddenly feeling awkward. "Anyway, I hope that he was able to help."

"It was a she."

"I'm sorry?"

"The vet was a she. Miss Fennaway."

"I stand corrected, Mildred. In any event, I hope that she was able to help."

"Not especially. Anyway, did my cards arrive?"

"Indeed they have, all 44 of them!"

"Well, that's good news. I've had a terrible day so far."

"I'm pleased to say that they have exactly the same cat on the front as the one you saw yesterday."

A big smile stretched across Mildred's face for the first time that day. She put her bag down and dried her eyes. "That really is pleasing news. Thank you."

"Not a problem, I've got them back here for you; just bear with me a jiffy."

He pulled across a very old and dusty looking curtain and disappeared out to the back of the shop.

She glanced down at his newspaper. 'Witnesses Sought Following Bus Accident.' Mildred read the title of the article, instantly remembering that Mr Franks had mentioned about an accident recently. 'Police are requesting for people to come forward following a fatal accident on Benbow Street. The Police investigation is ongoing but they have been forced to concede that all CCTV of the incident has disappeared. There are currently no witnesses despite Benbow Street being a popular place for tourists and locals alike. The unnamed victim…' "That's odd" Mildred muttered to herself.

Looking around, she noticed how unkempt the shop was. She had never really noticed it before. The labels with the prices on were all handwritten with a black marker pen. The lino on the floor was turning up in random places and pictures hung on the walls that were quite discoloured. Why there was a faded 'Monet' picture in a frame in this shop was anyone's guess.

"Here we are, Mildred." He placed the stack of cards that were wrapped individually in cellophane onto the counter.

Mildred lifted one of the cards and sure enough, they were exactly the same. "Oh, that is amazing, Mr Franks. I'm so happy," she said, turning the card in her hand.

Her smile quickly disappeared from her face as she read, 'Printed words inside say HAPPY BIRTHDAY.' Her eyes flared open. In a panic, she threw the card on the side and grabbed another off the pile.

"No, no, it can't be."

"Whatever is the matter, Mildred?"

"These are birthday cards!"

"Yes, that is correct, exactly as you ordered." He reached under the counter and held up the one from the previous day.

She snatched it from his hand; it read exactly the same as the others.

She closed her eyes in utter disbelief.

"Well, did you not know it was a birthday card, Mildred? Did you not check?" He rasped with stuttered laughter with his hands on his hips. "I thought it highly odd to order 44 birthday cards at once, but who am I to ask. Each to his own."

"Her own!" Mildred snapped, closing her eyes in annoyance.

"What now, Mildred?"

"Each to her own!"

Mr Franks looked down at his counter.

Mildred let out a large sigh and looked down at the floor again. "I'll take them. Would you happen to have a black felt-tip pen as well, please?"

Mildred paid and made her way to the door. She didn't offer a goodbye.

She started down the road muttering to herself. "You're going to a gathering and want to make a good impression and instead you give everyone a birthday card, you stupid woman!" She stomped her way home.

"Seriously, could this day get any worse?" Her stomping came to a halt as she noticed the boys at the bus stop. She about turned and took the long route home.

+-+-+-+

Nubia's news was still sinking in as they sat in silence.

"What exactly did Fennaway say, Nubia?" the Reeve enquired.

"She spoke very quickly as she knew that she was being watched. She informed me that one of our own, the cat named Nahla, is suffering." She puffed, still out of breath from running.

"Was she scanned?" The Reeve questioned.

"Yes and the results were exacting. The sensors detected her pain centre was coming from the region of her heart; it is as foretold."

"Okay, okay, let's not get ahead of ourselves." The Keeper gently interjected. "It may just be bad timing, that's all. Nothing more."

"Fennaway insisted the readings on the Signapher device were quite clear, Madam Keeper." The Curator asserted.

They sat motionlessly.

"Which Elder is Nahla with? I struggle to remember where each cat has been placed and with whom," the Keeper asked, looking at the Curator.

"She is with Mildred, from Rocke Road in Shrewsbury. A 9th degree Elder; one of the new intakes." Nubia said, biting her lip and fidgeting in her seat.

"This is indeed perturbing for any cat but for such a young one to be displaying these signs..." said the Keeper shaking her head.

"Yes and Mildred will not even know her real name as yet." The Reeve nodded in agreement.

"Nubia, is there something else that you know or want to share with us?" The Reeve noticed her uncomfortable demeanour.

She looked up with a guilt-ridden face glancing between the Keeper and the Reeve.

"Curator, speak up now, please!" The Keeper spoke for the first time today with the authority that is becoming of her rank.

Letting out a large sigh, the Curator always wanted to know secrets but knew that she was entirely useless at keeping them.

"I had been advised to keep an eye upon the Mildred of whom we speak."

The Reeve looked incredulous as her eyes lifted to the ceiling. She shook her head to the left and right before resuming her composure. "Are you serious, Nubia? Security is my department."

"That it is, Reeve." The Keeper said, joining her in support of this statement as they both now looked directly at the Curator.

Nubia, clearly quite anguished, looked at both of them. "I was told to keep it a secret."

The Reeve slammed her hand on her desk. "This is outrageous, especially from you, the one who sticks to rules and conformity no matter what. You need to start talking right now!"

"Yes, I know, okay, okay." She scratched her head and gathered her thoughts. "I wasn't entirely sure of the facts and I didn't want to bother you with it," (she lied). "The source can be unreliable at times, so I just wanted to check it. That's all, nothing more."

"I was unaware that you had sources Curator. In fact, I was unaware that we even had 'sources' within the Order." The Keeper's eyes were fixed firmly upon Nubia and her voice was filled with concern.

Nubia was struggling to maintain eye contact with either of them, the Keeper, due to her importance and rank and with the Reeve, well, just because she just didn't like her. She knew that she was very much in the wrong.

The Reeve leaned forward on her desk. "Curator, you will talk to us."

The Curator closed her eyes and gathered her composure.

"I was recently contacted by a very senior Elder who informed me that she had been told a great event of imbalance was about to happen. She was very concerned that the prophecy of old and the foretelling of the stopping of our time and dominium were imminent."

The Reeve and the Keeper both looked at each other in amazement.

"Dominium?" The Reeve smiled and lowered her chin towards the Keeper, "dominium, you say? Which dominium do you speak of?"

Nubia struggled to maintain her composure and could only offer a softly spoken reply. "Us Reeve. Our dominium. Our place here, at the end of our time."

Upon hearing this, the Reeve slumped back into her seat, eyes wide, looking at the Keeper.

"Okay, Nubia." The Keeper raised her right hand as an offering of peace and calm.

Nubia looked up towards the Keeper.

"These are truly dreadful words that you speak, Nubia. In any event, they should never leave this room, but you must tell us more about what you were told."

"I promised that I would look into it and promised not to tell anyone."

"Well, why was I not told about this?" questioned the Reeve in some astonishment.

"Because you are new, a new breed that does not follow tradition as it should be." Nubia snapped. "Look at the way you dress, like you are wearing a suit for business. You are not a banker and you are not trusted by all you know."

The Reeve slammed her hands on her desk. "Ridiculous! This is outrageous!" She looked towards the Keeper for support.

"Now, both of you, stop and calm yourselves!" The Keeper pointed towards both of them with her cane. Deep in thought, she leaned over to the Curator. "Who told you about this Nubia?"

"Oh, Madam Keeper, please do not ask. I promised that I would not repeat her name."

"I'm quite sure that is the case, but you have gone behind the back of the Reeve, who has the support of her Order, the Grand Council and myself. These are very profound statements you are making. So, I ask you again, who told you this?"

Nubia's hands were now in a ball resting on one knee as she twitched excessively, debating what to do.

She let out a huge sigh. "It was Lady Ebonee," she said, looking down at the floor.

"Lady Ebonee from Dundee; Lady Ebonee, who is a member of the Grand Council?"

Nubia nodded a couple of times, still looking at the floor.

"Oh well, that explains it then." The Keeper shook her head. "She may well be a very respected member of the Grand Council, but she is as nutty as a fruitcake. Her unique take on the 'prophecies' has to be heard to be believed Reeve," she said with some amusement, "don't get me wrong, I love and admire her deeply. Still, the older she gets, the more wayward she becomes."

The Keeper was still shaking her head, but her face was quizzical. "Most unnatural for a Member of the Grand Council to behave in this fashion and bypass others and the ranks of order."

"Maybe the others would not have believed her, Madam Keeper," the Reeve said, looking at Nubia as she leaned forward on her desk. "Maybe she knew that someone else would, someone who lives in deep paranoia of the prophecies and the passing of time, maybe someone that would do her bidding."

Nubia looked up, angered by her statement.

"I did what I believed to be right," she snarled.

"I'm sure you did Nubia, but this sheds a whole new light on things!" the Reeve said, now looking directly at the Keeper. "So, tell us how exactly were you going to do this? How exactly were you going to look into this?"

The Curator swallowed and looked at them both with a shameful expression etched across her face.

"I made contact with Jessica, who is the elder of Daphne..."

The Reeve practically threw herself back in her chair, rolling her eyes.

She let out a couple of small unintentional laughs, "Oh, this is all starting to make sense now."

"What, what is it?" the Keeper asked, looking confused.

"Shall I say or shall you?" the Reeve bluntly threw the comment at the Curator. "Well...?" The question hung in silence for a couple of seconds.

"Don't worry, Nubia, I'll fill in the blanks for you!"

Nubia looked down to the floor averting the Reeve's eyes.

"I'll tell you what our Curator did, Madam Keeper. A week ago, she asked for navigational enhancements to be made to Jessica's car. Then she requested for her to have her own personal navigator. I didn't think the request was that unusual, as she will be promoted to a Degree Level 6 Elder at the gathering tomorrow. This will give her a higher level of security access. So I asked for my security team to do just that and make the adjustments that she requested. However, what is unusual is that she summoned Jessica for a private meeting only two days ago. Invitations to headquarters for an Elder holding only a Degree Level 7 status is out of the ordinary. It all makes sense now. Is that what happened here Nubia, am I somewhat close?"

"She is about to be made a Degree Level 6!" Snapped Nubia. "But yes; that is what happened. It is as you say." Nubia nodded her head a couple of times and sighed.

"So, you've either told Jessica about the prophecy of which she is not of the appropriate rank to hear, or you've asked her to spy on Daphne and Mildred. Am I right?"

The Curator shifted in her seat, gathering her thoughts.

"No, I've asked Jessica to keep an eye on Mildred and to report anything unusual to me. Daphne is none the wiser."

"And we were none the wiser too, it would appear," the Keeper said, looking at Nubia.

"As I say, Madam Keeper, I thought I was doing the right thing!"

The Reeve and the Keeper looked at each other, slightly unsure of what to do next.

"Let's keep some calm as the event has already happened now. There is nothing we can do to change this. However, it may well be worthy of an internal investigation some other time." The Curator continued to hang her head in shame.

The Reeve looked towards the Keeper. "I do not know Lady Ebonee, but I have heard rumours about her 'thoughts' away from the Council. Do we think there is any validity in what she is saying?"

"Yes, indeed..." The Curator was cut short by the waving arm of the Keeper.

"It is highly unlikely..." She was then cut off by the Curator.

"But the prophecy states there will be three events and this bears the mark of the first."

The Keeper looked furiously at Nubia for cutting her off.

"Indeed, it does. The prophecy foretells that one of our kind will bear hallmarks of pain from the heart 24 hours before the union of the Grand Council of the Enlightened."

"Such as a gathering?" The Reeve put forward, "but the Grand Council are not meeting tomorrow."

"Whilst that may be true, Reeve, they will be present at other gatherings all over the world and therefore it could be considered a collective union."

"Could it be entirely possible that here, within this region, Nahla is the one showing the pains of the heart?"

"Nahla is a special cat...." Nubia mumbled before being cut off again.

"All of the cats I present are very special Nubia. There have been no indications thus far that Nahla is any more special than the others. If this is to be, time will tell." Her words lingered in the air as she looked directly at the Curator.

"What would you wish me to do, Madam Keeper?" the Reeve said.

"We must not get ahead of ourselves. This may be a coincidence of time and nothing more. In the meantime, we will remain calm. The passing of Lady Tempest is a concern and the cat displaying great pain. Not to mention a senior Elder making these sort of claims. But for now, they are just claims. Nothing more, nothing less." The Keeper tried to remain calm for everyone's sake.

The Keeper was deep in thought. She knew that the events sounded very suspicious. Still, she also knew that the Curator had a tendency to panic unnecessarily. She knew she would need to be careful with her words from now on.

"If there is any truth in these claims, there will be another event this evening. That is what was foretold. Until such time we remain calm and conduct our affairs as we always do – Yes?"

"Yes, Madam Keeper," said the Reeve. Nubia nodded, biting at a fingernail.

"Good. Reeve, will you store the scroll in the archive, please?"

"Yes, Madam Keeper, I will be very happy to."

"Good!" the Keeper responded, balancing on her cane as she stood up. The Reeve also stood up, but Nubia remained seated, chewing her fingernails.

"We have been a presence for good for thousands of years, through many times of adversity, even at its most stubborn. There is nothing to say that anything is going to change to that effect." She looked at both of them. "And on that note, I bid you both farewell. Reeve. Curator," she nodded to both of them.

"I'll see that Raysmau guides you out, Madam Keeper."

"So be it." She gave the Reeve a half-smile.

On the way out of the door, she glanced over at Nubia, who hadn't moved from her seat. Her face was filled with fear. Her words had clearly not reassured her.

Chapter Sixteen:

BEHIND THE GATE OF RAYSMAU

HEADQUARTERS
THURSDAY LATE AFTERNOON

Duat offered little resistance as he knelt down and put his hands behind his back. He listened to the familiar sound of cuffs being put across both of his wrists.

"Make sure those gloves are still secured, Gamila." Alian, one of the Reeve's elite security team, known as the Escarrabin, instructed her fellow security officer. Duat was lifted back to his feet by his cuffs, his palms covered by the leather gloves.

"What are you doing over here, one who calls himself Duat?" The tone of the questioning was reasonably hostile.

His head was bowed down and could not be seen under the hood of the full-length cloak that identified him as an outcast.

Alian moved around to face him. "I will ask you again, for the last time, what are you doing here?"

Duat remained motionless.

Alian bowed down slightly in an attempt to look Duat directly in the face. Partially seeing his chin and jaw was enough to make her grimace. His saliva ran freely down his face without him having the ability to wipe it away.

"Last chance, Watcher."

"I am more than a Watcher," Duat muttered under his breath.

"Oh, really?" Alian nodded to Gamila. "Pull his hood down."

Duat instantly contorted in pain as the bright August sun bore down on him. Unable to protect his eye, his head flayed left and right, his arms wrestling against the cuffs as he tried to get to his feet.

"Hold him!" Alian yelled as Gamila put a foot on the back of his knees, forcing him to kneel down again.

"There, as you should be, Watcher."

Alian crouched down to look directly at Duat and could see that the vessels in his huge solitary eye were swollen and multiplying at an incredible rate as he hissed in pain.

"Not so easy without goggles or a hood, is it? My, you are ugly, Watcher." Alian stood back and nodded for his hood to be put back over his skeletal-like head. The hood was replaced, shielding his eye from the sunlight.

The hissing noise changed to the more familiar high pitched cry that Watchers made when under threat. His breathing was gaining momentum again as his convulsions started to ease.

"There, you see, we can be reasonable. So much for your statement, you are clearly the same as the other Watchers."

Alian nodded for Gamila to bring him back to his feet.

Saliva ran between the gaps in his teeth and the two misshaped dark crevasses, separated by the thinnest bone that represented something of a nose flared up and down. He was breathing heavily and sounded like an animal in distress.

"I will ask you again and for the very final time, what are you doing over here, Duat?"

He remained motionless, having gathered his composure.

"Madam Raysmau informed me that the Curator reported that you were seen in this area only two days ago. Why is that?"

Alian was angered that no response was forthcoming from the Watcher. "I see!"

Frustrated with his lack of compliance, she leaned in closer. "In fact, I see very well with both of my eyes, Duat." A smirk appeared across her face only to be met by a deep hiss by way of his response.

"Before you go back to your rightful place below, you have an appointment with Madam Raysmau." She stepped back from the Watcher. "Take him away."

Gamila grabbed the handcuffs with her left arm, pushed at his shoulder with the right and started walking him back to the manor house. Alian watched Gamila lead him away. He offered no resistance despite his strength. She looked up behind her at the great statue of Salma. Why Duat had been here again for the second time in days, she had no idea.

Duat was escorted unceremoniously into the manor house through the private doorway used by the Escarrabin. He knew that Alian had now caught up behind them, hearing the unmistakable footsteps of her heavy footwear on the tiled stone floor.

As they entered the grand lobby, Duat looked up from under his hood and could see six Clerics sitting at their desk. There was a scattering of what his captors referred to as 'the Elders.' Movements within the lobby had stopped as everyone looked on at the events in front of them. Duat was ushered towards the archway that led to the quarters of the head of security.

As they drew close, Alian leaned forward and pressed the intercom.

"Control, go ahead," was the quick response through the speaker.

"Control, this is Escarrabin Alian, with a prisoner, requesting to see Madam Raysmau."

There was a short pause as the request was considered, followed by the sound of heavy locks moving from the door and the sound of a gate scraping across the stone floor.

Under his hood, Duat twitched a smile at the simplicity of their security measures.

The heavy door opened automatically as another member of the Escarrabin appeared, looking very unimpressed at the sight of the restrained Watcher.

Alian stepped forward to her fellow Escarrabin. "We need to speak with Madam Raysmau. This Watcher has been roaming again."

A frown appeared across the face of the security guard and gatekeeper.

"I see. Please wait here Alian, I will see if she is available." She pressed a button on the wall and the door started to reclose.

The two Escarrabin spun Duat around so he was facing the lobby for all to see. The six clerics were reasonably unmoved, but the Elders were looking on and talking amongst themselves.

Duat surveyed the lobby's pillars and architecture and the supposed 'art' that graced the walls. Other guards began to appear, having heard of his presence in the grand lobby. Duat looked up to the first-floor balcony to see two other security guards and one solitary Cleric were watching over him. The saliva ran down his chin to the floor. His breathing was heavy, which must have bothered one of the guards who forced his head back down.

The heavy door started to reopen as Duat was spun around and led into the security chamber of Raysmau. He looked up to meet the gaze of the security guard who had let them through. A very uncomfortable expression appeared across her face as she looked back at him. His head was pushed back down again to see the very worn sandals he was made to wear and his filthy, long and chipped toenails.

Duat was pushed and dragged to the doorway of Raysmau's office. He lifted his head as the gate swung back across the floor behind him.

It wasn't the first time he had looked on at Raysmau sitting behind her desk. She had very pale skin and was still dressed in her formal robes. He had been told that the Keeper had been here at the manor house earlier today.

Duat was led towards her desk and his hood was pulled down so she could look directly at him.

She had seen him before, so his appearance didn't surprise or shock her. He knew that the way he looked made others uncomfortable; that is, those who are not used to seeing him and other Watchers in their natural state. The head of security had knowledge and experience of such matters and some intellect too apparently; much to his amusement.

Her jet black hair was tied up neatly and secured by a leather band, giving the appearance of a long tail emerging from the back of her head. The lower half of her face and neck was covered with a dark mask moulded to her face, which was the custom for the head of security for the Order.

No doubt a futile effort to display the colours of the light and dark against the paleness of her skin.

He acknowledged her by slightly turning up the left side of his mouth, awaiting the words of wisdom that she no doubt would offer him this time.

She raised her hands behind her neck and unclipped the moulding that freed the skin around the lower part of her face.

Raysmau broke her stare from him to look at the security guards as the mask fell onto the desk.

"Well?"

"Ma'am, this Watcher was found wandering the gardens again. Nowhere near where he was supposed to be, around the great statue of Salma."

"I see." She returned her gaze to the Watcher, expressionless.

A snort from Duat disrupted the silence provoking her to speak as she watched beads of dribble fall to the floor. "Watcher, you've been in my chambers before and yet you are brought to me again. How are you to learn if you are not punished?" She leaned back in her huge, heavily carved wooden chair, resting her right elbow on an armrest and moving her thumb and fingers around each other as she spoke. "Your duties here are maintaining the garden around the lake, not towards the front of the house. Now, I'm told you have been found in this area a second time. An area that is out of bounds to you. Why?"

The Watcher stared forward and said nothing.

"I'm addressing you, the one who calls himself Duat."

Maintaining eye contact, he sneered in his deep voice; "You cannot order me around like a dog or like these imbeciles that try to chain me." He nodded to his left and right ensuring that the security guards knew what he thought of them.

Alian and Gamila scoffed.

"No? You think differently of yourselves?" he said, looking at them both in turn. His deep voice was broken up by the sound of saliva moving in the gaps of his teeth. "You are valueless, worthless and of no purpose. You just serve her." He nodded in the direction of Raysmau, "and that Reeve upstairs!" He returned his gaze to the centre to study Raysmau's reaction.

Having been on the end of Duat vocalising his thoughts once before, Raysmau was unmoved. "I am all too aware of the vileness of your mouth Watcher. What concerns me is that many Watchers have stood here in this room over the years, but you are the most disruptive and lack the most discipline. Today's excursion in the gardens will require punishment and the punishment you receive will teach you discipline and order. You have not been here very long. For your sake, I hope you are a fast learner and that you will fall into line. Do I make myself clear?"

Duat was expecting this reaction.

Raysmau leant forward in her chair, maintaining her stare with calmness in her tone.

"Let me be clear with you Watcher, if it were my decision, you would all be banished for eternity. You talk of purpose and yet you have none yourself. You are the remnants of a bloodline that was crossed with vileness and evil a very long time ago; I'm amazed you still survive, let alone why."

"Our numbers are much more than you realise, slave of the Reeve. The Order will learn this in time and very much to your personal cost." The gaps appeared in his teeth again in what resembled something of a smile as the Watchers' familiar hiss emitted from his mouth.

Raysmau looked at her security team and sniggered with laughter.

"Of course, you are referring to the so-called prophecy? The end of our time and the onset of the darkness of yours? Where you and your 'kind' will rise from dark places and your ugliness walk across the dying plains of the world, which you will then call your dominium?"

"That is not the name we call it." His words silenced their sniggering.

Raysmau slumped back into her seat and resumed the circular motion of her thumb and index finger.

"It disgusts me to even set my eyes upon you. The paleness and thinness of your skin, that oversized vein that runs to your eye that is full of nothing but poison."

Gathering her thoughts, she softened her tone. "There are always cures for poisons and you are no different from the others. It is you that will learn in time!" There was anger in her eyes. "Take him below!"

She gave the instruction at a volume that probably would have echoed around the grand lobby outside of her doors.

Alian and Gamila immediately grabbed him by his cloak and handcuffs.

"Not all poisons have cures, slave. The futileness of your ticking clocks is nothing compared to when the last grain of sand falls." He spat towards Raysmau as he was spun around and led towards the door.

"Oh, Watcher," she said as the security guards turned him back around again to face her.

"You know it does occur to me that we have not been in the below for quite some time. Maybe it is time that I ordered my team to search those caverns that you dwell in."

She stood up and walked around to the front of the desk and stood in front of Duat, her huge frame bearing down on him. "I personally have not taken the lift down for quite some time."

Duat considered tormenting her further but thought better of it. The last thing that he needed was her below ground right now.

"Nothing further to add?" She brought her face toward his. Saliva ran down his chin as he snarled.

"You are a relic of the past and relics remain buried and consigned to history. If you are brought before me again, your punishment will be severe and life below will become difficult for you as well as the others!" She stepped back from him and sat on the edge of her desk.

She nodded at Alian and Gamila to take him away and they escorted him out of her office. Duat turned his head to look at her one more time as she sat motionless on the edge of the desk before his hood was pulled back up. He was dragged back into the main lobby, ready to go to the lift that only goes down.

Staring at her friend for any positive signs of change, she ran her hand down Missy's belly for the hundredth time that day. "I don't know what to do to fix you, Missy?" She looked helpless as the twitches and spasms of her cat continued.

She looked at the cushion she had made of the innocent cat that Missy was sprawled out upon. In two minds as to what to do, she remembered that she had 44 cards to prepare. She slumped back into the sofa, remembering her failure to even get a simple thing like choosing an appropriate card right. She had visions of the other Mildred's ham and cheese sandwiches, even worse, the other Mildred's cat treats and cupcakes. Except for the clock ticking in the kitchen, nothing else could be heard as she looked around her front room at all the old furniture and the bits of paper that she had hoarded.

I used to wear make-up, she thought, pondering her life. She looked down at her wrinkled stockings and scuffed brown shoes.

She shook her shoes off, stood to her feet and headed to the kitchen.

She went to the fridge and looked inside at the three plates of stacked fish paste sandwiches and tugged at the cellophane of one of them. Taking out a solitary white bread sandwich that was curling at the sides, she brought it to her mouth and took a small bite. Looking towards the ceiling, she closed her eyes then looked back down at the sandwich. It tastes like fish paste, she thought, throwing the remainder on the side. She kicked the fridge door closed forgetting she had taken her shoes off. Feeling instant pain, she hopped around the kitchen holding her foot. "Ouch!!" she yelled in anguish and frustration. Wincing in pain, she threw herself down on one of only two chairs next to the kitchen table.

Red-faced and deep in thought, she bit her lip as her toes throbbed. She could see the cards on the side and the solitary black marker pen next to them.

Her initial plan was to write a personal message inside a card for each member of the club. That plan was now on hiatus. Now she would be crossing a line through the words 'Happy Birthday' and printing the words, 'from Mildred with best wishes.' She shook her head, knowing they were going to look terrible, really terrible. She didn't even know the names of the other members. It was meant to be a way of introducing herself. She knew that she would have to write 'from Rocke Road' after her name as there were so many other Mildreds.

She pondered why there were so many Mildreds, Jessicas and Daphnes. There weren't any Emmas, Joannes or Sharons anywhere in sight, which she found odd. She lowered her head with a frown as she questioned herself on this simple thing. Until now, she had never really considered it.

Outstretching her right leg to flex the toes of her throbbing foot, she winced; she had had enough. It will just have to be fish paste sandwiches and that's that! She got up, went over to the side, grabbed the cards and placed her less painful foot on the bin's pedal and held them over it. As the lid opened, she saw the picture on the front of the card. Pedal to the floor she glanced over at Missy, her heart beating ten to the dozen and a wave of guilt came over her for attempting to throw away such a beautiful thing. She took her foot off the pedal, picked up the black marker pen and sat back down. She opened the first card and threw the cellophane over her shoulder onto the kitchen floor. The 'Happy Birthday' was as clear as day. She crossed it out with the pen and started to write.

She would do that another 43 times before bedtime and there would be quite a pile of discarded cellophane before she finished.

K.S. Horak

Chapter Seventeen:

THE STONE STAIRS OF THE BELOW

THURSDAY EARLY EVENING

The old lift juddered to a halt. The steel grill was pulled across and Duat pushed into his familiar surroundings of the below.

"Kneel down, Duat." The two Escarrabin stepped out of the lift behind him. He obliged, feeling the presence of one of them directly over him, removing his handcuffs and freeing his hands. Bringing himself to his feet, he pulled his hood down and turned to face them, wiping the saliva from his mouth and chin and shaking it onto the floor.

He stared at them as Gamila pulled the grill back into place. The lift automatically ascended to the central lobby of Loxley.

"Look at you both," he spat, "would you not rather take the lift back up?"

"The lift only goes down, Watcher," Gamila said, walking back towards him, "you know that."

"Clearly, it does not," Duat spoke as he rotated his shoulders and flexed his fingers.

157

"The stone stairs are a reminder to you and your kind that you need to walk to the above. You have to earn your right to walk on the outside."

"Now it is you that must walk to get back to what you refer to as 'the outside'."

He laughed at their ridiculous practices, spitting more saliva on the floor.

The Escarrabin looked at each other with some concession to this observation.

"Everyone below, whether it is us or your kind, have to ascend by way of the worn stairs. It is the way things are done." Alian flipped a succinct smile at the disinterested Watcher.

"Pathetic!" Duat spat, breaking out a little smile of amusement as his breathing became more audible.

"I'm so glad that we are entertainment for you, Watcher. As Madam Raysmau has stated, punishment will be coming to you!"

"We will see," he smiled.

Alian walked towards him. "You do not unnerve us, Duat."

"Are you sure of that?" Duat gave a broad smile, uncaring of the saliva running down his chin and the echoing hiss of his deep voice.

Alian stepped back a couple of paces upon hearing noises coming from the darkness behind him.

The familiar groans of the Watchers echoed around the chamber. Alian could see silhouettes in the dark moving towards them as the flames of the candle's, that offered little light, started to flicker. The echoing high pitched calls from the darkness became more intense as the shadows moved closer, multiplying. Alian and Gamila looked at each other, sensing volatility in the atmosphere; they were outnumbered by some margin.

"Alian!"

"I know, I know!"

Gamila reached behind her. It had been many years since a Scatterblade had been drawn within the grounds; they were carried mainly for ceremonial purposes now.

"Go back to where you came," Gamila shouted as a warning. She swallowed and raised her Scatterblade as three hooded figures appeared behind Duat. There were potentially many more as the volume of noise increased. They moved closer to the Escarrabin pulling their hoods down one by one. Both of them could see the gaping holes of their noses and the warm mist emitting from them as their breath met the cold of the below. Her eyes flitted between them, staring directly at the pulsing vein that led to their singular eye. It was then that the other figures in the shadows came forward.

There was a sudden loud roar from deep in the below followed by multiple bangs, the sound of which made two of the Watchers turn to look.

The hairs stood up on the backs of the necks of both of the security officers. Duat, however, did not move or flinch; only his breathing could be heard.

"You are unnerved slaves; I can see it." He said, taking a step towards them, his eye pulsing as the loud roar came up again from the depths, echoing all around them.

Gamila pointed the Scatterblade at Duat, her hands shaking uncontrollably as the adrenalin raced through her veins.

"That will not help you. You cannot win; we are many." He removed his gloves and let them fall to the floor. Holding up the turquoise, pulsing palm of his right hand, he took a step forward.

Gamila jumped, feeling Alian's hand on her shoulder.

"We should go!" She dragged at Gamila's uniform, pulling her towards the worn stone staircase.

Duat lowered his palm with a menacing smile as he watched them move quickly up the stairs in retreat to the upper doors.

Alian reached the top of the stone steps first, ripping her glove off to push her palm against the scanner as hard as she could. The scanner moved up and down her palm. She glanced behind her, relieved that they hadn't been followed. "Come on, come on," she yelled at the scanner.

They both fell through the door into the grand hallway as the locks gave way. They pushed back on the door, trying to speed up the automatic mechanism that would seal it shut again.

An Elder at the end of the grand walkway stared at them both quizzically as they forced the door closed. Two Clerics at a desk, just off the walkway, also looked on.

"Well, don't just sit there. Help us!" Alian screamed.

The Clerics ran to the door and started pushing.

The door sealed and the symbol to the right turned green and all four of them let go. Gamila fell to the ground breathing heavily and nodded at the Clerics who made their way back to their seats. "You okay?" she asked Alian, who was equally out of breath, alarm written across her face.

"I'm not sure. What happened down there was horrible?"

Gamila nodded, "I've never seen them be so confrontational; they are usually so quiet. Something is going on." The Elder watching over them stared on in alarm.

"We had better report this to Raysmau" said Alian. "You drew your Blade. It will be seen as a weakness. You showed fear."

"I'll be honest, Alian, I was scared. Maybe we shouldn't mention it."

They sat gathering their breath, realising they were creating a lot of attention. Gamila spoke as quietly as she could. "What do you think made that noise from below; I've never heard that before or anything like it?"

"I have no idea. It came from somewhere very deep; somewhere none of us have been in a very long time, if ever. I hope that is the last we hear of it."

Mildred's cards had taken so long to write that Bang Goes Your Money had long since finished. Mildred glanced over her shoulder from her couch to see 44 neatly stacked birthday cards and breathed out a sigh. She ignored the 44 pieces of screwed up cellophane all over the kitchen floor; they could wait. She stretched out her hand to relieve her writer's cramp and looked at Missy by her side. There had been no change and she was clearly still in some discomfort. She glanced over at the rear end of her telephone and considered calling Fennaway's again or maybe even the other vet that Mr Franks had mentioned earlier on.

Fennaway's assertion that it was probably just a bug was doing very little to reassure her as she felt Missy's tummy worryingly. It was approaching 9 o'clock and getting on for her bedtime. How on earth could I possibly sleep with my friend in so much pain, she thought, watching her hand rising up and down on her cat's belly.

"It's no good. I've got to call Fennaway's Missy. Something needs to be done!" She got to her feet and snatched at the phone. She redialled, having no idea if the landline office phone would be answered at this time of night. She did not have the personal mobile number that she had seen her talking on earlier in the day.

The phone only rang twice before it was hastily answered without the annoying answering service this time.

"Hello Mildred," came the instant response.

"Dr Fennaway, it's Mildred from... how did you know it was me?"

Kamilah banged the phone against her temple in disgust of her error. "Well, Mildred, it's only because we spoke earlier, so I guessed it may be you, dear." She smiled to herself, pleased with her response.

"But didn't you say that you had another client to see after me?"

There was a muted pause.

"Well, er, yes I did, but that turned out to be a false alarm. It can happen around these sorts of times if you understand me?"

"No, not really. What sort of times are those?"

Kamilah screwed up her face again, "I mean the time of the year; that sort of thing, dear."

"Oh, right. Okay."

"Anyway, how can I help you?"

"Well, thank you for taking my call at this hour. I didn't think you would still be in the office right now."

"Well, as I say, at these times I need to be on-hand to help my very special clients."

"Thank you, Kamilah," although Mildred had no idea why she would be referred to as a 'special client.'

"You are most welcome, dear. Now how can I be of assistance? Is Missy still unwell?"

"Yes, she really is and she doesn't seem to be improving. What do you suggest, please?"

"Well, the most important thing is to keep her warm and give her lots of love."

There was another period of silence as Mildred shook her head and rolled her eyes.

"Is that it? Is that all you can suggest? I don't think Missy hugs are going to fix her, Doctor Fennaway!"

"You say that, Mildred, but hugs are good. It's been medically proven."

"Really...by whom may I ask?"

"Look, I sense your concern, but these bugs do pass in time, you will see."

"Doctor Fennaway, I am truly sorry to say this, but I'm upset and very concerned. I think I need another opinion."

"Whatever do you mean, dear?"

"I heard of another vet in this area. I think I will call them."

"No, no, no! Do not do that, Mildred. I implore you!" Kamilah's voice was stern and full of concern, so much so that Mildred pulled the phone away from her ear in shock at the outburst.

"Why ever not? It's my cat. I can do as I choose."

"It's not your..." Kamilah regained her thoughts. "It's just that vets, us vets, have a code and we do not exchange clients. It's an unwritten rule. That's all I mean, nothing more. Would you like me to speak with her?"

"The other vet? I do not know if it's a her. I've not called them before?"

"No, your cat dear, would you like me to speak to Missy?"

Mildred's eyes widened as her mouth fell open. She pulled the phone away from her ear again.

She could hear muffled words coming from the cat's head on her phone, "Mildred... Mildred, are you still there?"

She placed the receiver back to her ear, still in stark amazement. "Yes, I am still here."

"Let's just try?"

"Just try what, Dr Fennaway?"

"Put the phone to the cat's ear, please."

Mildred giggled slightly in amusement. "Really?"

"Yes, really."

"Okay, I think I will." With that, she placed the phone over Missy's right ear. If anyone could see me now, she thought, shaking her head at the absurdity of the situation.

She focused her eyes on Missy and could hear faint noises coming from the phone, spoken words of some kind. The smile quickly drained from her face as she watched Missy's legs stretch out at the same time. Her right eye opened slightly before reclosing quickly. Mildred could still hear sounds emitting from the phone before they stopped abruptly and Missy's legs relaxed.

"Mildred... Mildred, are you there?" The muffled sounds of the vet could be heard from the other end of the phone.

"Yes, I am still here. What on earth was that?"

"She will be fine very soon, I'm sure of that."

"But what exactly just happened? Missy opened an eye."

"I just happen to shine a little when it comes to cats, dear."

"Shine, what on earth..."

"Have you ever read about people who talk to horses, Mildred? Did you ever see the programme with the lady who said she could speak with dogs? Well, this is no different. I have a way with cats, that's all."

"But those people are bloody lunatics!"

"Not so, Mildred. Not so at all."

Mildred's mouth remained agape.

"Anyway, I must go, dear. Please do not worry, your cat will be fine come morning, I'm quite sure of that. It's as I said, just a bug."

"Well, I..."

"Must go. Goodbye for now, dear."

The phone went down at the other end, but Mildred clutched onto it, hoping for further words from the doctor. None were forthcoming. She looked at Missy. Her heart was still racing and she was clearly still in some discomfort. Apart from the ticking from the clock, the house was silent. You could have heard a pin drop.

The Curator sat at her desk, looking at the swinging pendulum of her clock. It had just gone 9pm and she looked like she had the weight of the world on her shoulders. She had been locked deep in worry ever since the Keeper had left earlier.

She wrestled with the thought of contacting her friend on the Grand Council, but given the probable investigation following her conversations with Lady Ebonee and her subsequent actions, this was probably ill-advised. This new Reeve and her embracing of technical 'things' probably meant that she would listen in on her phone calls from now on. She would have to be careful and not risk anything unless she had to.

Collectively, Lady Tempest's passing, Nahla's pain and Lady Ebonee's predictions were becoming quite unsettling. In fact, she could feel stress pains in her tummy as she moved, which caused her some discomfort. Locked deep in thought whilst biting at her nails, she was startled by her phone ringing. She shook her head and glanced back at the clock, wondering who on earth it could be at this hour.

"Yes, what is it?" She answered the phone with some ill-patience and rudeness."

"Nubia it's Kamilah."

She leant on her desk, pressing her phone to her ear.

"Nahla has got worse, much worse. I've communicated with her and it may well be the sign. The sign of the predicted, Nubia."

The phone fell from Nubia's clammy palms. The time of the gathering was approaching. She looked nervously at her clock again, although it told her what she already knew. It was three hours before midnight and counting.

Chapter Eighteen:

INDEBTED TO RATS

LATE THURSDAY NIGHT

A watched clock never tells the time, or it was something like that, Nubia thought as she mused over the old saying she had heard a long time ago. Nevertheless, she watched on intently as the minute hand of the ancient clock rested at two minutes to midnight.

Her shoes were off and her legs tucked firmly under her chair as she sat waiting. She was about to gnaw at her fingers again when she noticed how worn down her fingernails were. She snatched them away from her face as she recalled some of her interpretations of the prophecy.

The words spoke of three signs and only three that bore the hallmarks of the beginning of change and a change of order.

The gates of those who thrived in darkness would open and those that would come forth would seek to eradicate the world of all that would not do their bidding. In so doing, they would consume the light and plunge the world into a place of chaotic ruin and evil, creating a new level of dark rule.

The first sign would signify illness and the great pain of one of their own and would show itself 24-48 hours before a Grand Council meeting. A Council that had been bound by secrecy for thousands of years to ensure the prophecy never came to pass.

She recalled that over the last 700 years or so; only on two occasions had all three prophesied events materialised. Events witnessed, not just by the Order, but by those on the outside, those who were without knowledge. On both occasions, they had even recounted events in their historical literature, albeit not knowing the significance of what it really meant. She struggled to raise a smile in recollection, knowing that those who led their lives outside of this great Order had been protected from darkness for almost as long as time had recorded.

Her face was a picture of anguish as she recalled one occasion when they of the dark places were very nearly successful in achieving their goal. The cats of the Order were key in maintaining the Order's survival and the equilibrium that exists throughout human existence right up to the present day. Those outside of the Council and the Order were oblivious to how close they nearly came to perishing. They owe us an enormous debt of gratitude and the cats had prevailed.

She was not sure if what was happening to Nahla was potentially the first sign. The Keeper claiming that it may just be timing did little to ease her considering the words were spoken with concern. Nerves were always tested when gatherings were taking place. It was an uneasy time for the United Kingdom's national Headquarters as well as other Headquarters the world over.

The second sign would cause much concern, although the second requires the third if the prophecy were to be complete.

The second sign would show itself at midnight. The timing is not a coincidence. On this day, gatherings would be joining in unison in a worldwide celebration of tradition and their upholding of order and balance. The prophecy foretells a second sign or event showing within the same time zone as the first. Therefore, it would have to be midnight if Nahla was carrying the prophesied pain. She gripped her desk with both hands watching the clock hands with every passing second. She didn't even blink as she saw the minute hand reaching the 12 o'clock position. She started to wince as she listened.

Tick...

She momentarily froze as the clock hit the midnight hour, then turned her head straining with her ears to listen below. Clocks all over the house could be heard chiming. She slowly let her hands fall away from the desk and settled her breathing. She stood up and walked over to her window to look outside. The night sky was perfectly clear and the flickering stars could easily be seen wherever she looked. Standing on her couch, she craned her neck left and right. There was nothing out of the ordinary to be seen.

She walked quickly back to the clock and studied it. The hands were moving as it approached a couple of minutes past 12 o'clock.

Relaxing her body and taking a deep breath, she put a hand against the wall and bowed her head in relief. She went back to her desk and practically collapsed in her seat, falling forward to lean on both elbows, clawing at her hair with both hands. Letting out a huge sigh of relief and glancing once more at the moving clock, she remembered the bottle of Scotch that she had tucked in her desk. It was reserved for special occasions, this was almost certainly one of those.

A toast was probably not in order, but a good measure was. Taking out a tumbler from her desk along with the half-empty bottle, she poured herself a large measure.

Looking at the glass fondly, she sat back and shook her head; she was mightily relieved and tired from worry. Thankfully, Nahla was not the first sign, after all.

She sat back in her chair, looked up at the old ceiling and fell asleep almost instantly.

A few hours had passed as Duat sat alone with his thoughts. Earlier events were still on his mind as he contemplated the fear he had witnessed on the faces of the Escarrabin. The 'mighty security of the Escarrabin' he mused, shaking his head at their uselessness.

Their reaction to withdraw and their reliance on their Scatterblades amused him greatly. Their actions were not unexpected; they had not been tested in a very long time.

They were of little threat to him and his strength was ever-evolving. It was time the Watchers took a stand. Their incarceration here in this place was out of fear, he knew and those above knew that others roamed on the outside waiting for the one to unite them. Their roaming was often without purpose, their ambitions quelled by the Order. They needed unison.

Movements in what they call 'the below' were silent now. In the dark hours of early morning, the sounds would be active again, the tunnelling, the anger of being held against their will and their lack of freedom to roam. The one that lay further down was becoming more unstable. It was angry and needed passage.

He could hear the slight sound of scurrying on the dirty stone floor outside the entrance to his chamber and beckoned the rat over to him.

Picking it up, Duat looked closely into its dark eyes. "So strong, you are survivors of old, ruthless as well as cunning, we are indebted to you." He pulled his hood down and lifted the rat to his face. Watching its nose twitch, he could see its front teeth were dirty and worn; its tail had wrapped around his left hand.

"I have something for you, my friend." He clenched his right hand, then reopened it and stared at his turquoise palm, which was alive with movement. He brought the rat towards his palm and held the rat directly beneath it. A drop of blood rolled down his hand, which he placed millimetres from the rat's head and watched it drop into the rat's eye.

"You may have your time again, my friend, as we will have ours. I know you will never be far from us." He put the rat down gently on the floor. "Now go." The rat ran from his chamber as Duat looked up towards the stone ceiling.

"It must be near." He walked towards the wall of his cell and placed his right-hand flat against the stone. Closing his eye, he could hear light pacing movements from above coming down the walls into his palm. He concentrated further.

"Any time now... any time now." He waited patiently, knowing that the time was imminent. His mouth opened in anticipation as the saliva fell between his misshapen, broken teeth.

Dozens of chimes travelled down the wall as the clocks above talked to one another from all over the house. His eye was now open wide as he took a couple of steps back from the wall, knowing that overhead the clocks were chiming the hour of midnight.

He walked over to his ancient set of weighing scales that a long time ago may have passed judgement rather than weigh precious stones. He picked up the large hourglass to the side of the scales and smiled as he looked at the bottom vial full of sand. He placed it on the table and crouched down to meet its level, inhaling deeply as he turned it over.

The first grain of sand had fallen.

Nubia jumped with a start, abruptly awoken by the sound of ringing. Her neck was incredibly stiff. She opened and closed her mouth a couple of times and grimaced. She looked at the undrunk glass of whisky on her desk, realising that she must have fallen asleep. She looked at the clock face and noticing it was 1.09 am, wondered who on earth could be ringing at this hour.

"Yes." She answered in a tired and croaky voice.

"Nubia, is that you?"

"She recognised the broad Scottish accent instantly. She coughed a couple of times to clear her throat. "Lady Ebonee?"

"Yes, tell me, are your clocks ticking? Have there been any signs?"

Still half asleep, Nubia looked at the clock again. "Yes," she coughed, "yes, the clocks are fine."

"I bet our beloved Nahla is still unwell, though. Is she?"

"Well, yes, the last I heard, but that was..."

"It is as I thought! Many have struggled to interpret the great foretelling..."

"Lady Ebonee, I really do not think we should have this call right now. The Keeper knows that I have been talking to you," she interrupted.

"Yes, I know, these things get back to me and it's high time they started to listen to me. I get mocked, you know."

Nubia let out a deep sigh. "Lady Ebonee, I may be subject to an investigation and this phone call may not be private if you know what I mean?"

"How so? Don't worry about that. Anyway, it is as I foretold, your clocks are fine."

"If you knew the clocks would be okay and there is no second sign, why did you ask for me to keep a watch over Mildred?"

"Well, your clocks are not fine deary far from it; they haven't reached their destination yet."

Nubia had a vacant expression on her face with the phone pressed to her ear, looking at her clock. "Respectfully, Lady Ebonee, whatever do you mean?"

"Well, it's not the last minute of the last hour yet, is it?"

Nubia shook her head, "I'm sorry, what was that?"

"The last hour. That is the foretelling, not the first hour."

"Lady Ebonee, I…"

"Please ensure that the new Reeve of yours is prepared. This will be a big test for her. I must go. Bye, deary."

Nubia heard the phone click at the other end. The phone fell out of her hand onto the desk. With a pained expression across her face and her tummy jangling with nervous pains, she was locked deep in worry again.

Nubia looked across her desk; the tumbler of Scotch was just where she needed it.

Chapter Nineteen:

THE DRAWING OF THE SCATTERBLADE

FRIDAY 7AM

Despite the warm air of the August morning filtering its way through the open window, Mildred was lying in bed with the sheets pulled all the way to her neck.

She hadn't slept well with so much on her mind; trying to sleep was almost pointless. She was worried about Missy and very concerned that her symptoms had not improved. Deciding to give up on trying for any more sleep, she looked at the end of her bed. Missy was still there unmoved from where she laid her down last night. Pulling her knees up to her chest, she contemplated how much she always loved it when Missy slept at the end of the bed, as rare as it was. But this morning was not one of those occasions and Mildred felt great discomfort watching her cat in so much pain.

She was torn as to what to do for the best, feeling waves of guilt for even considering going to the gathering. She could not leave Missy like this all alone. If she started feeling better, then, of course, that would be fine, but looking at her now, that didn't look to be any time soon.

She was still perplexed and somewhat perturbed by the very odd comment, 'I just shine a bit' from the vet who tried to have a conversation with her cat and may well have done just exactly that.

"Missy... Missy!" She gently rocked her, but her cat just lay there, her tummy rising up and down. She flapped her arms at a loss. "Well, I guess that I do not shine at all then, eh, Missy!"

Mildred got up to go to the bathroom. Staring at herself in the mirror, she could see bags under her eyes caused by tiredness and the dark discolouration of her skin that surrounded them. She washed water over her face and noticed the fresh lines that had appeared and stared at how unkempt her hair was these days. Her face was pale and looked a picture of sadness as she tried to break a smile. The smile was short lived as fresh wrinkles appeared around her mouth. A sad face made her look younger, she contemplated as the water drops fell from her face into the sink below.

I haven't worn makeup in a very long time, she thought, assessing her age and the battle damage with the few grey hairs sprouting around her hairline.

She opened the door to the tallboy and looked inside. It was sparse. All that remained was an unused flannel, the medication that she had not taken in some time, an old pink lipstick and a near-empty and very out of date pot of foundation.

She ran a hand through the knots in her hair and let out a sigh. Middle-aged, old furniture, no makeup and a sick cat, that's my life. How on earth did it get to this?

She walked back into her bedroom with her hands on her hips and stared at Missy. She had a duty to her only friend in the world.

That talking cat woman had better have some answers.

Outside of her chambers, Raysmau could hear her gate being moved across the stone floor as she got to her feet and left her office.

"Good morning Ma'am."

She nodded at her security guard as the main door opened to let her out.

There was a lot more activity in the grand lobby area this morning. Gathering days were always a test for her security team. She would need to spend some time with the Reeve later talking through any last-minute security updates.

Lady Safiya's arrival back at the Manor House did not call for pomp and ceremony as she was here more often than not. Still, Raysmau always made a point of greeting her. Dressed in her usual uniform that bore the mark of the head of the Escarrabin, she stopped and bent down on one knee to brush over a very slight marking on one of her boots.

She nodded at the Clerics on the main reception desk to open the front doors.

The huge doors started to open and she could see Lady Safiya was nearly at the main entrance doors already. Behind her, the chauffeur-driven car was already moving away.

"Good morning, my Lady," Raysmau nodded. She noticed that she had no bags with her.

"Hello, Raysmau." She responded quite curtly, clearly not in the mood for talking.

"Are you okay, my Lady? You look troubled."

"One of my level and age is always troubled Raysmau," she stopped walking and looked up at the Head of Security, "in fact, I do not recall a day when I was not troubled with something." She resumed walking and Raysmau stepped in line with her.

"Tradition, everything is always about tradition. These gatherings are sometimes more trouble than they are worth. We should bring Elders that are to be elevated here, give them their cats and be done with it. Watchers are out there Raysmau, these gatherings create attention." She stopped walking again. "Far too many chatterboxes Raysmau, you understand what I mean?"

Raysmau was unsure whether to smile or not, so she just offered a blank expression.

"I'm not altogether sure what you are referring to, Ma'am."

"No, of course, you're not," she responded, not surprised by Raysmau's usual diplomatic response.

"Rumours, rumours, rumours of prophesied events that have not come to pass, that is what I'm referring to. Too much chatter!"

It did, of course, occur to Raysmau that Lady Safiya, a Degree Level 1 Elder and Head of Loxley Manor, was now doing a bit of gossiping herself.

"I see," Raysmau added with a hint of a smile for reassurance. "Well, I can assure you that I do not hear these things, Ma'am."

Lady Safiya looked up at her. "Mmm, well, I guess that's something then. Could you ask a Cleric to send up some tea for me, please? Apparently, my bags are being dropped around the back."

"I will see to it personally." Raysmau watched one of the most Senior Elders in the country head off to the stairs that would take her to her offices and living quarters.

Raysmau was just about to walk off when Lady Safiya turned to her.

"I trust my cats are okay?"

"I'm sure they are quite fine, my Lady. I've heard nothing to the contrary."

She grunted, turned around and kept walking.

It was always a pleasure greeting Lady Safiya, Raysmau thought with a twinge of amusement as she nodded towards a Cleric for attention.

The Curator heard a knock at her outer door. She stepped out of her private quarters into her office. Her door had already been opened and there stood the Reeve in her familiar pose. She leant against the door frame, one leg crossed over the other.

"I suppose you are here to gloat?"

"Why would I do that, Nubia? We should be happy there has been no second sign."

She took a few paces forward, inviting herself in.

Nubia looked her up and down. She was wearing one of those ghastly business type suits again and except for the badge on her lapel, there was no other indication of her rank and title. Nubia grunted with disapproval.

"So, I trust that your clock is fine? The ones downstairs seem to be in order."

Nubia sat at her desk, deciding not to look up at her. "My clock is fine, Reeve."

"Good, good."

Nubia could feel the Reeve looking around her office and probably looking at her as well.

"I'm assigning two of my Escarrabin to the local gathering earlier than scheduled, just as a precaution."

"I see, but I have no idea why are you telling me this, Reeve. You've made it clear that security is your domain."

"I'm just informing you that I'm keeping a good eye on things, today of all days."

Nubia looked up, sensing the Reeve knew something.

"Good, I'm very glad to hear it," was all that she could think of saying whilst looking at her, wondering if she knew that Lady Ebonee had been in touch again.

"Anyway, I was just passing by. I'll carry on my rounds." She turned to leave, glancing back over her shoulder. "I'm glad that your clock is fine," she added before disappearing out of view.

Nubia was staring at the now vacant but still very much open door. She got to her feet and gently pressed it closed. In the short time that she had been here, never had the Reeve just been 'passing by' as her quarters were at the end of the corridor, in any event. She was up to something; she was sure of it.

Alian had arisen from her bunk over two hours ago and it was still a few hours before her shift was due to start. There were three other bunks in her room, one of which was currently being used. She quietly slipped into civilian clothing so as not to disturb the sleeping member of the Escarrabin and made her way out of her room.

Standing in one of the corridors of the Escarrabin security block, she ran one hand through her hair and rubbed at her eyes with the other. Her night had been one of interrupted sleep.

Based towards the rear of the Manor House, the security block could contain anything up to sixty members of the Escarrabin. However, it was very rare that it would be full. They would regularly travel, protecting various headquarters and members of the Order the world over.

There were currently twenty-six Escarrabin based at Loxley Manor, although Raysmau had informed them that more were arriving later in the day; usual protocol on gathering days. She walked barefoot down the corridor, stretching her arms above her head and yawned, turning into a corridor on the right.

The door where Gamila stayed was already open and she was not surprised to see Gamila sitting on the end of her bunk. She nodded towards her to come outside as she could see that two others were sleeping in the room.

"You couldn't sleep either?" Gamila said, looking at the reasonably tired appearance of Alian, who shook her head in response. "I think we need to report what we saw."

Alian nodded in agreement. "And include that you drew your Scatterblade Gamila. You did threaten a Watcher with it."

"I know. I've been trying to weigh it all up. Duat will probably blab it out with pride to Raysmau anyway when given his punishment. It would just be a matter of whether she believed him or not."

"Other Watchers saw it though who could support his words, although their words are often full of lies."

Gamila nodded and they stood in momentary silence.

"Okay, get dressed. I'll meet you back here in 20 minutes and we'll go and see Raysmau," said Alian, receiving a nod from Gamila; she had pondered all night on the previous day's events. "Alian, what was that?"

Alian turned to her. "What?"

"That noise. The noise and the banging from the below. What do you think it could possibly be?"

Alian shook her head and bit at her lip. "I have no idea, but it can't be good. Something very dark from an older time. I've heard rumours before but never really paid them any attention."

She turned around to walk off. "See you back here in twenty."

Gamila leant against the doorframe; her pulse had risen. Explaining what had happened to Raysmau was one thing; being ordered back below to conduct a search and establish what lay underground was another.

The Watchers were bowed on both sides as Duat walked into the holding area on the first floor of the below. He walked past all of them, looking towards the stone stairs and the empty lift shaft.

Turning around to face them, he pulled his hood down and held his right hand out directly in front of them.

"Rise, my friends." One by one, they looked up at him and the moving turquoise complexity of his right palm. He was not like them.

"This has been planned for a very long time." He walked forward to them. "For far too long you have been bound by chains. Our numbers are growing. When those on the outside hear of me and my presence here, we will unite." He looked to his left, addressing the Watchers one by one. "The time of change has already started. The time and realm of the Watchers is now." He looked to the right. "Those of the above are unaware of the powers I possess, powers that have grown considerably since my voluntary incarceration here. I feed off this place and these walls and I know what lies below."

The Watchers looked at each other, taking in everything they were hearing. They had not been led in a very long time.

"What lies below has awakened from a very long sleep. It feels my presence here. My strength and my powers grow, and I offer it hope."

Duat lashed out at a Watcher with his left hand, grabbing his cloak and bringing him down to his knees.

Pulling down his hood, he placed his right palm on the top of his temple and pressed. "Do you see?" The Watcher was reeling in pain. "DO YOU SEE?" he yelled. The Watcher's torso went into spasm, his head shaking looking upwards, as his eye streamed in pain that he was powerless to break away from.

The other Watchers looked at each other with concern and took a step backwards, witnessing one of their own in great pain. His arms were flailing at his sides, but the strength of Duat held him down. He let go and removed his palm from the Watcher's head. The Watcher fell to the floor, shaking.

Duat brought his palm up to his eye as the patterns of turquoise began to fade.

"Rise, my friend."

The Watcher on all fours came onto his knees and looked up at Duat, his eye was bloodshot and he was breathing heavily.

"Well?"

"I see, Master." The Watcher lifted his hand, removing the saliva from the gaps of his mouth.

"Tell us."

"Master?"

"Tell us of what you saw."

"Fire! Fire on water and us walking among those outside."

"You see outcome, my friend."

"The Escarrabin, their master and the Order have little knowledge of our numbers. Our numbers multiply; they do not even know how many of us are here below."

Duat looked down at the kneeling and scared Watcher. "You have seen greatness, my friend. From now on, I will call you Bellator." The Watchers' heads all moved together upon hearing the familiar sound of the lift moving from above. Duat looked at Bellator. "Get up."

"Know this, for those who are about to come out from that gate, their time is precious and withering by the minute."

✝✝✝✝

Raysmau, for the second time this morning, could hear the gates moving outside of her office. Frowning, she looked up at her clock; she was not expecting any visitors or arrivals at this time. There was a knock at her door.

"Come."

Raysmau was looking at one of her security team. "What is it?"

"Ma'am, Escarrabin Alian and Gamila request to speak with you."

"Now? I have a lot to do today, as have you for that matter." She got up from her chair and walked around to the front of her desk. Perching on the end of it, she looked at her guard.

"Very well, send them in. It had better be important." She swished a hand out in front of her.

The security guard stepped back a few paces and leaned around the corner to speak with them. "She'll see you now. She doesn't look too happy about being disturbed, though."

"Doubt we will make her day much better," said Gamila stepping forward with Alian into Raysmau's office.

"Thank you," Raysmau said with a curt tone towards her guard. She was now looking directly at the two Escarrabin in her office in what was clearly an unplanned visit. The door was closed behind them.

"So?"

"Ma'am, an event happened yesterday that we thought you should be made aware of." Gamila spoke with concern etched across her face.

This was met with a deep frown from Raysmau. "An event?"

Both Gamila and Alian looked at each other.

Not always known for her patience, she stared at both of them. "Well?"

Alian swallowed. "Well, Ma'am, yesterday afternoon."

"Late afternoon," Gamila interjected.

"Yes, about late afternoon, you may recall that we found a Watcher in the gardens at the front of the house, not where he was scheduled to be."

Raysmau had a blank expression on her face. "Of course, I recall. What of it? Punishment will be assigned in due course."

"There was a little more to it afterwards." Alian looked uncomfortable as she spoke.

Raysmau shook her head. "Well, proceed, Escarrabin. There is a lot to do today."

Gamila took it upon herself to continue. "We took him below as usual, but he was not alone."

Raysmau had a confused look upon her face. "Well, who was he with? What are you talking about, Gamila?"

"He was not alone in the below."

"There were more Watchers down there; we couldn't say how many as it was too dark and we didn't have our vision goggles with us. We think maybe more than we have accounted for." Alian spoke as a couple of beads of sweat developed on her temple.

Raysmau opened her mouth to speak.

"That's not it, Ma'am. They amassed together."

Gamila was nodding in support of her colleague's statement.

"Amassed together?" She shook her head. "Get to the point." Raysmau's lack of understanding was testing the tone of her words.

"We felt very threatened. It's the first time both of us has ever seen anything like it."

"The Watcher who calls himself Duat is having some form of effect on them, some form of influence, Ma'am," Gamila added.

Raysmau crossed her arms and blinked with a vacant expression.

"And that's not all, Ma'am."

Raysmau shook her head a couple more times, ushering them to continue.

"There is something else down there, something very deep. We both heard it," Alian said, trying to maintain composure.

Upon hearing this, Raysmau's relatively relaxed posture changed within an instant. She leant forward as she spoke. "You heard what exactly, Escarrabin? Speak up!"

They both looked at each other. Gamila decided to speak on their behalf.

"We could not possibly guess, Ma'am."

Raysmau put a hand up. "You are going to have to do a damn sight better than that. I'm not going to make decisions or go to the Reeve with 'you heard a noise.' What exactly do you think you heard?"

"Something large, something from the deep, a depth that neither of us has ever gone to and maybe no one has for quite a long time." Gamila looked down at the floor as she spoke. "It was moving."

Raysmau's face was full of disbelief. "Are you sure of this? Alian, do you support this ridiculousness that I'm hearing?"

"Yes, Ma'am, I do. We were forced to retreat."

"I am also duty-bound to tell you that I drew my Scatterblade." Gamila lifted her chin up and fixed her eyes on the wall behind her superior.

"And did you?" She was looking directly at Alian. "No, Ma'am, I did not."

"Did you threaten any of them Gamila?"

She took a step forward, "Yes, Ma'am, I did."

Raysmau stared directly at Gamila, speechless with what she was hearing. "The drawing of a weapon on the headquarters grounds is strictly prohibited unless there is an undeniable risk to life, something that has not occurred for a great many years, a great many..." She now looked at Alian. "Was there an undeniable risk to life?"

"I believe that events had the potential to escalate. The drawing of a weapon allowed us to escape safely, Ma'am."

"Escape? Escape, you say? The Escarrabin do not retreat, even more so on our own grounds!" Her anger brought her to her feet. They both looked upon the towering figure of Raysmau.

"Then you had better add that into your report," she snapped.

"Yes, Ma'am," they both spoke in unison.

"You are both not due on shift for a few more hours yet. I suggest you go back to your quarters and I want both of you to submit your reports to me immediately. The Reeve will have to be informed of this as a weapon was drawn. Do I make myself clear?"

"Yes, Ma'am."

"If what you are reporting is accurate, this is a worrying development. However, I want your reports and we will take an appropriate level of action. Did you see anything to explain what the noise was?"

Gamila spoke for them. "No, Ma'am, but the noise or noises sounded like it was somehow contained below."

All three of them stood in silence as Raysmau rubbed her temple.

"Well! What are you waiting for? Off you go, there is work to be done."

"Yes, Ma'am," they said at exactly the same time as if it had been rehearsed a hundred times before. They both took three steps back, nodded their heads and left the office, closing the door behind them.

Raysmau went back to her heavy chair and sat gently into it, resting her right elbow on one of the supports and twiddled her fingers round themselves in contemplation. Watchers considering attacking, an unexplained moving noise below and weapons being drawn in defence. There was much to consider about this unprecedented event. She would defend the Escarrabin's actions if, and only if, what they reported was an accurate reflection of events, but that would be difficult to determine.

She had heard stories of the below from her predecessor. For that reason, she didn't completely discount what they were saying. The stories had been passed down through generations of the elite Escarrabin at Senior Level. Every time there was a vow of silence that these stories, of probable fiction, did not escalate to the point that they filter down the ranks.

Raysmau had some decisions to make and action would need to be taken. How she was going to explain this to the Reeve, she did not know.

Chapter Twenty:

TALKING TO CATS

FRIDAY MID MORNING

"Good morning Mildred and how are you today?"

Mildred pulled the receiver away from her ear, staring at the phone again in frustration. Clearly, if she were calling, she would not be alright.

"Missy is still unwell; I'm very sad to say, Miss Fennaway."

"Well, I'm most surprised, dear. These bugs would usually have passed through by now. Has she eaten anything?"

"No, she hasn't eaten a thing!" Mildred was losing patience, which was most unbecoming of her. The dismissive attitude of the vet was not helping one bit. "She hasn't moved all night!"

"Well, how very peculiar. Let's see then, have you tried spoon-feeding her some fish? Cats love fish, you see."

"I know very well they like fish! If she hasn't moved all night, she doesn't require dinner right now. I'm very worried Kamilah and your words of reassurance are not helping."

"She may have overdone it and is just getting some rest dear, would you like for me to talk to her again?"

185

"No, trying to talk to Missy is not going to help."

"Well, dear, I really think that it would not hurt to try."

"I'm getting a second opinion. I'm getting a second opinion I tell you, and I'm going to ring the other vet! This...this...what is happening is not natural for any cat and your solution is to have a chat with her?"

"Now look, Mildred, that really isn't necessary. I can always come over..."

"No, thank you very much. I'm going to call someone else. Goodbye, Miss Fennaway!"

Mildred hung up the phone. She was breathing so hard that her chest was rising up and down and her teeth were clenched. Her legs dangled off the edge of the bed as she flexed her toes (including the sore ones from the previous night). Upset and exhilarated that it was the first time she had stood up to someone in a very long time, she almost didn't think she had it in her. She shook her head a little, stopped grinding her teeth and got up to find an old phone book. She knew that she had it somewhere downstairs in one of the paper mountains.

"Missy, I will be back in a moment." She leant over to her cat and stroked her down one side. She could feel that her heartbeat was still very irregular; she shook her head "we are going to fix this!"

Downstairs, she looked at her cat-shaped phone on the sideboard and the masses of phone numbers, receipts and information flyers that she kept 'just in case.' She picked up a pile of papers and pushed them to the side, revealing an old, discoloured phone book.

"Okay, let's see what we can find." She started flicking through the book, looking for veterinarians. What was the name of the one that Mr Franks had said, she thought to herself but could not remember. She came to the V section of the book. Veterinarians, found it! Surprisingly, there were a few in her area but, she saw an advert for Castle Hollow Veterinary Practice and instantly remembered it as the vet that Mr Franks had mentioned.

Grabbing at the cat phone she picked it up and dialled the number. Whilst the call was going through, she looked back up the stairs, worried about Missy. The phone was answered at the other end after four rings.

"Castle Hollow Veterinary Practice, how may I help you?"

"Oh, good morning. My name is Mildred and my Missy is very unwell and has been for over 24 hours. Can a vet come and see her, please?"

"I see. May I call you Mildred?"

"You may. Can you help at all? I'm very worried."

"I'm quite sure that we can. Let me take some details and I'll see if Dr Sarah Belloch can pop around to see you. It will not be for a couple of hours though. Is that okay?"

"Yes, that is fine, but as soon as you can, please. I need a second opinion."

"A second opinion. Has another vet been to see you, Mildred?"

Mildred brought the phone away from her head, frowned and closed her eyes. She recalled that Dr Fennaway said that vets do not like to take on one another's work.

"Yes, briefly, but she hasn't been very helpful, I'm afraid."

"Oh, I'm sorry to hear this. May I enquire as to which vet came to see you?"

"Yes, it was Kamilah from Fennaway's Veterinary Practise."

"Mmm, that's odd, I've never heard of her and I've been the receptionist here for over four years," said the stranger on the end of the phone.

Mildred's concern grew as she heard this.

"Well, nevermind, Mildred. I may be mistaken. Let me take your number and the details of what is wrong and I'll arrange for our vet to come and see you. Missy is a cat, I presume?"

Mildred gave the particulars to the friendly voice on the other end of the phone, happy that Dr Belloch would be calling somewhere after 11am. She walked back up the stairs and sat next to Missy, placing a hand on her head. "Please don't worry, my lovely friend. Someone is on the way for you."

She stroked Missy repeatedly on autopilot as she stared at the wall. How could one vet not have heard of another within the same area? It was true that Fennaway's was some miles away, but how could they not have even heard of her? There was something very odd going on here.

Nubia's phone was ringing again. She reached over to answer it.

"Nubia, I think we may have a problem. In fact, I'm certain of it."

"What's the matter, Kamilah? Has there been some development with Nahla?"

"Well, of a sort in there has been no change in her condition from yesterday."

Nubia silently gnawed at the stumps of her nails.

"Are you not surprised by this, Nubia?"

"No, not fully. I can't, I can't really talk about it over the phone."

"I see. Has there been a second sign, Nubia? The clock in my office is fine?"

"No, there has not, but it may be that the time of passage is not over yet."

"What! Are you sure? This is news to me. I thought the prophecy stated that a second sign would have shown by now. If that hasn't happened, Nahla's condition is most odd and defies any possible explanation."

"I can't really say." She looked around her office to check no-one was spying and whispered into the phone. "I'm just saying that we may not have reached the final hours when a sign may show, that's all." She pressed the phone to her face. "Is there another problem other than Nahla still being very ill?"

"I just spoke with Mildred on the phone and she practically hung up on me. Whatever I say does not reassure her. She thinks Nahla has some form of bug and a serious one at that." Unaware, Kamilah was now whispering into her end of the phone too.

"Why is this a problem?"

"She has threatened to call another vet in for a second opinion."

Nubia's eyes flared and she coughed, almost choking on her words. "You can't be serious. That can never happen, Kamilah. It would be a massive security risk. Who knows where all of this could end up?"

"I know, I know. She won't talk to me. I did offer to go over and see her but she wants no part of it, or me, I feel." With paranoia, Kamilah glanced behind her to ensure no one was listening. "I spoke with Nahla last night."

There was silence at the other end.

"Hello, hello?" Kamilah's voice reached out into the silence.

With a hand on her head. "You did what?" Nubia said in utter disbelief.

"I spoke very briefly to Nahla."

"What! Are you demented, for crying out loud?" Nubia's voice had increased dramatically. She spun around on her chair, making sure no one had suddenly appeared. She returned to a whisper, concern in her voice. "You can't be serious. What possessed you?"

"She mentioned last night about getting a second opinion. I had to do something."

"Well, you certainly did that!" Nubia rested on her elbows. "Okay, so tell me exactly what happened."

"Well, I was on the phone, so I couldn't see Mildred, but my best guess is that she thinks I'm a lunatic."

Nubia shook her head a few times as her face fell into her hands. "You know that Mildred is a 9th Degree Elder and does not understand these things. She doesn't even know the name of her cat, Kamilah. What were you thinking?" Nubia sat back in her chair, checking the nails on her left hand to see if there was anything left to bite. "What an absolute mess this is, Kamilah. If Nahla is seen by another vet and those heartbeats are detected, they will take her away; you can bet your 9 lives on it. If Nahla's condition is what we suspect, the vet may call in others to make further assessments." A pained expression suddenly appeared across Nubia's face. "Kamilah, a discovery like this could even get into the press."

Nubia was horrified; delicate matters such as these reaching the press could lead to questions being raised. "She'll be seen as some sort of extraordinary cat, even if she does get better. They would question Mildred, and she may mention that she is a member of the Chamber. She's not aware of our Order as yet, but nevertheless, awkward questions could be asked."

Nubia knew that anything associated with the Order, no matter how tenuous, could lead to questions being raised in the press and needed to be handled by the security arm of the Order. They are exceptionally careful with these things.

"This needs to be contained, Kamilah. No chances can be taken that could expose our kind." Nubia spoke with forcefulness in her tone.

"Shall I inform the Reeve as security is her area?"

Nubia's face scowled as she thought for a couple of seconds. "No, it's okay. I have someone close to Mildred on my side. We will look into this. In any event, we need to ensure that another vet does not take Nahla away. If that happens, there could be severe consequences and it could spark a chain of events."

Nubia shifted in her seat, deciding very quickly to take the initiative. "I'll take care of this. Please keep me posted if you hear anything else, and Kamilah, this is very important; whatever you do, do not tell anyone about this."

"I understand Nubia, you have my assurance as ever, but my Signapher was quite clear, you know. It is as prophesied, the heartbeats were unmistakable; Nahla doesn't bear the mark though..."

"No, the one who comes bears the mark. The one who bears the pain will have a part to play in the future - how much and what part they take is unclear. What is clear, however, is that the prophesied cat will carry the mark as well as the beats of two hearts. Whether those hearts are to be a force for good or evil, only time will tell."

"But only if there is a second and third sign, Nubia?"

"Indeed, but for now until the second sign, if there is to be one, Nahla is carrying that pain; the prophesied pain of two imbalanced hearts fighting against each other."

"The poor dear must be in terrible pain."

"No doubt."

"Leave this with me; I know just who to call."

"I'll leave it with you and if I hear anything else, I will let you know. Goodbye."

Nubia placed her phone back upon its cradle.

The pain of two hearts where only one exists, Nahla must be in extraordinary pain. The Curator sat back in her chair, crossed her legs and put her hands into a ball on her knee. Nahla's suffering could be a prediction, Nubia thought, watching the swinging pendulum of her clock and listening to the gentle ticking noise. If the prophecy is to be believed, the only way Nahla's pain will stop is when that clock does. If Nahla's pain is eased, then the pain of others is just about to start. The Curator leaned over and picked up the phone.

She wasn't entirely sure that the phone call was private, but it was a risk she was willing to take.

Nubia could hear the phone ringing at the other end, "come on, come on."

"Yes hello."

Nubia breathed a sigh of relief. "Jessica, its Lady Nubia from Headquarters."

"Oh, hello, Lady Nubia. How are you today? It's nice to hear from you." Jessica's voice was one of surprise by the unexpected call, even more so on the day of a gathering. You would think she probably had other things to be attending to.

"Jessica, I'm not so good, to be honest and I need to talk to you about a most private development that could have serious repercussions. I'm going to entrust you with this most special assignment."

"Erm okay. I understand." She didn't understand and a wave of uncertainty moved through her. She thought it best that she sit down.

Nubia looked around her office again, concerned about privacy or possibly a lack thereof. "Do you have anything further to report on Mildred?" She whispered.

"No, nothing further, my Lady. I spoke to Mildred on the phone recently. I'm picking her up to take her to the gathering later today."

"How recently did you speak with her Jessica, it's quite important?"

Jessica leaned forward on her chair; something was clearly up. "A couple of days ago. Why do you ask? Is everything okay, Madam Nubia?" She was developing the nervous shakes in her hands again.

Nubia leaned into her phone and crouched down, ducking beneath her desk. "Did she mention her cat to you at all?" she whispered.

"Missy? No, she didn't mention her."

"I think you mean Nahla. She has become very ill and we are greatly concerned."

"You are concerned about Nahla being ill? It is always heartbreaking to hear of any cat being unwell, especially one of our own, but is this a problem of significance or something?"

"It may be... it may be." Nubia popped up from behind her desk to check the coast was clear. She ducked down again and continued to whisper. "I'll get straight to the point. We have reason to believe that she may be calling another vet instead of Fennaway."

"I'm sorry Lady Nubia, I'm struggling to hear you. Could you speak up a little, please?"

Nubia closed her eyes and bit her lip, trying to gather patience. "Mildred may be calling a different vet instead of Fennaway."

"Well, why would she do that, Daphne her Elder should have told her to only call Fennaway?"

"It's complicated. It is vital that if another vet goes to her home she does not take Nahla away. Do you understand Jessica? Vitally important."

"Yes, I understand." She still didn't have a clue what Lady Nubia was talking about.

"Jessica, I need you to get over to Mildred's house and keep her under surveillance."

"Surveillance!" Jessica was horrified, not knowing the first thing to do.

"Yes, that is right, surveillance."

Jessica gulped and sat upright. What could I possibly know about surveillance, she thought. As if this week had not been strange enough for her already.

"Go over straight away and report back anything you see, but only speak to me. Do you understand, Jessica? Only speak with me."

"Erm, okay. I'll do that," Jessica spoke in a very soft tone and stood up with purpose, a clueless gesture.

"Oh and one more thing. Your cat Khepri; take her with you as she looks like Nahla to the untrained eye, just in case you have to swap them!"

Jessica's eyes opened wide in shock, "Excuse me? Swap them?"

"No ifs or buts, Jessica. This is a matter of priority for the Order. You are entrusted with this task."

"Yes, Madam Nubia, I will do my best."

"Yes. Do your best, oh and one very last thing. Make sure you take your mobile phone with you. Fennaway, may need to speak to Khepri."

Jessica's eyes opened even wider, "Excuse me?"

"Your cat Khepri, Fennaway may need to talk to her to explain everything." The silence was not lost on Nubia. "Well, your cat is not a mind reader, is she now. See sense, Jessica. I'll send you my direct number now."

The phone was hung up at the other end.

Jessica stared at her phone and wondered what on earth was going on. Dumbfounded, she ran a hand through her hair and sat back down. The small, rude lady had elevated her pulse again.

Surveillance on Mildred, Nahla sick, Fennaway talking to Khepri? She sat cross-legged stared at the floor beneath her feet and took a deep breath. Looking to her right, she saw her three cat bowls and bolted upright. Her eyes scoured the kitchen and an anxious look appeared on her face.

Where the hell was Khepri?

Chapter Twenty One:

DR BELLOCH FROM CASTLE HOLLOW

FRIDAY MORNING APPROACHING 11am

Jessica tore out into her front garden with an oversized spoon in her hand. Reaching into the recycling bin, the clanging of empty cat food tins falling onto her pathway could be heard the length of the street. She held the chosen one a hoist.

"MUGSY," she screamed, "MUGSY," There was no sign of her.

She panicked, looking up and down her road. "MUGSYYYYYYY," she yelled as loudly as she could, bashing the tin can with the spoon. She took in a deep breath and at the top of her voice, bellowed, "MUGSYYYYYYYYYYYYYYYYY." She hadn't realised she was kicking her legs out to the sides to encourage her diaphragm to give her more volume. She looked up and froze. Some of the neighbours were staring at her. A few doors down, a man switched off his lawnmower and stared over with a puzzled look on his face.

She coughed under her breath a couple of times, unsure what to do with her neighbours staring as though she had just escaped from some sort of institution.

"Why do you think she needs her cat so urgently?" one neighbour asked another.

"No idea. She's not right that one!" The other neighbour replied, shaking her head.

"Aww, come on, Mugsy. Where are you?" Her voice was now at a much-reduced tone as she stomped her oversized heels a couple of times.

She tried to ignore her neighbours as she stood, hands on hips, looking up and down the road. "Come on, Mugsy. Where could you be?"

It was no good and time was of the essence. She placed the tin and spoon on the garden wall and gently called out, "Khepri." She glanced across the road, knowing she was now the centre of gossip. "Khepri." Another quiet attempt.

Suddenly, her cat appeared through the neighbour's garden, hopping over the wall and stopping at her feet. She looked down at her cat shaking her head. "You know, for the sake of appearances, it would be really helpful if you responded to Mugsy sometimes! Come on." She walked to her car and opened the passenger door, "we are going for a drive." Khepri glided casually over to the car and hopped up onto the passenger seat. Jessica fixed the seat belt, closed the door and walked around the front of the car, muttering to herself. "Apparently Fennaway wants to have a conversation with you as well." She put the navigator into its cradle and the car moved off.

Out of her windows, she could tell the neighbours were clearly talking about her. In the rearview mirror, she studied her own reflection, thinking about the craziness of everything that was going on.

"What the hell do I know about surveillance?"

The car disappeared from view and the man who had been cutting his lawn looked at the other neighbours across the road and shrugged his shoulders before starting his lawnmower again.

Mildred was peering out of her front room window in the hope that the vet was on her way. She had brought Missy downstairs in anticipation of the vet's arrival, laying her on the couch with her head propped up gently on the cat cushion.

She walked into the kitchen, looked up at her clock and saw the minute hand approaching 11 o'clock. She pulled a half-empty litre bottle of milk out of the fridge and placed it on the side next to the kettle. Noticing that she had left the fridge door open, she walked back over to it and peered inside at her plates of fish paste sandwiches. They were curling at the ends more so than yesterday.

Sighing, she closed the door and returned to put her kettle on the gas.

Opening her tea canister and taking out a single bag of English breakfast tea, she dropped it into her cat mug and stood waiting for the kettle to boil. It wasn't breakfast time, but hey ho.

She was still wrestling over whether to go to the gathering or not. It had been on her mind throughout her troubled night's sleep and still remained with her since getting up this morning.

It's not right, it's not right at all, she thought as she prepared her tea. I can't go out when my Missy is feeling like this. I must cancel, I'm sure the other members will understand. She sat back and looked over at the bundle of Happy Birthday cat cards on the counter. A sad expression appeared on her face. I meant well and wanted to feel like someone again, she thought.

She got up and went over to her pedal bin and stood hard on the pedal so the top remained open. Sitting back down, she took the teabag out of the cup and balanced it on the end of her teaspoon and aimed at the bin. As if the spoon were a catapult she flicked it at the bin and watched the tea bag hurtle past the bin hitting the wall behind with a splat.

She watched in dismay as the stained brown water ran out of the bag, down the wall to the skirting board, before the teabag gave up clinging to the wall and fell to the ground. Closing her eyes and letting out a large sigh, she looked down at her mug with the picture of a smiling cat. She spun the mug around, so the cat disappeared from view. There would appear to be little to smile about today.

✝✝✝✝

Sarah Belloch ended the route on her satellite navigation system, having reached her destination; number 1 Rocke Road. Turning the engine off, she picked up the notes from the passenger seat, which the receptionist had previously handed to her.

She had taken a quick glance at them earlier but decided to read through them again. From the new client form, she could see that the cat's name was Missy and the owner was called Mildred and she was not registered with the practice. Symptoms included: breathing difficulties, unresponsive to stimulation, not eating and looks to be in pain.

She could see that the cat was a British Shorthair and was approaching three years old. No medication had been prescribed so far, but a scribbled note explained that another vet had already visited. She re-read the note to be sure. It was rare for an owner to see a second vet, irrespective of the type of animal or breed.

She looked at the surrounding area where she had parked. The bush outside seemed to have been cut quite recently, but the rest of the garden looked very unkempt and overgrown.

Holding on to her notes, she grabbed her bag from the passenger seat and stepped out of the car. It was a reasonably quiet road, there were a couple of kids at the bus stop further down, but all in all, it was pretty unremarkable.

She opened the small gate and walked up the short, overgrown pathway to the house. She couldn't help but notice that the house next door had a beautiful, well-maintained front garden.

She knocked on the faded blue door and took two steps back. As she waited, she looked over at the paint flaking on the windowsills and the cobwebs hanging in just about every crevice the house had to offer.

Movements could be heard from behind the door as she prepared her face for smiling. The door opened and a woman dressed way beyond her years stood in the doorway.

"Hello, are you Mildred?"

"Yes, I am."

"I'm Dr Belloch from Castle Hollow Vets," she took her identification card from her pocket and held it up for Mildred to see.

"Oh, thank you so much for coming. My Missy is in a terrible state. Please do come in." Mildred stepped back, holding the door open.

Dr Belloch stepped forward and was immediately hit by the oddest smell that made her nose twitch and her eyes squint. What on earth is that she thought, putting her hand to her mouth.

"Please do come in. Missy is right through here."

It was not the first time she had been in a house that carried a unique smell, but this was a combination of mustiness mixed with fish. It was very overpowering. She moved into what looked like the front room and saw an old TV set, sparse old furniture and the most incredible mound of receipts and other scraps of paper. Over on the couch was her cat, Missy, wrapped up with her head on a pillow.

"Well, hello, Missy," Sarah said with a smile.

"Oh, she can't hear you. I'm sorry."

Sarah turned around to see that Mildred was very serious with her statement.

"Yes, I see. I'm sorry. I always like to say hello when I meet a new animal, a new client if you will." She nodded and offered a smile that fell reasonably flat. Now a little red-faced, she crouched down beside Missy and placed a hand on her. "Well, let's see what is wrong with you then."

"Would you care for a cup of tea? The kettle is hot," asked Mildred.

Sarah turned her head around to look at Mildred and smiled. "No, I'm fine, thank you. I have just come from another call and had one there, but thank you all the same."

"Are you sure? It's no trouble. I know that you are here to help."

Sarah smiled back at her. "Well, I'm certainly going to try."

"Would you care for some fish paste sandwiches? I have plenty."

Sarah turned back around to look at Missy and closed her eyes.

"So that's what the smell is?" She muttered to herself.

Raysmau studied Gamila's and Alian's security reports of events in the below the day before.

Although they should have been written independently, they were both near word perfect. She frowned as she compared the two accounts. It was not the first time security guards had colluded with each other to reach the same conclusion.

A Scatterblade being drawn within the grounds of headquarters had not happened for a very long time. To that end, it needed to be reported higher up the Order. Raysmau would always do her best to defend her team if she believed their actions were correct. Still, the fact that they both felt threatened would need to be investigated further. There would be no avoidance of that.

Although he had not been there long, Duat was unlike any other Watcher she had ever met and she'd met her fair share over the years. There was something different about him. Yes, he was arrogant and ill-disciplined, but she had seen these traits in other Watchers in the past; Duat was different. They did not like being kept here; that was a fact. Sooner or later, one would be disruptive.

She placed the reports back on her desk and sat back in her chair. In truth, she didn't know how many of them were below and doubted anyone did. The Reeve hadn't been in post long and it would depend on whether her predecessor had provided any clarity on the matter. Throughout history, the Reeves have remained very private. Raysmau was aware that the Order of the Reeves knew a lot more about this old building and its secrets than she ever would. If this new Reeve were like others from the past, they would only ever consult among their own kind.

Raysmau had met other Reeves at her former placement and when they had travelled from other countries to visit the UK headquarters. When they visited Loxley, all meetings were under lock and key. To her knowledge, details of what was discussed were never recorded.

The possible noise from the below concerned her greatly.

A part of her wanted her two members of the Escarrabin to be wrong, but she doubted it. Mistakes can be made but not for something like this and given the 'cloudy' history of the below. She knew they were both good soldiers and their reports would be somewhere near accurate.

During a very private moment, her predecessor, Mandisa, recounted that secrets of old had been left in the depths of the below. A resting ground of the past and from very dark times.

It is in those depths where they should remain. Mandisa had informed her that, to her knowledge, much from the past had never been recorded. 'Sometimes, dark events want to be forgotten; they need not be dwelled upon.'

Her predecessor's duty was to inform her that only the Reeves knew more exacting details of past events. This information was only passed to the next in line. When a Reeve passed, their secrets and knowledge were taken to the grave.

She recalled on one occasion, Mandisa taking her hand. "I have never been to the very bottom of the below; it makes me shudder to think of it." Mandisa's hand had shaken slightly as she looked at Raysmau. "Only ever go if you really need to, Raysmau. Those grounds have not been walked upon for a very long time and do not need to be disturbed if they lie in silence. Matters that have never been recorded do not need to be reopened, do you understand?"

There was no avoiding this. Raysmau would need to see the Reeve straight away and could only hope that she did not send them all to the below.

She knew roughly the way to Mildred's house. Although she had never been, Jessica was quite familiar with the area as Mildred only lived a few miles from her. All the same, the navigator sat in its cradle with a road map on it. She felt relieved to be in control of her own car again as no instruction had been put into it.

She looked down at Khepri asleep on the passenger seat of her car. "Guess you have no idea what's going on, do you?"

Khepri purred slightly.

"Surprised to hear that you are so at peace, I thought you didn't like the car Khepri."

With that, Khepri opened one eye.

"Oh good, you are still with us then, don't suppose you can advise me on surveillance skills? You can just about get into anywhere when it suits you."

Khepri's eye had already reclosed.

Jessica shook her head. "Thanks for all your help!"

It wasn't long before she saw the sign for Benbow Street.

Turning in, she passed the Futility Pub and could see a shop up ahead, she indicated to pull over. "We'll continue this chat later, shall we?" She stopped in front of Franks Convenience Store, looked down at Khepri, fast asleep on the passenger seat and opened the window slightly for some air. "Don't go anywhere now, will you?" she muttered before locking the car and turning to look at the peculiar looking shop.

The bell tinkled as she entered. She could see a man directly in front of her reading a newspaper behind the counter. He looked up as she offered him a slight smile. My word, Jessica thought to herself, looking at the most bizarre layout of any shop she had ever seen. Her nose twitched; it smelt of musty old floorboards. She looked down at the old lino and torn pieces of old carpet, but she couldn't be too sure where the smell was coming from.

She needed to equip herself for this afternoon's surveillance. It had just gone 11.15 am, so it wasn't afternoon just yet, but she had better get a hurry on.

What on earth do people need for surveillance? She chewed at her teeth, thinking about the last detective programme she had seen on TV. Cover the eyes, she thought to herself, yes, that's right, I need some glasses to disguise myself. She stopped walking and closed her eyes in annoyance; realising that she had left her sunglasses at home, she stomped one of her heels on the floor. Mr Franks was now watching, disturbed by the noise.

"May I help you with something?" he rasped.

"Yes, maybe. Do you sell glasses?" Jessica watched as she saw the man let go of his newspaper and walk over to her.

"You'll need an optician for that and I'm no optician," he said with a combination of a laugh and a rasp as his body rocked backwards and forwards with his own amusement. Jessica did her best to offer a slight smile in response to his 'humour'.

"I'm all out of sunglasses after the weather we've had, but I do have these."

She watched him walk to the other side of the aisle, where he lifted up a clear plastic bag for her to see. "These any use to you?"

Jessica's smile fell from her face as she saw the large framed black glasses with a red nose attached to them.

"What do you need them for, may I ask?"

"Er...a children's party?" she offered, more as a question than a statement.

"Oh, in which case these will be perfect," and he thrust the very noisy plastic bag straight towards her.

Jessica took the bag, her face a mixture of expressions as she held it up, staring at the big red nose fixed to the glasses.

"You'll look a right clown in those!" he rasped as she lowered the bag down to waist height.

He walked back towards his counter and briefly turned back to her.

"Never cared for clowns much," he said, shuffling back behind his counter.

"Do let me know if you need anything else?" Jessica gave him a curt smile.

She walked up the same aisle and noticed a box on the bottom shelf; 'Children's Binoculars With Up To x3 Range!' She grabbed the box, tucking it under her arm.

What else? What else? A Newspaper! She would definitely need a newspaper to hide behind. She walked past the counter and dumped the binoculars and glasses on top of Mr Franks' newspaper before eyeing up the newspaper stand.

"I can recommend today's Shrewsbury Gazette and Herald," he said, wiping her items to the side off his newspaper.

"I'm sorry?"

"Today's Gazette and Herald."

She looked at him, puzzled.

"For your newspaper."

"Oh, I see. Thank you. How big is it?"

"How big? I've never thought to look at how many pages," he shrugged.

"No, I mean, how long, is it a long paper? I need a long one?"

He looked at her with some confusion. "You mean a broadsheet? Well, there's the Midlands Farmer?"

"That's fine then, thank you, I'll have one of those."

"You like farming, do you?" he couldn't help but ask, looking at her expensive clothing. She smiled back, casually.

He lifted his arm and pointed behind her. "You'll find it over there, next to the cards."

Jessica noticed that he looked very confused, but she didn't have the time to think about his problems. She went over to the corner where he had pointed, looked down, saw the newspaper and bent over to pick it up. As she looked up, she saw a card of a beautiful cat and froze, it looks just like Khepri! She smiled and took it off of the rack; the likeness was uncanny. She took the card and the newspaper and dropped them in front of the man.

"How much do I owe, please?" She reached into her jacket pocket for her purse.

"Well, let me see." Totting up her purchases, he noticed the card. "Well, I never! It's like two buses coming along at once."

"Excuse me?"

"Your card with the cat on it. I sold 44 of these to someone only yesterday."

"44? That's a lot!"

"I've never sold so many birthday cards!"

"I'm sorry, it's a birthday card?"

"Yes, it's a birthday card."

"Oh, I didn't realise. I'll leave it then." Jessica pushed the card to one side.

"Well, without the card, that will be £11.50, please."

Jessica opened her purse and pushed £15 in notes across the counter. "Thank you, keep the change. Must dash." She grabbed her glasses, binoculars and farming newspaper and headed towards the door.

Mr Franks watched her struggle in her heels as she moved quickly on the uneven floor towards the door, practically throwing herself through it.

As the door closed, he looked down at the unwanted birthday card and shook his head, "out of towners!"

Chapter Twenty Two:

CLOWN NOSE AND THE SHEEP DIVING CONTEST

FRIDAY MORNING APPROACHING 11.30

Sarah Belloch could see first-hand that Missy was in some discomfort as she gently stroked her head. She tried to conceal it from Mildred as best as she could, but a frown appeared across her forehead all the same. She had never witnessed a cat remain asleep in this much discomfort.

She continued to run her hand down Missy. "She's a very beautiful cat, Mildred."

"She's my world doctor. Please do help her."

Sarah smiled at Mildred, trying to offer some reassurance. "I'm sorry to ask some general questions, but has there been anything different about Missy's routine that you are aware of? Has she been outside a lot or eaten anything unusual that you can think of?"

"I'm not aware of anything different. She often goes out at night. She thinks that I do not know, but I do." Mildred offered the doctor a smile.

Sarah returned the smile back. "So you can't think of anything that could have led to Missy being unwell?"

"No, nothing at all."

"I see." The vet placed her hand over Missy's heart and immediately froze and her eyes widened. "I must ask you, Mildred, I was told that you had seen another vet. May I enquire what they said?"

"Well, nothing really. It looked like she ran some form of a device over Missy and said it was a bug and that she would be okay soon."

Sarah turned in an instant to Mildred. "A device, what sort of a device?"

"I really could not tell you, I'm not a vet. It was a handheld scanner of some sort. The vet very quickly put it back into her bag and told me that she had taken a blood test?"

Sarah frowned again but chose not to conceal it this time. "A handheld scanner?" She took her hand away from Missy's torso with some surprise and shook her head slightly. "I've never heard of something like that, something that could determine what is wrong so quickly. May I ask what veterinary practise you use?"

"Fennaway's, it's about 15 miles from here. They were recommended."

"Fennaway's?" Sarah looked up in thought. "I've never heard of them, Mildred. How odd! How did you say you heard about them?"

Mildred clammed up a little upon hearing this question. "A recommendation from a friend."

"I see," Sarah nodded, noticing Mildred's lack of eye contact.

The vet looked back at Missy. Placing her hand over her heart again, she looked at Mildred and smiled. "I'm sure everything will be fine."

She reached for her bag and took out a stethoscope. Checking that the diaphragm was clean, she placed it over Missy's heart and pushed the tips into her ears.

"Well, that's somewhat reassuring," Mildred said, leaning over the vet.

Sarah removed the tips from her ears. "I'm sorry, Mildred. What did you say?"

"You are using your stethoscope to listen."

Sarah had a look of confusion all over her face. "Well, yes, Mildred, I have to listen. Why would you say that?"

"Oh, it's just Kamilah Fennaway had one of those but didn't listen to Missy's heart until I asked her to."

Sarah, who was crouched down over Missy, leaned forward to Mildred, "Excuse me?"

"I know. Strange, don't you think?"

Sarah nodded slowly. "Yes, I find that most peculiar." She turned to face Missy and continued to listen through the stethoscope, moving it around her chest as she closed her eyes in concentration.

Sarah's eyes snapped open as she pulled the diaphragm away. 'It can't be,' she thought to herself, replacing it immediately whilst keeping a watch on Missy's face.

She swallowed and performed the same movements three times to be sure. Pulling the buds from her ears and letting the stethoscope sit around her neck, she hesitated before looking Mildred in the face.

"Is everything okay, doctor?" Mildred peered over the doctor's shoulder. "Doctor?"

Sarah turned to face Mildred. "It's very early to tell, but I must be honest with you Mildred, there is an irregular heartbeat that concerns me." She turned back to Missy, stroking her gently. She had never seen anything like this before.

"Would you mind if I just make a phone call, please?" She said, standing to her feet.

"No, I don't mind. My phone is over there," she replied, pointing at the cat phone on the side.

"Well, actually, I'm just going to step outside. I just want to speak to one of the partners at the practice. Just to get a second opinion, you see."

"Should I be worried? Kamilah, the other vet, checked Missy and went straight outside to make a phone call as well."

Sarah stepped towards Mildred and placed a hand on her shoulder. "I'm sure it's fine, Mildred. It's always good to get a second opinion. It's quite common, really."

Mildred was not convinced she was telling the truth. "Well, okay, if you need to."

"Thank you, Mildred. I'll just be a moment."

Mildred watched as the vet headed to her front door pulling her phone from her pocket. She ran straight to the window to watch and could see a look of concern on the vet's face. She glanced over at Missy.

"Missy, what on earth is going on?" She turned back around to look at the vet but could not hear a word that was being said.

"I'm telling you, David, it's unmistakable. I can clearly hear the distinct sound of two heartbeats, both beating at different paces. The cat is in pain to the degree that she appears unconscious. Her body is twitching constantly and her eyes are closed. Have you ever heard of such a thing?"

"No, I certainly have not. That's a first on me," the voice replied.

"And that's not all. Another vet called by that I have never heard of. She ran some sort of scanning device over the cat and said that she would be fine soon. How strange is that? She gave an instant prediction without taking her away for observation."

"Scanning device? What sort of scanning device?"

"I have no idea. Mildred clearly doesn't know either. She's very concerned about the whole thing."

"I'm not surprised." There was silence at the other end of the phone. "You'll need to bring the cat in for further checks. If what you are saying is true, we will need to investigate this urgently."

"Yes, I agree. I'll bring her in."

Sarah looked up, noticing a car pulling up on the other side of the road. She turned back to the house to see the shadow of Mildred, watching her from behind the old, stained net curtains.

Mildred continued to watch, raising her hand to her chest as she studied the vet's body language in her garden. She looked back over to Missy with sadness. "I think she is going to take you away from me, Missy."

Jessica parked up her car on the opposite side of the road from Mildred's house. "I'm a natural at this," she exclaimed with some pride looking down at Khepri, who was still sound asleep. She could see a lady that she didn't recognise on the pathway outside Mildred's house talking on the phone.

I'm guessing that's her, she thought to herself, the unwanted vet. She leant down to the footwell on the car's passenger side and grabbed her surveillance equipment. Tearing open the binocular box, she ripped them out of the cellophane bag, brought them up to her eyes and started twiddling at the plastic centre dial. "Khepri, these are useless," she said, looking at the grainy image in front of her eyes. They did work a little; she could see a stethoscope around the vet's neck.

Putting the binoculars down on her lap, she pulled the oversized glasses out of their bag, pulling at the red nose, trying her best to remove it. "Blimey, it won't come off!"

Such was her enthusiasm that the car was beginning to rock, but the red nose remained firmly fixed to the glasses. They'll have to do, she thought, putting them on and grabbed at the newspaper. She pulled it up to her eyes so the nose was covered.

"Who you speaking to, I wonder?" Jessica glanced down at her clearly disinterested sleeping cat. "Bet she's speaking with someone about Nahla." She continued to watch when she noticed the lady looked over. Jessica quickly pulled the newspaper up to hide her face. She pushed her fingers through the paper to make a hole so she could look out; "that was close!" She noticed the lady on the phone had turned around facing Mildred's house. "Okay, no harm done. Khepri, I'd better call Nubia and let her know I'm here."

She hit the dial option and the phone began to ring at the other end. "Exciting all of this, isn't it, Khep...?"

"Hello, who is this?"

"Lady Nubia, it's Jessica. Just to let you know, I'm in position." I think that's what you're supposed to say, she thought to herself.

"Who were you talking to?"

"I'm sorry, my Lady. What was that?"

"Who were you talking to as I answered the phone?"

"Oh, I'm sorry," Jessica's face flushed, "I was talking to Khepri."

"Really, I'm not aware that you have the gift – do you?"

"Er... gift Lady Nubia, I'm not sure what you mean?"

"Well...can you talk to cats?" her tone was impatient.

"Well, to be honest I always talk to my cats." She shrugged her shoulders a little as the newspaper slipped down.

"That's not what I mean," she rolled her eyes "can they understand you?"

"Well, sometimes, I think..."

Nubia shook her head. "Obviously not. Nevermind, it would have saved us some time. So what do you want?"

"I was just letting you know that I'm here and there looks to be another vet here too. She's speaking to someone on the phone."

"I bet. Call me when you've been able to exchange the cats. Fennaway will call you in a minute."

"Lady Nubia, Khepri is my cat. I'm not comfortable with this."

"Nonsense, it's for the good of the Order and very important. You must get Nahla at all costs. Nahla must not be taken away, at all costs, Jessica. See that it's done!" The phone went dead.

Jessica pulled the phone away from her ear. "My word, she is so rude." Jessica hadn't realised that the newspaper had slipped whilst she was on the phone. She looked over to see the vet looking directly at her. She dived beneath the paper and peered through the hole.

"David, I'll explain to Mildred that her cat must come in for overnight observation. Look, I've got to go. There is a lady in a car wearing a clown nose, watching me from across the street. Something very odd is happening over here."

"A clown nose?"

"Yep, I'm not kidding. I'll see you in a bit."

Sarah stepped forward to take a closer look before returning to the house.

Jessica waited until the vet was out of sight before lowering the newspaper.

"Well, I guess I'd better do my research." She grabbed her phone and typed the inscription on the vet's car into Google, Castle Hollow Veterinary Practice. She waited patiently for results. Jessica immediately noticed that the vet's practice was not very far away. She went onto the 'About Us' page and there she was, the woman on the phone, the woman she guessed she was going to meet somehow. "Dr Sarah Belloch BVSC graduated blah blah blah. Well, that's her Khepri, that's our girl. They are not far away, so we won't have a lot of time."

She put the phone down and looked at Khepri. "I guess it's just a waiting game now." How she was going to get to Nahla, she had absolutely no idea. I hope Fennaway has some ideas when she calls, she thought to herself as she scanned the newspaper.

'Foul Play Suspected At Sheep Diving Success.' Shropshire farmer Royston Dingle is being accused of foul play and the use of performance enhancing drugs is not being ruled out, following his continued success at the annual sheep diving contest. "I refute any suggestion that I have been cheating" he said to the Shropshire Farmer. "I live and work next to the River Severn and my sheep often like to dive in, it's natural for them."

Mr Dingle went on to state "Spend an afternoon at my farm and you'll see them dive off the river banks for a swim. They love it! I'll sue anyone who claims otherwise."

Things have certainly been hotting up...

Jessica was abruptly interrupted by her phone ringing. She answered immediately.

"Hello."

"Jessica, it's Kamilah Fennaway."

"Hello, Lady Fennaway, nice to hear from you; Lady Nubia said that you would be calling. May I ask, have you ever been on surveillance? It's just, I have a question...?"

"Surveillance? What on earth would I know about surveillance, Jessica?" she said, interrupting, "listen, put Khepri on the phone, would you?"

Jessica pulled the phone away from her ear. She can't be serious.

"Jessica... Jessica."

Jessica put the phone back to her ear.

"I understand that time is of the essence, so if you will please."

"Er, yes, hang on a moment." Jessica pulled the phone away from her ear and looked across to Khepri, who was still asleep. She rocked her slightly. "Khepri, wake up." Khepri opened her eyes and sat up.

"It's for you," she said, shaking her head and rolling her eyes, placing the phone by Khepri's ear.

Jessica could hear muffled noises coming from her phone and watched as Khepri's eyes widened and blinked as if she understood everything that was being said. Khepri looked up and nodded her head. "What on earth does that mean? Are you done?"

She threw the glasses with the clown nose on the dashboard and brought the phone back to her ear. "Kamilah, what exactly just happened? Is everything okay?"

"Yes, fine, Khepri knows what to do. Now make sure you get Nahla. Goodbye."

"Kamilah..."

The phone went dead. Jessica threw the phone on top of the glasses on the dashboard and looked over at Khepri. "So, we're sorted now?" Her cat stared back at her. "I'm glad you know what you are doing because I'm absolutely clueless!"

"Sorry about that Mildred, I hope you do not mind my making a phone call to the office."

"No, that is fine, Doctor. May I ask your thoughts, please?"

"I know that this will upset you, but I've detected an unusual heart rhythm with Missy and to be safe, I want to take her to our clinic where we can assess her further. We must establish what is wrong, and we have specialist equipment at the surgery."

"Surgery? You're not going to operate on her, are you?"

"For now, Mildred, I'm not fully sure what is wrong with Missy, but you needed to call us. To be honest, the other vet you called should have done something similar."

"Oh, I see." Mildred looked at Missy and could feel her hands shaking slightly. "I've not been without her for nearly three years now, Sarah." Mildred could feel her eyes starting to well up and brought a hand up to wipe her nose.

Sarah placed a supporting hand on Mildred's shoulder. "We will do all we can for her; she will be in the best place with the right people. We will find out what is wrong."

"I see, thank you." Mildred could feel that she was going to cry. "Please be careful with her. She's my friend."

"We will, Mildred. Honestly, she will receive great care. I need to go to my car as there is some paperwork that I need you to sign. I'll get a carrier for Missy so I can take her straight away. I'll leave you with my personal mobile number and you can call me anytime. As soon as we can establish what is wrong, we will call you, of course."

Sarah was still holding Mildred's shoulder, "Is that okay with you?"

Mildred nodded, unable to speak.

"Okay, I'll just be a minute," she gently smiled.

Sarah walked towards the front door and Mildred crouched down beside Missy, placing a hand on her head. With tears in her eyes, she ran her other hand down her body. "Please don't leave me, Missy."

Sarah walked down Mildred's pathway to her gate and pressed the remote for her car to unlock itself. The sound of the boot opening automatically disturbed a wood pigeon in the tree above as a couple of loose leaves fell to the ground. She removed a carrier from the boot and placed it on the pavement whilst she sorted through the paperwork that Mildred would need to sign. She glanced over at the car opposite. Someone was still reading a very large newspaper. She put the paperwork inside the carrier along with a blanket and walked back up Mildred's pathway.

Jessica pulled the newspaper back and looked down at Khepri. "Right, she's obviously taking Nahla away. We must be ready!"

Ever since the phone call, Khepri remained upright. "Well, whatever she said to you, I hope it works out and you know what you are doing."

She paused momentarily, placing a hand on her cat. "Please don't take any risks, Khepri. You are my cat and I love you; it upsets me that you are being asked to do this. What on earth am I going to do next?" They both looked at each other, one more confused than the other.

Having explained the paperwork, Sarah looked on as a distraught Mildred signed her name where she had been asked. "These copies are for you, Mildred." Without words, she reluctantly took them from her. "I want to leave you with my business card as well; you can see my personal telephone number here at the bottom," she pointed out where her direct line was. "I know that you are upset, so call me if you need to. She is going to be in the best place, I promise."

Mildred wiped her eyes, doing her best to maintain some composure and just nodded. She crouched down to look inside the carrier. "Get well soon, Missy. Please!" She reached out at the grill that her cat lay behind, stood up and looked at the vet, nodding again. Sarah put a reassuring hand on Mildred's arm before putting her work bag over her shoulder and picking up the carrier. She headed towards the door, which Mildred was now holding open for her.

"I will call you, Mildred. I promise, as soon as I can."

"Okay, thank you, Sarah." The vet nodded and walked down the pathway to the gate. "Do you need a hand with the gate, Sarah?"

"No, I'll be fine, thank you, Mildred. Goodbye for now."

Mildred closed the front door very gently and went straight to the front room to look out of the window. Sarah's car was parked on the bend just out of sight, but then maybe that was for the best. She collapsed onto the sofa, picked up the cat cushion and held it to her chest. Tears were running down her face. "Oh Missy, what has happened?"

Sarah placed the carrier on the back seat passenger side, where she could keep an eye on Missy throughout the journey. She secured the carrier as best she could. Her work bag and the signed paperwork were now on the front seat next to her.

She started the car and indicated to move away, noticing the occupied parked car opposite and the large newspaper.

Jessica peered from over the top of the newspaper. "Here we go, Khepri!" She threw the newspaper to the side and started the engine. Following the vet down Rocke Road, she felt it best to leave a little distance, not wanting to give the game away. So far, she had been so discreet, but only one thing was paramount in her mind.

How on earth am I going to be able to get Nahla?

Chapter Twenty Three:

ACTIONING THE SWITCHAROO

Raysmau left her office, clutching the two security reports.

Closing the door behind her, she passed by the security control room on her right. One of the Escarrabin jumped up upon seeing her "Ma'am."

"Don't worry. I can do the gate for myself, unexpected meeting."

"Yes, Ma'am, if you are sure."

"I am." She pressed the wall-mounted button as she drew near to the gate, the familiar sound of metal moving over stone filled the corridor as it opened. She walked through, glancing at the reports until she reached the exit door. She brought her right shoulder down towards the illuminated crest as her pin badge connected and the heavy old doors opened inwards. She took a quick observation of those in the lobby area, knowing that more Escarrabin would be arriving within the next couple of hours. Those on shift were in their allotted places and the Clerics were busy with the administration.

A couple of Elders, deep in conversation, nodded as she passed; the sound of her heavy footsteps was unmistakable. She noticed two Escarrabin keeping a close eye on a Watcher cleaning one of the far stairways down the grand walkway. Everything appeared to be in order. The lift was where it was supposed to be and not below ground. Satisfied, she headed up the stairs for her meeting with the Reeve.

Raysmau knew she would have to choose her words carefully as she gave her account of the events of the day before. The reports told their own story, but she was apprehensive about the outcome of them. Being sent into the below was now a high probability and the Reeve may command such action. This, in recent history, was an unprecedented act. She considered what she would do if she were the Reeve. She hated to admit it, but if she were, she would probably send everyone below for a thorough investigation of the noise that had come from the darkness deep below. What such a beast is, how it got there and if it is secured, she had to confess to herself that she had no idea. All she knew was the warnings of her predecessor.

As she approached the Reeve's doorway, she looked back to the quadrangle at the four Clerics who seemed to be busy, with what she didn't know. Still, the Curator always seemed to keep them occupied.

She took a deep breath outside the Reeve's grand and scarred door before knocking three times with her knuckles and taking a couple of steps backwards. She didn't notice that one of the Clerics had looked up as she surveyed the grand old door. All of the scars and the stories they told went back many hundreds of years. The cracked and repaired old seal in the centre of the door was one of the stories she did know about.

The door was pulled open and Raysmau was surprised to see the Reeve standing there, having opened it herself.

"Good morning, Ma'am," Raysmau nodded.

"It's almost afternoon, Raysmau. I was surprised to hear from you. Come through. I trust this is urgent."

They passed through the Reeve's corridors. Raysmau could see that the doorway ahead into the Reeve's office was already open.

"Come in, take a seat, Raysmau." The Reeve ushered her towards a chair already placed in front of her desk.

"Thank you, Ma'am."

"What's troubling you, Raysmau? We have plenty to do today."

Raysmau watched the Reeve shuffling papers on her desk; her focus was elsewhere.

"I know, Ma'am, but I felt it prudent to bring something to your attention."

The Reeve looked up and took her seat opposite Raysmau without saying anything.

Raysmau looked at the Reeve with confidence. "There was an event yesterday which in itself may not be remarkable, but it led to an escalation."

The Reeve frowned, "An escalation; is this not something that you can handle?"

"On this occasion, no, Ma'am. It needs your consideration and possibly that of the Grand Council."

The Reeve sat back in her chair. Raysmau had her full attention. "Have a couple of the Escarrabin fallen out again?"

"No, Ma'am." Raysmau gave a gentle smile. Drawing her breath, she proceeded. "Yesterday, two Escarrabin found a Watcher around the great statue of Salma. As I say, that in itself may not be remarkable, but it's the second time it has happened and it was the same Watcher on both occasions. He was scheduled for duties over towards the lake."

The Reeve put her hands behind her head, ushering the head of the Escarrabin to continue.

"It is the nature of this Watcher that concerns me. He has been brought before me and is due to be disciplined, although I feel discipline would not affect him. He is not like the others."

The Reeve brought her hands back down as she heard this. "Really, how so?"

"A feeling that I have. He's arrogant, but there is something else about him. He has a deep disdain for us."

"Well, that's not uncommon among Watchers."

"Indeed, but he's different."

"I see. Presumably, there is more to this?"

Raysmau swallowed. "Yes, Ma'am, that is not all. Two of the Escarrabin took him below after he had seen me and they claim that he threatened them."

"Threatened them, our Escarrabin?"

"Yes, Ma'am, he affects the other Watchers as well. I have it here in their reports for you to see."

Raysmau leaned forward and placed both reports on the desk. "The two Escarrabin felt they were in danger and one of them drew her Scatterblade."

The Reeve's eyes widened. "You can't be serious Raysmau, drawing a Scatterblade, on Watchers in the below?"

Raysmau sat in silence, briefly letting the words sink in. She knew this would not be well received.

"With the absence of security cameras, Ma'am, we only have the accounts of the Escarrabin to understand what the Watcher was doing and why he was around the great statue of Salma."

"I get resistance on this from the Grand Council, Raysmau. I agree with you on this matter and cameras should be installed. If it were solely my decision, security matters would be taken a great deal more seriously. To my knowledge, a Scatterblade has not been drawn within these grounds in a very long time!"

"Indeed, but there is also something else, Ma'am."

The Reeves's eyebrows rose as she leaned back in her chair with her hands back behind her head again. "Well, let's hear it!"

Raysmau took a deep breath. "The two Escarrabin claim they heard something in the deep, far in the deep, something of old and not of this place. It was moving."

The Reeve lowered her arms feeling an instant rush of adrenaline pass through her, "Are you sure of this, Raysmau?"

"I must report my concerns. I do not know the full history of events in days gone by in the below, but something has awoken down there, something not natural."

The Reeve took her eyes away from Raysmau and looked down to think. A Watcher had been seen twice by the statue, something was moving in the deep and other Watchers were becoming unruly. She looked back up at Raysmau.

"I'm sure it's nothing!"

"Ma'am?" Of all of the reactions she expected, this was not one of them.

"The Watchers don't like being told what to do at the best of times. See that he is punished. Leave your reports here. I'll read them through and come back to you."

"Yes, Ma'am. You don't want any further action at this time? A Scatterblade was drawn!"

The Reeve smiled at Raysmau. "No, that's fine, but thank you for letting me know."

Raysmau stared back at her superior, lost for words.

"That will be all, Raysmau." The Reeve raised her tone in authority and tilted her head, looking directly into Raysmau's eyes.

"Yes, Ma'am." Raysmau stood up, nodded and took a couple of steps backwards before turning around to head for the door.

She headed out towards the grand door of the Reeve as a scowl appeared across her face. What was that? No further action and dismissing the noise from below as nothing, she pondered.

Throughout her working history, she had never seen a Reeve fail to take decisive action. Something was not right; there had to be more to this. Raysmau did not like being kept in the dark.

As soon as the Reeve was certain that Raysmau had gone, she leaned forward and brought a hand up to her mouth with worry. Taking deep breaths, she bowed her head, pulling her fingers through her hair. The Reeve knew some of the history of the below and the dark stories of old. She rested her hands on her temple and considered everything that Raysmau had said. Reading the reports would make no difference to the outcome of her suspicions; she knew exactly what the Watcher was up to. She leaned across her desk and grabbed at her phone. Looking up at her clock, she knew that her Head of Order would be one hour ahead of her. She sat patiently listening to the phone ring at the other end.

"Si, buenas tardes."

She drew a deep breath of relief. "Ma'am, it's the Reeve of Loxley."

"Yes, Reeve, what is it?"

"I must speak with you urgently."

✝✝✝✝

Sarah Belloch turned to look over her left shoulder at Missy lying in her carrier; she could see the occasional paw twitching. In all her years of training and having worked for Castle Hollow for the last two years, she had never witnessed such an event. As she drove towards the surgery, she estimated that she could be there in 15 – 20 minutes, with traffic permitting.

David Fullerton, the senior partner, knew she was on her way for a second opinion. Sarah had huge ambitions and love for her job. She hoped to be a partner of Castle Hollow in the future or, better still, have her own practice. However, this certainly was a mystery. She hoped to give some relief to Mildred later by way of good news.

As she approached the line of traffic at the lights, her thoughts turned to Mildred. There could be no doubt how much Missy meant to her, as all cats do to their owners. A little shiver ran through her spine as she was still trying to get the tingling of the smell of fish paste out of her nose. I can't believe anyone still eats that, she thought to herself. As she stopped in the line of traffic, she noticed a car closing up behind her in her rearview mirror.

"Khepri, what are we going to do?" Jessica estimated that the vets' practice was probably only around 10 minutes away from looking earlier on the internet. "If she takes Nahla into the surgery, we are never going to get her out!"

She glanced down at Khepri, who was still sitting upright in the front seat. As the lights turned green, she maintained what she considered a reasonable distance behind the vet's vehicle.

The speed of the car reached 30mph. Jessica knew she was running out of time. With one hand on the steering wheel and the other clutching a lock of her hair, she knew full well that it wouldn't be good if she let Nubia down. "You know, Khepri, I have no idea why this is so important. It must be devastating for Mildred that Nahla is so unwell, I would be devastated if it were you, but why we are on this mission, I have no idea." She continued to follow the vet down the main A5 road, knowing full well that Castle Hollow Vets was now only a few streets away.

They stopped at a roundabout and she could see there were two cars in front of the vet.

"Right, decisive action Khepri, we'll need to ram her." She looked down at her cat, who turned to look at her. "Well, you got any better ideas?" Khepri blinked and curled her tail. "Well, what was that? An agreement to my plan or what? Oh my days, what am I doing?"

Jessica looked in her rearview mirror at the cars that had stopped behind her in the line of traffic. She looked out of her windows for Police but could not see any. Pulse racing, she screwed up her face and almost closed her eyes. "Brace for impact Khepri!!" She took her left hand off the steering wheel and placed it on her cat to protect her. The vet's car moved forward to the front of the queue.

"Here we go. We're going to ram her!" Making a yelling noise, she drove directly into the back of the vet's car, hitting the bumper at about 3mph. "Phew! You okay, Khepri?" She reversed the car back slightly.

"What the hell?" Sarah Belloch felt the knock to the rear of her car. She looked in the rearview mirror and could see a car backing away, the driver flapping her arms and leaning into the passenger seat. Turning around to check on Missy, she could see that she was unmoved. She looked back in her mirror to see the driver getting out of the car.

Jessica leaned over and opened the passenger door of her car slightly. "Right, Khepri. Do what you need to do. Please be very careful." A sad expression spread across Jessica's face as she undid her seat belt. "Right!" She got out and took a few steps forward towards the vet's car. Not surprisingly, there was no sign of any damage. Think, think, think, Jessica's mind was in mental chatter.

She looked on to see the vet taking her seat belt off, obviously about to get out of her car. A car horn sounded from the line of traffic behind, but no-one was watching. She quickly kicked her heel through the rear quarter light sending pieces of red plastic to the floor as the vet climbed out of her car.

"What on earth happened there?" the vet exclaimed.

"I'm so so sorry. I don't know what I was thinking. I must have just lost my concentration!"

To her left, Jessica could see Khepri walking towards the rear of the vet's car.

"I'm sorry. It was my fault. Hands up." Jessica smiled.

"I'm not sure what you are smiling for?"

Jessica watched as she saw the vet crouch down to look at her broken light on the floor.

"I'll just check this side." Jessica made her way to the left rear of the car and crouched down. She glanced around to the side and could see Khepri sitting, staring at the car door.

"Is everything okay there?" Jessica said, trying to make conversation with the vet whilst reaching out her left hand to open the rear passenger door.

"Not really. You've done some damage."

"I'm sure it can be fixed," Jessica said, stretching to pull on the door handle. She was relieved to find the door unlocked.

She looked at Khepri and tilted her head to the right as if to say, 'go on then, get in.' She watched Khepri jump up into the vet's car.

Jessica stood up to look at the vet. "I'm very sorry about all of this. What is your name?"

The vet starred back quizzically. "I don't understand how the light broke. I barely even felt you hit me."

"Yes, quite strange that. I must have been at an angle or something."

Jessica looked through the rear windscreen to see Khepri pulling at the cat carrier.

Sarah was starring at Jessica. "Strange that there isn't a mark on your car, don't you think?"

"What? sorry?"

"Your car, there's not a scratch on it."

"British car see, made of strong stuff." Jessica smiled.

"I think you'll find these are made in Japan now."

"Oh, really?" Jessica was looking around, unsure of what to do next.

"Well, I guess we had better exchange details. I trust you are insured?"

"Oh yes, please do not worry about that," Jessica offered a reassuring smile.

"Bet you don't have a no claims bonus, do you?"

Jessica noticed the look of displeasure all over the vet's face as she walked back to her car door.

Jessica's eyes flared with worry as she looked through the glass to see Khepri getting into the carrier. She realised that she would now see two cats in her carrier if the vet looked on her back seat. Beads of sweat formed on her brow.

Sarah leant into her car and reached over to her bag, dragging it onto her front seat, looking for a business card. Jessica looked at the floor at the broken plastic from the light and then looked back up again and could see the vet bent over, looking into her bag.

Cars were now passing them by and their occupants were looking to see what had happened. Jessica kicked broken pieces of plastic under the rear wheel on the driver's side when no-one was watching. She quickly retracted her foot as she saw the vet approaching her.

"Here is my card with my details on it. I will need yours."

"Yes, of course. I'll just get those for you, but you know we should clear up this plastic; someone may get a puncture. I can see some under your car too."

The vet couched down and frowned at the broken bits of plastic around her wheel.

"We really should pick this up," Jessica announced.

"Yes, you are right." The vet replied, extending her arm underneath the car. Jessica took a few steps to her left and leaned into the slightly open passenger door. Khepri nodded to her from inside the carrier. Jessica leaned in and gently lifted Nahla from the carrier and closed the passenger door. She placed Nahla on her chest and tried to cover her with her black suit jacket.

As she closed the car door, Khephri pushed her paw through the carrier and pulled the cage shut.

"Okay, I'll get those details for you now."

The vet stood up, holding pieces of the plastic in her hands. She was startled to see a cat's head resting on the chest of the woman who had hit her car.

"What the..? Where did that come from?"

"What, sorry?"

"The cat, I didn't see it there before."

"Really? Oh, I take my cat everywhere with me. As a vet, I thought you would have noticed."

"Wait a second."

Jessica's heart was in her mouth as the vet threw down the pieces of plastic, opened the passenger door of her car and looked inside. Missy was still in there, asleep and she could see her paws twitching.

Jessica gulped and offered a smile, "Now, let me get those details for you." She walked over to her car, opening the passenger side door and gently placed Nahla on the seat. "Oh, my poor dear, you do not look well." Jessica was shocked to see Nahla's paws shaking, clearly in some discomfort.

She opened her glove box and took out a pen and a scrap of paper, closing the door behind her.

She leant on the vet's car to write down her details. "I could pay you cash for the damage if that helps."

Sarah didn't doubt it, looking at the expensive clothing the stranger was wearing. "No, you know what, I think we'll do this the official way. Something is not right here!"

"Whatever do you mean? I'm sorry. I told you I was careless, that's all."

"My last call, where I just came from, there was someone in a car outside acting suspiciously. Do you know where Rocke Road is?"

Jessica took a step back. Her heart was racing again.

"Erm, I'm sorry, Rocke Road, no I've never heard of there."

"Are you following me?" The vet walked over to Jessica's car and peered in. She could see a cat asleep on the passenger seat as well as large glasses with a clown nose fixed to them on the floor. The vet turned around to look at Jessica, hands on her hips.

"As I say, something is not right here. For the second time, are you following me?"

"I have no idea what you mean. You must be mistaken!" Jessica had a pleading look on her face as the angry vet walked back to her car and opened the driver's door, reaching for her bag.

Jessica took a couple of steps towards her car. "Well, I'll be on my way then."

"Not so fast!" The vet held up her phone and took a photograph.

"Excuse me, what are you doing?" Jessica questioned whilst trying to hide her face.

"You tell that ex of mine to leave me alone. The next time he hires a private investigator, tell him to hire one that knows what they are doing!"

"Well, I really..."

"And what sort of a responsible pet owner drives around with their cat in their arms, eh? Maybe if you concentrated more, you wouldn't have accidents. If you don't care for yourself, then think of your pet. Do I make myself clear?"

Jessica blushed. "Erm, yes."

"You'll be hearing from my insurance company."

The very angry vet climbed into her car and pulled away.

Jessica looked to the sky and let out an almighty sigh. That was close! She was distracted by a car horn that reminded her she was standing in the middle of the road, still creating an obstruction. Quickly gathering her thoughts, she checked her heels were not damaged and walked back to her car.

As she climbed in, she immediately placed her hand on Nahla's head. "I have no idea what Nubia has in store for you, but I hope she can make it all better and this was all worth it."

She started the engine and drove the length of two streets before pulling over to make a phone call. Thankfully, the phone didn't ring for long.

"Lady Nubia, I've done it. I've completed the mission objective and I've done the switcharoo!!" Jessica was ecstatic with pride.

"You've done what?"

"The switcharoo!"

"A switch a what?"

"I've switched the cats."

"Why didn't you just say that? Right, get over here immediately. I'll send an instruction to your navigator."

"Lady Nubia, you are a good hour from me and I need to get back. I'm supposed to be taking Mildred to the gathering in a few hours."

"You'll make it; I trust you have your pin with you for the gates?"

"Yes, my Lady, I always carry it with me. I'm not sure if I will have enough fuel."

"Then get some! When you get here, the car will bring you to the back of the house again. I'll also have something for you to take away with you."

"Take away with me?"

"Yes, of course. You want Khepri back, don't you?"

"Yes, my Lady."

"Good. When the time is right, you'll need to switch the cats back again!" She hung up the phone.

Jessica put her head in her hands; she hadn't thought that far ahead. The very idea of having to re-encounter the angry vet made her feel nauseous. No thanks and nothing for my efforts, she thought as she looked down at poor Nahla.

The navigator flashed and the peddles moved below her feet. She sat back in her seat. It would appear she had little choice; it looked like she was off to headquarters again.

Chapter Twenty Four:

THE GREAT STATUE OF SALMA

FRIDAY APPROACHING MIDDAY

Although her head of Order, Lady Berenike, spoke fluent English, the Reeve didn't speak a word of Spanish. Regardless, she chose to talk slowly, as some words were not easy to say in any language.

"Can you talk privately, my Lady?"

"Yes, I'm in my office. What is troubling you, Reeve of Loxley?"

"I've been informed about a worrying development. We have a Watcher who may be becoming active and disruptive and not like the others; ordinarily, my head of security would not bring this to me. However, on two occasions, the same Watcher has been seen around our great statue of Salma. Now, this in itself is one thing, but he is causing unrest below with the other Watchers and there is reason to believe they may be becoming hostile. He is trying to unite them."

She could hear her superior breathing down the phone. "Please continue."

"It has just been brought to my attention that yesterday there was an incident below and one of our Escarrabin drew her defence weapon. My Lady, during this process, the sound of something moving was coming up from very deep below."

"This is unsettling. What sort of noise do you think was heard?"

"I was not present, my Lady, but it was described as unnatural. An assumption has been made that it could be something from the past, from long in the past." The Reeve could only hear breathing through the phone receiver. "There is something else. One of our own has become very ill and our Curator believes it could be the first sign of the prophecy. The timing of a gathering of everyone worldwide is suspicious and my concern is that the timing is not a coincidence. Is it possible the actions of this Watcher has brought something back from the past? His presence around the statue concerns me."

"This is a very worrying development, Reeve. You know what lies protected beneath the statue. It is unlikely that he has somehow discovered what is below it; potentially trying to gain access would be of immediate concern and a security priority. One of our own becoming ill at the same time does not sit well with me. You were right to call."

"That is why I seek your counsel on this matter, my Lady."

"It would be an unlikely event that a Watcher could have gained access as they do not know or should not know about these things. If this information has come into his possession, then we have a serious security breach."

"Yes, someone may be helping him."

"Has the Watcher been assessed through the usual protocols?"

"He has, but the manner of his arrival here was unusual. He was seen not far from our main gates. We have cameras outside and the Escarrabin caught him and brought him in."

"So this is a Watcher who knew the location of your headquarters and effectively surrendered?"

"Yes. Putting it together, it is becoming a little unnerving."

"Indeed. I've never heard anything like it before. He wanted the Escarrabin to catch him. Reeve tell me, what of his hands, especially the right hand? Have you seen any discolouration, a turquoise-like colour?"

"I can't answer that. We are very wary of their hands. The usual measures are taken to cover them with gloves."

"I see. Well, that must be looked into, but Reeve, you must find out if he has gained access below the statue. If he has, I know what he is trying to do with everything that you have told me."

"Please continue, my Lady."

"I know that your predecessor would have told you about the days of old, especially the dark ones, much of which like to be forgotten. What she may not have told you is that a great many things were buried below Loxley, well more sealed away if the truth be told; they were very dark days indeed."

The Reeve adjusted herself on her seat, pulling her left hand through her hair in concentration.

"Over eight hundred years ago, a wall of iron was built in the very deep. It was built to close off everything that lay beyond, to ensure that what lay behind it and the secrets of old would never resurface. If what you are telling me is that noise from beyond there has been heard, and you have potentially a Watcher trying to unite them, this is of grave concern. The prophecy has spoken about three events and you have already described that one of our own is very ill. Presumably, she is suffering the pain of two hearts?"

"Yes, my Lady, we believe that to be so."

"Then it is vitally important that you get to the statue immediately. You know where the room of keys is once you are inside?"

"Yes, my Lady, I do."

"Once inside, you should see two very old large bronze keys that have no place with the others; they are both four-sided keys designed with extra security in mind. Both will be needed to open an access point within the wall of iron. That doorway within the iron wall has not been opened for hundreds of years; there is no guarantee that it will open at all. It is so old. The Watchers do not have the strength to challenge us, but if this one of whom you speak is gifted and can unite them, what lays beyond that wall of iron is what he will need to set them all free. That is a presumption on my part unless there is another goal that we are not yet aware of."

The Reeve sat back in her chair, considering the sudden mass escalation of events.

"Reeve, our foremothers, would have taken extra special precautions, I know this. No one person would be able to open that doorway alone, whether they are exceptional or not. There would be a third key and for safety's sake, there would be no reference to it within your grounds. I will need to refer to the ancient archives here to establish where that key is."

"I understand, my Lady."

"It is doubtful, but if your Watcher has somehow found the third key, this will need to be escalated to the Grand Council immediately."

"Yes, my Lady."

"For now, go to the statue and establish if the keys are still there. If they are, matters may not be as bad as they may appear. Once you have done that, call me back immediately. I now have some work to do in the archive."

"Yes, my Lady, of course. I shall go straight away."

"Reeve, whatever you do, be very careful. If this Watcher has gained access, someone is helping him. Do not trust anyone or discuss these matters with anyone but me at this time."

I understand fully. I will come back to you as soon as I can. Thank you for your counsel, my Lady."

"I'll speak with you soon, Reeve of Loxley."

The phone disconnected at the other end as the Reeve placed the phone back in its cradle.

She paced up and down in silence, deep in thought at what might be. Glancing up at the clock pendulum swinging back and forth, she considered if Nubia, the paranoid Curator, had been right all along.

+++++

Sarah walked into the reception area with her work bag over her shoulder and Missy in the carrier. She looked at the receptionist, who smiled at her as she answered the phone, "Castle Hollow Veterinary Practice, how may I help you?"

She walked towards a door marked private in search of David, the practice's senior partner. "Is David in his office?" she asked Julia as she passed by her. Julia was also a partner.

"Yes, he is. He tells me that you may have an interesting case."

"I certainly have. He's not kidding."

"May I join you? I would like to see."

"Yes, of course. Please do. Another opinion couldn't hurt."

Julia followed Sarah towards David's office. Sarah peered her head around his door to find him sitting at his desk, typing on his computer.

"David, I have the cat with me that I told you about."

He looked up with a smile. "Excellent, it sounds most interesting, Sarah. Take her through; we'll have a look straight away."

As she left his office, Sarah could hear his voice from behind her. "How are you holding up, Sarah?" She stopped in her tracks and turned to look at him, taking a deep breath.

"You're not going to believe it. He hired a private investigator to follow me."

"You're kidding?" exclaimed Julia.

"And that's not all. She was wearing a clown nose and drove into the back of my car, breaking one of my lights."

Julia raised an eyebrow looking at David, who was in shock.

"You can't be serious," David said, his mouth aghast.

"Yep! She was driving around, holding a cat."

David and Julia looked at each other.

"A private investigator, wearing a clown nose, driving with a cat and she crashed into you?" David tried hard not to laugh.

"Well, that's about the mark of the man!" said Julia.

"Total loser!" Sarah responded. "He can't even hire a professional to do his dirty work." They nodded their heads in unison.

"Let's take her through," David ushered his hand towards the doorway of the next room.

"I took her photograph, the investigator."

"Good for you." David followed Sarah into the surgery. "If she continues to harass you, you should call the Police."

Sarah placed the carrier with Missy inside gently onto the counter. "Oh, don't worry about that, I intend to. Really strange, all of her clothing looked designer as well."

David shook his head. "Right, let's see. What have we here," he said, walking over to the side to grab a pair of disposable gloves. "Tell me a little about her, please."

Sarah took her notes from her bag, although she didn't really need them. "The cat's name is Missy and she's a British Shorthair, nearly three years old. She doesn't respond to stimulation, is in considerable discomfort and has been this way for over 24 hours. As you know, I detected an abnormal heart rhythm." Sarah took a step forward towards the table where David was leaning over studying Missy.

"I detected two possible heartbeats."

David looked up to Julia's frowning face and then to Sarah, "Two heartbeats, you say?"

"Yes. I've never experienced anything like this."

"And there has never been any history of any heart abnormality in the past?"

"No, apparently not, although we have never seen Missy before. She called some other vet first, called Fennaway," Sarah shook her head slightly. "I've never heard of a vet called Fennaway around here, have you?"

"Nope. Never heard the name. Must be someone new; so many coming out of college now," he said with a mischievous smile.

David looked down at Missy, watching her paws occasionally twitch. "It's almost as if she's unconscious. How strange." He walked to the side and picked up his stethoscope. "Samantha," he yelled, placing it around his neck. All three of them turned around as the receptionist came into the room. "Can you prep the room for surgery, please? Just in case."

Khepri's ears twitched as she heard this.

"Right then, Missy, let's see what is going on."

Khepri could feel the presence of the vet standing over her.

"Mildred will be devastated if the cat needs surgery."

David looked up, "Mildred?"

"Yes, the owner. She was almost beside herself, sad really. It's almost as if Missy is all she has in the world."

Julia shook her head, "It is sad, but I get it. I really do."

David shifted his attention to Julia.

"I'd much rather have my cats than a boyfriend any day of the week," she continued.

"I can relate to that!" Sarah said instantaneously.

"We are not all bad, you know."

"Rubbish!" Sarah and Julia said at the same time, "you're all as bad as each other!" Julia added.

David smiled, placing the earbuds into his ears.

"I think the news of surgery will come as a blow to her," said Sarah.

On hearing the word 'surgery' for the third time, Khepri decided she was done with her Oscar-winning performance and opened her eyes.

"David, her eyes have opened!" exclaimed Sarah.

David took a step back, looking down at the cat. "So they have. Imagine that. They were definitely closed before?" They both nodded.

All three of them watched as Missy extended her paws, straightened her tail and sat upright.

"Well, I never." David brought his head down to take a closer look at Missy. "Hello Missy, this must be very confusing for you. I just want to check your heartbeat." He put the chest piece on the side of the cat and listened intently. A frown appeared across his face as he looked up at Sarah. He removed the chest piece and performed the same movement three times before pulling the earbuds out, letting the stethoscope rest on his neck.

Taking a couple of steps backwards, he looked at Sarah. "There is nothing wrong with this cat, well certainly in terms of heartbeat. Her rhythm is fine, not abnormal in any way. I most certainly can't hear any signs of two heartbeats, Sarah!" Julia frowned, looking over at Sarah.

"That's not possible. I know what I heard and I know what I saw." She snatched the stethoscope from his neck and placed the buds in her ears. "I'm telling you, I know what I heard!" She put the chest piece on Missy and closed her eyes to listen to the regular heartbeat. "It's not possible!" She removed the earbuds and stepped back, looking up at Julia.

"You've been working long hours, Sarah," Julia said, taking a step towards her as she looked down at Missy. "With everything that has gone on, it hasn't been easy. Now you have a private investigator following you."

"That has nothing to do with my professional capacity."

"We are not saying that, Sarah." She turned around to look at David.

"David, please. I'm telling you what I heard."

"See it from our point of view. You now have Magnum PI on your tail wearing a clown nose."

"But you could see that she looked unwell when I brought her in."

"Indeed, for this reason, we will keep her in overnight and monitor her, but ask yourself this, does that cat look unwell to you?"

Sarah looked down to see Missy sitting upright, staring at her. "I don't understand. I just don't."

"Sarah." She looked at Julia. "Look, why don't you take the afternoon off. We'll call Mildred later and give her an update. Just leave the client notes with Samantha and come back in the morning so you can take Missy back to her. It's for the best." Sarah looked at Julia with her mouth open in shock, then to David, who offered the slightest smile and looked to the floor.

"I see." She removed the stethoscope from around her neck, gently placed it on the side and picked up the client notes and her bag. "Well, I'll see you tomorrow then."

"See you tomorrow Sarah." Julia watched her leave the room as she turned to look at her business partner with some concern.

She dropped the client notes on the receptionist's desk as requested. "Here, these are for you. I'm having the afternoon off."

"Really? Are you doing anything nice?" Samantha inquired.

Sarah turned around, looking quite angry. "Car repairs!" With that, she pushed the door as hard as she could to exit. She stopped in the car park and pulled out her phone, entering the password. Her anger grew as she pulled up the picture of Jessica; "I'm on to you!"

The Reeve made her way to the Escarrabin security wing reasonably undetected. Although members of the Order's security arm seeing her was not an issue, she did want to keep out of view of the Elders and especially the Curator.

The thought of an insider was deeply troubling; so much was weighing on her mind. She needed to be sure of her facts and did not want to create any panic.

She turned to make sure no one followed her as she approached the side exit doors that led to the gardens. She placed her pin badge to the scanner logo for the doors to open, stepping through as quickly as she could into the fresh summer air. Once outside, she waited for the doors to close before moving forward. Keeping against the wall, she moved forward, still checking behind her.

She could see a couple of Watchers in the distance tending to the gardens, wearing goggles to protect their eye from direct sunlight. The great statue of Salma was visible down the main driveway through the gardens. She trod carefully across the gravel; there was no activity at the front of the house. She did her best to avoid being seen by her security from the house's lower front windows.

The great statue was getting closer, an impressive shrine to her past and everything Salma did for the Order a long time ago. Under her leadership, she shaped not just how the Order functioned but also moulded the Reeves's relationship and their need for privacy and security. The Order was in peril in days gone by. Her diligence and intelligence sought to rid that from any future events.

As she passed the pyramid-shaped bushes, she could see the stone cats at the feet of Lady Salma coming into view; there were eight of them in total. The Reeve looked up at the enormous figure above her, running her hand along the top of the huge stone plinth. Lady Salma was cradling her beloved Alliaa in her left hand. Her right hand was held aloft with her palm facing forward as a symbol of resistance against the Watchers and the darkness they stood for.

Her pulse had elevated. Although it was a warm day in the height of summer, she was becoming unnecessarily clammy with anxiety. She took three deep breaths and walked towards the statue.

Knowing that Nahla was now on the way, Nubia prepared her couch to make it as comfortable as possible. She plumped up the cushions under her main window as best as she could and went into her private quarters for more bedding and pillows. Constantly standing on the couch to look outside had taken its toll.

If she were truthful with herself, she was not sure what steps she would now take. She had done the right thing in ensuring that Nahla was not taken away for assessment by anyone other than Fennaway. Still, she was not going to be able to ease Nahla's pain. Fennaway, would probably have to be called to headquarters to oversee her. These are trying times, she thought to herself, dumping the extra bedding and pillows on to the couch. In any event, it was stuffy in her office and some fresh air wouldn't hurt. She stood on the couch and leaned towards the window.

Bringing the window off the latch, she opened it outwards, welcoming the fresh Welsh air into her room. She closed her eyes, took a deep breath and inhaled. Enjoying the clean air, which was a change from the smell of musty old furniture, she reopened her eyes to see a figure standing in the distance next to the great statue. She rubbed her eyes and squinted in the sunlight, focusing on the figure looking upwards at it. Judging by the misplaced suit the figure was wearing, it was reasonable to assume that it might be the Reeve. Well, what is she doing over there? She jumped down and ran to her desk, pulling open one of the large drawers and removing the bottle of Scotch. She leant to the back of the drawer, pulled out a set of binoculars and flipped off their protective caps. She ran and leapt onto the couch.

Practically throwing the binoculars to her eyes, she focused pretty well everywhere except where she really needed to see. "Come on!" she chastised herself before the statue came into view. Looking around the base, she grimaced that she couldn't see anyone. She pulled the binoculars from her eyes to rely on normal vision and frowned as she rested them down on the windowsill and leaned forward out of the window. Shaking her head puzzled, she knew that she had not imagined it. "Where the hell did she go?"

Taking three deep breaths, the Reeve walked towards the statue and stretched her arms up against the stone plinth and pushed up onto her toes. She was almost at full stretch as she felt her way around the paws of the cats set in stone at the base of Lady Salma.

There were four cats on either side of the great lady's legs. The four the Reeve ran her hands over were against the left leg of the huge statue. Only three of them unlocked what she suspected Duat had been trying to access. Taking another deep breath, she pressed down onto the left paw of the first cat. She felt it depress into the stonework and took a couple of steps to her right, ignoring the cat next to the one she had just pressed.

The next procedure would be tricky as the left and right paw of the next two cats needed to be pressed simultaneously. Stretching like she was about to do a star jump, she pressed down on both paws and immediately heard a loud echoed thud from underneath the statue and the sound of moving stone.

She was immediately flatfooted again as she peered around the corner of the statue to see that the stone plinth to her right-hand side had moved inwards. She looked over her shoulder one last time and back at the house, then pushed against the stone. She heard the expected secondary click and the very heavy stone found its way onto the runners underneath. She pushed it over to the right and climbed into the very dark chamber that had appeared.

The Reeve could feel her heart pulsing as she had only been in here once before and didn't care for being locked in the pitch black, which she knew was about to happen.

She reached out to the large handle set into the reverse side of the stone and took a deep breath, gathered her strength and pulled the stone back over to close her in. As the stone moved on the runners, she placed both hands against it and pushed until she heard a loud echo of the sound of stone sitting back into place and the cat's claws above her resetting outside.

In the darkness, she crouched waiting, knowing that she could not stand yet for fear of banging her head on the heavy stonework above her.

She started to count down from ten, hating every moment of the darkness. Suddenly, an old motor started up from below and flickered light began to appear. She could now see the old staircase directly to her left and let out a massive sigh of relief as the beads of sweat fell from her forehead.

At the bottom of the staircase, the symbol of the Reeves lit up to the right of the steel door and she looked at the old wheel that she would need to turn to open it.

Still crouched down, she stretched her left leg out and shuffled towards the stairs until she had descended enough of them that she could stand up fully.

Taking some thirty or so steps, she went deep below the statue. Her mind had lost focus from the possible missing keys and was now concerned about what she would do if the old release mechanism to get out didn't work. No one other than the Reeves knew of this place. Of course, that was the real reason why there was no CCTV on the grounds, to protect the secrets of the hidden vault from others' prying eyes. However, once inside, there was no form of communication whatsoever and she could potentially be trapped here. This was something that she would need to address at a later stage.

At the bottom of the steps, the illuminated symbol shone above the protective casing of the scanner. There were no visible signs of anything forced. Unclipping the casing, so it fell forward, she put her right hand against the scanner and pressed with her left hand on the symbol, watching the scanner as it moved up and down her palm. As the scanner read her hand, she looked behind her at the ancient lighting system and shook her head slightly. If her predecessor had installed this level of security to gain access, you'd think a light switch at the top of the staircase would have been a consideration.

The scanner stopped and the illuminated logo of the Reeve turned green. She replaced the protective cover, held either side of the large wheel built into the centre of the door, put her body weight against it and started to turn.

The old wheel took some effort to move as she could hear the locking mechanism working from within. She continued to turn until she heard the sound of multiple locking points giving way. She removed her hands from the wheel and took a deep breath. Putting both of her hands on the door, she leant against it with her weight and pushed from her shoulders until the old steel door started to move forward steadily across the stone floor.

She heard a clicking noise as the lights of the vault flickered on one by one, revealing its various chambers. She could hear the humming of electricity echoing from the vault's far end from the sealed temperature-controlled rooms.

The huge expanse of the vault and its eight chambers hosted the Reeves' treasures that had been collected and stored for centuries. For all the steps that had been taken for their preservation, it was highly disorganised and priceless items would appear to have been left here in the past as if in a hurry. If the Reeve of Loxley had any part of this in the future, the varying chambers and its treasures would be logged and separated. Organisation is something the Reeves prided themselves on. Why Roman, Egyptian and other relics were stored in the same chambers, she had no idea.

As the Reeve walked forward, her footsteps echoing in the coldness of the vault, she headed for the room of keys glancing at various artefacts on the way. Some she recognised from archaeology programmes on television, which was painful to watch, knowing they were wasting their time looking for them.

She looked up upon her approach to the chamber on the far left, the only chamber with its own unique archway; the archway's centre keystone had an old faded image of an ancient key engraved into the sandstone.

The heat of the summer afternoon bypassed this place below ground and she shivered as she entered the key chamber, the sweat from her previous excursions now making her cold. The keys were not hidden and did not need to be. This was a private storage area. She walked over to an old desk in the corner of the chamber, with lines of keys hanging on the wall above it.

A couple of heavy, ornate, eight foot long, gold-carrying rods were propped against the desk. She carefully moved them to the corner as she studied the keys, looking for the two keys with four sets of teeth.

There were hundreds of keys from the old system that opened every door of the mansion. The pin badge door entry system had been installed a few years before, making all of these old keys redundant. Here they now lay discarded to the cold and dark of the key chamber.

She recognised a few of the keys that hung on the hooks. Some opened old chests and the smaller keys opened lockable books. She ran her left hand along the multiple lines of old brass and iron keys, some of which would have been centuries old, but none of them were close to what she was looking for.

Taking a couple of paces backwards, she brought a hand to her chin in thought and bit on her lip as she looked around the rest of the room of keys. Her eyes were drawn directly to her left, where she could see a couple of keys hanging in the far corner. Pulling her suit jacket together in the chill, she took a few paces and bent over to look at them. They were very old, but not what she was looking for. Her eyes were distracted by a word above them to the right. It had been scratched into the wall by hand and was very faded. She leaned in closer, allowing her eyes to focus on the barely readable word 'Ferius.' "Ferius?"

She shook her head. It had been a long time since she had spoken the language of old. She did not take her eyes off the faded singular word as she brought her right hand to it. Tiny particles of old stone fell to the floor as she rubbed it gently. She gulped immediately as two more characters came into view 'Inferius!' She let out an audible gasp and only one spoken word, "below." She looked down at the two empty hooks on the wall in dismay, "Oh No!" The keys were missing.

She felt the hairs stand up on the back of her neck as her breathing became agitated, knowing full well that their security had been breached. Stepping back and breathing heavily she looked at the floor, knowing that she would need the help of her superior and the Grand Council would now need to be informed.

Thoughts of self-preservation ran through her mind, knowing that this security breach had happened under her tenure. She did not know how anyone could have got in and bypassed the scanner, which could only be accessed by her hand.

She clung onto the archway wall listening to her heartbeat and the humming of the electricity. She had better check the doors of the temperature-controlled rooms to ensure that nothing obvious was missing from there as well.

Still breathing heavily, she walked over to the two sealed caverns and looked through the heavily fortified screen doors of both of them. Truth be told, as it was only her second visit and unless obvious, she would not know if anything else was missing. The cavern on her left had rows of books and protected artwork, but there was no sign of any forced entry. The second cavern had an old chest with a white sheet draped over it with a red cross in the centre. She bent down slightly and could see it had what looked to be gold legs. There were also a couple of sarcophagi, scrolls and other artefacts. This temperature-controlled chamber bore more resemblance to a tomb than anything else, but in any event, it did not look like it had been disturbed.

Taking one final look around, she headed out of the exit door. She pulled heavily against it until it rested, then spun the locking wheel around until it would turn no more.

Knowing full well that she would be back in darkness in a moment, her anxiety was increasing again as she reached the top of the stairs, taking hold of the iron lever to release the stone to allow her to exit.

Taking two deep breaths, she applied pressure on the lever with both hands and pulled it down as the electricity cut off. In the dark, she heard the stone move towards her. Cracks of daylight started to make their way through.

Exiting this place was one thing, but her troubles had only just started.

Chapter Twenty Five:

THE KEYS
OF INFERIOUS

FRIDAY APPROACHING 1.45PM

Having made her way back to her offices as quickly as possible, the Reeve was sat at her desk behind closed doors. There was going to be no easy way to explain what she had discovered. If her Head of Order was correct and the four-sided keys were supposed to be in the vault, they certainly were not now. She would have some explaining to do, knowing that fingers would be pointed at her.

There were no guarantees that Duat had them. There were no guarantees they were even there. Let's face it, they could have been missing for a long time. She needed to get her story straight to protect her own reputation. Her predecessor may have even removed them, but she had to be honest with herself. That would be highly unlikely.

She had to prepare herself by way of explanation; not easy when you do not have all the facts. If they had been there, the Reeve's security had been penetrated, but how could that possibly be? No one should have known about the vault, let alone how to access it from above and below.

Drawing her breath, she picked up her phone, hit redial and waited to hear a Spanish greeting at the other end.

She closed her eyes, knowing that security measures being breached had not happened at any headquarters the world over in a very long time. It would get talked about throughout her Order with much detriment to her personal reputation.

After listening to the phone ringing at the other end for thirty seconds or so, she gave up and slowly put the phone back down. Her Head of Order must be busy. She didn't mind that as it gave her more time to think.

Approaching 2pm

The car hurtled around the bend into the dead-end road that she now recognised; this time, there would be no faffing around looking for secret entrances. Jessica reached inside her jacket pocket, pulled out her pin badge and fixed it to her lapel.

She felt the brakes of the car depress beneath her feet as the car pulled to a stop at the semicircle at the end of the road.

Time being of the essence, Jessica jumped out quickly and went straight to the scanning post and bent over, her pin found the mark of the scanner immediately.

She looked around to ensure that she wasn't being watched as she heard the sounds of moving metal from beneath her feet as the trees in front of her gave way.

With a few steps, she was back inside the car, making a mental note not to bang the car horn this time as she went down the driveway.

Glancing across at Nahla, her paws twitching, she hoped that she may get some answers as to exactly what was going on. The car sped forward towards the grand archway and as she passed through, she could see the trees in her rear-view mirror moving back into their original place.

Staring at the expanse of the mansion house as it became ever closer, the building and their gardens were beautiful. When she has her own office, she hoped that she would be able to enjoy them more. The statues looked fascinating telling stories from the past presumably. It may even be that Lady Nubia may not be quite so rude once she settled in, but she doubted that somehow.

As the main entrance came into view, her car veered round to the left of the building. She could hear the gravel beneath the wheels being disturbed in, what would appear to be, the most silent places deep in the countryside of North Wales.

As the car veered to the right, at the end of the building, she could see Nubia at the door waiting for her.

She jolted forward in her seat as the car stopped abruptly, dust rising up from underneath the wheels. She sat in the driver's seat, waiting to see if Nubia would come forward. After a few seconds, it was clear she had no intention of moving. Jessica released her seat belt and opened the door to get out.

"Good afternoon Madam Nubia," she said without response as she walked around her car and opened the passenger door. "Come on Nahla, let's take you inside." She very gently pulled Nahla to her chest, holding her with both hands and supporting her head. She swiped at the car door with her backside to close it.

Why Nubia had a frown across her face, she had no idea.

"There you go. That wasn't so difficult, was it?"

"Well, it was quite challenging, if I'm honest, Madam Nubia."

"Pass the cat to me."

It was not lost on Jessica that, yet again, there was no please or thank you.

As Nubia took Nahla from Jessica, she studied the cat, its pain was very evident. "Oh, my poor dear," she said whilst stroking Nahla's head.

It was only now, in their second meeting, that Jessica had witnessed any emotion from the Curator of the Order. Maybe she was human after all, but the jury was out on that one.

"Right, we need to know when Khepri is coming back from the vets so you can change the cats around again. Mildred will know straight away that Khepri is not Nahla."

"Well, yes, my Lady, but how on earth am I going to do that?"

The Curator's frown spread as she looked up at Jessica and sighed, shaking her head. "Well, you are seeing Mildred later, aren't you? Ask her about the wellbeing of her cat; she's bound to tell you. They will probably keep Khepri in overnight for observations."

"You don't think they will do tests on her, do you?"

"Let's hope not. That could cause another problem. Monitor it will you? Let me know if you hear anything untoward."

Nubia turned around to walk back into the mansion. "Step in. I have something here for you that may help."

Jessica followed, wobbling on the gravel as she went through the archway into the dimly lit room. The door closed behind her.

"Over there." The Curator nodded at an old table on the left-hand side. Jessica could see what looked to be a very old camera. "Take that, just in case you need it."

Jessica walked to the table and picked up what she guessed to be a Polaroid camera. Confused, she turned to the Curator and shook her head. "I don't understand. A camera? It looks ancient."

"Far from it, 30 years or so is very young in our timeline; besides, you should never mock the old, Jessica."

Not for the first time, Jessica felt like she was being told off.

"That may buy you some time. You just press the red button with it pointed directly at your target."

"My target?" Jessica said with some shock.

"Yes, your target. The flash will disrupt the brain for approximately 8-10 seconds and no more."

Jessica looked back at the camera.

"It may help you do, what did you call it, a switcharoo?"

Jessica looked down at the floor in embarrassment.

"I assure you it works. I took it from the security wing of the Escarrabin earlier."

"The Escarrabin, my Lady?"

The Curator closed her eyes at her slip of the tongue. "Yes, the Escarrabin, our security officers. You will come to see them in time when you settle."

Jessica watched the Curator as she stroked Nahla and turned to walk away. "Let me know if there is anything that I need to be aware of Jessica."

"Um, yes, I will do. Lady Nubia, may I ask something?" Jessica watched the short stature of Nubia turn around to face her. "What is wrong with Nahla?"

"We don't know, but we can't have outsiders assessing our own. It's as simple as that."

Jessica nodded. "I see." She did not see at all and was reasonably sure that she was not being told the full story.

"Well, off you go then, you have a gathering to attend. You'll be a Degree Level 6 next time I see you."

Jessica smiled as she watched the Curator disappear with Nahla. "Let yourself out. Your car is ready for you." The Curator's closing words echoed throughout the old room.

Standing there holding the old camera, looking at the flickering candlelight, she felt a wave of discomfort in this creepy old place and quickly made her way to the exit.

The symbol of the Order was lit next to the door. She lifted her pin towards it and was relieved to see the door opening.

Her car was already running as she got in and took her seat. Pulling her door closed, the car immediately moved away. She watched the door into the mansion re-close and glanced across at the old camera on the seat where Nahla lay only moments ago. She cast a thought for Mildred and the worry she must have.

As the car pulled around to the front of the house and down the driveway, she looked up at the imposing frontage. A couple of floors up, a tall lady in a business suit was watching from above. I wonder who that could be. She didn't give it any more thought as the car took her back through the archway.

"Hello, is that Mildred?"

"Yes, Mildred speaking."

"Hello Mildred, I'm Julia, one of the partners at Castle Hollow Veterinary Practice."

"Oh yes, how is my Missy, please?"

"Well, I'm very pleased to say that she has made a full recovery and everything is well."

"She's awake and has stopped shaking?" Mildred said with excitement and glee.

"She seems completely normal, Mildred. Quite odd, actually. She just seemed to make a miraculous recovery. Funny, really, we did not know what was wrong and were talking about possible surgery when she just seemed to wake up. I'm sure our cats understand us some times."

"Well, my Missy is a very special cat."

"I'm quite sure she is," responded Julia, positive that she could hear clapping coming from the other end of the phone. "I can tell that you are happy Mildred and so are we, but to be on the safe side, we would like to keep her in overnight just for observation."

"Oh, really?"

Julia could hear that the clapping from the other end had stopped.

"It is customary, Mildred. In truth and I must be honest with you, we didn't do anything, but Sarah did mention an abnormal heartbeat, so for this reason, it's best to be safe. I hope that you agree?"

"Well, yes, I guess so. If you think it's best. I thought Sarah was going to call me?"

There was a brief pause at the other end of the phone before the voice resumed. "She intended to but has had to go out on another call. However, she will bring Missy back to you tomorrow morning."

"Well, that is good news Julia, I'm so happy I cannot tell you!"

"I'm glad to be the bearer of good news and you have our telephone number if you need to call us. You can email us too if you would like."

"No, just phone, thank you. I don't have a computer."

"Oh really, that's quite rare these days, but as you wish, Mildred. Call us if you need to. If not and everything is okay overnight, Missy will be back with you tomorrow."

"Yes, I'm quite old fashioned and do without technology, but I'm so, so pleased Julia. Thank you very much for calling."

"You are welcome. Goodbye, Mildred."

"Goodbye. Thank you."

She put the cat phone down with something to finally smile about, clapping her hands together with joy. Thank goodness for that. What a scare Missy had given her. She raised a hand to her chest and took a few deep breaths.

"I think a celebration cup of tea is in order." She laughed, realising that she was talking to herself with no Missy to listen to her. She went into the kitchen, turned on the gas and filled the kettle. As she turned around, her eyes immediately latched onto the cat birthday cards on the side.

She bit her lip in thought. Well, I guess there is no reason for me not to go to the gathering now.

Looking at her clock, she could see that it was approaching 3pm. Jessica was due to pick her up around 6ish.

A rush of excitement washed over her. She was going out to meet her own kind, lovers of cats, enthusiasts of cats and she was determined to have a lovely evening.

I guess I had better start to get ready, she considered, kicking her shoes off across the kitchen floor. There was much to think about, including what she would wear. She had better check her wardrobe again.

Approaching 4pm

The Reeve was back at her window, having heard the disturbance outside of other Escarrabin arriving at Loxley. They were scheduled to arrive today, but her mind was now on the use of them outside of their usual ceremonial duties. They may have a more serious role to play with troubling events of potentially missing keys and a rogue Watcher.

She watched them filter off to their side entrance into the Manor House. She had no idea why the near 6th Degree elder, Jessica, had visited again. She suspected that it had something to do with Nubia, but her thoughts were focused on the below for now. Anything else could wait.

She went over to her phone to try her head of Order again.

The phone must have rung at least twenty times. She was about to hang up when she suddenly heard a muffled voice at the other end.

"Hello, my Lady?"

"Si, Reeve. I am here."

"I did try to reach you earlier."

"I have only just returned from the archives. These things take time; I had to look very deeply into the past. Now tell me, did you go to the statue?"

"Yes, my Lady, I did." The Reeve swallowed and looked around her room to check she was alone. "The keys, I could not find them. I found two empty hooks that were below the word 'Inferious.' I suspect that is where they should be." The Reeve could sense the discomfort at the other end of the phone.

"Reeve, this is most serious!"

"I know, my Lady. Is there any way that my predecessor may have removed them, or they were moved to somewhere else?"

"I think that to be highly unlikely and we must assume not."

They both fell silent.

"Reeve, if those keys have been taken, that is one thing, but how could that Watcher have got down there and provided a successful scan of your hand? It is only your hand that allows the vault to be opened," she paused before continuing, "we have to assume that someone is helping him, someone who can access certain information. In any event, it sounds like this Watcher is well informed. This may have been planned for some time. Showing up outside your main gates and now the missing keys confirm that he wanted to be caught."

"Those thoughts had occurred to me as well, my Lady."

"Reeve of Loxley, your security has been breached while you are in control and you have not been in post for very long. This will not bode well for you."

Her face drained of colour. "Yes, I am aware of this, my Lady."

"The first thing to do is to find out if the third key is missing. The iron wall will not open without it."

"I understand. Have you been able to find out anything from the archives?"

"Si, I have. This is a two-part process. First, you need a key to open where the main key is hidden. If the Watcher had got to this key, you would probably already know about it, so it may well be safe."

"I understand. Where do I find it, my Lady?"

"It should be safe with Lady Safiya, your Head of House. She, however, will not know the significance of it."

"She has no idea?"

"No, but if the process has been followed, she will have it."

"Will she tell me where it is? How I can get to it?"

"No, she will show it to you."

"She will show me?" The Reeve replied with surprise.

"It is a small ring. She should be wearing it. Within the ring is a key. This will open the door that contains the main key and the priority key to the wall of iron."

"I see, my Lady. However, once I have the ring key, where is this door that is to be opened?"

"You are sitting on it, Reeve of Loxley."

The Reeve's eyes flashed as she quickly jumped up and took a few paces backwards from her chair.

"Retrieve the key and find within the chair where the master key is stored." The Reeve didn't offer a response other than a silent nod of the head. "Reeve listen, this is very important. Whether the key is there or not, what lies below will need to be investigated and action taken. As yet, I have not been able to find out what this creature is. I need to return to the archives to see if I can find anything that will help you. Do not, under any circumstance, go down there until you know what you are facing. For now, I suggest you speak to your head of the Escarrabin. Make sure they remain vigilant as you do not want to cause a panic, but do not go below until you have the facts to hand."

"Yes, my Lady, I understand."

"Go and see your Head of House. I will call you when I have found out more."

"Yes, my Lady, I will do that."

"Find the key Reeve and put a stop to whatever this Watcher is trying to do!"

"Yes, my Lady. I will do my very best."

"I must go."

The Reeve heard the phone disconnect in Spain. She placed her phone down, not taking her eyes off her chair. She pulled it back from her desk and circled it a couple of times, crouching down to look underneath it. How could this possibly be? She only bought it from IKEA a few weeks back and assembled it herself? She was feeling her way along the arm supports when she suddenly stopped, shook her head and looked up at the ceiling. "Idiot!" She kicked the chair to the side watching it glide across the floor on its wheels.

She let out a deep sigh as she went into one of the adjoining rooms and stared at the ancient chair that she had replaced. It was so uncomfortable to sit on, no matter how many cushions she put on it. It was heavy and cumbersome and looked more like a throne than something you would sit on in your office.

As she dragged it away from the wall, she felt along the heavy oak arm supports for anything that resembled a keyhole. Her Elder had said that it was a tiny key, so she felt her way carefully, but nothing was obvious. Crouching down to look underneath, the elaborate chair design carved into the dark oak wood made it very difficult to see. She took both of the chair's back legs in her hands and lifted it upwards, spinning it over to see the underside clearly in the light.

"Well, I never." In the top right-hand corner, there looked to be a small keyhole. She pushed at the panelling, but nothing moved; it was sturdy and clearly well made. Wrapping her knuckles on the wood all around the keyhole, she listened for the hollow sound of a hidden compartment. She considered a sledgehammer, as unethical as it may be to destroy this grand old uncomfortable chair. Taking a couple of steps backwards, she gave it some serious thought. Still, she knew the Order of old do not do things in half measures and there could be a security mechanism inside that could damage the key, even if it were there in the first place. It was no good and she couldn't delay any further. She would have to see the Head of the House. There was no way around it. She knew full well that Safiya would be asking questions and she didn't want to give answers at this time, not that she had many anyway. A security breach was very serious. If Safiya didn't need to know, then she would avoid the questions completely. It was troubling, but she would have to face up to it along with any other action that may be taken against her in the future. She needed to prepare for an awkward meeting.

++++

Mildred shuffled out of the shower and raced for her phone with an old towel wrapped around her. "Number 1 Rocke Road," she answered with a couple of puffs of breath.

"Mildred, it's Daphne."

"Oh, hello, Daphne, lovely to hear from you." She was indeed pleased to hear from her Elder.

"I'm just checking in. I trust that you are going to the gathering later on?"

"Oh yes, I'm very excited about it; although it was a close call, I very nearly wasn't going to go."

"Heavens Mildred, why ever not?"

"Oh, it's Missy. She has been terribly unwell. I've been very worried about her the last couple of days."

"Did you call Fennaway?"

"I did, but I was not very impressed with her level of service, so I called someone else."

"You called someone else, Mildred?"

"Yes, I called a vet at Castle Hollow. Much better."

There was silence at the other end of the phone.

"Daphne, are you still there?"

"Where is Missy now, Mildred?"

She could sense concern in her tone of voice. "Well, I'm very pleased to say that she is much better, but they are keeping her in overnight, just for safety; it's procedure apparently. Kamilah Fennaway tried to talk to Missy down the phone. Can you believe it?" Mildred was in fits of laughter as she spoke.

"Err, that is indeed unusual." Daphne gave out a small fake laugh.

Mildred continued to laugh before realising that her laughs were not being matched from the other end.

"Mildred, do you know whether this other vet will run tests on Missy?"

"Tests, Daphne? Well, I have no idea. I'm guessing not. I hope not. Apparently, as soon as Missy arrived there, she got much better. Strange, isn't it?"

"Yes, that is indeed very odd, Mildred."

It was not lost on Mildred that Daphne's voice became more serious the longer the conversation went on. She sat on her bed as the water fell from her hair, somewhat perplexed with this sudden change of tone.

"Anyway, I'm glad you are going, Mildred. I shall see you later on."

"Yes. Lady Jessica is collecting me. We should be there at around 7.30 I would think."

"Yes, I know. I saw her a couple of days ago and she did mention it. She's never given me a lift anywhere, so I'm guessing she has taken a shine to you, Mildred."

"Oh really? Well, that's nice to hear," although the use of the word 'shine' again was perturbing.

"Yes, isn't it?"

Mildred noted the words coming from her Elder were still somewhat odd.

"Well, must dash. I was just checking to see that you are okay. I look forward to seeing you later, Mildred."

"Thank you, Daphne. I look forward to seeing you too. Goodbye for now."

"Goodbye, Mildred."

Daphne terminated the call very concerned with what she had heard and pondered for a few moments.

Flicking through her phone book, she found her Elder's phone number and dialled it. It only took a few rings before she answered. It was evident from the background noise that her Elder was in the car.

"Lady Jessica, it's Daphne."

"Yes, I know, your number flashed up on my phone. I'm driving at the moment, you are on the speaker."

"Okay, I'll be brief. I don't wish to talk out of turn, but I've just spoken to Mildred, the one from Rocke Road that is and she tells me that another vet has her cat, Nahla."

"Yes, we are aware of it. It's all in hand."

"Oh, you already know, my Lady?"

"Yes, apparently Mildred didn't get along with Fennaway, but we have taken precautions. It was quite the security operation, but it would appear I'm a natural."

"I see." Daphne had no idea how Jessica could already know about this. "I just wanted to bring it to your attention, just in case any tests had been undertaken. I thought it prudent to let you know."

"Thank you and we do appreciate that, but it's all in hand, Daphne. I saw to it personally. Please do not tell Mildred."

"Okay, that's good and no, I won't say anything."

"I'm driving back from North Wales, but I should make it back in time to collect Mildred for the gathering. I'll see you later tonight then."

"Yes, okay, my Lady. I look forward to it, thank you."

"Thank you, Daphne. Goodbye for now."

As Jessica disconnected the call, her thoughts immediately turned with some concern to Khepri, hoping that no testing had been undertaken on her cat. She swallowed at the thought of it in worry, shaking her head to clear her thoughts. "She's too smart. She'll be fine."

Glancing at the navigator, there was still an hours drive before arriving home, dependent on traffic. "Car, can't you go any faster?"

It didn't and stuck to the speed limit as she crossed her arms and sat back, letting the car do the work for her.

✛✛✛✛

The Reeve had ensured her old fortified door was secured as she walked towards the lobby area. The four heads of the Clerics were looking down at their work in an all too familiar pose. As she passed them, she looked over to see what they were doing as they shuffled papers and wrote notes.

She passed by two other corridors before joining one of the grand staircases that flowed throughout the centre of the house.

The red-carpeted staircases and the viewing balconies in-between offered views directly to the glass dome at the top of the house and the grand lobby below.

The quarters of Lady Safiya could be found on the fourth floor. This was the most opulent part of the house. The quarters themselves were not open to other Elders and visitation was strictly by invitation only. As one of the most senior Elders in the United Kingdom, Lady Safiya enjoyed peace when she could get it and disliked being disturbed at the best of times.

As the Reeve headed across the fourth floor towards her quarters, two of the Escarrabin were guarding her entrance door. Their backs became immediately straightened and their chins lifted as they saw the Reeve approaching.

They both nodded together, "Ma'am," as she arrived at the doorway. She nodded back to them as the Escarrabin on the right opened the door for her. She followed the security officer into the waiting area and watched her leave closing the door behind her.

The Reeve walked forward to a solitary Cleric, who handled administration for the senior Lady of the House.

"I would like to speak with Lady Safiya, please."

The Cleric looked up at the Reeve. From underneath her hood she could immediately see the paleness of her skin and her white eyes.

"Do you have an appointment, Lady Reeve? I'm not aware of it? The Lady of the House is very busy today."

"I do not, but I must see her straight away."

The Cleric stood up. "Wait here, my Lady Reeve, I will see."

The Reeve nodded and took a couple of steps backwards to survey the grand surroundings of Lady Safiya's chambers.

The walls were covered in wooden panelling, but no artwork was affixed to any of the walls throughout. Only one solitary painting was hung on the wall behind the Cleric's desk of the Lady herself holding one of her cats. The Reeve stepped towards the grandfather clock. It was much older than hers and had discoloured slightly over the years. The pendulum was sealed within and could not be seen swinging back and forth, only heard.

The heavy wooden door to the left of the Reeve opened. "Please come through my Lady. She will join you shortly."

She watched as the Cleric stepped forward and ushered her into the sitting room. "Thank you," the Reeve said, passing her. The door closed. She took stock of the room while she waited.

She was stood on a wooden floor with a huge rug that covered most of the room. The chairs were old and no doubt very valuable. A huge chandelier hung above her. Old candleholders were fixed above the wood panelling on the walls, but the panelling only went halfway up the room's height. A stone layer rose above those up to the mahogany coloured, panelled ceiling.

Her eyes were distracted by a long yawn from one of Safiya's cats. The Siberian cat looked at the Reeve and with disinterest, immediately closed her eyes and went back to sleep upon a cushion on one of the grand old chairs. Alicia, her eldest cat, did not enjoy her sleep being interrupted. She suspected Safiya would not welcome the interruption either.

The creaking of floorboards could be heard coming from another room as Lady Safiya walked in, dragging her supporting cane with her. She used this on occasions when out of public view. Two of her cats followed her into the room.

"Reeve, I was just made aware that you wanted to see me. The Cleric tells me it's urgent."

"Yes, Ma'am. I'm very sorry to disturb you."

"Well, as long as it is important. We haven't spent much time together. I hope you are settling in well." She ushered her cane towards a chair directly in front of the Reeve, directing her to sit.

"Yes, and thank you, Ma'am."

"Truthfully, I'm glad of the break. Gathering days are tiring days, Reeve. So much going on at home and abroad, too much to organise." She gave a faint smile. "I feel old."

Perched on the end of the chair with her legs together, the Reeve offered a faint smile in response.

"So what is troubling you?"

"It may be something and yet it may be nothing, Ma'am."

"Isn't it always?"

The Reeve watched as the senior Elder took a seat, propping her cane against her chair. One of her cats jumped up on her lap.

"I don't wish to trouble you with much of it, but I spoke with my Elder in Spain today."

"Yes, I know of whom you speak, Lady Berenike of the Order of Reeves."

"Yes, Ma'am." The Reeve swallowed as she gathered her words. "She informs me that you have something I need. A key, to be precise."

The colour drained from Lady Safiya's face.

"I can tell that you know of what I speak, Ma'am." The Reeve watched as the Head of the House moved her right hand over her left.

"Why do you ask this of me, Reeve?" Her tone changed to one of caution and concern.

"Because I'm told that I may need it, Ma'am." She watched as she saw one of the most respected Elders look towards the floor in thought.

There was silence between them before she looked up to the Reeve. "Understand this. This key was passed to me by my Elder, who was hugely respected. It was passed to her by her Elder and so on and so forth. I was told, as was she, that if the day comes that the key is ever asked for, it would be because of times of great peril. So I ask you this, is this a time of great peril, Reeve?"

The Reeve thought long and hard about her answer. "I can only hope not, but there is something that I need to check and that key, the one that you wear on your finger, can help solve part of a problem."

The senior Elder smiled slightly, but it was not one of happiness. "So you know that it is on my finger, you Reeves are very well informed."

The Reeve was without words and could only offer a slight smile by way of response.

"I know that even an Elder of my level is never aware of all of the facts. I know how secretive the Order of the Reeves is. If I pass this to you, it's not because I want to. I pass it to you hoping that whatever it is that you know, you do the right thing."

She removed the old ring from her finger, studied it, placed it in the palm of her right hand and offered it forward. "I've worn this for a very long time. It is a tradition of times past, so please do bring it back to me if you can."

The Reeve stood up and walked over, bent down to her open palm and reached out to take the ring. "Not so fast, Reeve," she closed her palm again. "Are we in trouble? Do the Grand Council need to be informed of what has happened here?"

"All I can offer you, Ma'am, is confirmation of an investigation. If the time comes that decisive actions need to be taken, I will inform you as soon as it is practically possible. For now, I do not want to be responsible for alarm if it's not necessary."

"You are still asking a question of something that has been kept secret for hundreds of years, Reeve and as I'm not an old idiot, I have to conclude that the matter is serious."

"I will endeavour to find out, Ma'am."

She opened her palm and nodded for the Reeve to take the ring.

The Reeve slipped the ring into one of her jacket pockets, not wanting to examine it in front of Lady Safiya. "Thank you, Ma'am."

"You had best go and do whatever it is that you need to do, Reeve. I do not know what that key opens."

The Reeve looked on as Lady Safiya leant on her cane to stand up, her cat leaping to the floor.

"Do come back with answers Reeve, you all have your secrets, but we have some of our own too."

The Reeve gave a slight smile and nodded, heading for the door.

As Lady Safiya watched the Head of Security leave, she slumped back into her chair again. She had told the truth, she did not know what the key opened, but she knew that potentially peril may not be far away.

Chapter Twenty Six:

THE SERPENT'S WHEEL

FRIDAY AFTERNOON 4.40PM

Nubia stood propped against her desk, having smuggled Nahla into the mansion house. The black cat with the white-tipped tail lay upon her couch, but she was far from peaceful. Nubia had made her as comfortable as possible, but her discomfort was clear to be seen by untrained eyes.

Leaning over to her phone, she dialled the vet, the one she trusted that is.

"Kamilah, just to let you know, Nahla is here with me."

"Really, how did you do that in the end?"

"Never mind. I know people as well, you know." She spoke with smugness in her tone.

"I have no doubt, Nubia." A small ripple of laughter came from Kamilah. "What is her condition?"

"Not good. She is still as you described. If her condition does not improve, I may need to call you over, but in truth, I'm not sure what you would be able to do for her."

"It is difficult, Nubia, no doubt. The last time this happened to one of our own, events did not play out well."

Nubia chewed at her fingers. "Yes, I am aware of this despite how long ago it was."

"And what of Mildred?"

"She thinks her cat is at the other vets, which has bought us some time. How much, I can't be sure, but I should be able to find out more later."

"My phone is always open for you if you need me, Nubia, you know that."

"Thank you, my friend. I will come back to you if there is anything to update you with."

"Okay, we'll speak later on."

Nubia looked over at her clock. Jessica should be picking up Mildred in a couple of hours or so. Hopefully, she will be able to find out how much time they have and how long she can keep Mildred's cat at Loxley, before further potential problems arise. She was certain that she had done the right thing in protecting one of their own, but it was never far from her mind that in so doing, she may have created entirely new complications.

✝✝✝✝

It had been a few years since Mildred had worn any makeup. She hadn't worn any at the last two gatherings, but today was different. After the long week and the stresses of Missy and her mystery illness, she needed some pampering and importantly, to feel good again.

There were no fixes in her dresser for the wrinkles across her forehead or the crow's feet around her eyes. Still, she did have one lipstick and an old brush for her hair that had become somewhat unkempt of late.

She reflected on her earlier call with Daphne. Her tone certainly changed when she mentioned calling the other vet. She shook her head slightly; there were some strange things about the cat club. Maybe this evening will offer some more answers, or maybe she should start asking more questions.

Hair still a little damp from her shower, she tugged at it with the brush, screwing up her face as she pulled through the knots in her thick curly shoulder-length auburn hair. It was usually tied up, but this evening she would try something different. She had new(ish) clothing and wanted to impress, so her hair would be worn down and that was that.

The thickness of the matted knots would mean slow progress, just as well she allowed herself a couple of hours to get ready. With a deep puff of her cheeks, she let go of the brush, which hung tangled, swinging in her hair. This was going to be much more difficult than she realised.

Her doors were locked behind her as the Reeve stood over the heavy, cumbersome and now upside-down chair.

She reached into her jacket pocket and pulled out the ring key. In the privacy of her quarters, it was the first time she was to examine it. Her predecessors at Loxley had probably never seen it or even known of its existence. She held the small ring up to assess it. The design was crude, very old and looked uncomfortable to wear. She doubted it would fit any of her fingers and smiled slightly, imagining Raysmau trying to put it on.

She could see a tiny fold in the design that allowed the key to be worn flat against the finger. Using both hands, she very gently pulled at the ring, allowing the key to extend. Even at maximum extension, it must have only been an inch or so in length.

As the Reeve knelt down on one knee, she took a deep breath and placed the small key into the keyhole on the underside of the chair and gently turned. It was stiff and unmoving as she applied more pressure. The key started to turn slowly to the right and she heard a click come from within the chair. In the centre panel of the chair, a small, perfectly cut square of solid wood fell backwards into a hidden compartment that had appeared as soon as the lock gave way.

The Reeve's hand shook slightly with anticipation as she pushed it into the hole to pull out the fallen piece of wood from the hidden compartment. Taking the perfectly hand-cut square of wood out and placing it on the floor, she peered inside the compartment surrounded by dark stained wood. It was impossible to see into it. She bit at her lip. Placing her hand into something that she could not see filled her with some trepidation. As she was right-handed and in case there was some sort of protective measure, she sacrificed her left hand, pushing it forward and feeling around with the tips of her fingers.

The hole was not very deep. Her eyebrows lifted as she felt what appeared to be a cloth bag. She immediately dragged it out.

Back in her office, she sat at her desk and opened the folded cloth bag. There was a small waft of dust as it opened. The object fell onto her desk with a heavy thud. A perfect circle, about six inches round, made of what she guessed to be iron, lay upon her desk after being hidden away for hundreds of years. There was a centrepiece that was fixed from multiple points around the circle. She estimated the thickness of the centrepiece to be around two inches wide. The way the centrepiece was secured made the key look like some form of small steering wheel.

However, the creature's head in the centre of the circle she recognised straight away as one of the feared creatures of old; cats feared them as much as they feared rats.

She stared at the head of the serpent and knew straight away that she had found the hidden key. She looked up, now certain of knowledge and knowing. The wall of iron could not be opened and the Watcher was bound to fail.

Friday 5.06 pm

"Mildred, it's Jessica. Are you okay?"

"Oh, hello, Lady Jessica. I'm very good, thank you, feeling much better now. It's been a trying week."

Mildred was almost dressed and ready to go. Just a few finishing touches to be applied. She was still due to investigate an old tube of mascara she'd found.

"Really?" Jessica said, trying to act surprised. "Well, I've been out all day, so I should be with you in around an hour or so, I would think."

"Great, thank you, Lady Jessica. I'm very much looking forward to seeing everyone."

"You're welcome. See you in a bit then."

Mildred put the phone down and returned to the bathroom to assess herself in the mirror. Her shoes were the cleanest out of the three pairs she owned, her stockings were a little creased in places, but they would have to do as it had been some time since she had bought new ones. Mr Franks did not sell them. Even if he did, that was not a conversation she would contemplate having with him, so charity shop stockings sufficed.

She had ironed her brown pencil skirt and as she turned to look at herself in the mirror, she could see from behind that her stockings were really quite baggy at the back of her ankles.

She raised her eyebrows; there's no way she could not wear them, that would mean bare legs. She could see hairs jutting out through the old stockings, so she discarded that idea straight away.

Her white floral shirt was neatly buttoned. She admired her handmade creation, quite possibly one of the best cardigans she had ever seen; it would certainly be talked about.

She slipped on her long heavy jacket, which was lying on her bed. It was the height of summer, but she had been saying to herself all week that first impressions counted. Therefore, the fake fur stole would need to be added just the same. As she wrapped the stole around her neck and un-tucked her now brushed, long hair, there was still one remaining item, the piece de resistance. The beautiful black cloche hat with the red outline of a cat was to be worn with pride; she had paid £4 for it after all.

With the exception of her bag, she was ready. Although, she mustn't forget the invitation and the cards.

And of course the fish paste sandwiches.

The Reeve had barely let go of the secret key since unlocking the chair. It was reasonably heavy with a pattern of teeth throughout one side. She had not seen a wheel-shaped key before and presumed it fitted into a slot, which you turn like any other traditional key. She held it out in front of her, pretending to place it into something. By gripping the head of the serpent that came forward from the centre of the iron wheel, you could get leverage of sorts.

She placed it gently on the desk and picked up the phone. Her Head of Order had said that she would call her, but it could not wait given the circumstances.

She tried calling, but there was no answer at the other end. Her Lady must still be in the archives. Finding such information was never going to be a straightforward process.

The clock in her room struck 6pm; darkness would be falling in a few hours. Irrespective of what her Head of Order may discover, going into the below after dark was not an option. If this one Watcher was uniting the others, it was too much of a risk. They were most active after the light had fallen. This was when their strength was at its highest.

Feeling around her neck, she released the clasp of her necklace and removed the amulet that had sat on it, placing it into the drawer of her desk. Her silver necklace was reasonably sturdy and she hoped that it would take the weight of the key that contained the serpent.

If no one was to be trusted, she would have to wear it for now.

Friday 6.09pm

Jessica arrived at Mildred's, this time parking directly outside her gate. Memories of her surveillance earlier flooded straight into her mind. She looked at the passenger footwell, gasping as she spotted the huge glasses with the clown nose on the floor. She unclipped her seat belt and leant over, throwing them onto the back seat along with the binoculars and the newspaper.

She felt a tinge of guilt, knowing full well that Mildred had no idea that she had been there earlier and that her beloved cat Missy was not where she was supposed to be.

Play it cool, Jessica, play it cool, she repeated in her mind as she banged the car horn.

Mildred instantly came to her window after hearing the sound from the car outside.

Mildred's blue door opened and Jessica saw an arm appear and place a huge bag on the path outside. She watched with a puzzled expression as Mildred locked her door with her back to her. "Oh, my goodness, what is she wearing?" Jessica muttered as she saw Mildred struggle a little as she lifted the bag and waddled towards the gate. Jessica pushed the button to lower the passenger window as Mildred approached and leaned her head inside. Jessica was momentarily startled by the pink lipstick Mildred was wearing. As she smiled, she could see that lipstick was caked over some of her teeth too.

"Hello, Lady Jessica!"

Jessica's wide eyes acknowledged the overexcited and highly enthusiastic Mildred.

"Can I put my bag on the back seat?"

"Yes, of course, Mildred. Please do."

Mildred opened the door and immediately spotted the glasses. "Ha! What do you have those for?" Jessica looked in horror as Mildred picked up the glasses with the red nose.

"Oh, I went to a children's party a few days ago." It was the best that Jessica could come up with off the top of her head.

"He-he, bet you looked a right clown in those!"

Jessica looked back towards the road and frowned. "Yes, quite."

Mildred tossed the glasses to the side, placed her heavy bag down and got in the car.

"You will have to excuse the state of my car, Mildred. I'm not much of a car person."

"That's because you are a cat person."

Jessica tried her best to smile but found Mildred's pink teeth quite the distraction.

That's okay, Lady Jessica. I have bits and bobs around my house as well. We have to live comfortably, don't we?"

"Yes, we do." Jessica watched Mildred apply her seatbelt. She immediately looked Jessica in the face and beamed a pink smile. Awkwardly returning the smile, she spoke, trying to avert her gaze. "Please just call me Jessica, Mildred. No need for Lady."

Mildred leaned forward to her and clapped her hands with excitement. "As you wish, Jessica."

Slightly bemused, Jessica started the car and pushed down with the clutch. Mildred glanced down at the very shiny black heels that Jessica was wearing and noticed the amount of leg she was showing.

Mildred coughed under her breath, "well, you look nice, Jessica."

"Thank you, Mildred. It's just a little black number. It's not often that I get out."

"Yes, I know what you mean," said Mildred as she looked down at her wrinkled stockings and scuffed shoes. She waited for Jessica to return the compliment, but it didn't seem to be coming any time soon.

Jessica's nostrils flared as she looked around the car. "Can you smell that, Mildred? What is it?"

"Oh, ha-ha, it's fish paste sandwiches. I have three plates of them."

Jessica opened her window slightly. "Oh, I see, that's nice."

"It's not far from here, Mildred. I think we should be there in about 20 minutes or so."

"I've never been to Dovercote Mansion before; it sounds very grand indeed."

Jessica looked over and smiled. "I've been a couple of times. It's quite nice."

As they left Rocke Road, Jessica bit at her lips, knowing full well that she would have to ask the question fairly soon.

"So how is Na..." she corrected herself, "how is Missy?"

Mildred started waving her arms around, speaking at a hundred miles per hour, "oh, I've had the most traumatic time, Jessica. I can't tell you. Missy has been very unwell. I called the vet that Lady Daphne recommended. She was useless, so I had to call another vet. It's been a terrible couple of days."

"Oh, that sounds very upsetting. I would be lost without my cats." Jessica's mind had started to wander as she worried about Khepri.

"Something about an irregular heartbeat."

Jessica took her eyes off the road to look at Mildred as she said this. "That sounds troubling." Jessica returned her gaze to the front, deep in thought.

"They've kept her in overnight to observe her."

Jessica took a deep breath. "Well, that's good." Her heart was racing as she tried to figure everything out. "So when does Missy come back then?"

"Tomorrow morning."

"What time?"

Mildred looked straight at her driver. "Excuse me?"

"Oh, I'm sorry Mildred, what time are you expecting Missy back?"

"Erm, I'm not sure. Does it matter?"

Jessica smiled. "No, not at all. I just wondered if it were likely to be early. If so, we had better not keep you out too late tonight!" Well done, not bad, Jessica thought to herself.

"They didn't say and I guess they would have done, so I would presume mid-morning, so there is no rush. I do hope my Missy will be okay."

"So do I, Mildred. So do I."

Jessica's mind had wandered off again.

✝✝✝✝

"I know, it's the strangest thing. I've never seen a layout like it."

Thomas and Brooke both shook their heads in agreement as they set the tables.

"Only 45 guests, the bar is to remain closed and no food service."

"Maybe this cat club is broke!" Thomas quipped at his supervisor at Dovercote Mansion as they studied the seating plan provided in advance.

"Well, they paid the hire rate for the room in cash. They want eight urns of hot water to be provided for tea and alcohol is only on the tables with the fewest guests. I've never heard anything like it. Get this, as soon as they are here, they insist they must not be disturbed; all the curtains are to be drawn." Thomas and Brooke both looked at each other with some astonishment and laughed.

"The crazy cat ladies roam amongst us," Brooke giggled, prompting further laughter from Thomas and Mary, their supervisor.

"You know, get how weird this is." Brooke and Thomas walked over to Mary to listen as she looked over her shoulder and then lowered her voice. "It's ticket only right, for this cat meeting and they are bringing their own security."

"What! Ha-ha. Are you serious?"

"Very!" Mary responded instantly with laughter.

"Security for a cat club meeting? That's the state of the world now."

Mary looked at Thomas on hearing his remark, "and what would you know about that? You are barely out of school," she smiled.

"You'd be surprised!"

"I don't think either of us wants to know, thank you," Brooke replied as she finished setting one of the tables.

"Tom, can you check the projector is working okay, please? Apparently, they are giving some sort of talk."

"Pictures of cats probably. God, can you imagine the boredom."

Mary smiled and shook her head at Tom. "No, not really," she waved her arm for him to switch the projector on. "Anyway, they'll be arriving soon, so let's get a move on."

Mary stepped back and looked around the vast room that only held nine round tables, save the tables where the tea and food were going to be; whatever food they were bringing with them, of course. She was distracted as she looked through the windows and the doors that led to the patio area outside. She could see cars starting to arrive, double blinking in shock at some of the beautiful vehicles that were parking up.

"There must be some money in this." She turned her head to look at her staff and nodded towards the outside. "Maybe I should join this cat club!"

Shula and Kassia from the Escarrabin Order walked through the grand entrance of Dovercote Mansion towards the reception desk, where they were politely greeted by Michelle.

Michelle could not help but notice the two smartly dressed ladies approaching her. They wore suits and what looked to be sensible shoes. "Good evening ladies, how may I help you?"

"We are from the United Kingdom Kat Chamber. We are here to provide assistance for the meeting this evening." Kassia informed the receptionist with a short and succinct smile.

"I see. Your meeting is in the Dogpole Suite further down the corridor. You go past the bar area and come to two double doors. Go through there to a reception area, then it is the doorway to the left that will be directly in front of you. I understand the room is set up ready for you."

Kassia nodded. "Maybe you can show us all the same."

"I'd be happy to. Can you sign in here, please?" She pushed the visitor's book towards them.

"You do it for me," Shula said to Kassia.

Michelle smiled and looked on, noticing that the one that had just spoken hadn't made any eye contact and was constantly looking everywhere except towards her and the reception desk.

A frown appeared across Michelle's face as she read the names of Sharon and Tracy being written in and the remaining boxes on the visitor's book were left blank. She politely coughed and looked up at the writer as she put her pen down. "Do you have surnames?"

"No, just Sharon and Tracy. We are security, you see."

"I see, then you will not mind if I ask to see your security licenses, please?" The one that had ignored her was now staring into her face. "It's for my records, just in case something, well, something goes wrong."

The rude one, who she guessed may be Tracy, continued to look at her. "They talk about cats; it's not a boxing match. Besides, we are more of a concierge service for the elder members. They are quite old, so we help them."

"I see," she said with some suspicion. "Well then, you had best follow me. I'll show you where to go." Michelle looked down at the book again. "Sharon and Tracy, is it?" She was met by two short smiles. "This way then." Michelle walked the length of the corridor, hearing their footsteps behind her. "Sharon and Tracy, I wasn't born yesterday," she muttered to herself.

✛✛✛✛

"This is impressive, don't you think, Jessica?"

Jessica turned to face Mildred. "It is a lovely building. We have never gathered here before, but I think I mentioned to you earlier I have been here for smaller meetings a couple of times."

Mildred was looking all around in excitement as the car rolled down the driveway slowing on a couple of occasions to go over speed bumps. The Mansion House stood majestically in front of them on the beautiful summer's evening. She glanced over at a small lake as the car veered around to the left, where other cars were parked.

"Wow, have you ever seen cars like this, Jessica?"

Jessica smiled. "I have. They belong to some of our senior members. They have been involved within the club for much longer than you and I."

"Well, you've been involved for longer than me, Jessica."

"True, but as you see, I do not have a car like those. I don't really care for it. Have you never noticed the cars at the other gatherings you have been to?"

"No. I guess the parking area must have been somewhere else."

Jessica watched Mildred looking through the glass and could sense her excitement as she parked the car.

Jessica undid her seat belt. "Right, let's go inside, Mildred."

"Well, before we do, I have something for you, Jessica."

"Oh really?" Jessica smiled as Mildred reached behind and lugged her heavy bag to her knees. She reached inside and pulled out a card.

"For you!" Mildred handed the card to Jessica with a beaming smile.

"Oh! Why, thank you, Mildred. That's very sweet of you."

"Well, aren't you going to open it?"

"Yes, of course." Jessica smiled as she tugged at the envelope that revealed a picture that she recognised from the shop earlier. As she opened the card, she could see the clumsy writing inside. The printed words of 'Happy Birthday' had a line drawn through them and the card read, 'Happy Gathering,' Jessica smiled. "That's really very lovely, Mildred. Thank you very much."

"The cat on the front looks just like my Missy."

"And looks like my Khepri."

They fell silent, sparing a thought for their cats.

"You have a cat called Khepri, Jessica?"

"Yes, that's her real name."

"Real name?"

Jessica closed her eyes, instantly realising what she had said. She had to think quickly. "Yes, her real name. I have two names for her, ha-ha."

"Oh, okay. I think I would get confused with that. Anyway, I'm so pleased you like it."

"Do you mind if I leave it in here, Mildred? I can take it home later?"

"No, not at all."

As Mildred undid her seat belt, her bag fell open, revealing all the other cards. Jessica smiled, realising that Mildred was the one that the man in the shop had referred to earlier, the one who had bought 44 birthday cards.

As they got out of the car, Jessica picked up her bag and noticed an arm waving at them directly to her left, indicating they should proceed that way. Jessica took the lead, with Mildred dragging her bag in tow as they approached the two officers of the Escarrabin.

"Your invitations, please, ladies."

Jessica put a hand into her small clutch bag and passed the ticket over as she watched Mildred fumble with her jacket.

"Are you not hot wearing all of that, Mildred?"

"No, I'm fine, Jessica. It's here somewhere." The three of them stood patiently as Jessica observed the two security officers watching intently over Mildred's movements.

"It is here. I didn't forget it!" She said and bent over her bag. "Here, hold these, will you?" She passed both of the Escarrabin a plate of fish paste sandwiches. Shula looked at Kassia before they both turned to look at Jessica, who offered a small smile of embarrassment.

"Ah-ha, it was here all along!" Mildred pulled the invitation from her jacket pocket. She couldn't help but notice the two ladies holding plates did not look very impressed. She put the invitation in her mouth, took back the plates of sandwiches and craned her neck forward for them to take the invitation.

As she put the plates back into her bag, she tried to make amends. "Would you care for a sandwich?"

"No!" was the matter of fact response.

"Oh... okay." Mildred turned to Jessica and flashed her pink teeth as both invitations were read over and checked.

"I wondered could I keep mine as a memento, please?" Mildred asked.

"No!" was the terse response.

"Oh, okay."

"Thank you, ladies. Please go through."

Jessica stepped gracefully into the main room as Mildred trundled in behind her. "Jessica, the last couple of times I've been to one of these, the people at the front have not been very friendly. Are they members of the club?"

"No, well, kind of, they just help out with security, I think. They won't be part of the meeting. I don't know much about them. They are above my level, you see."

"Oh, okay." Mildred was distracted as she glanced around, instantly recognising a couple of faces from her local group. "Why on ever would we need security Jessica, we are here to talk about cats?"

Jessica smiled. "And that we will, Mildred. It's just a precautionary thing. It's supposed to make you feel more comfortable."

Mildred wasn't sure that it did.

"Let's go and get you a cup of tea and say some hellos."

"Yes, please, Jessica." Her tone was one of excitement again.

"Oh Mildred, just a little thing, please. Now that we are in front of people again, it's Lady Jessica. It's just a procedural thing."

Mildred looked at Jessica's smile and beamed one back with a shrug of the shoulders. "As you wish, Lady Jessica!"

"Come on, it looks like the tea urns are over there."

+++++

Mildred walked over to the tea area dragging her large bag behind her. She noticed Mildred from Merewood Close walking around the tables, taking out small cakes from a large white box that she was carrying. Mildred studied the cake supremo, gently place an individual cake next to the name cards indicating where everyone was sitting.

Jessica reached the tea urns first, having said a few hello's on the way. "What would you like, Mildred?" She noticed Mildred was looking the other way.

"Oh, tea, please, Jessica."

Jessica coughed.

"Sorry, Lady Jessica."

"What type of tea? There are many."

Mildred looked at the huge variety of different teas but was far too distracted by the other Mildred's cakes that looked so good. "Oh, whatever comes to hand, I don't mind. Thank you."

She turned back around, biting at her lip, considering whether she should place her cards next to the individual cupcakes.

"Hello, so you must be Mildred?"

Mildred had not seen the new Mildred from Alpine Grove approaching.

"Hello Mildred, how lovely to meet you, I recognise your voice from our phone call." The other Mildred had clearly arrived a little earlier as she already had tea in hand.

"So, did you bring your fish paste delights with you?" She took a sip of her tea and gave a patronising smile.

"Yes, I have them here, three plates of them. Do you know where I should put them?" She watched as the other Mildred smiled and looked towards the floor with some form of other answer in her mind.

"Yes, over there," she looked up and nodded towards a table with food on it. "You'll see mine; the crusts have been cut off and they are on my finest bone china plates."

Mildred watched her beam in pride. Her fish paste sandwiches came fully loaded with crusts and did not sit on expensive plates.

Mildred looked uncomfortably at the floor. "Well, that's good."

"Here you go, Mildred. Try this herbal tea. I like this one." Mildred looked up to see Jessica passing a cup and saucer to her. She beamed a big smile at the other Mildred, proud that a senior Lady had made a cup of tea for her."

"Hello, my Lady, I'm Mildred from Stratford-Upon-Avon."

Jessica turned around to see an outstretched hand from the new member of the club, she couldn't help but notice that she was dressed similarly to Mildred.

"Hello Mildred, I'm pleased to meet you." Jessica smiled and took her hand to shake it.

"So you both know each other very well then?" The new Mildred enquired.

"Lady Jessica gave me a lift here." Mildred beamed with pride, trumping the other Mildred and her perfect sandwiches.

"Yes, that's right. I'm the Elder of Daphne, who is Mildred's Elder. We are getting to know each other a bit better."

"Oh, I see. Well, that explains everything then. May I ask Lady Jessica, how many cats do you have?"

Mildred looked surprised by this question.

"No, I do not mind. I have three cats," Jessica responded politely.

The new Mildred's eyes widened; with three cats that would make her a Degree Level Seven Elder. "My my, Mildred, you do know some important people."

Mildred continued to smile, although she was somewhat confused by the conversation.

"Well, this is my first gathering so I must go and mingle. It was lovely to meet you, Lady Jessica. Don't forget to put your fish paste sandwiches out Mildred, I'm sure they will be a delight."

The sarcasm in her tone was not lost on Mildred as she watched her turn around and walk off. Jessica looked at Mildred and they shared a smile.

At the entrance doors, Shula was pacing up and down. "How many are we at now?"

"Thirty-six. There has been one cancellation, so just eight more to arrive."

Shula nodded at Kassia and looked inside the room. They had arranged for all members to enter through the side doors to avoid the main part of the hotel. As she looked inside, the ranks of Order were easy to distinguish and not just by age alone.

"You can see who's who. They don't blend together too well, do they?"

Kassia smiled, "they never do. The ranks don't mix. I suppose the same could be said of us."

Shula returned the smile only slightly as she looked at the variety of styles of dress. Those who were 8th and 9th Degree Elders all seemed to dress similarly; heavy coats, large bags and hats even in this heat. However, one did stand out even though she was dressed in the same way as the others. Shula watched and noticed her confidence as she worked the room. "That's the one who introduced herself, right?" Kassia poked her head around the door and looked to where Shula was nodding. "Yes, said her name was Mildred. Stratford-Upon-Avon, I think she said she was from."

"She looks like she is trying hard." Shula turned around and looked towards the parked cars. "Seems someone is after a promotion."

"It's possible; there is a naming ceremony tonight, so some of them will be." Shula sighed. "Standing on the doors, I could do without it."

"Could be worse; at least it's not raining," was all Kassia could offer in return.

Mildred was glad to be free of the fish paste sandwiches as she laid them out on the table next to the other Mildred's perfectly hand-cut sandwiches.

There was much to survey; plenty of sandwiches and Mildred's amazing cakes. She looked in some dismay at the curled up corners of her own sandwiches prodding one; the texture felt somewhat wooden.

Mildred hadn't lied; she did indeed own some amazing plates in comparison to Mildred's, which were different colours and sizes. Her sandwiches were standing out for all of the wrong reasons.

The chomping of her teeth was only disturbed by a voice from behind.

"Hello, Mildred!"

Mildred turned around to see Daphne's smiling face. "Oh, Lady Daphne. How lovely to see you."

"And you, Mildred. What have you brought with you then? They look like some fancy plates."

"Erm, yes, Lady Daphne, I have brought some sandwiches."

"Well, they look hand-cut as well. How lovely. Not sure about those ones, though."

Mildred followed Daphne's eyes as she looked at her fish paste sandwiches.

"I wonder who brought those? Anyway, yours look lovely, Mildred."

Mildred responded with a smile, deciding to take some credit for the perfectly formed sandwiches.

"I brought something for you as well, Lady Daphne."

Daphne smiled as she watched Mildred pick up her bag from the floor and passed a card to her.

"A card, Mildred. It's not my Birthday!" She laughed as she opened it and read the scrawled words.

"They didn't have happy gathering cards at the shop!"

"Well, I guess they didn't. Thank you very much, Mildred. The cat looks just like your Missy."

"And Lady Jessica's Khepri."

"Oh, Lady Jessica told you her cat's real name then?"

"Yes, apparently, her cat has two names."

Daphne smiled but decided to add nothing further to this.

"Well, it's a big evening for Lady Jessica, with it being her naming ceremony as well."

"Naming ceremony, what on ever is that?"

"Oh, she didn't explain that to you as well?"

"No, that hadn't been mentioned." Mildred looked a bit bewildered and not for the first time, with the unusual processes that seem to be involved in this club.

"Well, I was surprised when she offered you a lift; she must have plenty on her mind."

Mildred nodded in agreement, not understanding a word of it.

"Come over here and sit with me Mildred, I'll explain a couple of things." Mildred watched as Daphne turned around, heading for a table. She reached out with her left foot to slide her bag under the sandwich and cake table, picked up her herbal tea and followed.

Mildred watched Daphne pull a chair out for her. "Please do sit, Mildred."

"Thank you, Lady Daphne," she responded as she pulled at the chair and sat down.

"It's like this, Mildred. Naming ceremonies do not happen very often. They only happen when one of our ladies is promoted. I guess promoted is a word you could use for it."

Daphne could see that Mildred was studying her intently.

"From this evening, Lady Jessica will not be known as Lady Jessica any more."

Mildred tilted her head, confused, "well, what will she be then?"

"I don't know and I'm guessing that she does not know yet either, but in any event, she will be given a new name and that is what she will be known as forever more. It's quite an accomplishment."

Mildred looked across the floor at Jessica, talking away to some very elegantly dressed ladies.

"I'm confused, Lady Daphne."

"Well, we can't all be Mildred's, Daphne's and Jessica's forever, can we?"

Daphne looked at Mildred's face in a state of perplexity.

"I know this seems daunting to you, Mildred. It was for me at the start, but the longer you are with us, the more things are explained."

"I just like cats."

Daphne smiled. "Yes, you do, Mildred. We all do. We adore cats, but there is a lot more to the Kat Chamber than you realise. It will all become clear in time. Who knows, you may have a new name in the future."

Mildred recoiled slightly in her chair. "But I like being called Mildred."

"And I like being called Daphne, but it's not my real name. I hope to discover it in the future as you may as well. Has it never occurred to you that we all have the same names?"

"Well, I thought it was just a coincidence."

"Nothing is by coincidence Mildred, they never are. Your invitation to join was predetermined a long time ago."

Mildred watched Daphne nod as she said this and had a smile across her face by way of reassurance.

"It will all become clear, my friend, don't you worry."

Daphne stood up with her eyes looking towards the food table. "Let's go and try some of your sandwiches. They looked like bone china plates you have there, Mildred."

Mildred smiled and looked at the floor as Daphne walked away. This was odd, far too odd, as it dawned on Mildred what she had gotten herself involved in. Her concentration was disturbed as she heard the doors close from where she had come in. The curtains were pulled across. The two rude ladies who had taken her ticket walked across the floor. They both nodded at some of the more elder ladies and she watched them leave the room via another doorway. She looked on as everyone in the room was chatting away. Some of the ladies who were dressed similarly to her looked as if they were talking about cats. The other ladies that Jessica seemed to be conversing with looked to be talking about something completely different.

The room was now closed and she was here now. I may as well hear what they have to say, but she would have to reconsider her membership to this club. There was clearly something not right about it or the ladies involved within.

The Reeve reached for her phone, somewhat relieved to hear it ring.

"Reeve, are you alone?"

"Yes, my Lady, I can talk."

"Do you have the key? Have you found it?"

"Yes, my Lady, I believe that I have it. I've never seen a key quite like it."

"Is it safe?"

The Reeve put her hand to her sternum and instantly felt the iron weight press against her. "Yes, it is safe. Do you have news?"

The Reeve could hear deep breathing from down the phone.

"Tell me, Reeve, does the key bear a symbol on it or have a creature of some significance?"

"Yes, my Lady, it does. There is a centrepiece, which I think you need to hold to turn the key."

There was silence and more heavy breathing, "is it a serpent?"

The Reeve closed her eyes and spoke gently. "Yes, it is the head of a serpent." She could hear coughing from the other end of the phone. She knew that her Head of Order was worried as she muttered words of concern in Spanish. "My Lady, do you know what this is or what it means?" She could hear swallowing from the other end of the phone as her Head of Order gathered her words. "Whether it travelled here or was brought here, I do not know. I have had very little time and the archives are not easy to navigate. I need more time, but I suspect we do not have it."

The Reeve could hear the shakiness of her voice.

"It is a keystone species from long ago. It has but one purpose and this Watcher may and I repeat, may have been able to bring it back to being. How I do not know, but it is to be feared and it is enormously destructive."

The Reeve could hear the sadness in her tone as she spoke slowly and clearly.

"It is from a place, a guardian of the underworld from the time of the Order Of Ancients."

"So, you have been able to determine what it is, my Lady?"

"It has had other names, but more commonly, it is referred to as the Hydra."

The mouth of the Reeve fell open with an audible gasp. "But how can that be? The Hydra is a myth."

"No, Reeve, it is not. It never was. It is a true being from darker times."

She could hear her Lady taking a deep breath. "Your superior knew much of this as you will in time. Not all myths are myths. Some were created as a cover to conceal the real and save people from fear. The Hydra is just one small part of that cover and it is quite real, I can assure you."

The Reeve, dumbfounded, placed a shaky hand over her mouth, swallowing as she spoke. "And it has been here for all of this time?"

"So it would appear. I know some of the referred myths and what belongs to legend, but that is not to say that I know it all. This afternoon has proved that. I have no idea why it was brought or travelled to Loxley, but our own ancients thought it wise to keep it there. The wall of iron was no doubt built to ensure it would never rise again. Who knows what else may be down there. It requires a thorough investigation now that those secrets may be about to be exposed."

"Do we know more exactly about this Hydra? Can it be defeated?"

"Oh yes, it certainly can, but the documents I have studied do not discuss or detail its condition."

"Condition, my Lady?"

"Yes, its condition. We do not know whether it fought before it was laid to rest."

"I'm sorry, I do not understand?"

"I can only quote from what I know and not from what I see here, as those details have been omitted or are at another place. The Hydra will have a centre core and multiple heads, nine to be exact."

The Reeve looked towards the ceiling and shook her head. "Nine."

"Yes, the number nine is not lost on you and nor should it be. It has been a number associated with our Order from the beginning of the time of our existence. The number here is not a coincidence. It was meant to be. Look at the key, Reeve; I presume that the serpent head you mentioned is supported by nine individual spokes to hold the head in the centre?"

"Spokes, my Lady?"

"Yes, I think that may be the English word for it."

"Please bear with me."

The Reeve put the phone down on her desk and unclipped her necklace to look at the key in more detail. She held the centre core and counted the supporting rods that held the serpent in the centre. There were nine, her Head of Order was right. She lifted the phone back up and nodded her head. "Yes, there are nine spokes. You mentioned condition?"

"Yes, we do not know whether it fought at Loxley or was brought there from its natural domain in Greece where it lay under the earth at Lerna. The place often referred to as a gate to the underworld. As I said before, I have not had the time to establish these things, if indeed I can at all. Remove the head of the Hydra and another two will form. If it fought, we have no way of knowing how many heads it has."

"Oh, my word." The Reeve had to take stock quickly, "I have to ask again, can it be beaten?"

"Firstly, you have the key. Without that, it should not be able to get out. It is strong and of enormous power, but it has a weakness, one you cannot control or beat. It will be of its own doing."

"I'm sorry, my Lady, I don't understand?"

"It will need access to water. Unless there is some form of labyrinth beyond the iron wall with a watercourse, it will need water and it will need it soon. That is its weakness and can be its undoing."

There was silence between them as the Reeve considered everything she was being told.

"If it is freed, if the Watcher somehow succeeds to release it, you and the Escarrabin will not win, not down there, not in the darkness of the below. It will be a slaughter."

The Reeve's eyes closed. Her throat was dry. "May I ask why, my Lady?"

"You cannot fight the un-fightable within the confines below ground. Its rage will destroy anything you put in front of it and it will tear through your security doors and anything in it's path without mercy."

"Are our Scatterblades useless?"

"As a firing weapon, yes. It would need precision shooting to remove the heads. If the heads are not seared quickly, two more will grow. The use of pulse fire in the below may bring the whole lot down on top of you. The Scatterblades would have to be used as their original intention from the past as a sword weapon. The steel would have to be heated to sear the heads and that alone is far from easy. The blood of the Hydra is highly toxic and its own blood can be used to sear the heads, but that is hardly recommended. To try so would lead to certain fatalities."

The Reeve ran a shaky hand through her hair.

"And that is not all, Reeve. Poisonous fumes come from the mouth, so it is not beatable in the darkness of the below. It would be a slaughter unlike any we have seen in a very long time. Combine that with your Watcher and those he's united and the seriousness of this becomes paramount."

"So you are saying that we have to let it escape?"

"In part; your Watcher will know that it will take all of your efforts to destroy it and that it provides cover for him and his kind. He will not care for the beast. He intends to sacrifice it so they can all escape. All of this and the first sign of the prophecy does not bode well."

"No, my Lady, it does not."

"If it escapes, it will head for water."

"The lake?"

"Yes, it will destroy everything inside it and that is not to say that new serpents may come from it, but afterwards, it will not like the above and will need to go back below. It is on the outside that you may have a chance to destroy it with your pulse applications, but your Escarrabin must be ready."

"I understand, my Lady, well, at least, I think I do."

"I will need to refer this to the Grand Council for their views and you will need to hold tight. It will be dark where you are in a couple of hours and you will not have the time to prepare. I suggest you go at dawn when the Watchers are less active and find the rogue Watcher of which you refer to. Find him, find the missing keys and put an end to this. Let's hope the second prophesied sign does not show. If it does, you may have no choice but to act quickly."

"I will need to consult with Raysmau, my Lady."

"Do so. She is a good soldier and trusted, but at this time, do not tell her everything until we know more and I've spoken to the Grand Council. Use your judgement as to what to do, but keep the key safe at all times!"

"Yes, my Lady."

"Do your job Reeve and execute a plan to contain this as best as you can. I will be in touch soon."

"Thank you for your council, my Lady."

The Reeve put the phone down and with shaking hands, struggled to reattach her necklace. The key was safe, but he may come directly for her if the Watcher knows about it. She opened her desk and took out a pair of gloves in preparation for carrying her own modified spear.

There was much to consider, much to fear. Lives may be lost. They would need to be ready.

Chapter Twenty Seven:

WELCOME TO THE KAT CLUB

Mildred had to concede that Mildred's cakes were very nice. However, that would come as no surprise to anyone. She decided to stay at the gathering and was making the most of it.

At the food table, the cheese and ham sandwiches were being demolished at an increasing rate. The same could not be said for her fish paste sandwiches.

With a casual glance over her shoulder, she could see the two Mildreds in conversation, much like everyone else. It would appear that she had the food table to herself momentarily. She bypassed the cheese and ham as a silent protest. She shifted some of her own fish paste sandwiches onto the other Mildred's bone china plates to make it look like hers were going down.

Turning around with the third cupcake in her mouth, she could see Jessica talking with some other members. Mildred had seen them before at the other two gatherings that she had been to but had never spoken to them.

As she chewed away, it occurred to her that they had never spoken with her either. For a club that adored cats, they seemed to keep themselves to themselves.

Mildred picked at her teeth, considering the garb that Daphne had been talking about earlier. She was paying more attention than she had at the last two gatherings. Not so far away, there were huddled groups with lots of smiles, but the group that Jessica was talking to seemed to be absent of any humour. Their conversation looked serious, similar to the group behind her, almost like little splinter groups. It was strange to say at the least, as she picked chocolate bits out of her teeth.

Mildred was dressed in her best and yet no one had complimented her as she reached for just one more cake, pondering if it was her fourth or fifth. It didn't really matter; she wasn't dieting and did not care. With a mouth full of cake, she was drawn to a couple of small groups over at the other side of the room, the ones who dressed more elegantly. They wore jewels that hung from just about everywhere. Only one thing unified them other than their lack of smiles, a small pin badge that they all wore. It was worthy of closer inspection. She woofed down the cake, bent down below the table to reach for her bag and took out some of the cards. Let's go and see how friendly they will be.

She walked over to the group that Jessica was talking to. She glanced over to her right to see ham and cheese Mildred, eyeing her up suspiciously, not that it was any of her business in any event.

Jessica saw her approaching and lifted her right hand slightly to silence the group.

"Ladies, you may well have seen her before and I know that one of you, of course, is in the local meets, but if you've never met, may I introduce Mildred from Shrewsbury, just down the road from here."

Mildred beamed a big smile of discoloured teeth with cake stuck to them, along with fading pink lipstick. "Hello ladies, it's nice to finally meet some of you."

A couple of them winced but could not help but stare at what looked to be the remainder of many cupcakes gleaming back at them.

"Well, I've brought you all something!"

Jessica smiled as she watched Mildred, with all of her enthusiasm, distribute the cards. "It has a picture on it, just like my Missy."

"Well, that's nice. Thank you, Mildred," one of them said, although Mildred noticed that she was not given their names. "So how many cats do you all have then? I only have my Missy."

"Yes, they know you only have one cat, Mildred. You haven't been a member for very long. We all have three," Jessica added.

"You all have three? That's a coincidence."

Jessica met Mildred's smile, but there were no words exchanged. There was suddenly an air of some disquiet as the conversation stopped.

"Erm…well….okay, I hope that you all like them." Mildred nodded with an awkward smile feeling uncomfortable.

"Some of the ladies over there have six cats or more, Mildred."

"Jessica!" One of the ladies spoke in a serious tone looking at Jessica as if to say 'stop talking.' "Six!!! Wow, how lucky. I would struggle to remember all of their names, ha ha ha. You definitely would Jessica, as one of your cats has two names!"

The members of the group looked at Jessica as she winced and looked at the floor.

The ladies watched Mildred's fits of giggles peter out to an uncomfortable cough. "Well, I guess that I should be going then, plenty of people to see, much talk of cats."

Jessica gave her a smile but was the only one in the group that did.

"Well, enjoy the cards then." She forced a smile and looked over to one of the groups she had just been told had lots of cats.

As she trundled off, she could hear murmurs from behind and what sounded like Jessica saying something like 'she's still new, give it time.'

Mildred glanced across into a mirror on the wall to her right. In the reflection, she could see a couple of the cards had already been put down on a table, unopened. A deep frown stretched across her forehead as she wondered why so many of the members were so rude. It hadn't escaped her attention there were other clubs that cat fanciers could join.

She would try again by approaching the small group in front of her. Their faces looked very serious. As she got nearer, she heard them talking about something called Watchers, whatever that meant. They could do with someone watching them for attitude problems, Mildred considered with a slight smile. There were only four in this little huddle that fell silent with Mildred's interruption.

"So how many cats do you have then?" She thrust a card towards each of them. Mildred noticed they were all drinking red wine.

"What's this may I ask?" One of the ladies said to her.

"It's just a card to say hello." Mildred decided not to display so many smiles this time as she looked closely at the pin badge the lady was wearing. "Well, that's nice of you, thank you." The lady in question noticed that Mildred was not looking her in the eye and seemed more focused on what she was wearing.

Well, I'm guessing you must be Mildred then?" Another lady voiced. Mildred turned and was instantly close to her pin badge. She stared at the logo on it that matched what the others were wearing. "Yes, I am. I'm fairly new, only been a member for a few years," Mildred said with an excited smile that someone actually knew her.

"I see," was the response from another who appeared to be studying what Mildred was wearing, "that's a nice cardigan."

"Thank you, I made it myself."

"Ah-ha," the lady nodded.

"Ladies, ladies, please take your seats," was the voice over the microphone as the lights came up over a staged area that had been hidden. Mildred looked up at the huge crest of the United Kingdom Kat Chamber LIV that was now displayed proudly in the lights. There was a podium in place ready for a speaker.

"Well, I had best take a seat then. Enjoy your cards."

The ladies politely smiled back as she walked off.

"Rehema, how did you know that her name was Mildred?"

"I didn't. It was one of three guesses."

They sniggered among themselves as they took their seats.

"Jessica." Mildred cupped her mouth, conscious that the room had now gone very quiet. "Lady Jessica," Jessica looked over to her.

"Yes, Mildred."

"There is a seat over here if you want it?"

"No, Mildred, I'll be sitting here. I'll see you later, though."

Mildred was disappointed. "Yes, okay," she replied as she noticed rude Mildred staring at her.

She went to her seat, still clutching her cards and smiled at the other eight members sitting at her table.

"Did you enjoy my cakes, Mildred? I saw that you had some."

"They were a delight. You must teach me someday!"

"I'd be happy to. We'll work that out, a cake and cats day!"

"I'd love that. I'll give you a call to arrange it."

They both smiled together as they were interrupted.

"Did you try Mildred's sandwiches?"

Both Mildreds looked at the new Mildred, the owner of the expensive plates.

"Yes, I had one Mildred, I quite like fish paste." The response was met by a scowl. Mildred looked at her new cake-making friend, who gave a smile back and leant into her. "Ignore her Mildred, she's always like this on the phone as well, just ignore her."

Mildred pursed her lips and nodded as she watched the other Mildred turn in her seat to face the stage.

They all started clapping as Lady Skylar took to the stage. Mildred recognised her as she had spoken at the last two gatherings that she had been to. She was much older and had been a member for some years, apparently. Mildred had been told she was the owner of seven cats.

"Thank you, ladies and honourable members of the United Kingdom Kat Chamber. I welcome you to this gathering of the middle sector of the UK Chapter. I give special appreciation to our elder members, who have been with us for some time." There was further applause as Lady Skylar waved her hand towards the table at the front. The five ladies sitting there, looked over at the other members and nodded with an appreciation for the applause.

Mildred looked at the speaker's attire. She wore a long flowing black gown, jewels around her neck, jewels in her immaculately styled hair and black gloves that went to her elbows. Lady Skylar's appearance could not be more diverse than her own, her style of dress was more in keeping with the ladies on the front tables. It was not the first time she had noticed this as she surveyed the members on her own table and the one in front.

"Ladies, as some of you may know, I have some formal announcements to make later on, as well as some sad news to deliver to some of you, but I will come to that shortly. As is customary, we have a presentation for you to enjoy. I'm very pleased to say that Daphne from Stow-on-the-Wold in the Cotswolds will give a short slide presentation of her two cats. Let's give her a round of applause."

Mildred looked over to her Lady Daphne, who was clapping at the table in front. Another lady stood up and walked to the stage. Mildred shook her head slightly; so many Mildreds, Daphnes and Jessicas; she was still confused about the 'real name' conversation she had earlier.

"Thank you, Lady Skylar, for your warmth. It is always a pleasure to see you and my esteemed fellows."

Mildred shook her head and smirked on hearing 'esteemed fellows.'

"As we all know, we are brought here today for our love of cats, but also our love of the Order. It is through our strength and our determination that this great organisation still exists to this day." There was rapturous applause from around the room as Mildred looked at those sitting at her table clapping and nodding with beaming smiles. Mildred the miserable had even stood up for this comment. Two members from her table looked over. It suddenly dawned on her that she was the only one in the room not clapping. Mildred looked at them, nodded and starting patting her hands together, what for, she had no idea.

"Our love and our unity bring us together as one on this most important day." More applause from the members.

"And this evening, I am going to show you a short snippet of my home life and that of my two cats, Tale and Lilly."

Upon hearing this and the somewhat diverse names for cats, Mildred blew her lips together. It sounded like she was making some sort of repetitive farting noise as the lights dimmed and a screen lit up behind.

Daphne went into her presentation with much enthusiasm. It was well-received on Mildred's table and the one in front of her. Elsewhere, however, especially towards the front, other members were whispering to themselves with complete disinterest in the presentation.

The presentation was not dull. Daphne owned two beautiful cats and she had the same interests as her. Why she had called her cat 'tail' was anyone's guess. Mildred crossed her arms, looking at the other tables with even more confusion. Much did not add up and describing some of the cat appreciation club members as rude would be an understatement.

Raysmau had changed from her ceremonial robes and armour in her private quarters and examined them for any marks, blemishes, or dust. The old house was a dust magnet and like all Escarrabin, she took great pride in her presentation. She unclipped her neck chains and placed them gently on the dresser. There had been no reports of any note from her officers at the five gatherings currently taking place across the UK and Ireland. As far as she was concerned, no news was good news.

Her intercom sprung to life as she reached over and pressed the button to talk. "Yes, what is it?"

"I'm sorry to disturb you, Lady Raysmau, but the Lady Reeve is here and would like to see you."

"Please send her through into my office. I will be there momentarily."

"Yes, Ma'am."

Finally, we may have some answers to explain the Reeve's lack of decisive action from earlier on. What happened below needed to be fully investigated, even if her own officers had overreacted and required disciplinary action to be taken against them.

She reached for her gown and slippers. She had signed off for the day and was already in her underwear. The Reeve was arriving unannounced and would therefore have to receive her as she was.

On occasion, Raysmau had disagreed with some of the decision making of the previous Reeve. It was the same with her first placement as a Chief Security Officer of the Escarrabin in Italy. Her disagreeable views were always kept to herself. It was a delicate balance. All she could do was offer guidance and subtle views that would hopefully carry some influence. But what she saw today was a blatant lack of process and inability to make decisions when they were most needed.

She made sure her gown was fully drawn as she walked down the corridor that led to the rear door of her office.

The Reeve had her back to her, looking at framed pictures of elder Escarrabin from the past.

"Thank you for seeing me Raysmau, I appreciate you are off duty."

"A Head of Security is never fully off duty, Ma'am."

The Reeve turned to her with a smile. "No, I guess not."

"Please forgive me for how I am presented."

"Not at all." She was still smiling as she nodded towards the chairs for Raysmau to sit down.

Raysmau drew her heavy chair from behind her desk and sat down, curious to know what was so urgent that this conversation could not have waited.

"I would imagine you were surprised by my reaction earlier on today when you brought me news about the Watcher and what happened below."

Raysmau tilted her head slightly with her eyes fixed on the Reeve.

"It was more of a statement than a question; I would have been concerned or confused if I had been you."

Taking a seat, the Reeve recognised the familiar pattern of Raysmau in thought; as she twiddled the thumb of her right hand around her index finger.

"I will level with you, Raysmau. My actions earlier were because I needed time to think. I also needed time to consult."

"Consult, Ma'am?"

The Reeve nodded. "Unruly Watchers do not concern me. They can be dealt with. The drawing of a Scatterblade is indeed a serious matter and that we can deal with. It is the other matter that concerns me. I needed to take council with my Head of Order."

The Reeve looked Raysmau directly in her eyes as she continued. "Let me ask a question that I have never asked you and please be frank with me. Have you ever been in the below, right to the very bottom?"

Raysmau took great pride in never showing expressions, irrespective of the outcome, but this question concerned her. "I have been below, but not for some time. Never to the bottom, never into the depths; there has not been a need for it."

The Reeve got to her feet. "As I thought." She flashed a smile as she looked at Raysmau, putting her hands in the pockets of her suit trousers. She looked around the office at the old pictures on the walls and took a deep breath. "In my Order, we know a lot of the secrets of old and they are kept secret for good reason. Much is known of this place and that includes elements of history that is seldom talked about."

Her thumb had stopped turning around her fingers. "Do you know what it is?"

The Reeve took a couple of steps towards the desk and nodded. "I suspect what it may be."

"But this noise, this roar, the sound from below has never been heard before."

"No and I very much expect anyone who lives has ever heard it. It's something of old that has woken."

"Or been brought back?"

"Indeed."

"Do you have a course of action, Ma'am?"

"I'm taking it now by informing you. I also hope to have further information later. But in any event, darkness will soon fall and we cannot risk going below in the hours of darkness to investigate. Please remain vigilant and have officers guard the lift that goes to the below. Anything suspicious, no matter how small, please inform me irrespective of the hour."

Raysmau nodded. "Yes, Ma'am. I'll arrange that right away."

"Dependent on what I am told, there's a likelihood we may have to be battle-ready for a dawn search of the below. If so, we have to go right to the bottom as far as it takes us."

The Reeve looked at Raysmau's huge frame as she stood up. "Ensure the Escarrabin return here immediately from the gatherings. We may need all the help we can get."

"Yes, Ma'am. I'll see that a message is sent out."

The Reeve turned to walk to the exit door. "Oh, one more thing. Do this as quietly as you can."

Raysmau could see that the Reeve looked uncomfortable as she spoke. "Collect all of the body armour we have and include the biological suits, full face protection with breathing apparatus without exception."

Raysmau nodded with concern.

As the Reeve opened the door, she was stopped by the sound of Raysmau's voice.

"Ma'am, may I ask one thing?"

The Reeve stopped and looked over her shoulder and gave a slight nod of the head.

"What is it? What are we potentially dealing with?"

The Reeve was still looking over her shoulder but did not look directly at her Head of Security. "The Hydra." The Reeve left, closing the door behind her without a glance in Raysmau's direction; she presumed it was just as well.

✛✛✛✛

A ripple of applause sealed the end of Daphne's presentation. Mildred clapped along with the others from her table. However, the front tables were still lost in conversation and it was a lacklustre display of appreciation.

"Thank you, Daphne. We very much appreciate you welcoming us into your home and the lives of your cats." Daphne left the stage and took her seat as Lady Skylar continued.

The membership looked on as her body language changed and her face took a more serious stance. "As some of you are aware, we are missing a beloved member this evening. For those of you who do not know, it is my very sad duty to inform you that Lady Tempest regrettably was taken from us a few weeks ago."

Confused, Mildred leaned over to her right. "Where has she been taken?"

"I think Lady Skylar is saying that she has passed, Mildred."

Mildred looked with shock towards the stage at this news. Not knowing who Lady Tempest was, it was clear that others did as many heads bowed and in the silence of the room you could have heard a pin drop.

"Lady Tempest was admired and even for her level, she was known outside of this chapter and respected further afield."

Mildred's quizzical eyes remained forward, listening to every word that made little sense.

From the table in front of her a lady she did not know spoke up loudly. "What happened?"

The question was not lost. The speaker looked towards the front table and took a nod from the lady, sat in the centre.

"She was most unfortunately involved in a road traffic accident. At this time, that is all I can say, but we are looking into it."

Mildred bobbed her head back like a parrot and leant to her right. "We are looking into it? Doesn't she mean the Police are looking into it?"

The Mildred to her right shrugged her shoulders, obviously not understanding this odd statement either.

The room was distracted by one of the security guards that Mildred recognised from earlier opening one of the closed doors.

She leant her head in and looked at Lady Skylar, nodded and re-closed the door.

Mildred frowned, leaning to her right again. "I don't mean to speak out of turn, but Tempest?" She shrugged her shoulders. "Tempest? Why do they have such odd names?" Cake creation Mildred offered no response.

"However, what this does mean is there is a gap in our ranks. It doesn't happen very often, I'm most pleased to say, but order must continue and the Grand Council have made their decisions." They all looked on as she adjusted herself. "But first, we will have one minute's silence for our beloved friend Lady Tempest."

The room fell silent as everyone looked to the floor in contemplation. Mildred, however, couldn't help but notice the one cupcake left on her table. She eyed it, wondering if she could nab it with the same stealth as she had removed the flyer in the cafe about the woman who talks to animals. Her tongue poked slightly from her mouth when she noticed Jessica looking at her disapprovingly.

Mildred leaned forward, put her elbows on her knees and rested her head into her palms. Grand Council... honestly, she thought as she looked around at everyone else, somewhat gripped with anticipation before this moment of mutual silence. Lady Tempest, will Lady Macbeth pop up next? She thought, letting out a deep sigh.

She was distracted as the minute passed and bolted upright again. "Although it is with regret that this event happened before it was due, I announce to you all that this evening is Jessica's naming ceremony. Please stand, Jessica." There was rapturous applause around the room. Mildred felt somewhat compelled to lift her chin up as she put her hands together, mimicking a light clap.

She watched Jessica look around the room smiling and nodding politely at the appreciation from her peers.

"Jessica, please do join me on the stage."

The applause continued as Jessica walked up only three steps that lifted her above everyone else. She stood next to the podium. "My Lady, if you would be so kind?" came across the microphone as Lady Jomana got to her feet from the front table, holding in both hands what looked to be a large and heavy old sword.

"What the bloody hell is going on here?" The words slipped out of Mildred's mouth as a couple from her table looked directly at her in disbelief. Her hands shook with fear at the thought of witnessing some bizarre beheading ritual, but her thoughts soon shifted to how she would return home without Jessica. It would be a long walk.

As the sword was passed from Lady Jomana to Lady Skylar, they both bowed their heads to each other. Everyone watched as Jessica went down on one knee. Mildred looked on as her chauffeur for the evening showed far too much leg for her liking. The sword was placed on one shoulder and then the other. Words were exchanged in this action, but the Mildreds were sat too far back to hear what was being said.

The sword was handed back to the lady, who carried it with another nod.

Lady Skylar took her place back at the microphone. "Please rise."

Mildred stood up and was quickly pulled back down. "Not you, Mildred. She means Lady Jessica!"

Still in thought but feeling rather terrified, she took her seat again and watched Jessica stand up.

"Lady Jessica has passed. From now on, she will be known as Lady Suzanna." Everyone in the room stood up, cheering and applauding. Mildred could see a huge smile on Jessica's face.

Mildred was the only one who remained seated, but that was short-lived as eyes turned directly to her. "Yeah, woo, woo!" she joined in, giving something that resembled fist pumps in the air. It somehow seemed appropriate, as she looked around the room, to establish exactly where all the exit doors were.

There was no speech given and it didn't look like one was expected. Lady Skylar leaned forward to the new Lady Suzanna, kissed her face on both sides and presented her with a certificate.

"Can I check please, is that spelt with one Z or two?" Were the only words Mildred could discern across the microphone. Lady Skylar did not look impressed, so Mildred guessed that she had heard correctly.

The clapping continued as Lady Suzanna (with one Z) returned to her seat. She received many pats on the back from her table. Mildred watched as her Elder, Daphne, walked over to congratulate her.

"Yes, congratulations to Lady Suzanna, although you are now sitting at the wrong table!" Lady Skylar laughed as Suzanna stood up, smiling with more pats on the back and moved to the table in front, where she received handshakes and more applause.

"Ladies, this does, of course, mean that we need a replacement for Lady Jessica." The room fell silent. The members on the table in front suddenly froze as if it was an awards ceremony announcement on television.

"The Grand Council have agreed that Lady Daphne from Housman Rise in Staffordshire will be promoted to Degree Level Seven. Let's hear it for Daphne!"

The ladies at Daphne's table stood up to congratulate her. Mildred could see that she was practically in tears at this apparent promotion as she turned around and looked directly at her.

Mildred smiled back and gave little hand claps, nodding to her friend, the same 'friend' who had introduced her to this cult of lunatics. Mildred's mind was made up; as soon as those doors were opened, she was off, even if it meant she had to walk home. At least Jessica, now Suzanna, kept her head. God knows what happens if you get on the wrong side of this cat club.

Everyone looked on as Daphne approached the stage and received a kiss on either side of her cheeks. The speaker presented her with a certificate. There was no sword this time.

She was beaming smiles all around as she sat back down, this time at the table in front of where she had previously sat.

Mildred was picking at her teeth again, staring at the lone cupcake on the table. She looked at it, grinding her teeth, wondered if anyone would mind if she nabbed it. Well, I'm leaving afterwards, she thought, so who cares? She leant across the table and stuffed half of it into her mouth.

"Ladies, our final announcement for the evening before we all head off. As is customary, we have one more promotion to make from our Ninth Degree Elders." Mildred was looking at the half-eaten cupcake. It was a conundrum as she really would like to know how to make these but suspected after this evening she wouldn't see Mildred again.

"The Grand Council has spoken and they have made their decision, the new Degree Level is awarded to Mildred. Congratulations!"

Mildred was distracted as Mildred from Alpine Grove stood up with a huge smile and shook the hands of those on either side of her.

"Oh, I'm sorry, I do apologise. Ladies, I didn't say, the award is for Mildred from Rocke Road." Two of the three Mildreds froze for completely different reasons. "Mildred, it's you!" as she felt an arm on her shoulder still chewing on what had been left of the cupcake.

"Eh, you what?"

"It's you. Well done. You'll get a new cat now!"

Mildred looked up at the other Mildred, who was red in the face and looked furious as she slumped into her chair and stared at her.

"Well, go on, collect your award!" Mildred swallowed the remaining contents of her mouth and looked into the face of the cake master, who looked thrilled for her.

"Erm, okay." Mildred stood up to applause around the room. For all of her life, she had never been awarded anything. In that very moment, she looked across the room filled with smiles, well, except for one. She was so grateful that she was being appreciated.

She shuffled forward. Lady Daphne gave her a thumbs-up and Jessica on the table in front was full of smiles. For the first time in a long time, she felt happy, momentarily putting to one side the fact that she was going to leave as soon as she possibly could. She approached the stage and the three steps that would take her up to the imposing figure of Lady Skylar.

"Congratulations, Mildred. Very well done." The certificate was passed to her. It was similar to the one she had at home, except on quick inspection, the markings were different. She would need to look at it in more detail later on.

"Thank you, Lady Skylar. Would it be possible to say a few words?"

"That's not the usual protocol Mildred, but yes, if you would like."

Mildred looked across the room at the tables with seated occupants. She, too, had the attention of the ladies at the front. She looked nervously at the sword that lay on the table as she gathered her words.

"Well, fellow ladies and cat enthusiasts, this is an honour. I've never won anything before, so this is a huge surprise."

She could see the glaring face of Mildred at the back of the room. Daphne, looked to be egging her on.

"I love cats and I love my Missy. It's been a difficult week as she has been so unwell." Mildred noticed that Jessica (Suzanna) suddenly took her eyes off her and looked at the floor. "So this is very welcome. I would like to say that I also enjoyed the presentation that Daphne gave about her cats. They are very beautiful and I hope to have more cats in the future." Mildred noticed that two of the ladies on the second table closest to her leant in to speak to each other.

"She really hasn't got a clue, has she?"

Mildred could see they were sniggering to themselves but continued undeterred.

"Yes, I hope that one day I will get a Tomcat and have lots of kittens."

There were gasps around the room and the sound of a wine glass smashing as it was dropped to the floor. Mildred froze in the silence and looked at all the opened mouths and looks of horror.

"Erm..."

A muffled sound could be heard across the room as Mildred put her hand over the microphone and turned to Lady Skylar. "Did I say something wrong?" She leant into Mildred, put a hand on her shoulder and whispered into her ear. "I think it would be a good idea if you stayed back afterwards. A few things need to be explained to you. There is much that you do not know yet."

Mildred removed her hand from the microphone. "Erm, okay. Well, thank you, ladies. World peace, I guess," she shrugged.

She could see Mildred the miserable doing a facepalm as Lady Skylar gently pushed her to the side. "Let's hear a round of applause for Mildred." There were a couple of muted claps as she walked back to her chair and looked around the room to plenty of stares. As she went to sit down she heard the voice over the microphone.

"Mildred!" She turned around to see Lady Skylar pointing that she should sit at the table in front of where she had been. As she sat at the seat that Daphne had been in minutes before, she did not receive the same appreciation Daphne had received at her new table. She looked behind to see expensive plates Mildred shaking her head, staring at her.

Lady Skylar continued to speak, but her words were drifting away as Mildred read her new certificate and looked up.

There was some good news however, there were more cupcakes on this table.

Their phones had been set to silent mode, but they both felt them vibrate within their suit pockets. They read the message simultaneously. "Not usual that we are sent a reminder to return back to headquarters, is it?"

Shaking her head, Kassia looked at Shula. "Not that I recall. Must be something going on. Shu, how much longer do you think this is going to take?"

She watched as Shula gently opened the door into the gathering and quickly reclosed it. "The speeches have finished, so shouldn't be too much longer now."

"We could encourage them, of course," Kassia had a mischievous look in her eye, "now that we've had a message to return and all."

Shula nodded in response. "Okay, let's go inside by the exit doors. It may help them make up their minds."

The two members of the Escarrabin walked through the room towards the doorway that would lead the visitors out over the patio to their awaiting cars.

"You hungry?"

"A little. We're not really supposed to eat on duty."

"I know," said Kassia, "but look around; no one is really paying any attention."

"Alright, go on then. Pass me a couple of those sandwiches, will you?"

Kassia grabbed two sandwiches each. They tried to hide them behind their backs as they opened the doors to let the summer evening air drift through.

Kassia put one to her mouth as discreetly as she could, took a bite and then put her arm behind her back.

"You okay?" Shula had a slight smile across her face watching her fellow Escarrabin's face screw up in some apparent discomfort. She leant forward to the table and put the half-eaten sandwich and the spare one back on the plate.

"Whatever you do, do not eat those. Stale fish paste!"

Mildred was the last one at her table. Some had already left while others talked amongst themselves. The ladies from the front table rose together, a couple spoke to the 'smarter' dressed ladies on their way out. Mildred got up and walked over to the window to see that car doors were being opened for them; the nice looking expensive cars, of course. They travelled separately and all had their own drivers. 'Alright for some, I guess.'

Mildred took her seat and looked over at Daphne and the newly named Suzanna. They were in their own little clusters chatting away. Mildred shook her head and turned her attention to the emptying room. The tables were bare, give or take the odd glass. It didn't take long for Mildred to see that most of the cards she had given out remained on the tables. She shook her head at the rudeness and had no idea why she had wanted to impress these people.

Mildred the miserable approached holding her fish paste sandwich plates in her hands. "Well, you've got plenty left to feed your cats, Mildred!" She dropped them with a loud clang on the table.

"I only have one cat, Mildred, as you very well know."

The response was met with a sly smile. "Not for much longer."

She turned around to see if anyone was listening, then bent down to Mildred at the table. "You don't deserve this, you know, this rank of Elder that you now have?"

"I do not know what you mean, Mildred?"

"That's my point. This award is beyond you and way beyond your skillset."

"If you intend to judge me on my sandwiches Mildred, then you really do not know my skillsets," not that she had any idea what her skillsets were in the first place.

There was momentary silence between them but the anger on Mildred's face was not going anywhere anytime soon.

"And besides, the Grand Council elected me." Mildred had no idea what she was saying, but it seemed to do the trick as Mildred's face fell with more redness before she turned to leave, sulking.

Not sure of what to make of it all, she leaned forward and grabbed one of her own sandwiches off the plate. It only took a couple of chews to convince herself that her sandwiches really were awful.

"Ma'am, do you require our service any further this evening? I only ask as we have received a message to return to headquarters."

"No, thank you for your help." Lady Abrielle, Suzanna's Elder, nodded at Shula. "Is everything okay?" She asked with some curiosity.

"Ma'am?"

"Why would headquarters want you back quickly?"

"I'm not sure. The message didn't say, probably just another training exercise." Shula smiled.

"No doubt. You Escarrabin work hard. Thank you again."

"Thank you, Ma'am."

Lady Abrielle watched the member of the Escarrabin Order walk towards her colleague. They both left via the patio doors. She noticed the other one was carrying all of the invitations. Only a few members remained in the room. The three that had been promoted including her Suzanna and a couple of other Elders, who would need to explain the new responsibilities that came with such promotion within the Order.

She looked towards the far table at the lady wearing the cloche hat and the fake fur stole who sat alone engrossed in eating something. In all of her days, she could not recall being at a gathering where any of the members talked about cat breeding on the stage.

Abrielle went over to Suzanna, who was in conversation with two other elders more senior to her. "Have things been explained to you so far, Lady Suzanna?"

She smiled. "Yes, my Lady, everything is in order."

"Good. That's good to know," she looked over at Mildred again. "In view of what happened earlier, I think she is ready for the chat now." Suzanna turned to look at Mildred, who seemed more interested in the food on the table than anything else.

"Yes, my Lady. I think you are probably right."

"I know that strictly speaking, you are considerably above her Degree, but you know her and a friendly face will help. Take Daphne with you. I understand she is her Elder and you are hers."

"Yes, that is correct. I'm very pleased that Daphne has moved up as well. She will be a great asset in the future. I'm positive of that."

Lady Abrielle looked at Suzanna with a smile. "The Grand Council always chooses wisely."

"Yes, my Lady." Suzanna could not help but grin in agreement. "Congratulations on this evening. I will see you soon. I'll leave you to your chat."

"Thank you, my Lady. It was lovely to see you again."

Suzanna walked over to Daphne. "Everything okay?"

"Yes, we are fine, thank you. It will take a while for me to get used to calling you Lady Suzanna from now on."

They both smiled as Lady Sherine, who Daphne had been talking to, said her goodbyes.

"It looks like we are the only ones left now."

"That's probably a good thing Daphne, we need to have a chat with Mildred similar to the one I had with you a few years ago."

They both looked over to Mildred, who was now looking back at them. "Yes, after her speech this evening, I think that is a very good idea."

Raysmau picked up her mobile phone and read the message. Her security officers in Scotland were the last to report back. Except those on driving duties, all members of the Escarrabin were making their way back to headquarters. She was mentally preparing herself to brief them all in the morning. It would be some hours before many of them made it back.

Some will not have had much sleep, but a show of ranks and strength will be necessary. There would be much fear about going below and there was no shame in admitting it. She questioned whether to inform them about a possible encounter with the Hydra.

Her team were far from stupid and the protective measures they would have to wear would be indication enough that this was far more than a search and detain exercise. She would have to consult with the Reeve, but her feeling was that her team would need to know the facts or the facts as they may appear.

There was much to consider and darkness was starting to fall outside. The dawn of a new day could be a test that her kind had not seen in a long time. It was not a test that she was looking forward to.

✛✛✛✛

Daphne and Lady Suzanna pulled chairs next to Mildred. It was hard not to notice the crumbs all over her.

"I must say, I do love your cardigan, Mildred," said Daphne. A comment received with some suspicion.

"I guess I need to call you Lady Suzanna from now on then?"

"You do," Suzanna said gently with a smile.

"Did you figure out how many Z's there are in your name yet?"

Suzanna laughed. "Yes, it's just one, apparently."

Suzanna and Daphne both laughed together, but Mildred just looked at the both of them. They regained their composure when it was obvious that Mildred appeared far from amused. Suzanna decided that it was time to press on with 'the talk."

"You must be a little confused about some of what has happened this evening Mildred. It's written all over your face."

"Confused would be one word for it; is this some version of the Freemasons or a cult or something? To be honest, I just wanted to join a club that appreciates cats."

Daphne and Suzanna gently laughed. "No, Mildred, I can assure you it's nothing like that. In fact, it is a great honour to be a part of this."

Mildred looked at Daphne. "And what exactly is 'this' Daphne?"

Daphne looked at Suzanna with a request in her eyes that she resume the lead. "I know this will not be easy for you, Mildred, but we and that includes you, are members of the Horde Of Light."

Mildred scanned both of their faces, then snorted with laughter, rubbing tears from her eyes. "Is this like one of those hidden camera shows or something?" Mildred laughed, searching the room for a camera crew. The seriousness on both of their faces cut her laughter short.

"I reacted in a similar way when I was first told, Mildred."

"I bet you did, Daphne. That is your name, isn't it, or will that be changing any time soon?"

Daphne smiled. "It will probably change in the future, Mildred, yes as indeed will yours. I have told you of this."

"Excellent, I have always wanted to be called, well now let me see, Mary or Joanna. Yes, I'd like that, Lady Joanna. Perhaps we could go the full hog and I could be called Douglas. Now that's a solid name. You can both call me that from now on."

Suzanna did not care for Mildred's patronising tone. "We do not take names from the world of men."

"I'll bet. What about Steve? Everyone loves a Steve."

"That's enough!"

Mildred jumped at the tone of Suzanna's voice.

Suzanna took a deep breath, lowered her tone and resumed with a more passive voice. "One does not simply join our Order Mildred and we are an Order that goes back over many centuries. You were selected to join us and you were always going to. You came of age a few years ago when Daphne, your Elder, first visited you."

She tilted her head back slightly and her eyebrows came together with bemusement or amusement; she wasn't sure. "Came of age? I became of age for many things and that was some years ago, quite a few in fact!"

"This is different. This requires maturity. Our numbers are exacting and your time was right. You were brought into the fold when a member passed on. We are always replaced, you see?"

"No, Suzanna, I really don't see."

"As you know from this evening, we recently lost one of our beloved members."

"Lady Tempest," Daphne interjected.

"Her passing meant a position needed to be filled and that was taken by me. Daphne has now taken my position and you have taken hers. That leaves a new position to be filled. You will become the Elder of the Lady who is selected."

Mildred shook her head, "I'm sorry, what?"

"You will be responsible for her, Mildred. You will go and see her as I did you."

"Well, I'm sorry, Daphne, but I thought you were barking when you first came round."

"Barking is a strange choice of word, Mildred. Cats don't bark now, do they?" Suzanna and Daphne both grinned.

"No, I guess they do not." Mildred's voice had become very quiet in all the confusion.

"Look, I know this is a lot to take in, but you are now what is known as a Degree Level Eight member. Daphne is now a Seven and I am a Six. The roles that we play are very important."

"What has this to do with cats and my Missy, Jessica?"

"It's Suzanna from now on if you please and it has everything to do with cats, Mildred. Missy was brought to you as she is one of our own. All cats are important, but our cats are special and you are her protector." Mildred shook her head again. "I think she does a perfectly good job of looking after herself, well except for this week, of course."

They both watched her as she looked towards the floor in worry.

"She'll be back tomorrow, Mildred and I'm sure she will be fine. I have something else to tell you and it's very important."

Mildred looked up at Suzanna.

She took a deep breath and looked Mildred directly in the eyes, nodding as she spoke. "Every cat has a name, Mildred, every cat without exception, whether they are one of ours or not."

Mildred raised an eyebrow and looked at Daphne, who nodded in support of this statement.

"Well, of course they do."

Suzanna smiled. "But they really do Mildred, they really do. Your cat, who is one of us, is not really called Missy. Her real name is Nahla."

Mildred looked back at Daphne, who was still nodding.

Mildred snorted a little. "What?"

"Nahla."

"Well, what on ever does that mean and why can't I call her Missy?"

"You can look up the meaning should you choose, but ask yourself this, have you ever called out the name Missy and she doesn't come to you, or you think she doesn't even hear it?"

"Well, yes, quite a bit actually, but cats can be like that sometimes. I don't think that is unusual; they are very independent."

"Indeed they are, as are we, including yourself, Mildred, when you think about it. You are very independent too and always have been. Cats prefer to be addressed by their real name. Try it when you see her; you will see. I guarantee it!"

Mildred was at a loss for words, well, polite words. "Okay, answer this, please. If that is the case, why did you not tell me her name at the start?"

"If it's of any consolation, Mildred, I asked the exact same question when I was told." Daphne reached over and put a hand on Mildred's knee.

"I'm not sure that it is, but please explain it to me."

"I will, well, in part. When a kitten is brought to you, it takes time to discover the world and what surrounds her. She has to find her own way in life and when you come of age, you are presented with her name. You have earned the right to know her name and in future you can address your cat correctly as you bond further. You are one. Does that help a little?"

Mildred shook her head. "I have no idea, to be honest, Suzanna."

Suzanna had noticed that Mildred had not addressed her correctly throughout the conversation, but this was clearly a lot for Mildred to take in. She would remind her to use her title later.

"Your cat will gather its own mould and through the early stages of its life, it is also independent until the time is right. Nahla's time is right now and the Grand Council has decided that your time is also now. It's a tradition that has gone back through generations and generations. We are not looking to change that any time soon."

"So, if I understand all of this correctly and I'm not sure that I do, you are going to give me a cat to give to a complete stranger?"

"She won't be a stranger now, will she, Mildred? She has been selected. Therefore, she is known to the powers above, if you will."

Mildred watched Suzanna do the inverted commas sign as she said this. She was looking at Daphne, who still resembled some sort of daft nodding dog, when another question came to mind.

"Where do the cats come from then? Like the one you are going to give to me?"

For the first time in this oddball conversation, Daphne looked at a loss and looked at Suzanna.

"I can't tell you that. I'm sorry."

"Well, why ever not, Suzanna?"

"Because I do not know the answer."

Mildred frowned again and tilted her head a little to the side with some disbelief. "Convenient don't you think?" She mumbled.

Suzanna shook her head and sighed. "But I do know this; our cats are brought to us by a Senior Lady called the Keeper. How they come to her or from whom is unknown to us all. It is a closely guarded secret. There are many secrets in the Order, Mildred."

"Such as?"

"Well, they wouldn't be secrets if I told you. I still have much to learn, but consider this. You will have learned of events throughout history, which you may have read about or seen on TV, such as the news. Whenever something happens, someone important addresses the nation through the media and often tries to give answers even if they do not know them."

"You mean like politicians?"

"Yes, they are one vessel of information or misinformation in some instances, but ask yourself this, has there ever been a cat far away?"

Suzanna sat back in her chair, confident she now had Mildred's attention and that her speech was going quite well.

"Well, I..."

"Think about names that are considered as great names in history; poets, authors, composers, Heads of State. Many of them were devoted to cats. Even here in this country, do you think it's a coincidence that you often see on the news that there is a cat in Downing Street?"

Mildred shrugged.

"They are our own Mildred, all of them and always have been. We are never far away and we stay there to ensure that order is maintained, well, at least where possible. We are always suspicious of key people who do not have a cat close by them, but it's always only a matter of time."

Mildred watched as both of their heads nodded in agreement.

"What order? What balance? I don't understand?"

"These are good questions, Mildred, you are asking the right ones." Daphne put a hand on Mildred's knee again.

"Mildred, regrettably, not everything is good; it never has been. On the outside of this place, some want to cause chaos and seek to poison the race of men."

Mildred raised her eyebrows and shook her head, "eh, what's that got to do with me?"

Daphne smiled, but Suzanna's face held a serious look. "These creatures are vile and want to create a world of darkness and disorder. That's where we fit in. We are the light that prevents the darkness."

Mildred could feel her lips trembling as she stifled a laugh that was trying to escape, but she managed to contain it. She would have a giggle later over a cup of tea at home.

"So we are the great protectors?"

"Something like that, Mildred. Yes."

They watched Mildred look down at the floor; she was obviously amused. "Mildred, look up, please."

She lifted her head to face Suzanna.

"They are called Watchers and they are a poisonous cast, a breed apart. We want to stop them from achieving their ideals."

"So at weekends, do I go Watcher catching or something?"

Daphne sighed. "Mildred, I accepted a lot of this better than you are. You will need time to think and adjust as I did. Have you ever wondered why you get paid by us every month? Do you think ordinary cat clubs pay their members?"

"Well, yes, I had thought about it actually. I thought it was kinda strange."

"Well, now you know. In fact, you will be paid more now that you are an Eighth Degree Elder."

"I see. Is it like hazard pay or something, as some of this sounds a bit dodgy?"

Suzanna gave a short and succinct smile. "I think that is enough for today. We can talk again soon after you've been able to take it all in."

Suzanna went to stand. "Lady Suzanna, you haven't mentioned the new addition."

Suzanna looked at Daphne. "Oh yes, sorry, Mildred, there is one more thing," she settled back into her seat again.

She looked at Mildred's confused face. "I do have some good news for you, though, something I know that you will be very happy to hear."

Mildred had no words and just nodded a couple of times.

"When the new kitten is brought to you for our new member, you will be brought one as well and it will be Daphne who brings it to you."

For the first time, Mildred sat upright, focused on what she was hearing. "I'm going to have a new cat?"

"Yes, Mildred, that is correct," said Daphne as they both watched a smile erupt over her face for the first time since they had sat down.

"As Lady Suzanna has explained, now that you are an Eighth Degree Elder, you have responsibilities and one of those is being presented with a new cat. We both will have a new one as well."

"So you will have three now, Daphne?"

"Yes and Lady Suzanna will have four."

"Four?" Mildred smiled. "You'll look like a crazy cat lady, Suzanna."

Suzanna looked on as Mildred cackled to herself. "That's not a term I care for Mildred, but I'll let you have that one this time." Suzanna stood up. "Besides, Mildred, from what you have learnt this evening, we are no ordinary ladies and far from crazy for that matter. We are owed a great debt from those on the outside." Mildred felt her shoulder being patted a couple of times by Suzanna's hand. "Time to go, much to do."

Daphne stood up and gathered her things.

Mildred, who was still sat down, turned around to Suzanna's voice. "Don't forget your sandwiches, Mildred. It looks like there are quite a few left. I'll meet you outside."

Mildred looked on as Daphne and Suzanna left the room. She slowly stood up to look through the opened doors they had just left through. She could see they were talking outside on the patio and she was 100% sure they were talking about her.

She looked across the abandoned room and heard the doors from the other side open as the staff came in to clean up.

She grabbed at her bag and collected her plates. Suzanna was right. There were plenty of sandwiches left, but she was more disappointed to see her cards were still there, either unopened or had just been left behind on the tables. She clenched her teeth as she walked around the tables to collect them and then walked back to her bag. Bending over she threw them in the bag as she heard muffled voices from behind her.

"Look, that is exactly what I mean. If you were ever going to describe a cat lady, that would be it." Tom nodded at Brooke as they both looked at Mildred's baggy stockings as she bent over. They both giggled at each other as she stood up and stared at them. She did not look too pleased.

They immediately stopped laughing.

Mildred knew they were making fun of her. One day this fun and mocking would stop. She was done with it. Tonight had reaffirmed it and her days of being the subject of ridicule were over.

Chapter Twenty Eight:

THE CLEAR SKY ABOVE ROCKE ROAD

FRIDAY LATE EVENING

Other than generalised pleasantries, hardly a word was passed between Mildred and Lady Suzanna in the ten minutes or so they had travelled together.

Mildred estimated they were only a couple of miles away from her home and she would be glad to be back. The evening and the week overall had taken a turn for the surreal.

Clearly, the newly named Suzanna had much to consider as she sat in silence. Mildred noticed that an Elder had passed documents to Suzanna earlier on in the evening after she had been named. They were presumably official papers or more of their 'secrets;' whatever that meant.

"So a new cat will be delivered to me then?"

Suzanna glanced across at Mildred. "Yes, that is the way it is, probably sometime tomorrow or the day after. It usually happens pretty quickly."

"I see. So what will be the name of my new cat and the other one for the new girl?"

"Lady Mildred, she is now a Lady, as are you."

There was silence again. Suzanna knew that Mildred wanted answers. "I will not know the names of either of the cats. That is not my role and at this early stage, as they develop from kittens to adulthood, I'm not sure who does know; the Keeper, I guess. A lot of practices are time old and their secrets are maintained and guarded. As you can tell, there are still matters of procedure that are beyond my knowledge."

"So, what will I call it then?"

Mildred was surprised to hear laughter from Lady Suzanna. "You can call her what you like, Mildred. It's a temporary name for you. In time the real name will be presented to you when you are both ready."

Mildred looked at the street lights and recognised they were only a few roads away from home.

"Does that all make sense to you?"

Mildred shook her head. "I'm not sure, Suzanna; it's a lot to take in."

"It certainly is. Some adjust better than others, but you have responsibilities now. You are a protector of cats."

"Like you?"

"Exactly, just like me. I've just been involved for longer, shall we say."

Silence ensued as they pulled into Rocke Road. Suzanna looked up to the sky. "Well, it's a beautiful summer evening Mildred, not a cloud in the sky." There was no response forthcoming, although she noticed that Mildred did peer forward to take a look.

The car stopped outside Mildred's home and Suzanna looked over to her. "You know my phone is always on for you if you need to speak with me. Daphne is your direct Elder and that is the usual process, but you can contact me if you wish. I want to take a keen interest in you, Mildred, as you adjust to things. We are like family."

Mildred nodded a couple of times, thinking about the 'bad forces' that were out there somewhere. Quite what that had to do with her and Missy, she had no idea.

She looked at Suzanna. "Is that why Fennaway was recommended? Is she one of us, this Horde Of Illumination?"

"Light Mildred, Horde Of Light." Suzanna saw Mildred shrug her shoulders and let out a deep breath.

"She is one of us, yes."

"You know I called someone else?"

"Yes, I am aware Mildred. Our cats are very special and Fennaway understands them. Please do not call others in the future."

"She can talk to them as well, apparently," she said with a shake of the head, looking towards the floor.

"That's as may be. It's not a gift that I possess."

Mildred looked up, raising her eyes. "A gift?"

"That's right, some of us are more gifted than others. You will have your own; you just don't know yours yet."

"I suspect it's not sandwich making," she replied, looking down once again and letting out a puff of air. "My Missy is back in the morning."

Suzanna looked on as Mildred looked up and glanced over to her empty house.

"I'm sure she will be fine; let's hope so!" Suzanna looked away with some guilt for the part she played in switching the cats earlier on. She had no idea how she was going to switch them back. Her thoughts started to dwell on Khepri.

"Well, I guess that I had better go." Mildred pulled at the door handle.

"Yes, tomorrow is another day, another day another dollar."

"Oh yes, apparently I'll be having more of that as well."

"Sorry, Mildred?"

"Dollars, money, although quite what I need it for is anyone's guess. Maybe I'll go on that game show I've been watching."

Suzanna smirked, "and which one is that?"

"Bang Goes Your Money, I quite like him."

"Oh yes, I know the one you mean."

"There is something oddly charming about him, well, for a man anyways." Mildred looked at Suzanna's smile. "Goodnight, Mildred."

Mildred stepped out of the car dragging her heavy bag full of cards and sandwiches. "Thank you, Lady Suzanna."

"You are welcome, Lady Mildred."

They both smiled at each other as Mildred stepped back to watch Suzanna drive off.

She was right. It was a beautiful evening as Mildred looked down her road, alone, in the peace and quiet. Even the bus stop was empty; the kids must have gone elsewhere this evening. She looked up at the sky as she unclipped her gate. It was cloudless and the stars shone more so than usual.

There was much to think about. She hoped a cup of tea would solve it, but in her heart, she knew it wouldn't. It would be her first night alone in three years and she didn't like the thought of it at all. She had missed her game show, of course. She considered investing in one of those video recording devices. Apparently, she would be a lady of some wealth now and then what, a computer, a car? The possibilities were endless. In all honesty, she was delighted that she would have a new cat, but that was all. Other than that, she wanted no further part of it.

Nubia sat at her desk transfixed by her clock. Her elbows and palms were supporting the weight of her chin; it was approaching 10.30. The midnight hour was rapidly approaching and she hoped that Lady Ebonee's predictions were not correct.

She bit down on her lip and looked at Nahla, who was still away in some other painful place. No matter what happens, Nahla would need to be removed tomorrow as Mildred was expecting her back.

She thought briefly of Khepri, standing in, but Mildred, like all cat owners, would know the difference between the two cats and explanations would need to be made. Some things can be very difficult to explain.

She was told earlier in the evening of Mildred's elevation to Degree Level Eight, she hoped that matters of her rank and title had been explained to her. She didn't know Mildred and had not met her, or at least in this time, but she knew that some new members struggled to realise that their former lives, pre coming of age, were nothing but blips in the past. Being brought into the Order was not a choice but a duty and she would have duties in the near future.

She reached down into her desk for the bottle of Scotch and collected a glass. Her nerves were being tested as she listened to the tick of the pendulum. She took a sip, enjoying the peaty taste from the Scottish Highlands and put the glass back down. She approached Nahla, who twitched in pain as her heart raced back and forth. Her mind wondered; The 'Great Nubia,' Curator of the Horde of the United Kingdom, drunk in charge of a cat with two apparent heartbeats. She shook her head at the thought.

She leant against the windowsill over where Nahla lay and looked out of the open window studying the beautiful gardens that were surprisingly visible in the Welsh moonlight. It was a clear sky, maybe the clearest she had seen in some time. She looked out at the stars as they flickered in the distance. They were different worlds and not all of them for good, but at least there wasn't a storm brewing. There would be no flashes of lightning or a blinding light; that was positive at least. It didn't look like there would be a sign from above as had been foretold.

The Escarrabin would be returning throughout the evening and into the early hours. Nothing untoward had been reported at this time.

She sat down, looking at Nahla with concern, hoping she would recover after midnight. Anytime before then would be of concern; an hour and a half would tell.

✛✛✛✛

Duat sat at the end of the carved rock that he used as a bed, focused on the grains of sand falling steadily through the huge hourglass. After nearly twenty-four hours of time passing, it wouldn't be long before they ran out completely.

"Bellator, come."

He could hear his servant's robe moving towards him as he approached the area that resembled his chamber.

He entered with his head bowed. "Yes, Master. How may I serve you?"

Duat was still leaning forward, focused on the hourglass. "It's nearly time. Everything is as planned?"

"Yes, Master."

"Go to our brothers and see that they are ready."

"Yes, Master."

"How many are there of us?"

"Twenty-seven Master."

Duat took his eye away from the sand, drew a deep breath and stood up as the vapour emitted from his mouth. He looked at Bellator. "Your time in chains is nearly over."

They were both disturbed by the banging coming from below in the deep. Bellator quickly turned towards the noise, pulled down his hood and spun around with a nervous gaze to see Duat's smile. "My friend grows restless." Bellator stared at his Master in confusion. Duat closed his eye and counted the multiple bangs that could be heard against iron. He smiled throughout, then looked up to the above. "Nine, it is untouched and perfectly formed." He returned his gaze, seeing the concern in Bellator's eye. "It is the sound of life behind iron; it too wants to be free. Like you, it does not belong in this place and wants to be outside beside water, not imprisoned by rock or iron and the will of others."

"I have dreamt of water, Master."

"You have dreamt of lakes of fire. What it seeks is something quite different." He stepped forward as his servant lowered his head again. "When it comes, keep clear of it. It means harm to the others that live above, but stay away from it. Let it carry out its will and determination and you shall be freed."

"Yes, Master."

Duat turned around to look at the hourglass again. "The bumbling efforts of the Elder to disrupt the inevitable were somewhat misjudged," he smiled.

"Master?"

He turned back around to look at the bowed head. "She who was called by the name of Tempest; it needn't concern you as it is no more, I saw to that."

"Yes, Master."

"Now go! Ensure all are ready. We move in the early hours."

"I will do that now, Master."

He turned back towards the falling sand.

"Serpents and rats shall be free again to roam, as shall we. It is foretold and inevitable; I have foreseen it."

Having just returned from the armoury and taken the opportunity to carry out an inspection, Raysmau was satisfied with what she saw. The battle armour was where it needed to be and nearby if the call from the Reeve was made.

Slight adjustments would need to be made to the night vision goggles if face masks and extra eye protectors were to be worn. That would be a decision that the Reeve would need to make in the event of the unthinkable.

As she entered her ceremonial dressing room, she knew that it had been some time since she had worn full battle armour. Some years, if she were honest. It had not been worn since her tenure at Loxley.

She removed her loose clothing she had worn in the armoury and walked to the glass case that contained her battle armour. She assessed the mannequin that wore it against her own frame and knew this may be a little tricky. Taking the key from her dresser, she opened the glass door and started to disrobe the mannequin. The sheer weight of the armour was hardly a surprise; how it restricted her movements could not be forgotten. The reality was that wearing it now may be more difficult than before. She placed the various layers on the chair next to her dresser and started to apply the protective undergarments and the steel-framed leggings. There was a short smile as she looked down at her size twelve feet and her socks with multiple colours. She drew the protective mesh over both of them. She was satisfied that her socks could not be seen by anyone before she summoned much-needed assistance.

"Layla, come into my quarters, will you? Don't bother knocking." She let go of the intercom button, knowing that the guard in her security office would be with her in a matter of seconds. She squatted up and down a couple of times, knowing that she could not be seen and stretched the protective leggings as much as she could as Layla walked into her chambers.

"Yes, Ma'am, how may I be of assistance?"

"Help me with this, will you?"

The Escarrabin looked a little confused. "Yes, Ma'am, with the battle armour?"

"I realised that I haven't worn it for a while and wanted to check it would still fit."

"Yes, Ma'am, of course."

"Put on a bit of weight since the last time I wore it."

"Well, if you have, I cannot tell, Ma'am."

Raysmau looked at her security officer with raised eyebrows.

Knowing that compliments were not being looked for, she walked over to the chair that the battle armour laid upon with a nervous smile. "Yes, Ma'am."

"Just lift that up, will you? It needs to be secured at the back."

She could see the look of shock upon the security officer's face as she felt the weight of the main armour that would cover Raysmau's upper body. "My arms need to go through together, so if you can lift it up in front of me."

The Escarrabin's shoulders shook from the weight. She held the armour aloft from underneath the armpits as Raysmau placed both arms inside. "You will see fasteners at the back that should secure it."

Layla let go of the armour as it fell upon Raysmau's torso, instantly gaining many kilos of weight.

Raysmau could see Layla's struggling in the mirror as she tried to pull it together as it pulled across Raysmau's chest and stomach.

"Nearly there, Ma'am."

"You won't break me. Just pull it!"

It was a struggle, but the fasteners were finally secured. Raysmau breathed out and could feel beads of sweat forming on her forehead from the weight, discomfort and how noticeably tight it was since the last time she had worn it.

"There, it fits no problem at all, Ma'am."

She frowned, feeling like a robot. "Well, I wouldn't say that."

Layla watched her Head of Order walk up and down the room, accustoming her body to the rapid weight gain.

"Thank you, Layla. That will be all for now. I'll keep it on for a bit."

"Yes, Ma'am."

Raysmau acknowledged the bow and watched her leave the room before blowing out as she leant against her dresser. "Who makes these things?"

The phone started ringing in her office. She sighed as she hobbled as quickly as she could in discomfort.

"Yes, hello."

"Raysmau, it's Lady Nubia."

"Yes, my Lady. Are you okay?" Raysmau looked at the clock and could see that it had just passed quarter to eleven. It was a bit late to be calling and rare to hear from the Curator in any event.

"Yes, I'm fine. Are you? You sound a little out of breath."

"Yes, Ma'am. Sorry, I was just doing some cleaning." She frowned, saying the first thing that popped into her head.

"I see. I've looked out of the window and not seen any of the Escarrabin return from the gatherings."

"No, my Lady, I'm not expecting them for some time yet." She puffed as she spoke, with no idea why she was being asked a question like this.

"That is as I thought, but just a question, if I may? When they are all here, how many of them will there be?"

Raysmau went to sit down but quickly realised that she couldn't, so she remained bent over the desk with the weight of the armour on her back. "Thirty-six by the headcount, my Lady." She frowned at the strange question. "Are you sure that everything is okay, Ma'am?"

"Yes, it was just a question. It's always good to know these things."

"I see." She really didn't, nor why she was being asked such a direct question about security. "Is there anything else that I can assist you with?"

"No, that's all. Thank you. I just wanted to be sure. I'll leave you to it. Thank you, Raysmau."

She replaced the receiver and straightened up her back with a grimace.

She looked at the closed door in front of her deep in thought about what was clearly not a generalised question. The Curator was worried and definitely knew something.

She wondered how many more at Loxley knew about these potential developments and hoped that things were not being kept from her. Her concern deepened as she looked at the ticking clock, hoping she didn't have to wear her armour all night.

It was a very late night for Mildred and approaching 10.30; it had been some time since she had been up at this hour. She sat down on her couch in contemplation. 'Dark forces,' 'bad things' she smirked to herself at the ridiculousness, of it all. She shook her head in amusement, wondering what planet these people were living on. She stared at the framed certificate on the wall, knowing that if she were to remain in the crazy cat cult, a new one would now be added alongside it.

Her hands went behind her head as she lay back in the seat, considering the obvious differences in 'rank' that she had witnessed this evening. At the two gatherings before, she had failed to notice the now stark differences between the Senior Elders and the others. The Seniors dressed differently from her and the other Mildreds, Daphnes and Jessicas. It was weird beyond belief.

The Senior Elders seemed to keep themselves to themselves as though they were a clan of some sort. They had drivers and dresses that were no doubt expensive. Even Jessica, who was now named Suzanna showed far too much leg and skin, like some other Elders. Probably something designer, not from the charity shops, where most of Mildred's clothing came from. At no time was she invited into conversations with the various clusters. She gained some nods after she was promoted, but that was about it. If she did overhear a conversation, it was never about cats, which was somewhat irregular for a cat membership club, or the Horde or whatever it was called.

If people on her street, like the kids at the bus stop, thought she was an oddball, this group were a pool table full of oddballs. And the jewels they were wearing, what was all that about? Like some sort of kings and queens, not that there was a man in sight. She smiled to herself as a picture came into her mind of watching television some time ago on a Saturday afternoon. She scratched her head. What was the programme called? She gave it some thought, oh yes, 'The A Team.' A couple of the members were dressed up in heavy jewels and chains, looking like the big guy on the programme that you didn't want to fall out with. She had forgotten his name as well.

"I love it when a plan comes together!" she giggled to herself. But there didn't appear to be any plan here whatsoever, just a collection of crazy people.

Nubia's body jolted. Her eyes opened, looking directly at the ceiling. She put her hands to her head and focused on the empty glass of Scotch. With everything going on, she couldn't believe she had nodded off.

Rubbing her eyes, she glanced over to the clock; it informed her it was only a few minutes before midnight. Her pulse elevated, knowing that in a few minutes all of this would be over. The prophecy on this occasion had failed. Her neck was stiff from having fallen asleep. She sat upright and immediately jumped up from her chair.

"Nahla!"

She looked at the shorthair cat standing on the windowsill with the white of her tail slowly twitching back and forth. Nubia immediately ran over to Mildred's cat. "Nahla, you're okay!" She smiled, but the cat showed no interest whatsoever, staring intently into the night sky. Nubia followed her gaze towards the stars. A shiver immediately ran through her. Her hands started to tremble as she used them to support her body weight as she leant over the couch and leaned against the windowsill.

"Do you know something?" She watched her tail that looked agitated in its movements. "Nahla, do you know something?" Nothing, no change, no sign or response. "NAHLA!" she raised the pitch of her voice and Mildred's cat turned her head slightly to look at her. "Good, so you understand me then? Do you know anything? Give me a sign." She looked into the deep blue eyes of the cat. "Should we be worried?"

Nahla looked at her for a few seconds and nodded before returning to gaze at the August night sky.

Nubia recoiled, shaking, placing a hand to her mouth in worry. She spun around to look at her clock. It was a couple of minutes before midnight as she swallowed and looked back at Nahla.

She stepped closer towards the windowsill, looking at Nahla, whose focus had not deviated from the night sky. Nubia looked across the Welsh skyline. Despite the differences in their languages, they both were terrified as the midnight hour approached.

Duat sat patiently as he pulled his hood down and inhaled deeply, closing his eye. Extending his right arm, he flexed his hand a couple of times and felt the power growing through him as his palm deepened in colour. He opened his eye and watched on at the life that moved through it.

He could hear the impatient movements deep below, sensing the anticipation outside his chamber from others who would consider him as their kind. He wasn't, of course, but they had uses and would be loyal soldiers for as long as he needed them; until the time was right.

Tonight they would do battle with the enemies of old; it had been a long time coming. Once the beast is free, it would tear through their defences. Their Escarrabin were no match for it. He placed his glowing palm to the wall and looked to his right at the two keys resting on the table. He closed his eye again to concentrate. There were nerves above, he could feel that, but the constant ticking overhead remained. He looked at the hourglass; it was not quite time, but he could feel it was very close.

Mildred woke with a startle and immediately sat upright in her bed; she put her hand to her chest and took a couple of deep breaths.

She had the most terrible dream and could feel beads of sweat on her brow. She leant over to her bedside table, picked up a hair tie and fixed her hair back, feeling dampness at the roots. She sat there in confusion for a moment, trying to remember what she had been dreaming about, but it was fading away. Wincing, trying to recollect it, she recalled a lake on fire and figures that were faceless or had their faces hidden. She wasn't sure; it didn't make any sense.

Looking around her room in the moonlight that poured through the window, she wiped at her brow. It was far too warm, it was August, but this was too much. She put it down to the global warming thing she had heard about. She stretched her toes, got up and went to the window to let in some air. There was very little breeze. The skyline was completely clear and silent as she looked at the moon that offered some reassuring light from the darkness of her dream. The first night Missy is away and it comes to this; terrible dreams. She was eager for her return and could not wait until the morning.

A rustling from the bushes next door caught her attention as she looked down to the garden below. She blinked and rubbed at her eyes. "Well, I never." She watched as a badger appeared, but she was more fascinated by the three cats in the garden, all looking skyward. She looked up at the stars and leant out of the window to see what they were all staring at. As she looked back down, the badger was looking directly at the sky as well.

She was fascinated by what she was witnessing. What a strange phenomenon; she looked skyward in anticipation with a smile, wondering, if Missy were here, would she be sitting with them as well. It was like they all knew one another.

Her smile was short-lived and instantly replaced by concern as two bright lights came into view, falling from above.

She rubbed her eyes as they came closer, flying high above her home. They looked to be on fire with white-lit trails coming from behind them. As they passed overhead, she looked down and watched the animals' eyes following the trail.

Both objects, still high in the air, flew over her home out of sight. She looked back down to the garden. The badger moved away, but the cats remained, their tails twitching in unison. Unlike Dr Fennaway, she couldn't speak to cats, but she had to concede they looked very nervous.

Duat's right palm was still pressed firmly to the wall as he focused deeply on what he could hear and feel coming from the above.

His breathing became more intense as he closed his eye and stretched out his fingers. His mouth opened with a hiss as he pushed further, running his palm throughout the building above. He stopped suddenly and opened his eye.

He breathed deeply as drool ran out of his mouth. A smile broke out across his face. The smile turned to anger as he moved his hand from the wall and looked at the hourglass.

The last grain of sand had fallen.

"Nahla, Nahla?" The Curator looked at the cat in anguish, then back to the clock. Midnight had passed, her clock ticked, but there were no chimes.

Her hands were shaking as she climbed onto the sofa to stare out of the window, looking as far as her eyes would reach.

She looked back at Nahla. "Is something going to happen. Nahla, is something going to happen?"

She looked deep into Nahla's eyes and froze as fear suddenly appeared in them. Her own eyes matched Nahla's fear as she spun around to look outside again. "Oh no, it can't be!!" Her knees buckled under her tiny frame as she fell against the couch. Two bright lights came into view, heading in their direction. They both watched the double light trail across the Welsh skyline. Nubia recoiled and put a hand to her face in fear as one erupted into eight separate falling stars that faded away. The one remaining ball of fire streamed overhead past the manor house. Nubia hung out of the window, watching it disappear into the distance before a bright flash of light lit up the skyline. It must have been seen for miles as the noise of a loud bang travelled towards them.

She collapsed on the sofa holding her chest. Nahla climbed down from the windowsill and stared at her. Nubia was shaking all over as tears formed in her eyes.

"Lights from above! A light will come from above!"

She steadied herself to her feet. "CLERIC!" She screamed at the top of her voice, "CLERIC!"

Her door flung open as the Cleric looked at the Curator, who could barely stand and was out of breath. "Get me the Reeve."

"Ma'am?"

"Get me the Reeve, GET ME THE REEVE!" She screamed as loudly as she could. The Cleric rushed out of the door, but she continued screaming even after she had left; "GET ME THE REEVE!"

Her voice travelled the length of the mansion house. Clerics and Escarrabin stopped working and looked at one another as her voice reached the corridor of clocks. There was a deep, cold echo as every clock within Loxley was silenced.

Time had stopped; they had ticked for the very last time.

The Reeve, in response to the Cleric's call, made her way towards the Curator's chambers. To have received an urgent call at this hour was very unnerving. She was surprised to see that Nubia's door was slightly open as she pushed it forward and poked her head inside.

Nubia was in some sort of catatonic state as the Reeve looked at the bottle of Scotch that was two thirds empty. She watched their Curator swallow another mouthful from the now empty glass.

"What's going on, Nubia?" She looked upon the short stature of the Curator who was leant against her desk, struggling for composure and breath.

"It's happening again, Reeve."

Her eyes looked damp as if she had been crying. She looked terrified. It was true, they did not have a great deal of time for each other, but it was worrying to see her in this state of pain and anxiety.

She spoke calmly and quietly. "What is happening, Nubia?"

"It's started."

"What has? I don't understand."

"Did you not see it?" Her eyes looked in pain and a little bloodshot from the tears.

She shook her head and raised her arms slightly. "See what?"

"Light. Light from above. The light fell from the sky." She was highly animated and flapping her hands, pointing towards the open window. "It crashed to the ground some miles away."

"What? You can't be serious. What did you see?" She walked over to the window and looked outside.

"The second sign, it is as foretold."

She turned around and saw Nubia pointing at her clock as more tears ran down her cheeks.

Horrified, the Reeve looked at the pendulum that had stopped swinging. "It will be the same in your office and everywhere."

The Reeve pulled back the cuff of her jacket and lifted her left arm. She tapped her watch. It had stopped at two minutes past midnight.

"I see it in your face Reeve, you know what this means, I have been trying to tell you."

She let her arm fall at her side and without words, sat on the couch underneath the window.

"Look."

She followed the direction of where Nubia was pointing to a black cat with a white-tipped tail, sitting quietly on a single seat. Until that very moment, she hadn't noticed her. Her eyes widened in surprise.

"Whose cat is that?"

"Mildred's."

The Reeve frowned and looked at Nubia. "Which Mildred?"

"Mildred from Shrewsbury."

"Is this the cat that was bearing the pain?" She looked at the Curator, who was now leaning against her desk and nodded. "Well, what on earth is it doing here?"

"I had to take action. I needed to intervene. I had to do the right thing."

She looked back at Nahla and swallowed whilst shaking her head in some disbelief. "Nubia, what have you done?"

"She was going to be taken away to a vet, not of our own. I had to take action. You have to believe me."

The Reeve's mouth hung open temporarily, her head still shaking. "I ask you again, what exactly have you done?"

"They would have run tests on her; we can't allow that. It might have exposed us."

The Reeve pursed her lips with a knowing expression. "Is that why I saw Jessica here earlier today," she looked at the non-ticking clock and corrected herself, "yesterday? I'm guessing her being here again had something to do with this?"

"Her name is now Lady Suzanna as I understand, and yes, she played a role."

"Nubia, you have to be honest with me. What exactly did she do?"

"I put her on surveillance and had her switch the cat with one of her own. She then brought Nahla here."

Flabbergasted, the Reeve slumped back into the couch. "You did what? You put one of our untrained ladies out on surveillance? Well, what a fine job I bet she did of that. Security is my department, Nubia. Are you insane, are you for real?"

"What is that supposed to mean?" she responded with some spite. "Is all of this real, are we for real Reeve?"

They both sat in silence to gain some composure.

"I remember some of it. The last time it happened."

The Reeve looked up at the Curator.

"My fear is justified. I know what happened the last time a light fell from above."

The Reeve crossed her arms. "Ridiculous that was too long ago."

She spoke softly in some discomfort, "I do Reeve, I really do."

The Reeve smiled but was shaking her head.

"It's not a laughing matter!"

"No, it really is not. You have memories of those times?"

"I do! That is why I was selected for this role. You think I panic and overreact, but I remember, I know what happens. That cat is one of us. It will have an important role to play."

The Reeve looked at Nahla, who was watching their every move. She didn't take her eyes off her as she spoke. "So, if I have this right, Mildred does not know that Nahla is here and Lady Suzanna's cat is now somewhere else?"

"Yes, that is correct."

She turned to Nubia. "With another vet?" She nodded in agreement. "They may run tests on her cat instead."

"It was an educated risk. Besides, I had Fennaway speak with her beforehand. Suzanna's cat Khepri was asked to help us."

"Asked or told?"

"We always ask and never assume Reeve. That is the way."

The Reeve leant forward onto her elbows in thought. "This changes things."

"Changes what? We need to act and act quickly. The second part of the prophecy has taken place right in front of my eyes. It cannot be a coincidence that it has happened here, right in front of us."

The Reeve nodded in agreement. "No, it cannot. There is something else very troubling happening that you are not aware of."

The Curator frowned. "How so, what am I not aware of?"

"We need to go upstairs to speak with Lady Safiya."

"Yes, I agree. She needs to know."

"She does, but that was not what I was referring to."

The Curator leaned her head forward. "Well?"

"Something has awoken in the deep of the below. What is happening cannot be a coincidence. We need to go into the below."

The Curator rocked backwards in shock. "Are you serious?"

"Yes now. Right now."

Duat had never been further into the below than where he had needed to. He had given his motivational talks to the others that dwelled within over the couple of floors below his own. His talks were full of venom, his words unforgiving; he had done well and could sense their anger at every turn. They bowed to him now, quite rightly and addressed him as their Master. He had won over their confidence in achieving what they had believed impossible. Their will to live beyond the walls and chambers was evident. He suspected many of them had been far below looking for a means of escape in the past.

Their language of Volemon and their own symbology had been carved into the walls throughout the lower floors. The first floor, where the Escarrabin would greet them daily, was left in the old dark and natural state.

Duat had been presented with facts and knowledge; he did not know about the Watchers tunnel when he arrived and did not care for how far they had progressed with it. That desire to be free rapidly gained him their support. They would do his bidding.

However, he did know that at the very bottom of the below was the original home of the Reeve's treasures they had stolen, it was not rightfully theirs. Their original stronghold must have taken many years of digging and carving with ancient tools to hide their secrets and wealth. Only on rare occasions would some of this wealth materialise to the outside world that was miraculously discovered in a field or a desert somewhere, no doubt for a price. Pirates that paraded as protectors; that was their only admirable quality.

He held his right hand up to an unlit torch and breathed on his palm. He watched the flames light up the area around him as he held the torch aloft. Safe in the knowledge that the two keys were in the pocket of his robe, he walked towards the stairwell. He could hear hisses all around him from the Watchers, seething in anger and ready for change.

The ancient stone steps beneath his feet were worn and uneven. He reached over to the wall on his right and removed another unlit torch, bringing the two of them together. The dark void directly to the left of the spiral stairs had no supporting rail. He leant over and dropped one of the torches over the side. He watched as the flames became more distant as it fell, much further than expected. The thud of it hitting the bottom took a couple of seconds for him to hear. He was not the only one to hear it as a roar propelled up the staircase followed by multiple bangs against iron.

The size of the beast would be of such enormity that it may struggle to fit up the staircase. He hoped its clumsiness would not bring the whole lot down upon them both.

He descended into the darkness with the torch held above him. His suspicions were correct. He ran his palm over the old Watcher's language. The others had the sense of touch but not like him. The acidic quality of their resin from their right palms had allowed them to leave their marks all over the wall as he progressed further down.

He could see the vapour rising in front of his eye as his breathing intensified in the coldness. The banging and noise from below became ever closer.

As he went down, he passed other doorways that had not been opened in a long time. He knew what lay beyond some of them, but they were not of interest to him right now. Free the beast, free the Watchers and in time, there would be a new order that would allow the others to come.

"I'm aware that it is late, Ma'am, but it cannot wait. I will also have the Curator with me."

Nubia looked completely confused as she watched the phone being put down. "Well, what is it?"

The Reeve stood up. "I'll explain when we get there; time is of the essence." She lifted the phone again, pressing another extension number. "Raysmau, just checking that you are up. Has your clock stopped?"

Nubia watched the Reeve's head nodding up and down.

"Yes, I understand. Stand by your phone. I may be calling."

The phone went down and the Reeve ushered the Curator to follow. "Make sure you close your door behind you Nubia, the cat needs to stay in here."

Unusually for Nubia, she was silent and struggled to match the Reeve's pace. The Reeve sensed her nerves. They were justified. She did not know what else was potentially going on in the below.

They ascended the stairs over two floors passing a handful of Clerics; most were resting at this hour. They arrived at Lady Safiya's quarters.

There was no knock at the door or pleasantries as the Reeve pushed the heavy door open. There was no Cleric to greet her this time either.

"Lady Safiya?"

"Yes, Reeve, I'm coming," was the reply from behind the door in her sitting room. The two of them waited. The Reeve looked down at Nubia, who was puffing a little from the quick, late-night excursion. Nubia looked up to her, her eyes wider than normal and still a little bloodshot. Their eye contact was broken at the sound of the heavy door being pulled open in front of them.

"Well, come in both of you."

The Lady of the House was dressed in slippers and a dressing gown, her hair unkempt. The Reeve's phone call had clearly disturbed her.

"Take a seat."

"Yes, my Lady." Nubia nodded as they both sat. There were no cats present on this occasion.

"I'm guessing your meeting with me earlier and the ring has led to something then?"

Nubia looked at the Reeve. "What ring?"

The Reeve sat upright, gaining composure and gathered her words.

"Yes, Ma'am, it did. I have troubling news."

The Lady sat down supported by her cane and waited in anticipation. She could also sense the nervousness of the Curator. "I see, well let's hear it then."

"I have had to consult with my Head of Order following the news of, shall we say, activities of a Watcher. He who calls himself Duat."

The Lady swallowed hearing the name. "That does not bode well."

"No, quite. I can't go into the fullness of what he may have done, but we suspect he has been able to obtain keys that open a gateway or a passage in the below."

Nubia looked over in horror. "What?"

"What gate? What passage, Reeve?" Lady Safiya enquired.

"In truth, I cannot be fully sure. We have reason to suspect that my ancestors, a very long time ago, created a form of a shield in the below. Behind that shield are secrets that have lain in rest for centuries. We suspect this Watcher may try to access this shield and free what lies beyond it."

Nubia froze with her mouth open as she heard this.

"This event is troubling enough, but this evening, Nubia witnessed what she believes to be the second sign of the prophecy."

"Yes, my Lady. It fell some miles away, flew right over us!"

Lady Safiya shook her head, not fully understanding what she was hearing. "What flew over? What was it?"

Nubia shrugged her shoulders. "I don't know, my Lady. A comet, a meteor or something." She lifted both of her hands, still shrugging. "My Lady, please look." She nodded at the clock behind Lady Safiya.

Safiya frowned and turned around to look at her clock. It said it was two minutes past midnight and the pendulum was silent. The frowned expression remained as she looked back at them both, leant on her cane, rose to her feet and walked over to her grand old clock. Turning the key, she opened the case and touched the static pendulum, pushing it to her left.

It swung back to the central position but no further. Her hand recoiled from it and she gently closed the case. She pressed her hand against the cabinet and bowed her head. Her back was still turned to them as she spoke. "Reeve, what time is it please?"

"I don't know, Ma'am. All of the clocks have stopped. I've not checked our computers to see if they will give us the time. It is an undeniable event."

Lady Safiya's head was still bowed. "The last time this happened, we lost great numbers."

"There was a light from above on that occasion as well. It was described as a comet by others on the outside."

She nodded gently, "Possibly, Nubia, but it was a different time then." She walked slowly to her seat. The Reeve noticed her hands shaking as she steadied herself on her cane to sit down.

"Tell me more of this Watcher. How has he obtained these keys to which you refer? I am not aware of such keys."

"No, Ma'am, you wouldn't be along with the full purpose of the finger ring you have worn for so long. My Order protects the Horde Of Light, but some of our measures are secretive."

"I'm aware of that, Reeve, but it still does not explain how he got them in the first place. I trust the key I gave to you is still safe?"

"Yes, Ma'am, it is."

Lady Safiya nodded as she looked at the Reeve and leant forward. "What did it open, you need to tell me?"

Nubia looked directly at the Reeve, shifting uncomfortably in her seat; she wanted an answer as well.

The Reeve tilted her head down and lifted up her hair, unclipping her neck chain. She pulled at the chain and the final key was revealed.

As the Reeve held it up, Nubia squinted at the perfect circle but could only see the centrepiece from behind. "What is that?"

"A Key."

They both looked at Lady Safiya, who had exhaled deeply as she looked at the floor. "The centrepiece Reeve, is it of the serpent?"

The Lady looked up to see the Reeve nodding. Her hand went to her temple in response. "What do you know of this Watcher, Nubia?"

Nubia frowned. "I don't, my Lady. This is all news to me. Security is the Reeve's department."

The Reeve lowered the key to her legs and gave the Curator an unpleasant stare. "And you haven't answered the question as to how this Watcher obtained the missing keys."

The Reeve did not care for the tone of Nubia's voice.

"The Order Of The Reeves does not concern you."

"But it does me."

They both looked at Lady Safiya. "Tell me what you know, Reeve. It could be very important."

"It would betray my Order, Ma'am."

"Better that than betraying all of us. If the prophecy is coming to pass, we need to take action. Tell me, Reeve, right now. What do you know?"

The Reeve looked at the floor and took a deep breath knowing full well that the Curator was staring at her. "We have a storage chamber within the grounds only known to my Order. Somehow, this Watcher we suspect, has gained entry and there is a possibility he has taken the keys. They open two of the locks of the shield in the below."

Lady Safiya's mouth opened in shock, as did Nubia's.

"Let me take a random guess. Would it be somewhere around the great statue of Salma?"

The Reeve shot an angry stare at the Curator.

"I saw you from the window. Ma'am, one moment she was there and then she was gone."

The Reeve flared her teeth. "Leave it."

"What do you keep there, hidden gold and treasures, I presume?"

"I told you to leave it. Something has to pay for all this. We may be an Order, but we still have overheads and costs."

The Curator shook her head. "And this Watcher knew what neither of us did? What a conundrum!"

The three of them sat in silence, composing their thoughts.

Nubia started shaking her head. "Oh wait, now it all makes sense. That's why there are no cameras outside. That's why there is no CCTV. It's for her lot to protect their treasure, to make sure we don't know about it."

"THAT'S ENOUGH, both of you!" They both looked at the floor in response to Lady Safiya's outburst.

"Both of you need to stop this, although I must concede Nubia, you do make a point worthy of some investigation."

The Reeve looked at the Curator with some aggression.

"When was this Watcher brought here?"

"He wasn't, Ma'am. As I understand, he appeared outside our gates."

Lady Safiya leant forward on her chair and looked over. "You can't be serious, Reeve?"

The Reeve raised her eyebrows; her eyes and lips twitched.

"So, a Watcher appears knowing our location and hiding places unknown to anyone on these grounds, except for you? Not just that, he was able to bypass all security measures that you had in place. I'm guessing that you have some?"

"Some, Ma'am?"

"Security measures in place?"

"Yes, Ma'am, there are."

The Lady of the House shook her head and slumped back in her chair. She brought her hand to her mouth in consideration of these facts. "Timing! Everything happens for a reason. He showed up here recently?"

"Yes, Ma'am, a couple of weeks ago. The Escarrabin brought him in and took him below."

"A couple of weeks ago?" The Curator frowned.

"Yes, why Nubia?"

She held her right hand up in thought, trying to process everything. A very concerned expression appeared across her face.

"Lady Ebonee, my Lady."

"Not her again, Nubia!"

"No, wait, Reeve. Let Nubia finish."

Nubia put a hand to her temple as she thought. "It was known to me that Lady Ebonee had a relationship with Lady Tempest."

"You've been talking to Ebonee?"

The Curator nodded. "Yes, my Lady, I have her ear."

The Reeve rolled her eyes.

"Lady Ebonee spoke with dear Lady Tempest quite regularly."

"Are you sure, Nubia, that's highly unusual? Tempest was only a Sixth Degree Elder."

"I know, but Lady Ebonee told me in confidence that Lady Tempest was investigating something. Something that left unchecked could escalate and have severe consequences for all of us!"

"She's losing her marbles, Nubia."

"That's the Keeper's words Reeve, not your own. You don't know her!"

"But I do and very well. She is a friend of mine, Reeve."

Nubia shot a patronising smile at the Reeve.

"So, what are you saying, Nubia?"

"Well, don't you see? Lady Tempest lost her life a couple of weeks ago and suddenly a Watcher shows up, knowing what he knows and knowing more than you and I, my Lady."

Lady Safiya looked at the Curator with concern.

"She was not knocked down by a bus. How could that be?" The Curator spat her words and shook her head back and forth. She froze and looked at the Head of the House. "She was murdered, Ma'am. She was murdered, I tell you!"

Lady Safiya put a hand to her mouth in worry.

"She knew something. She was onto something. This Watcher probably did it!"

The Reeve spoke softly. "Nubia, Tempest could not have known about the vault and how to access it."

"Well, maybe she did, or maybe she didn't, but she may have known that this Watcher did know and was trying to stop it!"

The Reeve shook her head. "Well, why wouldn't she speak to me? Security, as you state, is my department?"

The Curator looked increasingly angry. "Well, maybe she thought that she couldn't. It would appear that you have secrets to hide as well!"

The Reeve sat back in her chair, diverting her eyes. She was not going to rise to this, particularly as the Curator may actually be right in some of her estimations.

Lady Safiya held her palms up. "Okay, let's remain calm, please. I need a moment with this."

"What are we dealing with, Reeve? And what is that third key for?"

The Reeve chewed at her lip. "My Head of Order had to go deep into the ancient archives. Her investigation is not yet complete. However, in light of events that have taken place this evening, I feel that we need to act."

"You are referring to the potential second sign."

"Yes, Ma'am. I am."

"I'm aware that one of our own was baring pains of two hearts. Do we know of her status now?"

The Reeve looked directly at the Curator, who gave her a pleading look not to say anything. "Yes, Ma'am, we believe that she is now better, which is an added worry. Her recovery is as foretold."

Nubia looked at the floor, grateful to the Reeve.

Safiya nodded, not knowing that the cat was only two floors below her. "I see. So, tell me about the key."

"From what I've been able to establish, the shield below is a wall of iron. The two missing keys need to be inserted at the same time to open a doorway within the wall. However, countermeasures, as always, are put in place and this is one of them." She lifted the circle of iron from her legs and could feel the roughness of the patterns on the reverse side that formed some kind of combination. It was an assumption, but she guessed the unique design would allow the key to lock into the wall and then be turned.

Safiya pointed at the Reeve. "But he does not have that?"

"No, Ma'am, he does not. Without this, the doorway should not open."

The Lady of the House smiled briefly.

"You think that he does not know this?"

The Reeve nodded, "the doorway was never meant to be opened by one person. This is why this key was kept a secret away from the others."

There had been a brief moment of silence before the Reeve resumed. "However, I am concerned. This key and both of the others are very old. There is no guarantee that they work, or any countermeasure in place will work either. We do not know if the doorway will open or whether the iron shield will hold and could possibly be destroyed. But, of course, that is not the only reason why we must act."

Safiya nodded. "What is it the Watcher wants? What is he trying to get from there?"

The Reeve took a deep breath and avoided the Curators gaze. "It's more what he is trying to set free."

The Curator's chin prodded forwards. "What?"

"It only came to my attention today that sounds have been heard from the deep of the below. The sounds are unnatural. Something has awoken from beyond the wall of iron."

The Curator looked in panic at Safiya, who looked down before she spoke. "I asked you before if the symbol on that key was of the serpent. Is it something to do with the enemy of old? Is that symbol a warning?"

"Yes, Ma'am, I believe it is."

Safiya rested her elbow on the side of her chair and placed her hand to her chin, closing her eyes. "What is it? What is this beast?"

The Reeve swallowed and looked at the Curator and then at the Lady of the House. "It's possible that it may be the Hydra."

Safiya's hand moved from her chin and covered her eyes.

The Curator's face was in equal measure of terror and laughter. "THE HYDRA, are you demented?"

"It is as I have been informed, Curator," the Reeve retorted.

She spoke with laughter. "That's ridiculous. How could it possibly be here, and why, for that matter? Honestly, your Order at times is more of a hindrance than a help." She shook her head in disgust. "The Hydra being here, that was thousands of years ago."

"Remember that as well, do you?"

"Don't patronise me!"

"ENOUGH!!" They were silenced by the loud voice that cut over them. "You are both ladies of the Order. Act like it!"

They both looked on as the Head of the House's hands quivered. Her voice wavered as she spoke. "There are no other ladies here. They have all been to their gatherings this evening. How many Escarrabin are present, Reeve?"

"When they all return from their duties from last night, there will be 36 Ma'am." She nodded clearly in discomfort.

"We will need them."

Nubia looked in shock. "My Lady, do you believe any of this?"

"Ma'am, I believe we need to act quickly. I was going to wait until dawn, but given what is happening right now, I don't think we can."

Safiya nodded and got to her feet. She turned to look at her clock.

They both stood up as their senior rose.

The Reeve was looking for a response. "Ma'am?"

"I need to get changed." She turned to look at the Reeve and nodded, heading to the door with her cane.

The Curator swallowed as she looked at the Reeve, decisively walking over to a desk. She reached for the phone.

She waited patiently for a few seconds before it was answered. "Raysmau, this is the Reeve. We are at diligence." She slowly put the phone down and looked at Nubia.

"It has started."

K.S. Horak

Chapter Twenty Nine:

WALLS OF VOLEMON

Watchers have their own unique smell, a smell that those above described as one of decay, but what he could smell right now was something entirely different.

The thin skin around the two gaps in his skull where a nose would have been a long time ago twitched. He was not immune to this smell as the thin skin over his forehead displayed faint frown lines of nausea.

No one had been here for a very long time. Even the etchings of the language of Volemon had stopped on the wall some way back.

The chamber was dimly lit from the torch he had dropped from above and the one he held in his left hand. Duat surveyed the dark iron wall that absorbed most of the light. He suspected the smell was coming from what lay beyond on the other side despite the cold and dampness. Reasonably encouraged, this suggested that the wall was not as sealed as it probably was when constructed. The beast that lay beyond could not have eaten; the smell of decay must have been from something consumed a long time ago.

He could hear movements beyond the wall and the hissing sound of multiple heads as he looked around the holding chamber. He could see two old torches on his left and right, secured into the rock, each held by a large iron ring. He would take advantage of those.

He wiped saliva from his mouth as he lit the torches on both sides of the chamber and focused on the seal of the Reeves. It was now clearly visible and engraved into the ironwork.

He read the two words that accompanied the seal 'Tenere Immortus,' words from the old language roughly translated as 'hold of the undead.' The left side of his mouth turned upwards slightly in amusement of their fickle ways.

He walked forward to the wall and placed his right palm on the ironwork closing his eye to concentrate. He waited a few seconds, but nothing could be felt or heard. He reopened his eye and hissed. He could not communicate directly with the beast; something within the wall stopped him from doing so. The beast had awoken shortly after his arrival at Loxley, but he didn't understand why he couldn't communicate with it.

He removed his palm and stepped back, hearing a large bang against the wall of iron. The roar that followed was deafening as multiple thuds echoed throughout the chamber. It was growing restless. He may not be able to communicate directly, but it sensed his presence and no doubt could feel that freedom was imminent.

The wall was strong; there was no doubt about that, given the unflinching barrage of weight thrust upon it from the other side. He looked across the length of the wall with some concern. There was no obvious sign of a doorway as he walked its entire length. The temper and noise from the other side were relentless as he waved the torch around, straining his eye for something to assist him.

He knew the entry point for the keys would not be obvious. He searched as quickly as he could. The beast may well have sensed or heard his presence, but he could not be sure of controlling it once free. If he couldn't, he would need to protect himself. That would not be an ideal situation as he needed it by his side, at least initially anyway.

He was drawn to an intricate carving cut out in the rock on the right-hand side of the wall. He waved the torch in its direction. Even from a distance, he recognised it instantly as the serpent Goddess and shook his head with concern. "The Uraeus," he snorted.

He moved towards the cobra upright on its tail. He had no fear of serpents, but they did. Its placement here could not be a coincidence.

He focused on the unusual shape of the head; the mouth open much wider than would normally be possible, even for a snake.

He was trying to concentrate, but the noise was overwhelming from the other side of the wall. He did not know why the Reeves would have taken the time to carve out something with so much detail. Presumably as a warning to others.

The multiple sounds of impact upon the ironwork were becoming too intense to focus.

"SILENCE!" he yelled at the top of his voice with no effect. "SILENTIUM!" "SIOPI!" The roar subdued to a hiss and the occasional rattle of a head against iron.

It appeared that he had some form of control after all. He studied the rock carving of the serpent, but he couldn't see any entry point for a key or keys.

He turned as he pushed saliva from his mouth to the floor below. As he watched it descend, he noticed a perfect circle cut into the ironwork. He lowered the torch and crouched down, pushing his fingers into the circle. It was only an inch or so deep. He removed dust and dirt and could feel there were rough abrasions inside the circle. He stood up and moved backwards. He could feel the thin skin of his forehead rising again, but this time with confusion rather than nausea.

He glanced back at the head of the rearing cobra. The cut-out circle would not be there by chance, but it meant nothing to him. However, with the Reeves, nothing happened by accident; it must have some form of purpose.

There were a couple of large bangs against the wall again. "SIOPI!" Duat's voice grew more impatient as the sound of hissing echoed around the chamber. Time was critical and he needed to find the entry points as quickly as he could. The combination of the serpent and the carved circle meant something. It must be close. Knowing that the Reeves may have some form of countermeasure in place, he chose to sacrifice his left hand just in case. He ran his fingers in circles over the ironwork. He recoiled his hand on a couple of occasions in response to the aggressive banging coming from the other side. The beast was becoming more hostile. He could not be sure if he would have control over it. The longer this took, the less likely it would be. The wall was still holding, but he would not be able to penetrate it for all of his powers unless the key inserts could be found.

His frustration was growing with the fear that he was losing control. His own hiss of anger was not on a par with the sounds from the Hydra but in that moment, it was the only common ground they shared.

He watched the steam emanating from his mouth and yelled out in a temper, stamping against the floor. He reached into the pocket of his robe in desperation and held the keys in front of his eye. As he did, he felt a draft upon him coming from the direction of the carved serpent. He turned the keys towards it and looked over his shoulder to the right. One of the torches fixed to the wall had started to flicker.

Still holding his own torch, he separated the two keys in his left hand and held them towards the head of the serpent. There were two turquoise coloured stones in the eyes of the serpent that, until that point, he had failed to notice. They glowed against the flickering light. He placed a key directly over one of the eyes of the serpent's head, noticing for the first time there was a tiny jewel carved into the base of the key. He moved the head of the key in a circular motion over the turquoise stone set into the eye and turned to look over his left shoulder. He hissed in satisfaction as he saw the faintest flicker from a tiny turquoise stone set into the iron wall. He rushed over to where he had seen the light flickering. It was low down on the wall. He crouched down to see the tiny coloured stone, but there was no keyhole. He dropped the torch to the floor and felt around it. He left a key on the floor to mark its place. He ran back to the serpent and placed the other key over the other eye of the snake. A similar reflective light flickered above the other one in the wall, just further to the right of the one he had just discovered.

Returning to the wall, Duat was positive he had cracked the Reeve's code. With both arms stretched, he could feel both of the small stones set into iron. He pressed against them. Instantly, he heard movement coming from within the iron wall and a small opening appeared. He emitted a hiss with his own success.

He brought his eye level to the opening and could see two very old keyholes cut into the ironwork. He knew instantly they were designed to fit the four-sided keys.

He drew a deep breath at the importance of the moment as he felt the wall shudder as the beast hit against it from the other side.

"Soon, my friend." He blew the dirt off the key that lay on the floor and inserted them both simultaneously. He took a step back in consideration as he rubbed the saliva from his mouth and closed his eye. With a smile, he reached out and turned them both to the right. He could hear sounds of old locking mechanisms moving within the wall. He opened his eye and pushed against the keys in anticipation of the parting of the wall of iron.

The echo from the locking mechanism could still be heard, but nothing was happening. He tried turning them the other way, but there was no movement. The keys were locked into their ports. Grimacing, he applied all of his strength to the keys as a breeze drifted over him again. In the stillness of the chamber, he could see the torch to his left started to flicker.

He let go of the keys and turned around to look at the flickering torch. The right hand torch flickered in equal momentum.

"What, what is it?" he yelled in a temper at the torches. He was suddenly drawn to the head of the serpent. He swallowed deeply as something glowed from one of the teeth of the open mouth. He rushed towards it. He pressed on the stone imbedded into the tooth and immediately a light flickered to his left from the centre of the cut circle.

In anguish, he rushed to it and pushed the circle cut into the iron, his saliva running uncontrollably.

"NO, NO, it can't be!" He hit out at the circle. He put both of his hands to his head as the banging from the other side started again. The chamber was full of the sounds of multiple snakes angrily hissing in unison. He spun his head around, looking at the torches. He must have missed something; there were only two keys he was certain of that. "WHAT IS IT?" His yelling and rage were becoming uncontrollable when all of the noise suddenly stopped within the chamber.

He looked at the head of the serpent and then to the flashing of the stone set within the circle in the wall. He stood in the silence, breathing heavily when the faintest sound started to make its way down to him from the above.

He rushed out of the chamber to look up the stairs and could see shadows moving in the dim light at the very top. This was followed by the sound of Watchers in pain. Their howls started to make their way down to him. He turned to look at the wall and shook his head in confusion. He had no idea what was happening. Just then, a sound travelled down the stairs that he knew the meaning of.

He looked back up from the darkness of the base of the staircase as the sound became louder. "It can't be! It can't be!" He ran back to the wall and grabbed at both of the keys. He put his entire weight on them to the point that they may bend or break. Suddenly, he heard sounds of movement from the head of the Uraeus and stopped instantly. Breathing heavily, he could see the light in the circle was flashing. The mouth of the serpent began to move and became wider. He stepped away from the wall hearing the Hydra bellow at full volume forcing him to put his hands over the holes where his ears would have been. He stared at the mouth of the serpent as liquid began to spit outwards from it. A mist started to form within the chamber.

He swallowed and stepped backwards. Even with his ear sockets covered, he could hear the almighty roar of pain from behind the wall and dozens of rapid bangs against it. There was one more bellow that sounded more like a scream, then silence. The beast retreated. It was gone.

"NO, NO!" He put a hand to his nostrils and forced himself against the keys once again. The chamber started to fill with noxious smoke. Duat's eye watered as he coughed and spluttered, spitting saliva and phlegm across the floor. He retched in pain as he fell against the wall from the poison in the air. The two torches flicked once more then immediately went out.

He dragged his way out of the chamber and fell at the base of the staircase. He looked upwards at shadows moving quickly above. Coughing, he started to pull himself up the stairs, the noise from the above becoming ever closer and more apparent.

Holding his midsection and covering his mouth, he steadied himself to his feet and started to climb slowly upwards. He looked behind him; the noxious smoke was not following and was contained within the chamber.

As he ascended, he knew he was right about the noise he had heard below. The further he climbed, the louder it became. He slumped to the floor, trying to regain his breath. Still holding his midsection in considerable pain he looked up from his bloodshot eye. He knew the sound and knew what it meant. It was undeniable.

The general alarm had been sounded as his head slumped against the wall. He had failed, the beast would not be freed and the Escarrabin were coming.

Still partially dressed in her battle armour, Raysmau had put the phone down and walked as quickly as she could to the security control room. The door was slightly open as she pushed her way through.

"Escarrabin Layla and Amera, we are at diligence. Sound the alarm immediately."

They both looked at each other. "Ma'am?"

"Now. That's an order!"

"Yes, Ma'am. May I ask, is this a drill and shall we continue to monitor the cameras outside the grounds?"

"This is not a drill, Amera," Raysmau looked briefly at the floor, "and no, the problem is already here." She looked up at both of them. "Use of pulse fire is authorised. Issue the instruction through your terminal to the weapons store. The Scatterblades on charge, make sure they are primed."

They both looked at each other again. "Yes, Ma'am, right away."

"I will give a short briefing at the muster point in ten minutes. Make sure all Escarrabin attend without exception."

"Yes, Ma'am. The security block will be notified immediately. Many have not yet returned from their duties, Ma'am."

"I'm aware of this," she snapped, "send a message to their navigators and phones to return to headquarters as quickly as they can."

"Yes, Ma'am. Activating now, we are at diligence."

Raysmau pointed her hand forward. "Open the outer door, will you."

"Yes, Ma'am, doing that now."

Raysmau left the control room, headed through the security gate and waited with some irritation for the outer door to open into the main lobby. Security measures outside the manor were tested once a month. She hoped they would work without a hitch.

She looked up towards the balconies as the general alarm sounded, echoing throughout the building. Only two Clerics sat at the main desk at this hour. They looked at each other and lifted their heads with concern towards Raysmau. "Stay at your posts unless otherwise instructed and secure the Cleric's residence."

"Yes, Ma'am."

She watched the fingers of the pale hands direct instructions through their computer terminals, locking down and securing the Cleric's sleeping area. Only those working would now be within the main part of the building.

As she stepped into the centre of the lobby area, the steel shutters slid down over the windows of the lower level of Loxley. She could hear the very old portcullis moving beyond the main doors. She waited patiently for the sound of their closure before moving back into her quarters.

Only a short drive away from headquarters, Kassia was in fits of laughter. Shula, the more serious of the two, couldn't help but smile.

"Honestly, she did not know it was ancient wine. In fact, it probably wasn't wine at all. It was made by monks or something. It was far stronger than usual and she thought it would be a good idea to see if pulse mode was working. Destroyed a desk and the tapestry behind it caught fire; it took three of the girls to put it out."

They carried on laughing. "She didn't get away with it, though."

"What happened to her?"

"I got a message from her not so long back. They sent her to Alaska." Kassia was still laughing.

"Alaska?"

"Yes, punishment presumably; didn't think she would like the cold and solitude." Kassia ran a hand through her hair, still laughing.

"And does she?"

"Does she what, like it out there?"

"Yeah."

"She loves it. The views are amazing. She goes into the mountains during her time off. She's still not allowed a Scatterblade, of course."

"Ha-ha, I bet."

They drove to the bottom of the secluded road towards the semi-circle of trees. Kassia held her pin badge up to a hidden scanner as they sat, watching the trees move to the sides and the view of the Manor open up in front of them.

"That's odd, look." Kassia looked forward.

"What are all of the floodlights doing on?"

They drove under the archway towards the house. Shula leaned forward.

"Am I seeing this right?" She strained her eyes as the house became closer. "Is the portcullis down?"

"Lower level windows are secured as well."

They were both drawn to their navigator that displayed a new message as Shula read it aloud. "We are to return to headquarters immediately." She looked at Kassia. "Something must be going on."

"Navigator disengage!" Kassia's coded voice overriding its control. She took charge of the car and sped up. "I'll get us to the security block as quickly as I can. I do not like the look of this.

"No, me neither."

"Reeve! Reeve!" Panicked, Nubia tore into the Reeve's office.

The alarm ringing throughout the building was becoming too much for someone who remembered events of the past.

She was not in her office, so she pushed her way into her private quarters. She could see the Reeve in her dressing room, half-dressed in battle armour.

"Well, don't knock, will you."

"I'm sorry, Reeve, do you mind if I stay with you? I don't feel safe."

"Why, the Watchers are below. There is nothing to indicate at this time they have escaped and as unlikely as that would be, they would run anyway. They have no interest in you, Nubia."

"That's as maybe. I'll just feel safer."

"As you wish, but you stay behind out of harm's way. When at diligence, it is for soldiers, not for Curators, clear?"

She nodded, fearful of everything happening so quickly. "Yes, I understand."

"I've told Raysmau what she needs to know. She'll be giving a briefing in the security block in the next few minutes. I have authorised the use of pulse weapons."

She watched the Curator nod in acceptance and could see the worry across her face. "Don't worry, Nubia. We are fully trained for this." She opened her ceremonial cabinet and took out her modified spear. "This spear has never been fired as an act of aggression." She could feel the worry emanating from Nubia. "I'm sure it won't be tonight."

"If the beast has got out, things could be terrible."

She stopped dressing and nodded. "It could be, but if my Head of Order is correct, that wall cannot be opened without this. She pulled at the chain that hung around her neck. Nubia could see the tip of the secret key appear from under the Reeve's blouse. "The only way anyone is getting this from me is to take it from me, understand?"

Nubia nodded and swallowed hard.

"And that is not going to happen." She continued affixing her upper body armour that proudly displayed the crest of the Reeve in the centre of her breastplate.

She took a hair tie from her dresser drawer and tied her hair up at the back.

"Nubia, ring downstairs and have a couple of Clerics watch over Lady Safiya until after the briefing. We'll send a couple of Escarrabin to her directly afterwards." Nubia nodded and headed out of the room to use the Reeve's phone in her office.

She lifted her helmet and placed it over her head. The red ceremonial mane hung from the back. She dragged the frontage down to protect her jaw and mouth. It would be impossible for her to wear breathing apparatus and her traditional face protection, so she would have to judge that as things evolved.

Nubia came back into the room. "Front desk is arranging two of the Clerics that were still on duty to watch over Lady Safiya. Their sleeping quarters have been locked down, so only a few are active within the building."

"Good." She put on her heavy gloves, flexed her fingers and picked up her spear. She couldn't help but notice the Curator was looking at her differently. "What is it, Nubia?"

She smiled. "You are dressed properly for a change. You look like a Reeve." Nubia could not see the faint smile that had appeared from behind the mask.

"Careful Curator, you almost paid me a compliment."

"I won't make a habit of it."

"I don't doubt. Let's go to the briefing."

✝✝✝✝

Gamila rushed into the weapons cache and collected her Scatterblade from the Quartermaster. "What's going on?"

"Just take your weapon Escarrabin, use of pulse fire has been authorised. Move to the muster point immediately."

She looked behind the Quartermaster to the clock on the wall that had stopped.

"Yes, Ma'am." She ran to catch up with Alian, who was ahead of her. "Alian, do you know anything?"

"Not a thing other than Raysmau is giving a briefing very soon."

"Do you think this has something to do with what we told her?"

Alian looked at her and nodded. "I suspect so, but why now and at this hour, I have no idea. Something has happened."

"Did you notice the clock in the weapons store and my watch? They've both stopped."

"Mine too. It's not a coincidence."

"It looks like everyone is being called. How many of us are there, do you think?"

"Don't know. I'm guessing about twenty. Many won't be back from last night yet."

They both entered the canteen to see other Escarrabin talking to one another whilst others were coming in behind them. Gamila looked over to see the familiar face of Kassia entering the room with Shula; both were dressed in what looked like business suits.

"Well, you don't look ready."

"We've literally only just got back. The portcullis is down. What's going on? Everyone is reporting in."

"Don't know, but we had to report to Raysmau earlier that Alian and I had been in the below. There's something down there."

Kassia smiled. "You what. You're joking, right?"

Alian shook her head. "Afraid not."

Shula shrugged her shoulders. "Guess we'll find out now."

Raysmau walked into the room wearing full battle armour.

The Quartermaster also entered, "Attention!"

The Escarrabin all stood to attention with their Scatterblades by their sides. They looked on as the Quartermaster stood on tiptoes and talked into the ear of Raysmau. She nodded. "So this is everyone, for now, nineteen in total?"

"Yes, Ma'am."

"Right, Escarrabin. At ease."

She watched them all partially relax as she did a quick visual inspection of their battle dress.

"I'll tell you what I know. You all must listen. Firstly, this is not a drill exercise."

She could see that she had all of their attention.

"Information passed to me by the Reeve, who will be joining us shortly, is there have been a series of events that we do not determine to be a coincidence. I'm not going into all of those right now as this could be time-critical and we will be moving immediately. There is a potential that something is in the below. Something from the past may have awoken."

Mumbled speculation was heard. Raysmau held her hand up to silence the Escarrabin.

You are all members of the elite Escarrabin Order. You have undertaken your training and studies about the history of the Horde Of Light and why we protect them. Their heritage, their legacy, depends on us to ensure that darkness does not prevail. You will not find in any text or your training manuals what may be happening here right now. There is suspicion and reason to believe that a carcass may have been buried deep in the below, in an area none of you has seen. That carcass may have awoken."

There were further looks of concern around the room, but this time in dignified silence.

"There are actions of what we believe to be a rogue Watcher. He may have played some part in this. How and why we do not know as yet, but it is enough to be a concerning development. The creature was buried a very long time ago, some of you may have heard of it and as such, you need to know. It is an old enemy of the past, a serpent creature and we believe it to be what is known more commonly to you as the Hydra."

There were immediate audible gasps around the room.

"The snake demon?"

"Not a demon, but if awoken, it will act with ruthlessness and will need to be destroyed."

Raysmau turned to the sound of footsteps behind her. The Reeve entered in full battle dress, accompanied by Nubia. Raysmau felt the mood of the room change in an instant, seeing the senior Head of Security dressed for battle.

"However, the Order Of The Reeves a long time ago put security measures in place and we believe that this Watcher does not have the necessary tools to release the beast. We will go into the below as far as we need to." She paused for breath, letting her message sink in among the concerned faces.

"None of us can be sure how many Watchers lie below. That will change as of this evening. We will conduct a full search. All Watchers are to be detained. The rogue called Duat is to be brought before me. Understand this. You are to take no chances. The Watchers, despite their bloodline, are controllable within this secured environment. If this Duat is uniting them, we know from history they can change and adapt quickly. All of you will be issued with extra protective gloves. Make sure you and they wear them before you apprehend them. Once in gloves, cuff them and bring all of them up to the central lobby as we need to detail them. Security has been too weak here for too long. That also changes today. As we are at diligence, the lift down is disabled. Against usual protocol, the door leading to the stairs below will be opened from this side to use the stairs down. However, it will seal again behind you and you will need to use the scanner to exit upon your return. Those functions are not disabled. Watchers are to be brought up the stairs. We will construct a cordon within the lobby for their detention. Are there any questions?"

"Does it breathe fire, Ma'am?" All of the Escarrabin turned to look at Kassia.

"Blimey, Kass, what have you been watching?" Alian said, shaking her head.

Kassia shrugged her shoulders. "Well, I don't know!"

Raysmau frowned, unimpressed. "It is said that the breath of the beast and the fumes from it, is highly toxic. You will all be issued with breathing apparatus and eye protection. I must reiterate, we do not think that it can escape. Pulse fire from your Blades is not to be used below unless in an emergency. If so, at the lowest level of pulse. Ensure your pulse dials are set properly. If the beast is free, your Blades should be used as their original intended purpose as a sword weapon. You are trained for both. I will issue an order if sword application is needed. All of you carry out comms checks to ensure your earpieces are secured. Do so now. Any problems, report to the Quartermaster. Escarrabin, Amera and Layla are in the control room; speak with them, but only if you need to. Maintain radio silence as much as possible."

Raysmau surveyed the room and nodded. "That'll be all. Carry out your checks and collect the rest of your equipment. Don't forget the gloves. I'll meet you in the lobby as quickly as possible. We move immediately."

Raysmau turned to the Reeve, noticing the quivering figure of Nubia hiding behind her. "Madam Reeve, is there anything you wish to add?" Raysmau watched the iron mask of the Reeve move slowly to its left and right.

"That's it, Escarrabin. Collect your gear and move to the lobby. Shula and Kassia get changed immediately."

Raysmau turned back to the Reeve. "Ma'am, they will know we are coming now as the alarm has been sounded."

The Reeve nodded slowly. "Fear Raysmau, fear."

She had no doubt they were in fear, but if it had been her decision, she would not have alerted them. Going into the darkness when they are most active was bad enough. If they were trying to unite, this was going to be a very difficult test.

If the beast had been freed, losses were inevitable.

Raysmau depressed her talk button on the front of her breastplate and lowered her chin to speak. "Control, silence the alarm. I can't think over it."

The general alarm was silenced. Without the sound of clocks, there was an eerie silence within the central lobby. The Reeve looked at Raysmau. "Are you ready?"

She nodded in response. Her anxiety was fully justified as she surveyed the assembling Escarrabin.

Raysmau spoke loudly to ensure she was heard. "Has everyone comms checked?"

"Yes, Ma'am," was the collective response.

"Ensure your Scatterblades are primed and be mindful of our rules of engagement. No one discharges fire unless a threat to life is imminent. Sword application will be on my order."

She turned around, hearing movements coming down the stairs. She gestured with her head to the Reeve to turn around.

Lady Safiya was making her way down the stairs.

"I'll speak with her," the Reeve said quietly. Raysmau nodded and continued to brief the Escarrabin.

The Reeve walked to the bottom of the staircase and pushed her face guard up to face Lady Safiya, who had a Cleric on either side of her. "My Lady. Respectfully, this is not the place for you right now."

"Oh hush, Reeve. I'm not going to miss this. What is happening right now will have to be reported to the Grand Council in any event."

She was now at the base of the stairs and level with the Reeve. "I know what you do is with all of our best interests Reeve and your Order are secretive and wise, but you know that I do not have to take instructions from you." She smiled, looking directly into the Reeve's eyes sat between the iron nose protector that came from the Reeve's battle helmet.

The Reeve smiled ruefully back at her. "Very well, my Lady. Let me insist that two Escarrabin replace the Clerics."

"That's fine, thank you, Reeve." She turned either side to the Clerics and thanked them.

"Clerics, your quarters are sealed off at the moment. Wait on the upper landing under the dome for now."

"Yes, Ma'am." They both nodded their heads in response to the Reeve's instructions and walked up the stairs.

"I will also ask that the Curator joins you as well Ma'am. I don't want her below."

"That is also fine. I guess I'll just wait here then."

The Reeve smiled and nodded to the Lady of the House and walked back to Raysmau. "Assign two to watch over Lady Safiya, please."

"Soad and Yara come to me."

Both guards came quickly towards her. "Please watch over Lady Safiya, don't leave her side for the duration."

"Yes, Ma'am," they responded at the same time.

The Reeve stepped to the right of Raysmau towards the Curator. "Nubia, I wish for you to remain with Lady Safiya while this takes place."

"I would like to see what happens, Reeve!"

"You are not trained for battle. Wait with the Lady. That is non-negotiable. I don't want you going below. Besides, you are not dressed properly."

"But Reeve…"

"End of discussion, please. We have to leave."

She watched the Curator sulk off towards the stairs. She looked back to Raysmau and pulled her face protector back down.

Raysmau had finished speaking to the Escarrabin, who were now ready for the order.

"Raysmau, this is your operation, your soldiers; control lies with you unless I deem it necessary to take operational command. Is that clear?"

Raysmau pulled down her face protector, checking that her night vision goggles were in place on top of her helmet.

"Yes, Ma'am. That is clear."

"Good. Then let's proceed."

✝✝✝✝

Coughing regularly, it was slow progress up the stairs. In pain from his bloodshot eye, Duat had no choice but to use the wall for support.

The alarm was still ringing above. As he looked up the stairs, the moving shadows were becoming more impatient and agitated. He would need to control the Watchers quickly. He stopped climbing and steadied himself. "BELLATOR!" he yelled as loudly as he could, his voice echoing around the cavern of the stairs. "BELLATOR!"

He could hear shuffling above him and looked up to see a dark shadow moving down towards him. The Watcher's face appeared. "Master!"

"Come to me!"

Bellator moved as quickly as he could down the spiral staircase. "Master, what happened?" He put out an arm to steady Duat, who was unbalanced and fell against the wall. "The Reeves and their countermeasures, I underestimated them. I was not in possession of the facts. I've inhaled something, but it will pass."

"Master, where is the creature? The brothers are restless, awaiting your command?"

"It is below, but it has retreated. That is why you do not hear it anymore." He coughed. "It could not be freed, not now anyway. They have many secrets and much is buried and hidden away down there."

"But Master the noise from above, are they coming?"

He smiled as saliva ran down his chin. "Oh yes, they are coming," he steadied himself and started to walk up the stairs, "but do not worry, you and I will be fine, the others... not so much."

There was concern in Bellator's eye. "But we need our brothers. We need them on the outside."

"We will, but this is not over. The evolution of the new realm has only just started. Their prophecy of change is taking place as we speak. It is unstoppable."

"Prophecy, Master?"

"Their fears, the stopping of their time. Come, my friend we must go up to greet them. Follow my instructions throughout and you will not be harmed." He looked at Bellator. "You shall be leaving here tonight."

Yes, Master. Thank you, but they will be coming in force. The brothers are sure of that."

They both stopped talking as the alarm above fell silent.

"I am more than what I appear to all of you. We are leaving this evening. I can't stand their vileness any longer."

Bellator bowed his head. "Yes, Master."

"Come, my friend, we must unite the brothers. We do not have much time."

Raysmau pressed the talk button of her radio. "Control receiving?"

"Yes, Ma'am, loud and clear."

"Override the door."

"Activating override."

The Escarrabin heard the security locks free and the button outside the door changed from green to red.

"Shula, take front. Masika and Suma behind her." She nodded at both of them to do as she instructed. "Masika, scan the area once below on your movement tracker and stay close to me."

"Yes, Ma'am."

"Suma, monitor for gases." She raised her voice, "everyone affix gas masks and eye protection. Other than those on detail up here, everyone goes down." Raysmau nodded at Shula. "Open the door and proceed inside." She watched the Escarrabin sling her Scatterblade over her shoulder and with gloved hands she picked up two heavy magnets with handles from the floor. She fixed them to the door and pulled.

As the door started to open, the cold air from below drifted into the lobby. The Escarrabin lifted their weapons, the silver chrome reflecting the light from the chandelier above.

Shula jammed her foot against the door to hold it open. Reaching for her Scatterblade, she moved through the door's opening. At the top of the stairs, she looked over the drop to her left and pointed her weapon downwards. Masika and Suma followed behind her. They started down the stairs in formation.

Raysmau nodded at Lotfia to move through. "Keep a check on your scanner until we've found them."

"Yes, Ma'am."

Raysmau moved through the door to the stairs, followed by another thirteen Escarrabin and the Reeve.

They descended the stairs to the first floor below ground. Raysmau surveyed the area and the darkness of the chamber.

"Spread out." She ushered them all to separate before placing her arm back to support the weight of her Scatterblade.

"Masika, movements?"

She looked into her handheld scanner and moved it to her left and right. "Negative, Ma'am."

"Suma, emissions?"

"Negative, Ma'am. Air is breathable."

"Keep masks on for now."

The Escarrabin moved forward, checking the expanse of the vast empty chamber and its cold stone walls.

Raysmau nodded towards the officers at the front. "Proceed to the stairwell."

They moved collectively towards the stairs at the opposite side of the chamber. Shula pointed her Scatterblade down the stairs and gave a hand gesture for the others to follow as she disappeared out of sight. "Rashida and Kissa, stay up here at the top of the stairs."

"Yes, Ma'am," they replied, content in the knowledge they would not have to proceed further. The Reeve nodded to both of them as she passed by, her finger over the trigger release button; her spear was fully primed for battle should she need it.

As Shula reached the bottom of the stairway, she ushered for the others to catch her up quickly. The second floor below was as dimly lit as the one above. Light bulbs hung from old wiring crudely tacked to the walls. Many of the bulbs were not working and those that were offered the faintest light reassurance. She moved across to her left to let the others enter the chamber. This was as far as she had been below ground, much like the others. The silence was eerie. The occasional sound of dripping water could be heard from somewhere, probably from a leak above ground.

She waited patiently for the others to fall in line behind her, but they were taking orders from Raysmau.

"Any movements showing?"

"Negative Ma'am, this floor is quiet. There's nothing here."

"Suma readings, please."

Raysmau watched her shake her head. "Nothing. It's all clear; air is breathable."

"Alian, come to me," she beckoned with her hand.

"Yes, Ma'am."

"The noise that you heard before, it was from this floor?"

"No, Ma'am, the one above; that is as far as we come to collect and return the Watchers. The sound would have been coming from down there, presumably." She pointed to the stairs at the end of the chamber that Raysmau had to strain her eyes to see.

"Masika, go to the stairs with Shula and check for movements below. Use your night vision goggles if you need them."

"Ma'am." Masika nodded, holding her movement detector out directly in front of her.

The Reeve had now moved up directly behind Raysmau. They both looked around the old chamber that lay in perfect silence.

Raysmau pointed forward. "Proceed." They all moved to the stairs.

It was not lost on the Watchers that Duat was hurt. He had rushed his instructions as they gathered in silence on the third floor below ground. They stood in a semi-circle and Duat took his place directly in the middle in front of them. He spoke as quietly as he could, his strength returning quickly. "Remember what I told you all, do not resist at first and wait for my command. Some of them will be assisting us. It is me they want. I will surrender to them." His smile was ruthlessly fake. "Keep your hoods up. They will probably try to cuff us and make us wear gloves. Remember, they will not fire unless they are losing control. It will be me and me alone that will provoke that control."

They heard movements directly above them. Duat looked furious as one of the Watchers let out a hiss.

Shula stepped backwards on hearing the noise of the Watcher and turned to Raysmau. "Contact!" she whispered.

Raysmau indicated for them to go down the stairs. Shula lowered her Scatterblade, took two grenades from her belt, pulled the pins and looked at Raysmau. She nodded as both of them were released.

The Watchers could hear the sound of the two light grenades bouncing down the worn stone of the stairs. Both grenades settled directly in front of them. Duat spoke at volume as it didn't matter anymore. "Do not look at them. Shield your eye!" The Watchers bowed down, looking at the floor. A huge blast of white light sparked across the dark chamber. The noise of the second explosion travelled throughout the below. "Open!" hissed Duat as soon as he had heard the second blast. The Watchers all recoiled at the intense light, shielding their eyes.

"Go, go, go!" Raysmau yelled as Shula rushed at the stairs, immediately followed by Masika and Suma. The rest of the Escarrabin descended on mass to the floor below.

The Reeve reached the bottom of the stairs to see drawn weapons pointing at the semi-circle of Watchers. She could not tell how many of them there were, maybe thirty or so. The chamber was in silence save the hissing that was still coming from the two grenades. She could see the Watchers were still struggling against the intense and sudden light that lit the chamber. She had not been down here before. She took in the huge area that had been cut from the rock. There were tunnels directly to the left and right and stairs further ahead.

"Suma readings, please."

"The air is normal, quite breathable."

Raysmau smiled below her mask. The Watcher had failed; the Reeve's security measures must have worked.

"Remove masks." It was an educated risk; if the beast was loose, they would have known about it by now.

Raysmau stepped forward to the recognisable skull of Duat. "Is this all of you?"

He hissed as saliva ran from his mouth. "Raysmau, the heart and soul of the Escarrabin," he laughed loudly and spluttered a cough.

"Stop laughing, Watcher."

"You should address them by their real name, by what they are really called."

"They?"

He continued to laugh. "Slave of the Reeve, that must be her right there." He nodded to the figure behind Raysmau carrying the spear. "All that armour, you must be fearful?" His mouth opened wide as more saliva fell to the floor.

"Shut up, Watcher. I will ask for the last time. Is this all of you?"

"Shut up? And you want answers, Raysmau? Your arrogance and incompetence is the true value of the Escarrabin."

"Incompetence?" The Reeve moved forward. "It is you that didn't get what he came for."

Duat hissed. "You know nothing."

"We know what you tried to free below. You failed."

"Failed?" It is your kind whose time has run out. Tell me, Reeve, how are your clocks? What time do they tell you?"

There was murmuring behind. The Reeve heard one Escarrabin say to the other, 'how could he know that?'

"Enough of this." Raysmau was running out of patience. "On your knees, Watcher."

She pointed her weapon directly at Duat. He looked at the gleaming chrome work of the Scatterblade against the dimming lights of the grenades as she moved her finger over the trigger.

"As you wish." He moved slowly down to his knees.

The Reeve watched from behind her mask. She didn't like it. He was conforming too easily.

Raysmau nodded at Shula. "Gloves. Secure him first before the others. He is lying. There will be more."

Shula released one of her hands from her Scatterblade, reached into a pocket behind her leg armour, pulled out a pair of leather gloves and threw them at Duat's knees. "Put them on." She returned her hand back to her weapon and pointed it directly at him.

Duat picked them up with an arrogant swagger and looked at Shula with a grin. "Stop smiling, Watcher. It makes you look even more ugly if that is at all possible."

He separated them and went to put one on his left hand. "I assure you that I am far from what your kind call ugly. I am beauty."

The seriousness of the atmosphere was disrupted momentarily by a few sniggers from behind where Shula stood over Duat.

"Silence!!" Raysmau instructed.

Shula was not amused in the slightest. When she saw the right hand was gloved, she stepped closer to him. "Put your hands behind your back."

Duat surveyed all the weapons pointing at him as he put his hands behind his back and closed his eye to concentrate. He could feel movements through his right arm down to his palm. Strain lines appeared across the thin skin of his forehead as he focused.

He could feel his palm burning through the leather glove. Bellator, standing behind, could see flashes of turquoise against the light within the room as the smouldering leather came apart and fell to the floor.

Shula slung her Scatterblade over her shoulder. "Do not resist," she commanded as she reached into a different pocket and pulled out a pair of cuffs. Duat turned to look at Bellator and smiled. "Eyes front Watcher, or should I say eye?" She crouched down, took hold of his left wrist and put the cuffs around it. She reached for his right hand. As she touched it, she immediately felt a wave of heat pass through her. Duat secured his hand to hers and looked at her. "I am ready. Are you?" The heat had frozen her movements. He ripped his right hand away from hers and brought it down upon her forehead. Shula shook uncontrollably as deep red blood vessels streamed across both of her eyes.

"Let her go, Watcher!" Raysmau commanded. "Let her go."

"Drop your hand," could be heard from multiple Escarrabin throughout the chamber.

He pulled Shula closer to him. "SERVATORUS!" he yelled as loudly as he could as spit exited his mouth all over her.

"Watcher, let her go or we will fire upon you!"

He let go of her laughing and dragged himself behind her using her body as a shield.

Shula stood up. Her shaking had stopped. He stood up to meet her gaze and looked into the redness of her eyes. "Do what needs to be done."

Her mouth was quivering as she turned to look at the Escarrabin whose weapons were all pointing at her. Looking from right to left across the chamber, their yells and words were unheard as she glanced down at her Scatterblade.

"Watcher, get away from her," yelled Raysmau.

Their yells of command echoed around the room.

"Shula, Shula!" Kassia screamed, "get away from him." She looked directly at her friend. "What has happened to you?"

"She's not herself," asserted the Reeve.

"Watcher, get away from her, or we will fire upon you," Raysmau yelled for the second time.

Still snorting his laughter, he stepped back a couple of paces with his hands held aloft. "As you wish, Raysmau."

The Reeve's eyes suddenly widened. "Look at his palm!"

The Escarrabin immediately focused on Duat's right palm; his laughter stopped in an instant. His mouth opened emitting the familiar hiss of the Watchers.

"SERVATORUS!"

Time within that moment seemed to pass slowly as Shula's mouth opened in anger. She brought the Scatterblade up towards her chest.

"Escarrabin, drop the weapon!"

Her face contorted in rage as she looked to the left of the room at two of the Escarrabin. She snatched the weapon up as the white pulse of light left her Scatterblade, forcing the Escarrabin to dive for cover. She screamed as the pulse struck the soldier on the left, sending her tumbling backwards.

"OPEN FIRE, OPEN FIRE!" The command was issued as the chamber lit up with the white pulses of the Scatterblades. Shula continued to fire, hitting the soldier second on the left. She fell next to her former colleague.

Pieces of stone fell from the ceiling; the blasts impacting against the walls sent rock hurtling around the chamber.

Duat crouched down as a blast passed him, striking the wall to the side of him covering him in dust and stone. He reached out for Bellator. "WATCHERS MOVE!" The black cloaks needed no further instruction. They were gone in an instant, scattering in all directions down the tunnels.

"After them. After them!" Raysmau yelled as she shielded her face from an indiscriminate blast from Shula. The ceiling rocked above her and some of the Escarrabin gave chase.

"SHULA!" she turned to look at her friend Kassia whose hands were shaking. "Drop it, drop it now!"

Shula hissed back at her and was immediately struck across the chest. Shula fell along with her Scatterblade.

As she dropped to the floor, Duat's hand stretched out and gathered the fallen Scatterblade. He disappeared down a tunnel, taking the Scatterblade with him. Kassia lowered her weapon; her hands were shaking with shock as she approached Shula.

"What are you doing?"

She turned to look at Raysmau. "I need to see if she is dead, Ma'am."

"Well, of course she is, she has passed over. Maintain your focus and get down that left tunnel. Masika, join her and continue to scan. We have no idea how many are here." Kassia swallowed and looked down at her friend.

"She was lost to us."

"Yes, Ma'am." She nodded a few times, her lips quivering.

"Make sure this doesn't happen to anyone else. Now get down that tunnel." She watched the two of them lift their Scatterblades and move to the tunnel on their left.

"Reeve, Ma'am, are you okay?"

"Yes, I'm fine." The Reeve stood up, brushing the stone from her breastplate.

"Rashida and Kissa, get down to us now." At the top of the first-floor stairs, Kissa and Rashida looked at each other and swallowed, having heard the exchange of fire below.

"Control receiving?"

"Yes, Ma'am. Go ahead."

"Send remaining Escarrabin down to us immediately, whoever can be spared, with a limited cordon around the lobby area. Ensure all doors remain secured."

"Yes, Ma'am, although most are with you. As others return from last night's duties, we will send them down."

"Received. Kassia, receiving?"

"Yes... pro... level...."

"Kassia, receiving?"

"...dark... movement..."

The Reeve and Raysmau immediately looked at each other as the sound of a blast came through their earpieces. The sound then travelled towards them from the tunnel. "We are losing comms and control down here."

"Yes, we are. Raysmau, look how many tunnels there are and that's what we can see directly. There may be more further ahead and we don't have enough soldiers. We can't send them in two at a time; we don't know how many we are dealing with and how many tunnels lay beyond. We have to concentrate on Duat; it looks like he went down there. He is the snake. We need to remove the head of the snake." She pointed at the tunnel behind where Shula fell. There was another sound of a blast from the tunnel directly in front of them.

"Yes, Ma'am and the other Escarrabin may not be back for some hours."

"Yes, I know. Tell me your thoughts."

"I agree, Ma'am. It could be a maze down here. We could be chasing them for hours; we have no idea how deep it goes."

"Agreed and..?"

"My gut feeling is that we have to call them all back and come here again in the morning with the full accompaniment of troops. We have already lost three." They looked over at the two Escarrabin that had fallen by Shula's hand. "Agreed, but we must get Duat tonight. We must get him now. Take him and the others will conform. He is unlike any Watcher I have ever seen."

"Lotfia and Suma, get down that tunnel and bring back Kassia and Masika. Rashida and Najla, both of you get down there. Bring everyone who gave chase back to this point. The rest of you search and detain Duat, don't go too far. If you find him, ignore the others for now. The Reeve and I will head down that tunnel. Once everyone has gathered and if you have not captured Duat, you all proceed down there to catch us up, understood?"

"Yes, Ma'am."

The Scatterblade had been passed to Bellator, but he was clueless how to use it. They were moving quickly in the near darkness of the tunnel. Duat turned to look at him and the two Watchers that had followed, the others had scattered in all directions.

"Give me cover."

"Master?"

"With the Blade."

"Master, I am sorry, but I have never used one of these before."

Duat snatched it from him. "It's not complicated. This button here is for the blade that extends at the end to make it a sword; we do not want that, so leave it." He held the weapon up to Bellator's face. "This is the trigger; you see here? That is the pulse fire control," he pointed at a controller. "The cave complex was not destroyed because it is at a minimum setting, so you turn it here. Only turn this far when I command, understand?"

"Yes, Master, I understand."

"At full pulse, it may take a few seconds to charge. It will tell you when ready." He passed the weapon back to him.

"How will it tell me, Master?"

Duat hissed in anger as Bellator stepped backwards.

"You will hear it!"

Duat walked away from the three Watchers. "Now, all of you provide cover for me. They will be following."

Bellator turned around, awkwardly holding the Scatterblade, pointing it towards the direction they had just come from.

Duat looked around the tunnel running his right palm against the wall as he walked. To his right, there was another passage in near darkness; his vision was good, but at the far end, it was pitch black. He had not been down this passage before. Stepping back, he looked at one of the cloaked Watchers, not being able to see his face. "You, what is your name?"

"Karawan Sire."

"What is down this tunnel?"

The Watcher moved to him and looked to his right. "There are further quarters down there. At the bottom there's a shaft that leads to the floor above, but it is sealed from the top, Sire."

"Sealed by what?"

"Some of us have tried to leave before Sire; the Escarrabin discovered it some years ago. They came down here with equipment that melted metal. It is a metal seal and strong. You would have walked over it above Sire, but you would not know that it is there."

Duat looked into the Watcher's eye, unnerving him instantly as he looked down. Duat had powers of communication, light and fire but not to break through metal plates by his own hand. He turned around, knowing that Bellator could as he looked at the chrome work of the Scatterblade. "Come, all of you, we go this way."

They had only taken a few steps when Duat stopped and turned to look at Bellator with the Scatterblade in his hand. Full pulse he considered; full pulse may open the iron wall below.

Bellator looked at Duat's gaze as he pushed saliva away from his mouth. "Master?"

Duat lifted his palm slightly for him to be quiet as he considered it. The gas below was deadly and he could not know whether it had cleared. It was unlikely in such a confined space. He chewed with his misshapen teeth, contemplating the risk; this was only the first phase in any event. His thoughts were interrupted by a noise in the distance that seemed to be coming closer. The Watchers turned to face it. "Leave it, let's go."

They watched Duat walk into the darkness of the tunnel and they duly followed.

The Reeve looked down the dimly lit passage, holding her spear in front of her. Despite the coldness of the place, her body temperature had risen from the weight of her armour. She felt the controls of her spear and pressed the button for illumination. The intense white light shone from her spear and they both watched in silence as she guided it throughout the length and across the walls of the tunnel.

"There are so many tunnels Ma'am, impossible to know where they went." Raysmau depressed the torch button on her Scatterblade, surveying the unreadable language carved into the walls and the various offshoots from the tunnel. She had night vision goggles attached to her helmet; though helpful, it was far better to work in light if possible.

"Ma'am, if we are proceeding down there, I insist I go first."

The Reeve looked at the size of the frame of Raysmau and concluded in an instant that her nobility was just and that she would make a useful shield if it came to it. A selfish thought of life preservation rather than cowardice, she decided that it was a good idea. "Please do."

Raysmau stepped forward and proceeded further into the tunnel. "Control, comms check." There was no response through her earpiece. "Control radio check, receiving?"

The Reeve moved forward, lighting up the far right-hand side of the tunnel as Raysmau lit the left. "Damn walls are too thick. It's just us for now."

They passed other tunnels and cut-outs in the rock that were the Watchers resting quarters. Now shrouded in eerie silence, Duat could feel the coldness of the place again. "How much further, Karawan?"

"The walls curve around to the right; the whole passage is one big circle, Sire. We were standing in the centre of it before the Escarrabin opened fire on us."

Karawan was right. The Watchers excavation skills were impressive, Duat concluded, as he felt the bow in the rock with his right palm. There was a short flash of light behind them that reflected off the damp walls.

"Master!"

"I see it, Bellator. They are coming but will not be in numbers. The rest of our brothers scattering saw to that. Karawan, move quicker and take us there."

"It's just a little further, Sire. Up there."

Duat looked at the long nails of the Watcher's hand pointing to a gap further up. They rushed towards it. "Bellator, stay behind me. If the Escarrabin appear, cut them down. They have never shown mercy to you, do not show it to them." Bellator dropped back behind the three of them. "Yes, Master."

They approached a cut-out area of the circle and Duat stopped the one Watcher he had not spoken to before. "What is your name?"

"My name is Zuka, Sire."

"Go up ahead of us. If this tunnel is a circle, they could come from the other direction as well."

"Yes, Sire."

The cloaked figure passed by them as Duat stepped into the cut-out and looked up. He strained his eye, looking at the seal of the thin shaft above.

"There are climbing holes cut into the wall, Sire," Karawan pointed at cut-outs in the rock for foot and hand placements.

"How could you have escaped through here if it only goes up one floor?"

"Others had a plan before, Sire, to lure the Escarrabin down below. While they were searching in the tunnels, some of us would climb up and go over the top of them. They found the shaft, sealed it and added the security scanner by the doorway some years ago. The plan was foiled."

Duat grunted, shook his head and placed his right foot into one of the cut-outs, he found a gap above that he could steady himself with and pulled his left leg up. Gripping old stone with his long nails was not easy. Stone chips and dirt fell to the floor as he pushed himself up.

Bellator and Karawan looked up at him, making progress as he whipped his left hand away as a broken fingernail fell towards them. The reinforced roof was becoming ever closer as he stretched as far as he could. He took one more lunge upwards and was immediately below the steel plate secured by the Escarrabin.

He ran his right palm across it; dirt and small particles of rock fell below as he made a fist with his right hand and gently hit against it. Listening to the noise, he hit it again at three different points; the seal was strong but not immensely thick. The Scatterblade would destroy this easily.

Closing his eye, he brought his hand down and thrust his right palm against the rock wall. The two Watchers below looked at each other as a turquoise glow emanated against the rock face. His face screwed up in concentration and he ground at his teeth, trying to get a connection outside. The grinding soon dissipated. He removed his palm from the wall, opened his eye and started to descend.

"Master, is everything okay?"

Duat was still looking upwards. "Pass me the Blade. Assistance has been summoned."

Chapter Thirty:

FLAMES AT THE LIGHT OF DAWN

Nubia backed up a couple of stairs, having heard the fire exchanges below ground. She looked at one of the two Escarrabin providing security for Lady Safiya. "What are you hearing? What is going on?"

"I'm sorry, Ma'am, I cannot say other than more support has been requested. There are some communication problems in the below."

"Well, many of you are still missing, not back from last night's duties!"

"Yes, Ma'am, I know, but given the circumstances, we need to take you both to a more secure area."

"Rubbish," Lady Safiya interrupted, "I'm too old to be hiding; besides, Watchers can be overpowered. If that creature was out, we would have heard it by now. Someone is resisting."

"Ma'am, we are not in a position to overrule you, but it would be prudent advice for us to move from here."

"What is your name, officer of the Escarrabin?"

"Soad, Ma'am."

She turned to look at the other one. "And yours?"

"My name is Yara, Ma'am."

"Look, if you both want to go and support your friends, I understand." Nubia looked at Safiya in a state of shock. "I really think they should..."

Safiya's hand lifted calmly to silence her. "Your advice is noted and will be on record. Whether you go or stay is entirely up to you."

They both looked at each other. "Lady Raysmau's order was clear that we should stay and protect the Lady of the House." Yara, looked at Soad for reassurance.

"And me!" Nubia interjected as they both turned to look at her.

"Settled then. We stay unless we hear more pulse blasts, that is." They nodded to each other as Yara looked up at the stairs. She lifted her weapon as her eye caught a movement.

"Yara, it's just a Cleric."

She lowered her weapon as the white-robed figure descended the stairs towards them. Her head was bowed and no words were exchanged as she passed. Both of the Escarrabin looked at each other.

"Cleric, where are you going? The manor is at diligence." Yara questioned.

The figure had reached the bottom of the stairs and turned to them still with head bowed. "I have an urgent message from the Reeve that I need to present to control."

Yara looked down at the Cleric with a frown from her elevated position on the stairs. "We have received no such instruction or message. There are comms problems below."

There was a brief pause before her head lifted slightly so the Escarrabin could see her chin. "That is why she messaged me through my terminal. It's important. I must deliver it right away, Madam Escarrabin," she said, lowering her head again.

Yara nodded. "Okay, you may proceed." She looked at Soad as the Cleric walked towards Raysmau's secured area. "You think Lady Reeve has her navigator with her or another form of communication?"

She came to her out of earshot of Lady Safiya and Nubia. "It's possible; we don't get told everything. Besides, they will probably not open the security gate to her anyway." They both turned to look at the Cleric as she walked into the archway. From the angle they were at, she disappeared out of sight, but they could see the right-hand side of the security door was closed.

"I guess we may get issued with another instruction then?" Yara questioned.

"It's possible. You want to take point or stand with Lady Safiya?"

"I'm happy here if you want to go up to her." They both looked up the stairs to where Lady Safiya stood. Nubia was peering from behind her, staring back at them, her face a bag of nerves.

"Still nothing."

"Keep trying. Three life indicators have flatlined, but I'm losing readings on the others, just intermittent blips. The below is too deep and signals are not coming through."

"Escarrabin, report your status. This is Control, receiving?"

Amera nervously looked at Layla with a shake of the head. They both leant over their monitors, waiting for signs of something positive.

A buzz was heard across the room and instinct tilted their heads to the monitor above, not that they had CCTV to assist them.

"It could be one of ours wounded or with orders. Go check it, will you?"

Amera reached for her Scatterblade. "I'll go look, back in a mo, keep trying comms."

She was shaking her head as she walked towards the gate. "It's times like this I really wished we had CCTV in this place." She pressed the speaker button. "Control, identify yourself, please."

"Cleric, Madam Escarrabin, I have an urgent message from the Reeve for control."

Amera let go of the button, frowning, looking at the push to talk button. How could she have a message? She pressed the button again.

"Tell me the message, Cleric. I am control."

"It's a written message, Madam. I have to show you."

Amera took a deep breath. The Reeve must have been wounded to write such a message; the Cleric must be a message runner. She entered the code for the outer door to open. The robe of the Cleric with her head bowed came into view. "Come towards me, approach the gate."

The Cleric walked towards her. "You don't need to bow Cleric, pass me the message; what is it written on?"

"My palm."

"The Reeve wrote a message on your palm? Is she okay, is she wounded?"

The Cleric nodded.

"Come closer, open your palm."

The Cleric put her right hand through the bars of the gate and opened her palm. "Do you see?"

The Escarrabin looked at the palm in confusion. "No, where is it written?"

"Look more closely!" The tone of the Cleric's voice deepened as she lifted her head.

"I see nothing, I can't see..." Amera looked up into the Cleric's face and froze, looking at her red eyes that were bloodshot with rage. "Do you see?"

Amera looked down. There were movements inside the Cleric's hand, turquoise patterns running across the lines of her palm. She let out a gasp and went to move away, but the Cleric reached for her arm. Immense pain immediately shot through her, disabling her movements as her Scatterblade fell to the floor. Her mouth opened to yell out as her body shook. The Cleric brought her palm down onto her forehead. The Cleric's mouth opened but made no sound as the Escarrabin tried bringing her arms up, but she was powerless. All her strength was draining from her as her eyes rolled and filled deep red in colour. The Cleric pushed harder with her palm as the Escarrabin spluttered and fell to the floor. She looked behind her; no one had seen a thing. She leant through the gate with her left arm and hit the control button to release the gate. The gate moved instantly and she stepped through dragging the Escarrabin's body out of the way so the gate would open fully. She was dead, but she had no use for her anyway. She glanced behind again, picked up the Scatterblade and headed towards the control room. Further ahead, she could see the doorway for Raysmau's private quarters. She brought the weapon up to her chin and wrapped her finger around the trigger. She knew control was the next door on the left. Steadying herself, she tilted her head to the right to see that the door was open. She could hear a voice inside talking, but only one voice.

With the weapon raised, she pushed through the door to find one Escarrabin attempting communications.

"Cleric, what are you..."

"Drop it, drop it now."

Layla saw the Scatterblade pointing at her and dropped the comms set on the desk.

"What is the meaning of this Cleric? What are you doing?"

The Cleric pulled her hood down, revealing her eyes. Layla froze in fear. "Raise the barriers," the Cleric spat in anger.

Layla did not realise it, but her head was shaking. "What has happened to you Cleric and where is Amera?"

"I am no Cleric and your friend is dead. I will not tell you again. Take us out of diligence and raise the barriers."

Layla went to move her hands to her terminal.

"Slowly!"

Hands shaking, she tried to speak calmly. "There is no escape from here whether they are open or not."

The weapon was moved closer to her head, but it was not close enough to try and disarm her. She pushed at the keys on her pad and a flashing button appeared on the screen that said 'Diligence.' She pressed enter and the flashing stopped. She bowed her head in resignation as the portcullis started to move upwards and the shutters over the windows on the lower floor started to lift exposing the glass.

The Cleric took a couple of steps back towards the exit and listened for the sound of the security shutters withdrawing. Satisfied with what she heard, she went back towards the officer of the Escarrabin and raised her weapon again.

The two Escarrabin on the stairs turned around, hearing the noise of the portcullis being drawn up and could see the security shutters moving from the ground floor windows.

Soad, who was standing to the side of Lady Safiya, looked confused and stepped down a few steps towards Yara. "Diligence could not have been lifted with the others below."

Two other Escarrabin, who had been guarding the doorway to the below, stepped forward into view and looked up the stairway to them.

"Something is not right," Soad pressed her push to talk button, "control receiving, control receiving?" There was no response.

"Try one more time." Yara couldn't hear any response in her ear either.

"Control radio check, over?"

Nubia stepped forward. "What is happening, Escarrabin?"

"We've lost communication with control, Ma'am."

Nubia looked up at Safiya in worry.

Soad looked at her fellow Escarrabin shaking her head. "Something is not right." She bowed her head in thought, but her eyes suddenly sprung back up. "Did that Cleric come back, the one who said she had a message?"

The look in Yara's face said enough as she spun to look at the entrance door to control. Even at the awkward angle from where she was standing on the stairs, it looked like it may be open. She lifted her Scatterblade. "I'll go check."

"Ma'am, I really think that we should move upstairs to a secured area."

Safiya looked into the face of her security guard, considering her opinion this time.

She could hear them calling for her in her earpiece, but the pointed Scatterblade stopped any response. The Cleric was breathing hard, staring at her.

"What is that?" The weapon was drawn closer.

"What is what?"

She heard the muffled noise again. "Take that out of your ear! What are they saying?"

"They are asking for me."

"Take it out and put it on the table. Now!"

The weapon was drawn closer as she slowly brought her left hand up to her right ear and glanced to the side of the desk at her own Scatterblade that was propped against it. She knew that if no response was forthcoming from control, it was protocol for it to be checked immediately and that others would soon arrive. Her movements were slow as she removed her earpiece and brought it forward towards the Cleric. She let go and it bounced on the edge of the desk, falling to the floor.

The Cleric hissed in anger. "Not clever!" Stepping forward, she stood on the earpiece, glancing down to check it was destroyed. The weapon was now only a couple of feet away from her head. Layla lashed out with her hand, disabling the Cleric's grip and moved the weapon away from her face. She pulled a fist and punched the Cleric across the bridge of the nose, splitting it open. The blow dazed the Cleric as she let go of the Scatterblade that fell on the desk. Layla's left arm went straight for her throat and gripped firmly, forcing her to lose balance. The Cleric fell backwards to the floor. Layla could see the bursting red in her eyes. "Enough of this!"

The Cleric's right palm was bursting with turquoise veins as she grabbed the gloved hand of the Escarrabin and pushed down.

"You are under arr..." Layla immediately felt uneasy as heat passed through her glove and up her arm. She started to convulse. The Cleric could see the fear in her eyes as the grip lost purchase around her throat. She rubbed the blood from her nose and brought her palm down on Layla's neck. As the Cleric leaned over her, Layla could see the anger in her eyes. She couldn't fight back as the pain inside her deepened. Turquoise veins came to the surface of her neck from where she was being held. The colours moved quickly towards her skull. "SERVATORUS!"

The Escarrabin's legs were shaking as her eyes turned colour. "Servatorus!" The Cleric let go of her and stood over the fallen body, reaching for the Scatterblade on the desk. "Get up, servant!" A thin line of blood fell from the right eye of the former officer of the Escarrabin as she looked up at her. "On your feet. NOW!"

She stepped back and watched Layla try to get to her feet; her body shook as she steadied herself against the desk. She pulled herself up. The smell of burnt leather from the smoking glove filled the air as the Cleric passed the weapon to her. "Get out there and kill the Escarrabin." Layla took the weapon. "Yes, Master." She watched Layla pass by her, weapon raised. "It's Ma'am," she hissed as she leant over the desk to study the security controls.

With her Scatterblade raised in defence position, Yara descended the stairs and made her way across the lobby floor. She stepped to the doorway of the secured area, bringing her weapon up to her chin. She could hear movement on the other side. She turned into the archway to see Layla with her weapon raised. "Control, why are you not at your p…" She looked down to see the deceased body of Amera next to the gate and back up seeing the anger in Layla's face. "Drop the weapon. Drop the weapon, now!"

A white pulse of light came towards her, striking her in the torso and throwing her body backwards into the lobby.

Nubia screamed, seeing the fallen Escarrabin.

"Escarrabin Contact!" Soad yelled as she dived over the body of Lady Safiya, forcing her to the floor. She looked down at the exchange of fire from the two Escarrabin below her and saw one fall. "My Lady, cover there now!" She pointed to a pillar on the first-floor balcony. She helped her to her feet and unceremoniously dragged her to the pillar, where they both hid. Nubia was shaking in a ball behind them.

Soad's weapon was aimed at the security entrance as she watched the archway and door being ripped apart. The pulse fire scattered stone and wood over the unmoving body of her friend. The surviving Escarrabin officer below had taken cover and was now engaged in a firefight. Unless the shooter responsible was cut down by the officer below, sooner or later, they would come out and Soad was certain of one thing – that when they did, she would not miss.

She stepped back from the control terminal, hearing the pulse fire outside and concentrated. Her deep red eyes started to flicker as she placed her right palm against the wall and waited.

Duat felt the positive sign of warmth run through him and recognised its meaning immediately. He rushed to the wall of the shaft and placed his palm on it, closing his eye. Somebody was trying to get through to him, but it was weak. He climbed halfway up the shaft and tried again, looking upwards as his palm received knowledge.

He let go and climbed back down. "Karawan, get Zuka back here. It is time. Bellator, give me that."

Bellator passed the weapon to him and watched Duat adjust the pulse control. The adjustment was slight. He didn't want the whole shaft collapsing. He stepped inside the shaft and looked at the seal above. Crouching down, he lifted the weapon to his shoulder and took a firm hold of the trigger. He drew in a breath; his hands and body were steady as he pulled his finger backwards. The shaft was instantly illuminated in white light.

As the pulse rose, he rolled out of the way as the explosion above echoed through the shaft and raced through the tunnels around them. The metal plate was blown off its securing bolts and the blast hit the ceiling above. Rubble fell down the shaft, creating a dust cloud that covered them both. Duat passed the weapon back to Bellator and leaned into the dust. He wiped his eye, waiting for it to clear, in any event, the shaft had held. The other two Watchers had rejoined them. "Now, we are leaving!"

The sound of the explosion stopped the Reeve and Raysmau in their tracks.

"It came from above!"

"Yes, it did, Ma'am. Watchers and probably Duat must be above us. We must go."

The Reeve nodded at her as they turned around. "Control receiving?" There was just static noise. "Escarrabin receiving?" Raysmau received muffled and indiscernible words from others below. "All Escarrabin, if you understand this message, report to the first floor below immediately." Raysmau and the Reeve raced towards the third-floor chamber as quickly as they could.

Duat reached the top of the shaft and cautiously looked across the stone floor. It looked to be clear. The occasional rock had struck him on his way up. He noticed the hole smoking in the ceiling above and glanced down to Bellator, who was climbing behind him. "Move now. It is clear." He stepped out of the shaft and looked at the steaming metalwork that had previously covered their exit path.

He walked forward, looking at the stairway. The Escarrabin must have heard the blast; it would not be long before they were here. He turned to see the figure of Bellator emerge from the shaft, the Scatterblade over his shoulder. "You provide cover... and we'll need that," he pointed a long fingernail at the Blade. The other two were soon to emerge as he focused on the stairs that led up towards the exit and nodded at Bellator. "Proceed up. We don't have long."

Raysmau could not be sure if the others heard her radio call; using caution they entered the chamber of the third floor. The bodies of the Escarrabin lay as they had fallen, but they were alone. "Ma'am, we must investigate above."

The Reeve held her spear in front of her, the light source showing them the way to the staircase which would take them up. The light grenades from earlier had long since died. Raysmau took the lead.

Raysmau switched off her torch and crouched at the bottom of the staircase, looking up with her Blade raised. She couldn't hear any movements above. She looked at the Reeve, giving her a silent signal to deactivate her torch and join her at the base of the stairs. They ascended in silence, smelling something burning from the upper floor as they reached the top. Raysmau stepped forward and visually swept the room. Her eyes were drawn to a smoking metal plate and a cloud of dust that was still spreading throughout the chamber. Small shards of stone fell from a hole in the ceiling. She gave a signal for the Reeve to join her as they both looked around the chamber. They appeared to be alone as they swept every corner and curve of the cold room. They both immediately looked up, hearing movements above. Raysmau instructed the Reeve to proceed to the stairs that would lead them to the floor directly below the manor.

Bellator had reached the first floor of the below and looked across the familiar room where the Escarrabin would collect them for 'duties.' The stairs were at the far end and he could hear pulse fire above. "Master, listen!"

"We are not alone my friend, we have help above," he beckoned the other two Watchers to move with them. "The door at the top of the stairs will be secured; the Blade will make short work of that."

"But the outer doors, Master?"

Duat looked at him and spoke with a hiss of satisfaction. "They are already open."

"Master. But then what? Where do we go?"

"We?"

Bellator looked confused. "Yes, Master, our brothers."

He leaned forward to him. "We are leaving this evening, but not everything has been completed. The others will be freed in time."

Bellator turned to look at the backs of the other two Watchers, who were looking in the direction of the stairs that led below. Duat's words were unheard to them. One turned to them. "Sire, movements below."

"They are coming, quickly to the stairs."

Soad looked down the stairs to where the other member of the Escarrabin was pinned down; pulse blasts had caused considerable damage behind her.

Crater damage in the ceiling had torn away some of the elaborate panelling. One window had been blown outwards and a chandelier hung delicately but mostly destroyed. Her weapon was still pointed towards the arch; whoever was firing from the other side was a terrible shot. She looked down to Ana, the Escarrabin, who had been returning fire, as she removed a grenade from her belt and held it upwards to inform her to be ready. She adjusted the strength dial of the grenade and spoke to Nubia and Lady Safiya without looking at them. "Don't look at it." She stepped towards the top of the stairs, put her Scatterblade on the floor, brought the light grenade behind her and threw it as hard as possible towards the archway. Hearing it bounce on the floor, she reclaimed her weapon and turned around to shield her eyes.

The sound of the blast rang through the chamber, chandeliers shook and artwork fell from the walls. Soad turned, pointing her weapon at the archway. Ana did the same. A figure fell through the arch shielding her eyes. Soad shook her head in disbelief as one of her own came into view. "Ana, hold your fire!" but the command was too late. She was sent reeling backwards, crashing against the door where she fell.

Lady Safiya looked on in horror at the downed Escarrabin. "What the hell is happening?" Soad looked down from the balcony to see Ana's weapon still raised. She had moved forward to check on the Escarrabin that had been hit earlier; she found no pulse. She moved towards the body of Yara and checked that the Escarrabin she had just shot had been killed. She kicked the Scatterblade away although she knew that she had passed. She stepped back towards the stairs to be met by Soad pointing her weapon at her.

"Soad, what are you doing?"

"You just shot one of our own."

"I'm telling you that was not one of us. She was the one that was firing at me and she killed Yara and Ruon."

Soad received the comment with shock on her face. "WHAT?"

"Ridiculous!" was heard from behind them as they looked at the tiny frame of the Curator. "I've never heard of anything so unbelievable."

"I'm telling you the truth, Ma'am, whether you like to hear it or not." She looked at Soad; her hands were shaking.

"Others have fallen below and we need to go down."

The Reeve and Raysmau had reached the base of the stairs. The sound of footsteps on stone could be heard from behind. They spun around as quickly as they could, turning their weapons towards the staircase. They were somewhat relieved to see the faces of Alian and Gamila.

Raysmau beckoned them over and pointed with one finger upwards as Gamila crouched to look up the stairs. She had seen the smouldering metal on the floor below with some concern. "Looked like a heavy pulse blast." Raysmau put a finger to her mouth to silence her.

Raysmau moved first, stepping forward onto the stairs whilst the other three followed closely behind her. As they approached the top, they all crouched down, with Raysmau indicating to Alian to move straight across the floor to provide cover. She looked into her eyes and spoke quietly. "Ready?"

She nodded and took a deep breath, bringing the weapon up to her chin. "Go!"

Alian stepped up and ran across the floor to the far wall. Raysmau moved at the same time to cover the near side. They could immediately see moving shadows in the distance on the far set of stairs. Alian gave a hand signal to move forward as all four of them moved to the stairs with their weapons primed.

Bellator was ascending the stairs and felt a hand on his shoulder. "Wait!" Duat turned around. Shadows in the dim light of the chamber were moving towards them and noise underfoot could be heard. "They are here! Bellator, come back, come back." Duat pulled him to the bottom of the stairs. "Don't get close to those doors." Duat looked at Zuka. "Come closer to me."

"Yes, Master?"

The Watcher walked down the steps to him. "We have to go, Sire."

He glanced towards Bellator and resumed looking into the face of Zuka. "Yes, WE ARE!" Duat pushed against him as he fell backwards down the last two stairs onto the chamber floor.

"Watcher on your knees!" Screamed Raysmau as the falling cloaked figure came into their line of sight.

The Watcher fell on his side and looked back up the stairs towards Duat. His mouth opened, bearing the nubs of his stained teeth as his hiss of anger filled the room. "Traitor!" he spat at Duat.

"WATCHER, ON YOUR KNEES!"

Zuka flicked his head instantly towards the Escarrabin and stood up enraged, moving towards them in aggression.

The pulse blast from Raysmau's Scatterblade sent him backwards. He fell, his dead, lifeless eye looking towards the stairs. Duat hissed as saliva projected from his mouth. "Bellator, full pulse, NOW!!"

Bellator turned the pulse control as far as it would allow and looked at Duat, who was pointing upwards ahead of them. "Destroy that door!"

He held the weapon upwards, waiting for the sound of notification that the weapon was ready; a double bleep was heard and he pulled at the trigger.

The recoil from the huge release of energy from the Blade sent him backwards against the wall as the pulse light travelled up the stairs.

Having heard Duat yelling the order for full pulse, Raysmau turned, screaming at the others. "Take cover, take cover!"

Duat crouched down and shielded his eye as the pulse struck the doorway above. The door bowed on impact. There was silence for a fraction of a second as time appeared to freeze. The whole building shook as the door was blown from its fixings and the lift shaft to the right collapsed. The explosion and wave of fire blew across the lobby and carried down the grand walkway. Chandeliers were torn from their holdings as the downstairs windows blew outwards one at a time as the fire rushed past them. Artworks on the wall were instantly ablaze as the dust made its way through the flames engulfing the floor above.

Duat opened his eye, feeling the heat soaring towards him as a ball of fire raced down the stairs at him.

Bellator and Karawan also saw the oncoming blast of fire. They threw themselves over Duat to shield him as the flames raced over them into the chamber. The ball of fire impacted Karawan's back as his cloak was immediately set alight. His screams were heard throughout the chamber as the fire blast raced down the tunnels of the below. The blast was short lived and quickly extinguished against the dampness and cold of the walls.

From Raysmau's order, the four Escarrabin had scattered for cover, shielding themselves behind pillars and rock. The fireball had passed by them, causing minimal damage to their battle armour. The Reeve moved from behind a pillar to see the flaming figure stumbling around the chamber. She looked on in anguish as her ears rang with the noise of his pain. She raised her spear and brought it upwards to her chest and pressed the button for the trigger release that dropped down from the spear. Wrapping her index finger over the trigger, she pulled back. The pulse of light struck the screaming Watcher, sending his flaming body backwards.

The screaming stopped as the lifeless Watcher fell to the floor. She lowered the spear looking at the flames that continued to burn the remainder of his cloak.

Duat had instinctively protected his right palm as the fire raced over him. Using his cloak with his left hand, he thrashed against Bellator, trying to put the flames out on his cloak. His own minor burns were of no significance, but that could not be said for Bellator. He could smell the stench of the Watcher's seared skin. He pulled Bellator's head back and looked into his eye. He was burnt and hurt. To what extent, he did not know. "Get the weapon. We are leaving!"

Duat had seen Karawan fall from the pulse blast of the Reeve and looked up at the remnants of the doorway that was still ablaze. The stonework that secured the door was long gone, scattered above.

Bellator reached for the Scatterblade in immense pain and gingerly rose to his feet. His cloak smouldered.

Duat helped pull him up. "Now, let's go!"

They both ran up the stairs towards the flames. A pulse blast raced by them, striking the wall, covering them with stone. Bellator fell through the former doorway. Duat moved through, shielding his right hand from the flames. Bellator had fallen on the stone that covered the corridor and the grand lobby. He looked up among the flames and dust to see Duat moving forward, "Master!" Duat turned to him and pulled his hood down. His saliva was frothing around his mouth, his eye bloodshot. "Get up!"

He reached for the weapon and stumbled to his feet as a chandelier crashed to the ground. He was surrounded by fire as artworks burned. Parts of the ceiling above him were still ablaze.

Duat paused in the fire and dust, looking towards security control. The figure of the Cleric emerged and started walking towards the opened gate with a Scatterblade in her arms. Duat beckoned her forward.

Nubia's hysteria had momentarily paused as she hid behind Lady Safiya. Soad's heart rate was still far from where it should be, following the explosion and fire blast that had ripped across the lobby, blowing the main outer doors partially open. She looked down through the flickering light of fire and dust at what appeared to be a figure coming into view. At the same time, a figure appeared at the entrance to Raysmau's archway. Soad raised her weapon.

"Wait," Ana grabbed her arm, "let her get closer." They crouched behind the balustrade and looked on. The pair of them appeared to be communicating.

As the Cleric stepped into the lobby, they could see for the first time that she was armed.

"That's close enough!" They both stood up from the stairs. "Drop your weapon!"

"Drop it now!" Soad screamed.

Quite disinterested by the threat, the Cleric casually turned her head to look up to the stairs at the two Escarrabin, who had their weapons trained upon her. She looked back to Duat, who nodded and stepped backwards out of view of the others on the staircase. Knowing the other Escarrabin would be on their way, time was short.

"KILL THEM!" he yelled at the Cleric.

She whipped the weapon around and fired, striking the wall next to the staircase, completely missing the two Escarrabin.

They both ducked for cover behind the balustrade as fragments of stone from the wall came hurtling towards them. The Cleric quickly stepped back into the archway. Pulse fire was immediately returned, striking the walls on either side, covering the Cleric with multiple stone shrapnel.

Alian could hear noises from behind her as two other Escarrabin tore into the chamber. She stepped forward out of hiding to meet them.

"What the hell just happened, Alian?" Rasida said as Kissa looked on in stunned silence. "A fire blast just raced by us down the tunnel."

"No time to explain."

"Proceed forward," yelled Raysmau as the six of them passed the two smouldering cloaks of the Watchers and made their way up the stairs.

"Alian, how many went through the doorway?"

"I only saw two, Ma'am."

Duat stood next to the damaged lift shaft looking at the thick cabling ablaze and the smashed remnants of the lift below. He turned to Bellator. "Can you run?"

"I can try, Master," he reached for the weapon.

Duat focused, knowing they had little time. His appearance as a Watcher was drawing to a close.

Bellator stumbled towards him. He was in pain and could feel the burns underneath his cloak, some of which had bonded to his skin.

"The slave will protect us," he pointed towards the main doors, "that is our exit."

"Slave, Master?"

Duat turned to him. "She has opened the doors for us."

He gestured towards the Cleric that they were heading for the doors as her dust and stone strewn cloak moved forward to the front of the arch.

Duat stretched his right arm out. "Pass me the Blade."

Bellator passed the chrome weapon to him as Duat communicated with the Cleric showing her where the dial for the pulse control was.

Suddenly, a pulse blast struck the wall next to her. She fell, having been hit by heavy stone. Duat froze momentarily, looking at the fallen Cleric. She pulled her hood down as she steadied herself back to her feet; her pale face that rarely saw sunlight had blood running down it from a head wound. However, the blood that coursed through her veins was strong and determined. Duat watched her moving the pulse control dial.

"Be ready, my friend."

"Yes, Master," although he had no idea where they were going or what they would do once they got there.

The Cleric stumbled forward with her weapon raised. They both watched her depress the trigger as the huge pulse blast left the weapon, taking her from her feet as she crashed against the battle scarred wall to her side.

The noise of the pulse emission sent the two Escarrabin diving to cover Lady Safiya. The pulse was nowhere near them as it struck the other end of the balcony with an almighty blast of light and fire. Nubia was screaming as the balcony crumbled and fell to the lobby below. The blast of fire soared upwards, scorching the balcony above. Stone and dust raced over their huddle, impairing their vision, but the fire was short-lived. The pulse control had not been fully turned; if it had, they would certainly have fallen as well.

The Cleric lay where she had fallen, the noise of falling masonry from the balcony filled the central lobby. Duat sensed the opportunity.

"Now!" They both rushed for the remains of the grand entrance doors. They pushed their way through the weight of the heavy oak doors with iron fittings that were still on fire. Bellator glanced around, hearing screams from above, but they were not being fired at. They felt the air of the outside move over them as they ran across the gravel driveway at the front of Loxley.

"Stop where you are!"

Bellator turned to see the Escarrabin moving through the doors surrounded by flames, their weapons trained. He counted six of them, but more were bound to follow. "Master, they are here!"

Raysmau indicated for them to move forward as she glanced over the heavily damaged frontage of the Manor House. Glass and stone were scattered as far as she could see and pockets of fire burned all around.

Soad lowered her weapon, relieved to see the arrival of some of her fellow soldiers moving across the lobby. She glanced down at Alian, who beckoned her to follow them. She turned to Lady Safiya.

"Are you okay, my Lady?"

"Are you serious? I'm far from okay," she gingerly rose to her feet, leaving Nubia wrapped in a ball behind her. She looked at the collapsed balcony, the flame scarred walls and the bodies below. "Get down there and finish this!"

"Yes, Ma'am." Ana looked at Soad and nodded towards the open doors below as they raced down the stairs.

Safiya looked around at the burning picture frames; their canvases had long since gone. She shook her head and looked down at the shaking Curator, who was still curled up in a ball. "Nubia, what on earth has happened here?"

Her eyes were watery, tired and scared as she looked up. "The prophecy, it is happening. It can't be stopped."

"But he didn't get what he came for."

"No... not yet."

"I must see this with my own eyes. Come Nubia and be careful of falling masonry."

Nubia struggled to her feet, watching Lady Safiya without her cane slowly weave her way through the rubble on the stairs. She was shaking all over and could feel the heat from multiple fires as she moved down the stairs. She didn't have the same confidence as Lady Safiya, but knew that she had to see what was happening.

Duat passed a flaming statue dragging Bellator with him. He ignored the calls from behind. He glanced around to see some of the downstairs windows were still ablaze and smoke was pouring into the sky above them.

The Escarrabin poured across the gravel, giving chase with weapons lifted.

"That's enough!" commanded Raysmau. "Stop where you are, right now!"

Bellator, hanging on the back of his Master, was looking at them as they stopped moving. The Blade was still in his hand, but he didn't have the initiative to know what to do next. He let go of Duat, who was still facing the other way, his palm alive and restless as he flexed his fingers.

The Escarrabin surrounded both of them in a semi-circle. "Turn around Duat, on your knees and you Watcher, drop that weapon." Duat recognised the voice of Raysmau and smirked as he ran his hand across his mouth, flicking saliva to the floor.

"Escarrabin are dead, Watchers are dead, all attributed to you. You have plenty to explain and you will do at the highest Order."

The Escarrabin could hear a deep laugh from the cloaked figure who still had his back to them. "Raysmau, warrior of the Escarrabin, you have no idea of what the highest order is," he turned to look directly at them. His bloodshot eye reflected the flames burning behind the Escarrabin.

"All of you and your ceremony, your uniforms and your armour did not save all of this," he hissed, "your security failed at every level. You are beaten, ill-educated and incompetent."

"That's enough!"

He looked at the Reeve, who stepped forward with her spear raised. "Watcher, drop your weapon now."

Duat looked at Bellator and nodded. "We do not need it, my friend."

The Reeve watched it fall to the floor. "On your knees, both of you."

The salvia from the smiling mouth of Duat hit the floor first as he moved down to one knee.

"Both knees and you do the same. Now."

Bellator, in pain, did as instructed.

"Both knees, Duat!"

He looked up to the spear pointed at him and into the eyes hidden behind the mask.

"We all wear masks, Reeve."

"Last time and I will not ask again, both knees now, or you will be fired upon!"

He watched the other Escarrabin move closer to him.

"NO!"

"What?"

He laughed as he spoke, "NO!"

He whipped his right palm towards the Reeve as a blinding white light burst from it. They were all instantly defenceless, shielding their eyes. The heat from the light became more intense and started to burn. They were forced back. Bellator shielded his eye and moved backwards on his knees, putting his burnt hands over his face.

"Master?" He looked at Duat, who had stopped laughing, instead, he was making noises of intense pain. Still partially shielding his eye, his Master turned to look at him. His body was shaking as he watched thin folds of skin fall from his skull.

"Master!"

He looked in horror at Duat's eye as it split in the centre and moved across his skull to form two eyes. The cuffs that had been fixed to his left arm fell to the floor. The two holes in his skull that were formally nostrils broke as a snout started to appear. His cloak split down the back and he fell to the floor with his back arched.

Yells of pain from the Escarrabin could be heard as they protected their eyes from the light and heat. Lady Safiya and Nubia appeared at the door and immediately covered their eyes.

In complete fear, Bellator yelled as loudly as he could, "MASTER!" He watched the back of Duat split in the centre as two black veins appeared that separated and grew outwards. His terror intensified as the wing-like veins split into different sections and grew downwards, flanked with skin and blood vessels. The light from Duat's palm was shaking and starting to fade. His voice had changed in tone as he looked at Bellator, "Come to me!"

Bellator shakily got up and walked towards him as he felt a claw grab hold of him. The light from the palm went out.

There was immediate silence as the Escarrabin lowered their hands. All that could be heard was the heavy snorting of a creature breathing. They looked at the two bright red eyes staring at them and froze; the other Watcher had a huge claw wrapped around his torso.

"What the hell is that?" One of the Escarrabin said in fear under her breath. The Reeve, hands shaking, slowly raised her spear again, but a deep roar almost sent them all backwards. The two veins extended and the cracking noise of bone could be heard from the creature's back. Bellator felt a rush of air over him as he was dragged upwards.

"OPEN FIRE, OPEN FIRE!" Pulse fire entered the silence of the night as a huge black tail whipped over them. The creature climbed up into the sky and flew away out of sight.

An order of cease-fire never came; it didn't need to. The Escarrabin lowered their weapons and looked into the clear sky. The light from the full moon shone across the Welsh landscape.

Raysmau turned on hearing gravel move behind her. Lady Safiya stood close by, looking upwards.

Alian was the first to speak. "What the hell was that? I've never seen a Watcher who, well, could do that!"

Lady Safiya could see the fear in the soldier's faces. She turned to the quivering figure of Nubia, knowing that Nubia understood what had just happened. She looked into her watery eyes.

"I'm telling you, that is not...."

"Enough." The Reeve cut Alian off and looked at Lady Safiya, who in turn looked at Raysmau and shook her head.

"I never thought my day would see what has happened here this evening." She looked down at Nubia.

"Ma'am?" the Reeve responded, removing her helmet. "That was no Watcher."

"No! No, it wasn't." Her response was softly spoken as she considered her words and looked at the nodding head of the Curator.

"No, Reeve, that wasn't." She looked forward again, "that was a Gatekeeper."

"MASTER!!" They all turned around to see the Cleric run out of the doors, waving an arm in the air. She was unarmed as far as Raysmau could see. "Lower weapons." She was running towards them, not caring or paying any attention to them.

"MASTER!!" She was screaming as loudly as she could as she ran past all of them and started down the driveway. The floodlights were still on as Raysmau looked at Rasida. "Strike her down."

"Ma'am?"

"Put her down. You saw her eyes. She is lost and a danger to us all. She is possessed by him. Now put her down."

Rasida looked at the Reeve. There was no counter command as she lifted her Scatterblade and brought it to her chin. The white-robed figure was now in the distance as she lifted up her sights and closed her left eye to take aim. She breathed in deeply and held her breath as she pulled at the trigger.

All of them watched the white pulse of light travel down the driveway as it struck the Cleric in the back. Instantly she fell upon the gravel. Rasida lowered her weapon and they watched the Cleric's right leg lift slightly as she pushed herself upwards to her knees. She looked up to the sky, muttering something as the turquoise veins faded. She breathed her last.

Rasida swallowed as she looked at the others in silence.

"Leave her there." The Reeve didn't question this instruction from Raysmau. The others looked amongst themselves and back down the driveway at the fallen Cleric on her knees.

Lady Safiya closed her eyes and looked upwards, taking deep breaths as she felt her hand being taken by Nubia. She reopened her eyes and looked at the Reeve. "He will be back, but not tonight. The Gateway has been opened. What happened here this evening is just the beginning." She looked down at the Curator. "Come, Nubia, let's get you inside. We will all reconvene in the morning."

They watched the two figures walk back towards the destroyed frontage of the Mansion. Lady Safiya didn't turn to them as she spoke and it was almost nonchalantly as she did. "Raysmau, please have someone put the fires out, will you."

"Yes, Ma'am," she responded, but her words were so quiet no one else would have heard. She looked at the Reeve, but there were no words they could exchange.

A gate from another place had been opened and this had been a failure on every level.

As the claws released their grip, Bellator fell a short distance, unceremoniously hitting the ground. Emitting the high pitched cry of a Watcher in pain, Bellator rubbed at his painful wounds, his thin skin pulsing and scarred with burns.

As the winged creature settled not far from him on the hillside, he crawled behind a gathering of rocks, fearful with no understanding of what had just happened. His bloodshot eye focused on the former Watcher, who had shape-shifted into something that he had never seen before; he was fearful of it.

Its long black tail covered in spines extended and the wings outstretched. An almighty bellow roared across the Welsh mountains.

Bellator sensed the creature was in pain. Shaking nervously, he could see the claw of the right hand glowing; it pulsed rapidly in a moving turquoise display. The creature brought the right claw up to its snout and placed it against its skull. A secondary roar echoed across the landscape as the winged beast started to shake uncontrollably. The wings withdrew towards its back and the creature fell on its side, contorting in pain.

Bellator winced and lowered himself further behind the rocks as the head of the beast started to change. The tail withdrew as the wings cracked and moved back into the torso. The talons fell away from its feet, resting on top of the stone. Slowly the figure of Duat started to reappear.

"Master!" Bellator gingerly got to his feet and moved towards the naked Watcher.

Duat was breathing heavily; his single eye had returned. The huge central vein that fed it pulsed as folds of skin moved across his skull as he completed his transition.

Saliva ran from Duat's misshapen teeth as he coughed heavily to the point of retching and pushed himself upright. "Over there," he coughed, "behind that tree, fetch them for me."

Bellator looked to his right at a small cluster of trees atop the mountain in Snowdonia. Still holding his burns, he moved as quickly as he could. Buried in the roots were a robe and a couple of pairs of strange-looking glasses.

Sitting upright and struggling for breath, the deep voice instructed, "bring them to me."

Bellator collected the items and with hands shaking, laid them next to Duat. He stepped back a few paces and watched Duat pull the robe over himself and then struggle to his feet. "You look shocked, my friend." He coughed and turned to look over the darkness of the mountainscape.

Bellator swallowed; he had no words. He watched Duat shake his head as he turned around to him.

"I underestimated them. We had no knowledge of a third key for the wall of iron."

"We, Master? I didn't know anything…."

"Not you, you fool. I refer to my kind, not the stupidity of what all of you have become, incarcerated in that place for far too long."

Bellator stepped back further in fear watching Duat shake his head with anger.

Duat lifted his right palm towards his skull; the turquoise patterns were fading. "You have no idea what you are; you have no idea what you were meant to be."

Bellator, still holding his burns, shook his head. "Master, I do not even know what you are?"

Duat snorted and turned around to face the mountains.

"You are hundreds of years old; your memory has been wiped from years of punishment by them."

Duat took a deep breath as he paused in thought.

"There was a great divide, thousands of years ago where battles were fought, ideals sought and where the world of men thought they could conquer and rule and in some part, they did."

He turned to face Bellator. "And then there were them, an army of women hidden in plain sight. They paired with others and fought against the change they called the supernatural; you are a bi-product of that change, that is why they punish you."

"I don't understand, Master?"

"No, you won't. Although there are others, like you, outside that place that do. Your bloodline was split by the Masters, divided into two. A new rule would have succeeded if it were not for them. What they call Clerics represent purity and harmony."

He paused with his thoughts.

"What you are is somewhat different."

He stepped forward to Bellator. "The Masters of the past destined you to be soldiers and prepared you for this new level of rule, replacing the world of men. We would have been rulers in our own right; it would far surpass anything they would be capable of. Such intellect was placed within you that your brain evolved over time; that is why you only have one eye, you see everything and you have extrasensory skills. That eye is all-seeing, providing you with wisdom for this life and the next."

Bellator shook his head and stepped back further. He and the other Watchers at Loxley knew they had been incarcerated for a long time, but he had no idea how long and how he got there. There were no recollections of the past. The other Watchers never spoke of the words he was hearing now. He had no knowledge of this 'purpose' that the shape-shifting creature spoke of.

"Your wisdom has evaporated, your brains and skills destroyed following thousands of years of persecution by the Horde Of Light. That is why they call themselves that. They believe they are the light path and now they cover you in darkness, so that powerful eye you have is blinkered and blind. Look at what you have become; your human form has almost left you, for that is what originally you were. You are disgusting and incomplete. I despise all of you for your failure. This form and how I appear now appals me; you are a failure of race."

Bellator stopped rubbing at his wounds. "Master, you had said about the rise of the Watchers and we all being united?"

Duat laughed, "Watchers...you don't even know what your race is called." He shook his head. "I told you what you wanted to hear. I thought that I would need all of you below ground to free the beast... I was wrong." He growled as he spoke.

"Master, what are you?"

Duat snorted; "If your brain was not so distorted, you would know."

Bellator shook with nerves as Duat moved closer to him.

"I am a Keeper of the Gate. Every few hundred years, a gap opens, allowing one of us to cross over into this realm. This has been planned for a very long time; other Gatekeepers wait for my success."

"Success Master?"

"To allow them to come."

He looked at Bellator's confused face. "The beast is behind the wall of iron to deny access to anyone to pass through. They bound the truth in secrecy and the prophecy was created as a cover of fear. The ancients of the Horde Of Light knew what is really behind that wall."

"And what is that, Master?"

Duat paused, hearing the words of the soldier without purpose.

"It's a portal, a gateway to the other realm. It's been there for thousands of years; they just don't understand what they are really protecting. If the portal is opened, the others will come and you, my friend, will regain all of what you have forgotten and lost. A new era of dark rule will commence."

Bellator lifted his head with purpose; for far too long, he had been punished, never understanding why. "What do we do now, Master?"

Duat paused in thought.

"They will be scared." His words were spoken softly. "In time, they may seek the help of others. When we succeed, it will be the end of their time. The stopping of their clocks is just the start. Before the end, they will all be judged."

Bellator nodded. He wanted revenge for the years of punishment.

"I can only change between the form of your race and my real identity." Duat's tone was full of regret. "A couple of weeks ago, I hid these glasses just in case." He nodded towards the ground at the two pairs of glasses that rested on stone. "You have not seen that type before. We will need them in daylight."

Duat focused on the ground as he thought.

"My brothers and sisters will be very angry. We need to take stock and re-gather; I have friends here as well."

He looked up at Bellator.

"We will plan our return and strike them where it hurts most."

Both of them looked across the mountainscape.

No further words were said between them as the dawn chorus started in the distance.

Saturday 5am

Raysmau was deep in thought. For the benefit of the Escarrabin, it was important that order was shown for those who remained. She had removed the ill-fitting upper assembly of her body armour. Still, the rest remained as she surveyed her office. Her door was still intact but closed.

She slumped into her chair. Much would be asked of her, but more so of the Reeve who had failed as the commander of security. Escarrabin had died, Watchers had died, a Cleric had died, the building frontage was partially destroyed. There was no walking away from this; they would all be summoned.

They would have to go below again later to recover the bodies and this time carry out a controlled search and round up all of the Watchers. With Duat, or whatever he really was, gone, she hoped for little resistance. Maybe normality would resume, but she knew that it would be brief.

She looked at the artwork on her walls depicting glories of battle from a former age. There would be no painting hanging anywhere in the future portraying what happened a few hours ago; she was sure of that. Her clock had not regained life and still read two minutes past midnight.

She cracked her neck back and forth and with composure, got up and headed to her door. Reassurance was what was needed now. Other Escarrabin who had since arrived from their duties last night wanted answers. She knew that answers to what she had witnessed would be in very short supply.

The other side of the door from the tranquillity of her office was difficult to take in. The corridor was destroyed from pulse fire. The main door had been blown apart and the gate had come away from the wall at the top. She looked to the floor and could see blood on stone shards, the blood, presumably, having lived within the Cleric.

She moved to the right to security control, an Escarrabin officer went to stand upon her entry into the room. She waved her arm. "Save it." The officer resumed her seat. "Anything outside, have you seen anything moving out the front?"

"No, Ma'am. I've been watching the CCTV and the road outside is clear. All is quiet."

"Good, please keep watching," she nodded and turned to leave.

"Ma'am, excuse me, but should we be expecting something? Will something else happen?"

Raysmau stopped and didn't turn around to the question. "After last night... yes, I think there will be more to come. Much will change from now. This Order has been dormant for too long."

She left the room and stepped between boulders of rock to look at the flame scarred door that lay in pieces.

Central lobby was a singed shadow of its former self, it was fixable, but it would take some time. The bodies had since been moved. She looked to the floor as the pin of one of the fallen Escarrabin caught her eye. Bending down to pick it up, she looked at the collapsed balcony to her right, the scorched irreplaceable artwork on the walls, chandeliers in pieces, marble now discoloured from soot and dust. It smelt of death in this former peaceful place.

Two Escarrabin were staring at her from next to the fallen lift shaft. She walked through puddles of water to them and looked down into the deep hole that fell below. "Any movements?"

"No, Ma'am, nothing has come up the stairs, nor have we heard anything."

She nodded. "They lie now in peace. They will be scared, but I suspect we will have to round them up later."

"And of the other, Ma'am?"

"Other?"

"The beast that lies below, what will become of that?"

She didn't know the answer and simply nodded at the two security officers. "I'm sure the Reeve has that all in hand." It was a lie but the best she could offer.

She walked away from them, knowing that talk would be rife amongst the Escarrabin and that it would spread to others in the Order all over the world.

The morning sunlight was coming through the open doors and the windows that had been destroyed. The fires were out, but the window frames smouldered. She could still see the fallen Cleric on her knees down the driveway. This night would make the history books for all of the wrong reasons. Judgements would be made and it would not be forgotten for a very long time. Everything was about to change.

K.S. Horak

Chapter Thirty One:

THE SCARRED COMET

CATURDAY 7.36 am

Mildred woke with a start and quickly opened her eyes, squinting and shielding them from the rays of the morning sun. Another worrying dream, the second this week. This time, the dark figure who wore a cloak, looked directly at her. She felt goosebumps over her skin as she recollected the events; she could only recall him having one eye.

She shook her head at the absurdity of it all and tried to clear the image from her mind.

She opened and closed her mouth a few times, "aarrgghh," as she chomped up and down. Her breath was offensive, even to her. She licked at her teeth and ran a hand through her tangled hair.

A smile appeared over her face as she kicked her legs a couple of times under her duvet knowing that Missy was coming home today. She had no idea what time it is and didn't know if she had overslept. Her alarm hadn't sounded as yet; it must be early. She neglected her toothbrush and dived down the stairs to the kitchen. She was horrified as she looked at her clock. "Two minutes past twelve, it can't be!" How she had slept in till midday, she had no idea. She looked down at her cat pyjamas. Missy will be here soon, she thought to herself, I can't greet the vet dressed like this. She launched herself back up the stairs for something to wear. Her best and quite possibly, her only friend in the world was coming home and she couldn't wait.

✝✝✝✝

Nahla lay curled up on the couch as Nubia looked down at her. "Quite how you can sleep, I have no idea. You saw it; you saw it fall from above. Nahla… Nahla!"

She bobbed her head up to look at the Curator. "Are you not fearful? Do you not feel our anguish?" She put her hands on her hips. She knew that Nahla understood what was happening, but there was little she could do about it. She chewed on her teeth and looked at the phone, then back at Nahla. "I guess it's time you went home," whatever time it was, of course. Nubia felt lost without the constant reassurance from her clock. She looked out of the window, making a judgement on the time by the height of the sun, then reached for the phone. The phone rang at the other end for longer than she would have liked.

"Yes, who is this?" A very sleepy voice spoke with a cough clearing her throat.

"Get up Suzanna, there is work to be done!"

Jessica scratched at her head, still coming to terms with her new name and coughed again. "Yes, my Lady, what time is it?"

"I have no idea, but I'm going to be sending Nahla back to you. She has made a full recovery from the pain she was in."

"That's amazing news, my Lady," she put a hand to her mouth and breathed into it and brought it up to her nose and squinted.

"About the only thing that is…"

"I'm sorry, my Lady, what was that?"

"Never mind, Suzanna, you'll find out in due course, as I'm sure everyone will. Look, I'm going to have a security driver bring Nahla over to you, so be ready to receive her in just over an hour and a half or so."

"Yes, my Lady, although I have no idea how to switch…"

"Just do it please, it's very important, Suzanna."

"Yes, my Lady, I will do my best."

"Yes, you do your best. Let me know when it is done."

The phone went down at the other end. Suzanna stared at her phone and shook her head. "That woman is so rude!" Still, at least Khepri was coming home; she had been worrying about her. She rubbed at her eyes but, unlike Mildred, went straight to the bathroom for her toothbrush.

Saturday Morning 8.58 am

Looking at the new quarter light on her car, Sarah pouted her lips in annoyance; the other woman should be paying for that really. She was undecided whether to chase it up or not. She had had enough hassle in her life recently and didn't really need any more.

She breathed out and looked upwards to the sign outside of her place of work; 'Castle Hollow Veterinary Practise.' She could see movements inside reception. Sarah suspected that she had been the subject of gossip after yesterday's events. She would have to shrug it off; it was as simple as that as she headed towards the main doors.

"Good morning Sarah," Samantha said with a smile.

She nodded and spoke quietly. "Good morning. Have there been any calls for me? My personal phone has been quiet, well as far as work goes, that is." She put her work bag on the floor.

"Oh, you still getting hassle from him?"

"I seem to attract them," she nodded as a clipboard was passed to her with some notes on them. Do you know if the shorthair cat called Missy has been okay overnight?"

"Fine, no problems at all as far as I know."

Sarah nodded. "Do you know if any testing was done on her, blood taken or anything else?"

Samantha shook her head. "I'm not aware of it as she appeared to be perfectly well when she got here, according to David."

"Mmm."

"Any reason why you would ask?"

She shook her head. "No, no, curious, that's all. I'm glad she is doing well. I have to return her in a bit."

"Well, the kettle is on if you want a cup of tea before you start."

Sarah smiled and picked up her bag. "Thank you, a cup of tea is in order I think. Do you want one?"

"No, I've just had my second already."

Sarah's smile continued as she let herself through the doors behind reception and looked down the corridors. All seemed quiet as she passed by the kitchen area and took a pair of gloves out of her pocket. She went to the back of the building to the kennelling area and looked through the small piece of thick glass in the centre of the door. It looked like no one was in there as she let herself in, closing the door behind her. She put her bag on the side and took out what she needed.

She passed by dogs, rabbits and reptiles before she got to the back of the large room where the cats were kept in their own area, a part-time cattery of sorts. She saw Missy immediately.

"Good morning Missy and how are you?" Khepri blinked a couple of times but never lifted her head that was resting on her front paws. Sarah turned around to check she was still alone, gathered a warm towel, took a needle from her pocket and unlocked the cage. "I'm truly sorry to do this, but I know what I heard." She ran a hand of reassurance back and forth down what she believed to be Mildred's cat and wrapped her in the towel, exposing a hind leg.

With clippers, she removed the smallest amount of hair that she hoped would go unnoticed. "I'm sorry, this will take just a second," as she depressed the needle into the cat's leg and watched the small vial fill with blood. She felt Missy tighten under her hand that gently supported her. "There you go, all done." She sealed the vial and put it into her pocket. She cleaned over the injected area and applied a small temporary dressing. "Mildred seems like a lovely lady; you have a good owner. She really cares for you; I want to make sure we do right by her. You're going home soon after I've had a cup of tea." She smiled as she spoke.

She closed the cage, locked it, went to the exit door and peered through the glass. The coast was clear. She closed the door behind her and removed her gloves.

She knew what she heard yesterday was a phenomenon worthy of further investigation.

Saturday morning 10.05 am

Suzanna sat in her car staring at the old Polaroid camera. Just push the button and click, I guess, she thought to herself. She put it on the passenger seat next to Nahla, who had been swiftly returned by a lady who had very little to say for herself. She wore a strange type of uniform and seemed anxious to get away.

She started the car and headed in the direction of Mildred's home. How on earth she would carry out a cat exchange for the second time, she hadn't a clue. Quite why this had been put upon her, she had no idea. So much didn't make sense and now the vet woman who has Khepri thought she was some sort of private detective.

It didn't take long before she was only a road away. Once again, she pulled up outside the shop from the land that time forgot.

Sitting there looking at the frontage of the old building and the faded paintwork, she clicked her back teeth together for inspiration.

"Mildred comes here all the time, doesn't she?" She looked down at Nahla. She didn't have the gift of cat language, but she was confident that Nahla understood what she was saying. She ran a hand across the back of the cat that stayed at Mildred's. "It's really good to see that you are better though, you had us quite worried."

She pressed down on one of the controls on her door panel, so the window came down slightly for some air. "I won't be long. I just need to figure out what to do."

She stepped out of the car in her gleaming heels, straightened her pencil skirt and pressed the remote to lock the car. The shop's windows looked like they could do with a good clean as she looked at the assembled items displayed in quite a disorderly fashion. There were posters all over the windows advertising concerts and postcards from people searching for missing animals.

She peered inside between two posters to make sure that Mildred was not in the shop. The man behind the counter immediately saw her movements and looked up at her. Her eyes flipped to the right to read a poster advertising a karaoke night at the Futility. She knew the pub was at the end of the road.

There was no sign of Mildred, so she entered, hearing the tinkling of the bell ringing above her head.

"Oh, hello again," the man rasped, "you like karaoke, do you?"

Suzanna turned to look outside the door before realising that he was speaking to her. "I'm sorry?"

"Karaoke! I saw you reading the advert. It's a good night out, doesn't matter if you can't sing!" He chuckled away to himself. She watched him adjust his trousers as he breathed out heavily.

"Oh no, I'm not really interested in that." She smiled and exited the conversation to look around the shop.

"Oh, right you are." He shook his head and continued reading his newspaper.

She wandered around the shop with no clue what she was looking for. It may be from years of protecting cats that her eyes were drawn to tins of cat and dog food stacked on an old shelf when she paused with an idea.

She walked over to the counter. "Erm do…"

"Farming paper is it today?"

"I'm what, sorry?" She had a confused expression on her face.

"You came in here yesterday, left with the Shropshire Farmer newspaper."

Her head tilted forward with puzzled frown lines across her forehead. "Oh, yes, no, I wasn't very interested in that," the man's face was reasonably perplexed. "I did read something about the sheep diving contest, though."

"Oh, yes," he rasped, "that's quite the scandal; everyone's talking about it." He leaned forward to her. "Apparently, the use of anabolic steroids or something makes the sheep jump higher… supposedly." He leant back and gave a satisfactory nod, having provided her with the local gossip. "Don't know what the world is coming to?"

"Erm, yes, well er, tell me do you have a cat lead?"

His right eyebrow raised. "Cat lead?"

"Sorry, I meant to say dog lead, for a small dog, with a collar."

"Right you are." He spoke in a soft but confused tone, "wait right there." He walked to the other end of the shop, murmuring something to himself.

He returned with a bright pink lead with a collar.

"That should fit any small cat. I'm sorry, I meant to say dog."

She looked up at him, smiled and took what looked to be a very expensive purse out of her jacket pocket. He noticed the notes inside it and the gold symbol on the outside, probably from some exclusive fashion house.

"How much is that?"

"I'll take eight pounds, please."

"Well, here's ten. Keep the change."

He picked it up. "Thank you, you can help yourself to another farming paper if you wish?"

She picked up the lead and headed for the door. "No, thank you, not much of a farmer."

The bell tinkled overhead as she wobbled on her heels and went through the door.

"You're not kidding," he muttered and looked down to continue reading.

She quickly got into the car, threw the lead into the front passenger footwell, then started the car. "Nahla, we are going for a walk!"

The car moved away from Mr Frank's shop heading in the direction of Mildred's house.

✝✝✝✝

Stockings, a brown skirt, blouse and homemade cat sweater were adorned as she looked out of her bedroom window with some curiosity. She frowned, looking up and down the road as it seemed very quiet for midday on a Saturday in the height of summer.

She looked at her alarm clock on the side, walked over and picked it up; two minutes past twelve? That seemed kind of odd as she must have spent ten minutes or so getting ready. She brought it to her ear but there was no sound of ticking coming from it as she placed it back down.

She shook her head, reasonably certain that she had wound it up yesterday. Oh well, it was a strange day, after all, so she probably did forget. She should put the kettle on just in case the vet wanted a cup of tea. It was the very least she could do.

She walked down the stairs into the kitchen, picked up the kettle and took it to the sink. The minute hand of the clock had not moved. She put the kettle down and took the clock off the wall. There was no ticking coming from that one either. She flipped it over and took the batteries out that she had only replaced a few days ago. "Bet they had passed their sell-by date as well," she scoffed, knowing that she would be taking those back to Mr Franks later.

She placed the kettle on the gas ring and walked into the front room to switch on the television; maybe that would tell her the correct time.

She could see a reporter speaking at a fast pace as she bent over to turn the volume up. It looked like an important news item, as it had 'BREAKING NEWS' in bold letters at the bottom of the screen.

"Well, that's a good question, Mary. The safety record is still intact to the very best of our knowledge, but authorities here are being very tight-lipped as we await some form of official announcement. There is still a 100% safety record that no one has been killed from falling debris or what is sometimes referred to simply as space junk."

Mildred cocked her head back. "Eh?" She took a seat.

"But early reports say these were functioning satellites?"

"Yes, we believe so. Experts are certainly doing some head-scratching as to how they didn't fully break up within the atmosphere. I'm no expert, Mary, but from those who know about these things, usually as satellites near the end of their lives, they perform a burn or an orbital manoeuvre. They are sent into what is called the graveyard orbit. Apparently, this movement takes less fuel than bringing them back to earth. For those that do, as early as 1971, over 260 craft have been directed to the South Pacific to an area often called 'Point Nemo'; the oceanic pole of inaccessibility. Mary, that area, the Point Nemo I refer to, is over 1,600 miles away from land."

"So, why do they do this?"

"Well, this is done with safety in mind, along with sending satellites into the graveyard orbit to try and minimise satellite collisions. But in any event, that would appear to be what has happened here, in the early hours of this morning."

"Do we know when there may be an official announcement?"

"As I say, Mary, everyone is tight-lipped here and the whole area is sealed off, but many are saying that events like this were not likely, but probable. I spoke to Professor Morgan Stephens from Lochnagar University on the phone earlier. He informed me that there are over 170 million pieces of so-called space junk flying around overhead. Granted, many are very small in size, but observers here say two balls of light fell. One disintegrated, breaking into many pieces that are scattered over 50 miles. However, the other did make land contact behind me here in North Wales."

Mildred's mouth fell open; it must have been what she saw last night as she put her head into her hands and rested them on her knees.

"As you can see behind me Mary, many have gathered here. You can read some of the banners they are holding up, welcoming what they believe to be an alien spacecraft. Henry Hubbard is here with me, who has driven over from Welshpool and saw the falling lights. So tell me, what did you see, Henry?"

"Well, I was outside right, having a couple of bottles of cider as you do, well quite a few actually; it was a beautiful evening. It had gone midnight when this bright ball of light flew over my house and I saw a ball of flame erupt in the distance. I hid under my garden table just in case it was a nuclear bomb. It obviously wasn't, or I wouldn't be here now, would I, ha ha ha? Anyway, I finished my cider and asked my mate Barry next door to give me a lift over here. I was a bit pissed, you see."

"Right, well, thank you, Henry, and so..."

"This is the new Area 51 this is."

"Thank you, Henry."

"They are here, I'm telling you and the guy over there told me he saw some sort of flying dragon last night. This is Wales's Area 51!"

"Yes, thank you, Henry and we do apologise for the use of bad language."

Mildred could hear Henry still talking in the background as the reporter cut him off and security moved him from in front of the camera. She could see people waving signs in the background saying 'Government Cover Up' and 'Aliens Welcome' amongst other stuff.

"In any event Mary, the Space Lawyers are going to be rubbing their hands with glee. According to Professor Stephens, the actual collision would have happened maybe as long as 24 hours beforehand."

Mildred was distracted by the kettle whistling in the kitchen and the clock on her television screen saying it was only 10.47am.

✛✛✛✛

It was quite late in the morning when Sarah was given her full itinerary for the day. As she worked through her notes, it would appear that she had a few calls to make in the afternoon. Knowing that she had said to Mildred that she would return Missy around midday, there could be no doubt of how much she loved her cat, so maybe an hour earlier would be welcome news.

She walked into reception with a carrier in hand and waited for Samantha to finish her phone call. She lifted the carrier. "Just to let you know that I'm taking Missy from out the back if you could check her out."

"Yes, bear with me," she tapped away at the keys of her computer, rolling her tongue as she read the screen. "Rocke Road belongs to Mildred. Does that sound correct to you?"

"It does."

"Great, I'll check her out."

Sarah nodded and headed out to the back as David appeared from his room.

"Sorry, I haven't seen you today Sarah, how are you feeling?"

"I was feeling fine yesterday, David. I'm just going to take Missy back to Mildred."

"Oh yes, the cat with multiple heartbeats," he grinned.

"That's not funny. I know what I heard and saw, David."

He still had a teasing smile on his face. "Well, I'm sure her owner will be glad to have her back."

"Yeah, I think she will. Catch you later."

She headed through the door with a little scowl on her face. Make fun of me, we'll see, she thought as she unlocked the kennel labelled 'MISSY' and removed the dressing from her leg.

"Come on now, time to get you back home. Hope you are not going to cause me any more trouble, Missy."

With surveillance experience under her belt and now prepared, Suzanna parked her car just a little way before Mildred's house on the opposite side of the road. It would be a waiting game as she tapped at her expensive watch that seemed to have stopped working, but it was commonplace that she would forget to wind it up.

"Guess we'll just have to sit and wait, Nahla." She crossed her arms, looking down the road and adjusting her rear-view mirror to see cars approaching her from behind.

She picked up the camera that fortunately had a strap attached to it and put it around her neck. "Suppose we had better get you ready then." She adjusted the collar and placed it around Nahla's neck. "This has been quite the security operation, Nahla, getting you back home. I do hope Khepri is okay," Nahla met her eyes, "and they haven't done any tests on her." She chewed her lip at the thought of it. "That could cause complications." She picked up the lead and attached it to the collar. "Let's hope not."

She ducked down to look out of the windows. There was no church with a clock in sight and the time on her phone seemed temperamental. It would have to be guesswork. No matter what, she could not be seen by Mildred. "Before midday. She said the vet would be back before midday." She shook her head, knowing that she should have asked the time from the strange man at the shop.

Fifteen minutes or so must have passed when she saw what she thought was the vet's car approaching in the rearview mirror. She ducked as the car passed.

"Well, that was quick work, Nahla. She's replaced the car light already!"

She picked Nahla up and checked no one was driving by as she got out and crossed over to Mildred's side of the road.

The brake lights of the car ahead were still on with the engine running. She sped up her steps, which wasn't the easiest to do with the footwear she had selected. "Right Nahla, I'm going to let you go. Please do play along." She lowered Mildred's cat to the pavement. "Keep up with me." They approached the vehicle as its engine was switched off.

Sarah got out of the car to see the very unwelcome face that she had first seen yesterday. "You again?"

"Well, what are the chances?"

"Yes indeed, what are the chances in an area you claimed not to know? You owe me a hundred pounds in damages."

Suzanna pondered, "I have some money in the car. Let me get that for you."

"No, that is not necessary, just please leave me alone and stop following me or I'll report you to the Police."

Suzanna's head recoiled back in shock. "The Police. Why?"

"I've told you I want nothing more to do with him. He must get over it, he..." She looked down at the floor with some surprise. "What are you doing?"

"What do you mean?"

"Why is your cat on a lead?"

"I'm taking it for a walk."

Sarah's eyebrows rose. "You are taking your cat for a walk?"

"Yes, don't you?"

"No." She shook her head and crossed her arms. Her body was ridged except for her tapping foot. "You really are the worst private investigator ever. Just leave me alone."

"Honestly, I have no idea what you mean, but look, I must pay you. Here, hold my cat." She stepped forward quickly, picking up Nahla and forcefully passing her into Sarah's arms. "I'll just be a moment."

"I told you that..." Sarah sighed as the strange woman moved away from her so quickly she didn't have a chance to stop her.

Suzanna opened her car door and hid behind it, reaching for her purse that was already in her pocket. She took out some notes. She looked up through the glass to see the vet staring at her, clicked the camera on and closed the car door.

Sarah glanced down at the beautiful cat. "Well, you are very pretty. You look just like Missy." She gave her own comment a moment's thought.

"Well, don't you both look beautiful together? I must take a picture."

"No, I don't think so, thank you. Here, please take your cat."

"No, I insist."

"You insist! I insist that you do not."

"Nahla, close your eyes!" Suzanna pressed the button and an almighty flash lit up the vet, who froze instantly.

Suzanna puffed and panted, taking a step back in shock. Not because the vet's mouth had frozen open, but because a woodpigeon had fallen from the tree above and bounced on its back on the pavement. Its legs twitching in the air.

"Bloody hell!"

She looked around quickly. No one seemed to be watching. She let go of the camera that fell on the strap around her neck, dived at the car and opened the door. "Hello, Khepri!" She flipped the catch on the carrier and took her out, holding Khepri under one arm. "Right, you go there." She switched the cats, disconnected the lead and placed Nahla into the carrier, closing the door. "Khepri, just stay there a mo." She was starting to panic as the vet wasn't moving, frozen to the spot. "Oh dear, I hope I haven't killed her." She looked behind again to see if anyone was around. She watched the woodpigeon's legs start to move. The vet blinked and wobbled, clearly disorientated, as she put a hand to her head, which she shook a couple of times.

"That's odd. I feel a bit queasy."

Suzanna's hands were shaking; the pupils of her eyes were as wide as they could possibly go. "Are you okay?"

"I'm not sure. Here, you'd best take your cat."

"Gladly, thank you."

The woodpigeon shook its wings and making a funny sound, flew off straight into the side of the vet's car, creating a small dent on the driver's side door. Suzanna, watching the pigeon and the vet, held her arms out to receive the cat. Sarah noticed the weird stranger was holding the cat lead and frowned. "Wasn't that…"

"Wasn't what?"

K.S. Horak

She stepped forward to Suzanna and snatched the Polaroid from the bottom of the camera. "I told you not to take pictures of me!" She walked to her car and tossed the Polaroid onto her car seat, "and if I see you around me again, no ifs, no buts, I'll call the Police!"

Suzanna nodded and lowered her head. "Okay, well, goodbye then."

The vet put her hands on her hips and watched the lady wobble in her heels, walking as quickly as she could to get back to her car. She shook her head in disgust. "Honestly!" She went to the rear of the car and opened the door. "Hello Missy, you are back at home. Come on now." As she picked up the carrier, she immediately distracted by a pink object on the cat. She held the carrier up to eye level and paused. "Were you wearing a collar before?" She thought it over and was fairly positive that Missy didn't have a collar. She looked over at the car in front of them, doing a three-point turn in the road, before it took off at some speed. She looked back into the carrier as Mildred's cat looked back at her.

Maybe all of this business in her personal life was getting to her, she was forced to consider it.

"Khepri, high five," she held her hand up, "job well done. Lady Nubia will be most pleased." She felt the money in her pocket and realised she hadn't paid the vet, "and it only cost me a dog lead, ha-ha!" She hit the gas and continued to giggle away as she looked at the dog lead on the floor that was minus a collar. Her giggling immediately stopped as she looked at Khepri's collarless neck and looked forward to the road. "Oh, no!"

Mildred bobbed at her window like a demented meerkat. She heard someone outside and rushed to the front door.

"MISSY! Sarah, please do come in."

She beckoned the vet into her front room. Mildred turned down the television as Sarah looked at the screen.

"What is going on?"

"Mmm?"

"On the television, looks like a news story."

"Oh, aliens have landed in Wales or something. Anyway, how's my Missy?"

Sarah blinked, her nose twitching at the fishy smell. She already wanted this day to be over. "Erm, yes, she is fine, Mildred. Quite strange, in fact, one may say quite peculiar all in all."

"Can I have her?"

Sarah smiled at seeing the excitement in Mildred's face. For all of the weirdness, there was no doubt how much Mildred loved her cat. "Yes, of course." She placed the carrier down on the sofa, unclipped the cage and took Missy out. "Here you go," she passed Missy over.

She watched Mildred cling to her cat like a mother to a newborn child as her eyes became watery. "Missy, I have been so worried about you!"

Sarah suspected that Missy would have a lot of hugs and loving today.

"Would you like a cup of tea?"

"No, thank you, Mildred. I really must go, I'm afraid. I have a busy day."

"That's okay, not a prob...Oh, you've given her a collar?"

Sarah swallowed. "Er, I, er really can't explain that, call it a present from us," she shifted her body uncomfortably.

"Okay, thank you, are you sure she is okay?"

Sarah nodded. She didn't know what else to say.

"Well, if you are sure. Thank you ever so much for what you have done." Mildred looked at the very simple smile across the vet's face as she picked up the carrier and headed for the door.

"Mildred, if there are any more problems, please call me personally on my mobile."

"Of course, I will. Thank you for bringing back my friend."

She smiled. "You're welcome, there will be a small bill in the post for you."

"Of course."

"I'd best be off."

She watched the vet walk down towards her gate as she closed the door and looked at Missy. She was ecstatic, clapping her hands together. Her friend was home and she was no longer alone. Life was good.

Sarah lent on Mildred's gate, trying to think everything through. Something was sorely amiss, but she struggled to figure it out as she went to her car and took her keys out of her pocket.

Unlocking the car, she rubbed at her eyes, noticed the Polaroid on her seat and picked it up. She was still rubbing her eyes when a noise of shock emitted from her mouth. The carrier fell to the floor with a crash as she held the picture to her face with both hands. Her mouth fell open in horror as she looked at the picture of her skeleton and what looked like a skeleton of a bird falling out of a tree behind her. She looked upwards to see a woodpigeon wobbling on a branch above her as she let out an audible gasp.

Feeling queasy, she swallowed and stumbled backwards a couple of times, looking back down the quiet road to where the other lady had driven off.

Her breathing was audible as she reached into her pocket for her phone and went into the picture files bringing up the photograph she had taken of the strange lady. She closed her eyes in thought. "Jessica!" She remembered what the lady had said her name was. She continued to stare at the photograph of Jessica as she brought the Polaroid closer to her face to look at the cat.

She was shaking her head in shock. Unlike herself and the bird wobbling in the tree above her, the cat's image was solid, not transparent and not skeletal. It also looked like the cat's eyes were closed.

She lowered the Polaroid and put a hand to her heart, trying to gain composure as a frown etched across her face. Blinking, she looked down. "Is that a bloody dent in my car?"

The woodpigeon flew away.

Two hours earlier

The Reeve sat with her head in her hands, dwelling on the lost Escarrabin, as well as the part she played in the events only a few hours before.

It was a disaster. Security penetration, lost soldiers, dead Watchers and who knows how much the damage to the Manor House would cost. She knew she would be called upon to give her account of everything, especially the realisation they may have witnessed the presence of a Gatekeeper, who had actually dwelled, for a short period, at Loxley. Where do I even start? She thought, shaking her head.

She would need to consult with her Head of Order, but she didn't want to as yet. She needed to think everything through and she was nervous about making the call. She looked up at the clock and wondered if they had also stopped in other parts of the world. If so, it may well be her that would be hearing from her Head of Order very soon.

She took a sip from her glass of water and returned it to her desk.

The security measures in place were not fit for purpose; that was a fact. She collapsed back in her chair, the one she had assembled herself, not the old heavy chair on its side next door.

She would need to consider it step by step. Firstly, how that Watcher, or whatever it was, got below the statue; that would be a good place to start. How he could have known about the chamber and even more so, how he could penetrate it using the hand scanner?

She went to pick up her glass and noticed the prints of her fingers on it; her eyebrows came together as she held it to her face. She let out an audible sigh, put it down and walked quickly to the side to look at her other glasses.

She held up a large wine glass that had not been washed and closed her eyes, seeing her whole handprint on it. She also noticed that one glass was missing... the Cleric had taken it.

She stepped back, shook her head and smashed the glass against the wall. Well, that was one question answered with many more to go.

47 minutes later...

She was dressed back in her business suit. The Clerics, who usually had their heads down with work, were now looking upwards at the slightest sound. They were unnerved and had every right to be. She had been summoned to Lady Safiya's quarters; no doubt the Curator would also be in attendance. Protocol would dictate that her Head of Security would not be present, but she would have preferred it if Raysmau was there for support. Difficult questions would be coming her way; a Reeve would not have been tested like this in generations. It would be of no surprise to her if she were summoned before the Grand Council. Being demoted or expelled was the least of her worries.

K.S. Horak

Lady Safiya's Cleric greeted her. There was no waiting around as she was shown straight into the sitting room. Sure enough, Nubia stood with her arms behind her back and Lady Safiya sat, this time, without a cat in sight.

"Ma'am." She looked at the short nervous figure in front of her and acknowledged her with a nod of the head. "Curator."

"Please sit, Reeve."

"Yes, Ma'am, thank you." She perched herself on one of Lady Safiya's expensive, antique single seater chairs.

"There's much to discuss, Reeve."

"Yes, Ma'am, there is."

"Yes, Reeve, there is!"

She flicked her eyes towards the Curator, who was shaking, her demeanour a mixture of anger and resentment.

"Come now, Nubia, we are friends here. Let's keep as calm as we can." Nubia looked at the floor. "Yes, my Lady."

"Reeve, our clocks have stopped, our home is destroyed and we've lost friends. In the middle of all of this, your Order has an unimaginable creature buried right below us. A creature so terrible that something crossed from the other side in an attempt to claim it or release it. My question is, why?"

The Reeve knew this would not be easy as she swallowed, knowing that the question in the scheme of things was a fair one. "It is difficult to explain the actions of the past, Ma'am and I am not aware of the facts, but I'm sure they can be established in time."

"How much time do you think we have Reeve before that monster comes back?"

"Nubia!" Lady Safiya raised her arms, "please let me ask the questions."

The Curator lowered her head.

"We need to know these things Reeve, members of your own security Order have been killed. The one who came, who appeared as a Watcher, had the power to communicate and convert. He obviously knew some of your secrets, starting with your hidden chamber right here on these grounds."

The Reeve chose not to look her in the eyes as she spoke.

"For too long, there has not been enough transparency between your Order and ours. After the events these past 24 hours, that will now need to change. We need to work together. Somehow that thing got to one of our own Clerics and poisoned her. The rest of the Clerics are terrified. We need to know what we are dealing with here. We need to know what is hidden away here. I have to report directly to the Grand Council, who are highly alarmed and that's an understatement!"

The noise of small shuffling feet came from the right-hand side of the Reeve.

"It just doesn't add up."

"Nubia, please!"

"No, my Lady. Please listen." She composed her thoughts and coughed to clear her throat. "That creature may have failed, but we lost one of our own in Lady Tempest and this chain of events happened very soon after. This Watcher practically handed himself to us and now we know why, but to what end? What did he want? To overrun our home? He clearly hoped to free the beast below to destroy us and our way of being, but others would come from the Order to protect us. The Watchers are in numbers and many more are bound to still be out there. What do they hope to achieve? The end of our kind, to take over the lands outside of this place, outside of our Order?" The Curator stepped forward. "So, I put it to you, Reeve, your Order put that thing down there a long time ago, that is now undeniable, but we need to know why. I think it was there to protect something else, something that you have not told us about."

The Reeve looked up as she stepped back to her original place.

The room fell silent.

Lady Safiya twiddled at her thumbs, considering what the Curator had just said and nodded her head. "I think Nubia has a credible point, Reeve. Before now, we have asked about simple measures such as CCTV to be added not just outside but inside this house. The world has changed. We do not feel as protected as we once did by your Order; last night is an example of that."

"My Order has protected the Horde Of Light for thousands of years. Don't you..."

"Reeve, that is enough! Know your place within this room as you address me!"

The Reeve's face reddened in anger as she looked at the slight smirk on the Curator's face.

"No one is dismissing what your Order has done for us Reeve, the Grand Council and I never would. We will always remain thankful, but the secrets you keep now need to come out. The prophecy is happening right in front of us, right in front of our very eyes. How can we fight if we do not know the facts? The third part of the prophecy has not materialised as yet, but I feel it is only a matter of time."

After a short pause and much to the Reeve's dismay, Lady Safiya was not done quite yet.

"Let's face it, there has been such a reluctance to go into the below. We had no knowledge of how deep it was or how many Watchers were down there. It's too disorganised and from what I hear, the whole area may now need to be sealed off and they will need to be housed elsewhere."

"Or we kill them off," Nubia mumbled under her breath.

Safiya's eyes widened in alarm. "Curator, don't ever speak like that. We are not murderers!"

Her smirk disappeared.

"But what purpose do they serve, my Lady? They are vile and poisonous. They have no place here."

"Everyone and everything has a place, Nubia. We do not kill because we do not like. That is what the others outside of this place do in their world and it is not an example that we intend to follow."

Safiya sat back in her chair, took a deep breath and looked at the Reeve. "What if what Nubia is saying is correct? Is there something down there, something we need to know about?"

The Reeve shook her head. "Ma'am, I am not aware of it. I was not aware of any of this until yesterday."

"Maybe your own Order do not trust you, Reeve."

She scowled at Nubia, "I am well thought of, Nubia. I suggest you remember that!"

"ENOUGH, enough! Both of you, please! I know you have your code, Reeve, but I have to ask you again is there anything we should know?"

"No, Ma'am, I am telling you all I know, but I need to speak to my Head of Order and maybe a trip to the archives must follow. Rest assured, we will get to the bottom of this and changes will be made."

"That thing Reeve, that creature came or was put here for a reason and I don't think any of us has the full picture, including you."

She leant forward on her chair to address both of them. "But we can be clear on one thing. It will be back; that is inevitable."

There was no response from either of them as they considered Safiya's point of view.

The Reeve took in a deep breath, knowing this was just the start of the questions that would be coming her way. Her thought process was suddenly distracted by a knock at the door behind her. She turned with a frown across her face to see the Cleric had appeared at the door.

Safiya looked up. "What is it?"

"Ma'am, Lady Fennaway is here."

The Curator's head bobbed up with some concern. "Fennaway is here?" as she looked at Safiya.

"I was unaware of her coming here Nubia. Do show her in."

Kamilah Fennaway walked through the open door into the centre of the room with her work bag in hand. She noticed the Reeve staring at her and instantly recognised the confused face of Nubia.

"My Lady." She nodded at Lady Safiya.

"Fennaway, what are you doing here? We are somewhat in the middle of a crisis?"

"Well, I couldn't help but notice Nubia. What on earth has gone on here?"

"Have your clocks stopped, Kamilah?"

She turned, hearing the Reeve's question and nodded a couple of times.

"So the stopping of time has affected more than just here." Safiya shook her head. "Kamilah, this is an unexpected visit. Pray, why are you here?"

"Do you not know, my Lady?" She looked at the three confused faces. "The Keeper is on the way here. She contacted me well over an hour ago. I'm not sure of the exact time as nothing works, but she said it was vitally important that I was here."

Nubia stepped forward. "The Keeper is coming here?"

Kamilah nodded, looking as confused as the questioner did. She shrugged her shoulders slightly. "She should be only minutes away."

Safiya squinted her eyes in thought. "Reeve, were you aware of this?"

"No, Ma'am, I was not." She stood up. "She must be greeted."

"I don't think she needs pomp and ceremony, Reeve."

She looked at the Curator. "All the same. Ma'am, may I use your phone?"

Safiya nodded. "Yes, please do."

The room was silent as she pressed a button on the phone that was shortly answered. "Raysmau, the Keeper is arriving in a moment. Please greet her and escort her to Lady Safiya's quarters."

The others could not hear what was being said in response. "No, no, just what you are wearing, there is no time and it doesn't matter in the scheme of things. Please post some guards outside the rubble so she can be guided in."

She put the phone down and placed her hands on her hips as the Curator voiced another opinion that hadn't been requested. "Something must be serious if she is coming here."

"Indeed," nodded Safiya, "the new cats are due here today, but she never delivers them herself. So, something else has made her feel the need to be here."

Raysmau had received the radio call that the Keeper's car was heading down the driveway. In the short time frame, she dressed as best as she could, but there would be no mistaking the tiredness in her eyes as well as her reasonably unkempt appearance.

As she stood outside on the summer's morning looking down the now calm driveway, it only took a brief glance behind her to see the damage to the front of the grand old Mansion House.

The smell of smouldering wood and crushed stone was still in the air. The building would take time to repair, but much had been lost that could not be replaced.

She took a deep breath to greet the important, unexpected visitor as her car weaved around the fallen stone on the driveway. The body of the deceased Cleric had been removed a couple of hours before. She looked down, momentarily dwelling on it.

As the car stopped, she nodded to the officer of the Escarrabin on driver duty, who did her best not to stare at the front of the house. She left her driver's seat to open the door for the Keeper.

She saw the familiar cane exit from the car door as she was supported by her driver and got to her feet.

"Morning, Ma'am. I was not aware of your coming."

"I notice you did not say good morning, but I guess there is nothing good about this."

Raysmau watched her look over the front of the house and the fallen brick, glass, and debris strewn on the grounds. She could see that she was very upset.

"It's worse than I feared. What has happened to this beautiful place Raysmau?"

"It's difficult to know where to start, but we will get to the bottom of this."

"Your Reeve will have some questions to answer. You can be sure of that!"

"Yes, Ma'am. She has my full confidence and answers will be given."

"Is Lady Safiya okay?"

"Yes, Ma'am, as well as can be expected. She waits for you upstairs."

She shook her head. "I'm glad that part of the building hasn't been destroyed as well. Here, give me a hand with this, will you, Raysmau?"

The Keeper nodded at her driver to open the door on the other side of the car. The security officer walked around the car and took out four large ceremonial carriers draped in black cloth; there was a carrying handle on top of each one.

The driver carried two in each hand and brought them around to her.

"Pass those to Raysmau, will you?"

"Yes, Ma'am."

Raysmau took the four square carriers from the security officer. They were not exceptionally heavy. "We need those upstairs. Show me the way."

"Yes, Ma'am. You will need to navigate through some of the blockwork and stone that has fallen, but the stairway up remains relatively intact."

"For now." She propped herself on her cane and started shuffling forward, noticing other Escarrabin outside watching over her.

Raysmau turned to the security officer, who was aghast looking at the damage, aware that some of her own Order had lost their lives some hours before. She nodded at the driver. "Please return to your duties."

"Yes, Ma'am." She closed the car doors and drove the car around to the back of the house.

The Cleric opened the door to let the Keeper into the room where she was greeted by the Reeve, Curator, the Lady of the House and their veterinarian.

"Do follow me, Raysmau."

All five of them turned to see the large stature of Raysmau enter the room holding four carriers, which they all recognised instantly. Upon seeing them, Kamilah instantly knew why she had been summoned; a look of worry etched across her face.

"Raysmau, would you please put those on Lady Safiya's desk?"

"Yes, Ma'am." She nodded, glancing at the Reeve, who didn't let it show that she was pleased to have her present.

She placed the carriers on the desk, turned and nodded. "Will there be anything else, Ma'am?"

"No, thank you, Raysmau."

Raysmau headed towards the door, offering a slight smile of reassurance to the Reeve. She leaned towards her, speaking very quietly. "I'll just be outside the door." She sensed the Reeve's nerves as her smile was reciprocated. "Thank you." The Reeve nodded as her Head of Security exited, closing the door behind her. The Keeper turned to confirm Raysmau's exit.

"Well, this is a fine bloody mess, isn't it?" She shook her head in anger. "Whatever happened here last night will be examined thoroughly. I'm advised that some of our own soldiers were lost, Watchers killed, the building destroyed and a Cleric somehow overpowered or seduced. Is this all true, Safiya?"

Safiya was still on her feet as she had risen to greet her old friend but resumed her sitting position with just a few words. "I'm afraid so, my friend."

She shook her head in disbelief.

"It's always good to see you, but you were not expected today. What brings you here other than the events of last night?"

"I needed to be here, Safiya, as I needed Kamilah to be here."

Kamilah looked at her curiously.

"Did you bring your equipment with you?"

"Yes Ma'am as you instructed."

"Good." She put her left hand on her hip and balanced on her stick with the right. "I'm not going to go into the process of how our kind are brought to me, but I am greatly concerned by something this morning, something of the like that I have never seen. Nubia, please go to the carriers on the desk and read the label on the one on the left, would you?"

Nubia nodded with some concern as she approached the desk and saw Lady Safiya stand back up. "What is going on here?"

"Safiya, in a moment, I think we will find out. What does the label say, Nubia?"

She looked up, "Daphne, Housman's Rise, Stafford, Staffordshire."

"Now read the one next to it."

Nubia fumbled with the tag tied to the handle of the carrier. "Suzanna, Porthill Crescent, Shrewsbury, Shropshire."

"And now the one on the far right."

"Daphne, Crosshouses Road, Much Wenlock, Shropshire. The new Lady, the one that Mildred from Shrewsbury will be the Elder for."

"Yes, that is correct. These are their new cats, but it is that one that concerns me." She pointed at the one whose tag had not yet been read out. "Nubia, please remove the cover."

She frowned, looking at the Keeper, her shaking hand hovering over the carrier. She took hold of the jet black cloth cover and pulled it back, lifting it away from the container. She recoiled in shock as the cloth fell to the floor from her hand.

Safiya shook and swallowed and there was an audible gasp from Kamilah. "Now, please remove the covers from the other three."

Nubia looked at the Keeper. Her eyes were full of fear as she pulled the cloth from them one by one and placed them on the table. She stepped back and put a hand to her mouth, her eyes welling up as she feared the worst.

The room was silent as they looked at the three gold caskets and the one the colour of turquoise.

"I've never seen anything like it!" Safiya was horrified as she looked at the elaborate and familiar carvings upon the gold caskets. She was not familiar with the one that had the serpents head engraved into it.

"Open it!"

Fennaway looked alarmed. "Ma'am, are you sure?"

"That is why you are here. As you know, I never see the contents of the caskets, I just arrange their delivery after they are presented to me, but given the events of last night, we need to be sure. I don't need to see the other three. But that one, the one that bears the enemy of old, I do. Kamilah if you please, open the casket."

Kamilah's hands were trembling as she picked at the catch to open the door. The Reeve stepped forward as the Curator took two steps back. Kamilah took a deep breath as she put her hands inside and brought out a small moving bundle wrapped in multiple cloths. She pulled at one of them, exposing the head of a tiny kitten.

"Her eyes are already open," but that was not unusual. She smiled as a tiny paw exposed itself to stretch. The kitten's mouth opened with a yawn. "You are very beautiful."

"Never mind that, Kamilah. Does it bear markings?"

Kamilah looked at the Keeper and refocused as she pulled away the layers of cloth to expose the kitten's body. She swallowed as she ran her fingers over the heart of the cat and closed her eyes as her head lowered.

Nubia was practically panting. "Well?"

The vet opened her eyes and solemnly looked at the Curator. She spoke so quietly the others struggled to hear. "Yes, Nubia, she does."

"Oh no… it can't be!"

They all watched as Nubia started to crumble, tears running down her face.

"Nubia, please! Kamilah, we need to be sure."

"Yes, Ma'am." She lifted her arms forward to Lady Safiya. "Would you mind? I need my bag."

Speechless, Lady Safiya held her arms out and brought the kitten into her chest, looking at the marking on her side. She hoped hair would grow over it in time.

The Reeve looked on in silence. The only sound in the room was Nubia's sniffles.

Kamilah reached into her bag and removed her Signifier and switched it on. Lady Safiya held the kitten forward.

"No, you hold it please, my Lady," She watched the screen display whilst running the device gently along the kitten's midsection. The unnamed kitten's legs twitched as the Signifier rested over the heart. The vet froze, closed her eyes and stepped backwards, switching off the device. She turned to the Keeper. "It is unmistakable. She has two heartbeats."

The Reeve let out a loud breath as Lady Safiya sat down. The noise of Nubia's tears became more audible as the vet wrapped the kitten in the cloth.

For the first time during their meeting, the Keeper shuffled to a chair and slumped down, her cane falling to the floor. They all watched as Kamilah returned the cat to the carrier and stepped back.

"So, it is as foretold, the one bearing the mark will come." She looked to the floor. The Keeper had little else to say.

"But this is the end, the end of our kind!" Nubia's words echoed within the room. If she were looking for support, she didn't find any. She wiped her hand across her nose. "Reeve, say something."

The Reeve looked up with nothing to offer.

"But the prophecy has now come to pass. We have to do something!"

"And we will, Nubia." Lady Safiya moved her eyes to the vet. "Kamilah, who is this cat bound for? Where is it going?"

Kamilah, who had just zipped up her work bag, looked over at Lady Safiya and let out a sigh. She walked to the casket and lifted up the tag.

"Mildred, Rocke Road, Shrewsbury, Shropshire."

"What!" spat Nubia. "Are you serious? She's a... she's new... she's only just been made an 8th Degree Elder!" Everyone was silent. "She can't have this responsibility; she doesn't know her backside from her elbow!"

"THEN SHE WILL LEARN!"

Nubia was instantly silenced by the tone of the Keeper and she stepped back further.

"I don't know who this Mildred is, but she had better be ready and she had better be worthy." They all looked at the Keeper. "For the time may come when we all have to look to Mildred. The future of our kind may well depend on it, for all of those on the outside and our Order."

"But... but Madam Keeper, she knows nothing, she barely even knows about us. Can it not go to someone else?"

The Keeper shook her head. "No, Nubia, it is as foretold. This is the way things are done. I do not know why she has been selected; these matters are not explained to me. I don't know why this is happening now. In time, we will discover these things. But let us all not forget that the one that bears the mark may be for good, but may also be for evil. This Mildred, this one of whom we speak, is now our highest priority. The time will come when she will be tested in the most difficult of circumstances," she turned to the Reeve, "this will fall under your jurisdiction."

The Reeve nodded in silence, biting at her lip.

"Wait, wait a second." Nubia put her hand to her temple as she thought, shaking her head. "I think there's something else."

"What do you mean, Nubia?" Lady Safiya questioned.

"Yes, there is definitely something else. That cat is going to Mildred in Shrewsbury."

"Yes, that is correct Nubia, we've established that. What is it?"

"Something is not right here, Madam Keeper and it all has to do with Lady Tempest."

"You've made your views very clear about what happened to Lady Tempest. What else is there?"

"Lady Safiya, Lady Tempest was in a place she was not supposed to be and we still do not fully know why she was there. But she was knocked down only a couple of roads away from where Mildred lives. Don't you see? She was on to something. She knew something!"

The room fell silent as they considered Nubia's words.

"The cat will need to be delivered and taken away from here as soon as possible. Given recent events, I think it would be wise to expedite that immediately."

They all knew that Safiya was correct.

"I'll take her."

They all looked at the Reeve.

"I'll take her to Mildred."

"Protocol dictates that an Elder passes the cats down, Reeve, you know that."

"Whilst that is true, Nubia, I think the events of last night and what you've just said about Lady Tempest changes things. I am comfortable that the Reeve is assigned with this."

Safiya nodded in agreement. The Keeper had spoken and Nubia knew the subject was now closed.

"Nubia, would you inform Mildred's Elder that there has been a change in the process this time. Just make something up. We do not want to cause unnecessary alarm down the ranks."

Nubia nodded reluctantly.

"You shouldn't need me to tell you, Reeve, but take others with you."

She nodded at the Keeper. "Yes, Ma'am."

"So it is settled." She balanced on her cane and stood up. Her face of usual steady calmness was full of emotion. "I fear for our time and what has transpired here. I must report to the Grand Council, as should you, Safiya. There will be great changes ahead that will affect all of us."

She turned to leave and headed towards the door. "From now on, we will all have to believe in Mildred. Look after her Reeve, or the time of the Watchers will be upon us all."

Except for Nubia's sniffles, the room fell silent again.

She screwed up her nose on opening the fridge door. "Wow-wee, that's a bit ripe!" She slammed the fridge door closed and ran her tongue over her lips, considering whether Missy would eat some of the leftover sandwiches. The larder was a little empty as usual as she looked for tinned cat food. "Guess I'll have to go and see Mr Franks, Missy. I need some new batteries for the clock anyway."

She turned around. "Missy?" She heard the cat flap close. "Now, how do you like that?" Mildred put her hands on her hips in disappointment. She was alone in her kitchen once again. "You've only been back five minutes!"

Nahla didn't hear her as she bounced down Rocke Road. She was moving fast, faster than she ever had, surprised with her own newfound strength. She knew exactly where she was heading, needing the solace of her den.

As she ran down Benbow Street, she shot past Mr Franks reading his newspaper outside his shop.

"Steady now!"

She heard his words, but couldn't see his shaking head of disapproval.

Entering the car park of the Futility, she quickly hopped up upon the wall and jumped down avoiding the glass on the other side.

Pulling the streams of ivy across, she entered the darkness of the damp and discarded den. She remembered very little of the last couple of days.

She looked at the etching scratched into the wall in front of her and lifted a paw towards her heart, there was soreness and her surrounding muscles were tired.

There had been dreams and partial amounts still clung to her mind. She lifted her paw to the wall and touched the image of the Egyptian looking cat. There had been faces hidden behind hoods, Watchers and a creature that could take flight against the backdrop of fire. But looking at the scratching now, there had been a warning and that is what she couldn't shake from her mind. Another cat was on the way and that she must be careful.

The navigator informed her that she was now on the road to Mildred's home. The car headed to the far end to find number one. She glanced into her rearview mirror at the two Escarrabin dressed in plain clothes in the car behind her. Their small arms weapons were sealed away in an untraceable compartment hidden within their car. Being stopped by civilian law enforcement and explaining their advanced weapons technologies could lead to some tricky outcomes.

The navigator flashed and her right-hand indicator signalled that the car was pulling in to park. As the engine stopped she put her arm over the two carriers, still covered on her passenger seat and released her seat belt. She looked into the mirror again. She could see that one of the Escarrabin was looking back down the road as the other watched her. Glancing to her right at the old gate directly next to her car, she couldn't help but stare at the state of the unkempt garden.

She stepped outside next to the gate and looked further down the road. A couple of young boys were making a noise at the bus stop, but that was about it. She looked up, hearing a noise from above to see a very unstable looking woodpigeon in the tree. Other than that, it all looked to be reasonably quiet for a Saturday afternoon.

She looked towards the house again at the state of the windows and the general condition. Protecting this property would take a lot of work, she considered as she closed her car door. She signalled at the two Escarrabin to stay in their car as she walked around to the front passenger door. She took both carriers out and placed them on the ground and closed the door. Feeling quite exposed, she checked one last time, looking behind her and further down the road. She locked the car, picked up both carriers and proceeded to the gate. With her hands full, she pressed with her backside against the gate that freely opened. She moved up the weed-strewn path.

The gate didn't close properly behind her, but it didn't really matter. As she reached the door, she placed one of the carriers down on the floor, gave the door a firm knock and picked the carrier back up again and waited.

Mildred's ears twitched to the sound of knocking and like an auto-response, looked at her un-ticking clock, as if knowing the time would tell her who was at the door. She scratched her head, not expecting anyone, but that was hardly unusual. She looked around the kitchen floor for Missy, but to no avail, she hoped she wasn't stuck up a tree again or worse. Through the frosted glass of the front door, she could see a tall, dark shadow waiting for her on the other side. She pulled at the catch and poked her head around.

"Yes, may I..."

She froze instantly as the tall lady in a black suit, that looked half hit-woman and half lawyer, stared back at her, wondering if she had done something wrong.

The stranger spoke gently with a smile. "Are you Mildred?"

"Well, I don't know. It depends who is asking?"

Her question was met with a little smile. "Please do not worry Mildred, I am from the Horde Of Light."

"Oh, another one of those crackpots!"

"Excuse Me?"

"Well, I..." Mildred glanced down to see that she was holding two containers. "Are they cats?"

"Yes, Mildred, they are."

The door flew open and Mildred's face was beaming. "Well, why didn't you say? Come in, come in. Excuse the mess. I wasn't expecting anyone."

She stepped in past Mildred, who held the door for her. The smell of the house made her eyes water. She instinctively went to raise a hand to cover her nose when she realised that she couldn't and coughed.

The door closed behind her.

"Are you okay? You seem troubled?"

She spluttered. "Yes, I'm fine, thank you. I'm just used to the clear Welsh air."

"You've travelled from Wales. I've never been to Wales. I would like to one day."

"I expect you will in time Mildred, the border is not far from here after all." The Reeve stood, not sure where to go next.

"Good, good, then follow me," Mildred unintentionally knocked her to the side in excitement, clapping her hands as she led her through.

The carriers were placed on the table and the guest looked around at what she guessed within the mess, resembled something that may be a kitchen.

"I'm sorry. You didn't say your name?"

Not used to being asked this question, she was taken off guard. With a faint smile, she turned to Mildred. "My name is Kiya, but most call me the Reeve."

Mildred laughed, "why on ever would they call you that?"

The Reeve clicked at her teeth, thinking what to say. "It goes back to a long time ago. We've been called different names in the past. It's a shortened term of sorts for the word 'Sheriff'."

Mildred was in fits of giggles. "Like in the Wild West, pistols at dawn, that sort of thing?"

"No, not really," was the short response.

Mildred's laughter faded away as her kitchen fell into an uncomfortable silence.

"Oh, I see, erm well would you like a cup of tea or a fish paste sandwich?"

The Reeve looked at her surroundings as well as now guessing what the smell was.

"No, I'm fine, thank you."

"Well, okay, so then... cats, cats, cats!"

The Reeve watched Mildred bobbing up and down like a cork on water.

"Yes, of course." The Reeve walked to the table and peeked under the cloth of the container on the left. She removed its cover to reveal the gold and elaborately detailed carrier.

"Oh my! My Missy was not delivered in one of those!"

"No, this delivery is a little different this time, Mildred." She unclipped the door, reached inside, lifted out a tiny bundle and unwrapped the kitten.

"Oh my again!" Mildred was practically jumping for joy. "She's beautiful. Well, I say that... is she a she?"

The Reeve froze. "Trust me, it's a she, Mildred." She passed the kitten over.

"Oh, I love her!"

"I trust you have a carrier for her?"

"Erm, what? Why's that?"

"Really? I presumed these things have been explained to you?"

Mildred was holding the kitten with as much care as could be possible. "How so? I do not understand?"

"Well, that cat is not destined for you." The Reeve looked at the tag on the carrier. "I understand that you are the new Elder for Daphne. This is her cat, which you are to deliver to her."

"Oh!" Mildred's face fell as she clung to the kitten. "Well, what if I want to keep her?"

The Reeve turned to her. Her body became rigid and her face more serious. "You must never say words like that, Mildred. Your path is clear and that cat is not for you. It is to be protected by another."

Mildred stepped back a little as the stranger suddenly looked more hit-woman than lawyer. She felt intimidated within her own home.

There was silence between them as it dawned on the Reeve that she had just unnerved the lady with the unusual dress sense standing in front of her. She drew a breath, smiled and looked at the other carrier. "This one is for you, Mildred."

Her smile returned with some curiosity. "Well, please show me!"

"Mildred, I have to explain something to you. This cat is special."

"Well, all cats are special, Kiya."

The Reeve, unused to being addressed by her real name, closed her eyes but offered a passive smile. She spoke with a soft tone in agreement with what Mildred had said. "All cats are special, the ones that are brought to you, the ones outside, the ones you see on television. Never forget Mildred that all cats are special." She stepped forward to her, "but this cat, this one that is being presented to you for safe-keeping, is very special. You must look after it at all times."

Mildred, still holding the other kitten, was a little confused. "Erm... okay."

She watched as Kiya removed the cover, exposing the box of turquoise.

"Oh, the box is a different colour from that one!"

The Reeve paused as she went to open the catch. "Yes, quite."

As the Reeve removed the kitten, she pulled away at the covers that had kept her warm. Mildred's face lit up. "But she's beautiful," she smiled, "it's a she?"

The Reeve's lips pursed. "Yes." She passed the kitten to her.

The Reeve stepped back and looked on at the joy in this relatively new member to the Order as she held both of the cats; it looked like tears were in her eyes. "This one is for me!"

The Reeve smiled and was surprised as she felt an unusual wave of emotion run through her. "Yes, she is for you, Mildred, and only you."

"Well, I can't believe it. I don't know what to say."

"No words are necessary. Just please look after her and the other kitten needs to go to her rightful owner."

"Oh yes, of course, I have no idea what to say to her, though," she giggled to herself. "I'll need to work that out. I remember when Daphne came to me for the first time, I thought she was a lunatic."

Mildred lifted her cat to her face and blinked a few times.

"There looks to be some sort of a mark on her?"

The Reeve was prepared for the observation. "I wouldn't worry, probably a birthmark. It can happen." Mildred looked at the Reeve, who was lying to her face. "Quite common, really."

"Oh, I see. It looks like some sort of burn?"

"Like I say, it's quite common."

Mildred's face had lit up as though she had just won the lottery. They both turned around on hearing the sound of the cat flap.

"Well, there you are, Missy. Come look, you have a new sister." She placed her new cat on the floor and continued holding the other.

Nahla looked directly at the Reeve as they acknowledged each other, something that Mildred did not spot in all of the excitement.

The Reeve smiled. "Well, I'll leave now and let them get acquainted." She picked up both of the carriers and instantly covered the one that bore the head of the serpent, somewhat thankful that Mildred hadn't noticed the markings.

"Shall I see myself out?"

Mildred looked at the suited lady who called herself the sheriff, now with three cats in her presence, thinking it could be her happiest day for a very long time.

"Erm, no, I can help."

"That's really not necessary."

Mildred watched the intimidating suited lady head towards her door. She stopped and turned to speak to her one last time. "Mildred, I have a strong suspicion that we will be meeting again. Please do be careful and protect the newborn." She stepped forward and paused. "Oh, and one more thing. Please be careful around those who wear strange glasses."

She looked at Kiya, the Reeve or whatever she was called, "well, of course!" She had no idea what the last comment meant.

The suited stranger smiled briefly and left.

Mildred was finally alone with the three cats. She felt happy and content and Missy was better, so she was thrilled about that too. This club, whatever it is, is filled with lunatics, but you know, they have just given me another beautiful cat, so I guess I should be thankful. She looked at the two cats on the floor, happy to be able to call them her own.

The Reeve made sure the front door was closed, bent down to pick up one of the empty carriers and moved down the pathway. She couldn't help but peek into the window of the kitchen. She looked through the dirty glass as Mildred innocently played with the cats. It had been a long time since she had seen someone so happy. In Mildred's blissful ignorance, the Reeve felt momentarily jealous of her happiness, but she knew that it would not last. This was a happy day for Mildred, hopefully, one that she would remember in the bad days to come. She bonded with her new cat, the one that no one from the Order knew whether it would turn out good or bad.

She looked up to the sky and took a deep breath and quite unbecoming of her, she thought that she may have felt a tear welling in her eye but was quick to dismiss it. Lives had already been lost, the prophecy had come to pass and evil was here. The image of the stranger through the window playing harmlessly with the cats was mesmerising to watch. "You have no idea Mildred and the time will come when you will play a great part for all of us." She stepped closer, watching her happy face as she picked up her new kitten. "Much will hang on your shoulders, Mildred and many will have to believe in you." She watched her kiss the new kitten that had been prophesied for hundreds of years. "I will believe in you, Mildred."

The Reeve stepped back, gathered her thoughts and drew a deep breath. There had been many emotions racing through her over the last 24 hours and she had many pressures to face. She regained her composure and headed towards the gate.

She unlocked her car, placed both the empty carriers on the back seat and walked over to the car where the two Escarrabin were waiting.

The window came down. "Everything okay, Ma'am?"

She nodded. "In the circumstances." She crouched down to speak to them through the window.

"Listen, I need you both to stay here and blend in. Observe everything, do what the others here do."

"Like get a dog?" One of the Escarrabin suggested with a slight smile.

The Reeve, with everything that had gone on, did her best to conceal her smile. "No, don't get a dog." It was a nice feeling to have a smile again, as brief as it was.

"Look, if a property comes up for sale or rent, I need to know. This road is now a major priority. I want to know about every person who lives here. I want to know what they do, where they go, what routines they have. I'll speak to Raysmau to arrange a shift rotation, but this property is now an immediate priority. Security measures will need to be added without her knowing; this place needs to be fortified."

She stood back up. "I need to get back to headquarters; it will take us some time to rebuild."

"Yes, Ma'am," they both responded, "we'll log everything."

The Reeve nodded and looked at them with some concern. "Also, keep an eye on the sky."

The Escarrabin both looked at each other as the Reeve departed.

Mildred did not like calling her Missy, Nahla; it didn't feel right.

She watched with curiosity as the tiny kitten wobbled on her feet. The bigger cat looked on at her with playful eyes.

"Missy." There was no response as she coughed slightly. "Nahla!" She had to confess that her cat looked up at her and she didn't know how she felt about it. She was still holding the kitten that didn't belong to her. "So, what do you think about our new friend?"

The tiny kitten blinked and then yawned, offering little assistance to the question.

Nahla placed a protective paw over her new sister as they began to get to know each other. Mildred wondered how such a young kitten would cope away from her mother, but much did not make sense in recent times.

Mildred jumped along with the kitten she was holding. "Nahla, she needs a name!" as her smile broadened.

With one hand, Mildred scratched at her head and dishevelled hair, trying to think of a suitable name for her new family addition. She brought the kitten up to her face and sighed, knowing that 'apparently' she could not keep that one as well. "Well, what do you think?"

She looked around the kitchen, trying to think up a suitable name as the two below her played and appeared to be happy. "Spatula... no...forks... no... blade... no. Oh, hang on." She reflected on the earlier news story and remembered the falling lights from the night before.

"Comet, I will call you Comet!"

Mildred was satisfied with the name and nodded in glee. She put the kitten on the floor to join the other two, took a deep breath and in happiness, looked out of her kitchen window with a smile.

If truth be told, Mildred knew that Comet would only be a temporary name as the Order had told her that every cat had a real name, and that's all cats, not just the ones in her kitchen right now, cats everywhere the world over. She smiled as she watched them play.

As life carried on outside Rocke Road, it would be some time before Mildred would discover her new cat's real name. But the time would come when she did and when she did, she would be told that her new cat's real name is Tempest.

UNITED KINGDOM
KAT CHAMBER

United Kingdom & Ireland Kat Chamber Sectors

Scottish Sector

Dundee

Northern & Northern Ireland Sector

Irish Sector

Wales & Middle Sector

Shrewsbury

Coningsby

Welshpool

Stratford-Upon-Avon

Lowlands Sector